PATRIMONY

Also by Toni Morgan

Two-Hearted Crossing
Echoes from a Falling Bridge
Harvest the Wind
Lotus Blossom Unfurling
Queenie's Place

PATRIMONY

A Novel By

TONI MORGAN

Adelaide Books
New York/ Lisbon

2017

Patrimony
A Novel
By Toni Morgan

Published by Adelaide Books, New York / Lisbon
An imprint of the Istina Group DBA
adelaidebooks.org

Editor-in-Chief
Stevan V. Nikolic

For any information, please address Adelaide Books
at info@adelaidebooks.org

ISBN13: 978-0-9995164-9-2
ISBN10: 0-9995164-9-3

Printed in the United States of America

For my husband, Ralph, who always believed.

Author's Note

During the turbulent sixties and early seventies, the call for Quebec independence created a political and social maelstrom in Canada. For nearly ten years riots, bombings, labor strikes and violent street scenes were part of daily life in Montreal, the epicenter of battle. The most radical of the groups pushing for the independence of Quebec was the *Font de Liberation du Quebec* – the FLQ.

Although this is a work of fiction, I have tried to remain true to the era and the events, including the October Crisis of 1971. Except for several well-known politicians of that era, the characters in this novel are purely figments of my imagination.

PART ONE

Chapter One

Marie-Catherine rolled onto her back and squinted at the glowing hands of her watch. Four AM. Without looking, she knew Marc's mattress was empty. She scrambled to her feet and padded to the window, forced open a few inches the night before to let fresh air into the musty cabin.

The silhouette of a large yacht loomed about fifty yards out in the Sound. A small fishing boat, it's chrome wheel gleaming in the moonlight, rocked close to the shore. The water around it looked like a million chips of broken glass.

Cloaked in the cabin's velvety darkness, Marie-Catherine breathed in the smell of salt water and pine seeping through the slit of open window. Outside, her brother and two men splashed into the shallow water of the Sound. Each picked up a box from the bottom of the fishing boat. The smallest of the three, a wiry-looking man with long ropy arms, staggered and readjusted his hold on the box as they splashed back to shore, across the short span of sand to the back of the orange and white rental truck.

They slid the boxes in with apparent indifference to the explosives, guns, or ammunition each contained. If the men spoke to one another, their voices were too low for Marie-Catherine to hear above the sound of the wavelets slapping against the flat sides of the boat and the sandy beach with a soft but steady beat.

The big man turned and Marie-Catherine inhaled sharply, recognizing him from the evening before. He'd stood on the pier next to the seafood restaurant where she and Marc stopped for dinner. Even though he'd worn mirrored sunglasses, she'd felt his eyes slide over her body as she crossed the oyster shell-covered parking lot behind Marc. She shivered at the memory of his intrusion into her personal sphere.

They'd barely been seated when her brother left the table. A moment later, she saw him through the restaurant's salt-streaked window, talking with the big man. She'd stared at the setting sun reflected in the man's sunglasses. Thinking about it, she felt a quick surge of anger. Typical Marc, he'd returned to their table without a word of explanation.

The big man slid another box into the back of the truck, straightened and swiveled his close-cropped head, peering toward the cabin. Marie-Catherine took an involuntary step backward. But only for a moment. Despite the man's threatening presence, the scene beyond the window was too riveting for her to resist. At least he no longer stared toward the cabin.

Marie-Catherine fingered the neck of her tee-shirt. Marc said they'd be back in Montreal in time for her to start school. She should feel more enthusiastic—she'd worked hard for the opportunity to enter the freshman class at the new University of Quebec at Montreal. She was happy about it. But it would be nothing like this. A frisson of excitement rippled through her. Fear, anger, excitement —she'd felt all those things, one after another, from the moment she and Marc had embarked on this trip to North Carolina to procure guns and explosives for the *Front de Liberation du Quebec,* the FLQ.

A mosquito whined near her face. She brushed it away and thought once again how proud she was to be even a small part in the fight for Quebec separatism. How great it would be when Quebec was independent from the rest of Canada, when French Canadians could finally rule themselves. It wasn't right that all the power was in the hands of the fifteen percent of Quebec's population that was Anglo.

The mosquito flitted off then looped back and settled on her thigh. Without thinking, Marie-Catherine brought her hand down, hard, on her bare skin. The sharp crack rang out like a gunshot.

The big man's head whipped toward the cabin again, his hooded eyes like a hawk's, searching for its prey. They locked on the cabin's window where Marie-Catherine stood, and then shifted to the cabin door. He started forward.

Marc grabbed his arm. The man, heavier than her brother by a good twenty pounds, shook him off. Marc grabbed the man's arm again. The man drew back his fist and hit Marc on the side of his head. Marc dropped to one knee, stunned. He shook his head before springing up.

Marie-Catherine went icy cold then hot. Blood pulsed in her throat, at her temples.

Marc dove at the man, grabbing him by the waist. The man locked his arms around Marc's chest, squeezing him.

Mari-Catherine held her hand to her mouth to stifle her scream.

Marc punched and kicked his opponent, but with little effect. The man was so much bigger.

If only Marc could break free—they could make their escape in the truck. She pulled her eyes away from the two men, now on the ground, the big man on top, to judge the distance to the truck. She caught her breath and gripped the windowsill, her nails digging into the rotting wood. She'd forgotten the other man. He stood at the back of the truck and slid in a box. When he turned and caught sight of the two grappling men, he dropped his head and charged.

Dear God. Marc didn't stand a chance against two. She had to help him. Spinning around, she made for the door. She darted a last look through the window just as the smaller man grabbed the big man's arm, hauling him off her brother. He pointed to the boat in the Sound and shouted something in a language Marie-Catherine didn't recognize. The big man stood and, with a grunt, dropped his balled fists.

Marie-Catherine sank to the floor, the breath going out of her like air from a deflating balloon.

The noisy abruptness of an engine starting up splattered the dawn. She sprang to her feet. Marc and the two men were in the little fishing boat, plowing through the water toward the sleek boat riding at anchor in the Sound. Minutes later, figures moved on the yacht's deck. Marie-Catherine strained her eyes in the growing light, trying to make out Marc's lean shape among them. Unable to locate him, she panicked, her mind ricocheting from one fearful possibility to the next: there'd been another fight; the men demanded more money; he'd slipped and knocked himself out, broken his leg. Something.

The deep throbbing sound of heavy engines floated across the water. The yacht began to glide away. Marie-Catherine's fingernails again dug into the windowsill. The yacht headed for the open Atlantic, leaving the little fishing boat to bob like a cork in its wake. After a few moments, it turned and headed toward the beach. In it, her brother sat alone. The rising sun cast a crimson glow across his face and body. When he reached the shallows, he jumped out and dragged the boat onto the shore.

Marie-Catherine stepped from the cabin.

Marc nodded to her. His jeans were wet past his knees and sand caked his shoes. He wrenched open the truck's door and climbed inside. "Let's go."

Marie-Catherine had no idea where the blue Ford sedan had been parked all night. Instead of behind them, where it had been the day before, now it remained a few hundred yards or a mile ahead as they passed through one small coastal North Carolina town after another.

The mesmerizing scene and its accompanying emotional high that held her at the window that morning had long-since faded. The truck's windows were rolled down and the hot, muggy air swept over her, enhancing the funky, kelpy smell coming from Marc's still-damp jeans.

Her sweaty legs stuck to the truck's hard vinyl seat, and she squirmed to find a more comfortable position. She fiddled once again with the radio dial, searching for something, anything to break up the monotony. All she got for her efforts was static from the radio and silence from her brother.

Hour after hour, Marc remained tightlipped, staring at the road ahead of them. She heaved a heavy sigh. Why was she surprised? Hadn't he ignored her most of her life? The twelve-year gap in their ages had apparently been too wide for either of them to bridge.

It was different with Henri. Only eighteen months Marc's junior, her brother Henri always had time for her. Lately, though, they'd been arguing a lot. Mostly over Marc.

"Marc isn't really interested in correcting injustice," Henri said. "Our brother and the rest of the FLQ won't be happy until English-speaking Canadians are on the receiving end of French-Canadian injustice." He'd called her a damn fool when she claimed Marc wasn't like that.

She pulled her legs up to sit cross-legged on the seat and heaved another sigh.

Ahead of them, the blue Ford disappeared around a bend in the road. She glanced at Marc. "Who's driving? I can never see the driver."

"You're not meant to." Marc pressed down on the gas pedal, and the truck slowly picked up speed. "Just do your part and don't worry about anyone else."

Marie-Catherine lifted her hands in the air. "But what is my part? If I'm not to know any of these people or know how they get here, and I'm not supposed to ask questions about your plans, why am I here?" She dropped her hands back into her lap.

Marc didn't answer.

She prodded him again. "Well?"

"Because together we look like a couple, like we're moving somewhere."

Blood surged into Marie-Catherine's cheeks. "You mean

I make a good front, a good cover? That's why you brought me along?"

"Yes."

His casual dismissal crushed her. She'd been so pleased when he'd asked her to come with him, convinced she finally had a chance to prove she could play a useful role in the fight for Quebec's sovereignty. She forgot any concerns she may have had about discovery and arrest.

Bitterness made her voice shrill. "I want to be more than that, Marc. I've told you before, I want to do something."

"Like what? What do you want to do?"

He looked and sounded annoyed, but she didn't care. "I want to be part of things, not just someone who sits on the sidelines and cheers, or an ignorant little tweety-bird other people use or hide behind."

Marc frowned into the mirror outside his window. "Well, you may get your chance right now."

"What do you mean?"

"A *flic* is behind us." He picked up the hand-held radio from the seat between them and thumbed down the button on its side. "I have something in my mirror."

Marie-Catherine dropped her feet to the floor and peered into the tall mirror outside her window. A brown car trailed some distance behind them. Sunlight glinted off the chrome-rimmed, ball-shaped light on its roof.

A voice crackled over the radio in Marc's hand. "How far back?"

"About a quarter of a mile. I just picked him up."

"Right," said the voice. Marc put the radio back on the seat.

Marie-Catherine watched the police car in the mirror. "It doesn't seem to be gaining on us." She turned to face forward again, trying to tamp down her alarm. She pictured the boxes in the back of the truck, could feel their weight dragging at the engine, slowing them down. She imagined that instead of the rental company's name on its sides, the truck was emblazoned with signs advertising its contents.

Just then the blue Ford blasted past in the opposite direction. Startled, Marie-Catherine whipped back to the mirror. The red light on top of the police car flashed on as the driver made a rapid three-point turn and took off in pursuit. Within seconds the blue Ford sedan had disappeared. Holding her breath, Marie-Catherine followed the flashing light on the police car until it was mere pinprick, finally dissolving from sight.

She took a shaky breath. "What will happen to him?"

Although Marc shrugged, a muscle in his cheek twitched. "Probably just get a speeding ticket unless he does something stupid. I'm more worried about us."

"Why? No one's following us now."

Marc tightened his grip on the steering wheel. "Right, and no one is out front running interference for us, either."

Chapter Two

From the top of the steps of Notre Dame Basilica, Henri gazed through the growing dusk at the throng of tie-dyed, jeans-wearing young people pushing, shoving, waving signs, and taunting fire hose-wielding riot police with shouts of 'pig' and 'fascist.' Five students with megaphones stood on top of an old gray milk truck, further stirring up the crowd.

They'd gathered to protest the jailing of Pierre Vallieres and Charles Gagnon, who'd been convicted of fatally bombing a Montreal shirt factory. Convinced of the men's innocence, the two served the students and many other French-Canadians as living symbols of Anglo oppression.

The milk truck, with *Vive le Quebec Libre* painted in red on both its sides, stood in the center of Place d'Armes, home to the Montreal Stock Exchange, the Bank of Montreal, and the cathedral where Henri stood. He thought the juxtaposition of the buildings spoke volumes.

Streetlights popped on. Their reflections glistened on the wet pavement. A blond, curly-haired boy, who didn't look more than sixteen, threw a bottle at a policeman manning a hose. The policeman responded by sweeping a torrent of high pressure water across the crowd. More bottles filled the air along with renewed shouting.

Henri moved a few steps down, wanting to get closer to the action. He felt pumped up, like he always did when he covered a story, especially one to do with Quebec independence. Much as he admired the students' commitment, however, he had the feeling the evening wouldn't end well. Their demonstrations rarely did.

"Set Vallieres free; set Gagnon free," the students on top of the truck chanted through their megaphones.

Somewhere in the crowd, a single voice began singing, *"We shall overcome...."*

Others took the hymn up and soon their voices carried above the shouts and taunts. Several policemen appeared to hesitate, looking around for instruction. Henri sensed the beginning of a subtle change in the tension-filled air.

A firebomb exploded in a sudden flash of light.

The students on top of the truck stood silhouetted against the twilit sky, for a startled instant still as statues in a game of blind-man's-bluff. The already muggy air filled with smoke and the smell of gas. The singing became ragged then died.

The police surged forward again, quickly surrounding the milk truck, trying to cut off the students on its roof. Their voices escalating, the crowd pushed toward the truck, too, reaching out to the five desperately trying to scramble to safety.

Through smarting eyes, Henri spotted the girl from the Student Union he'd spoken with earlier—knew her by the fiery red hair flying around her head, gleaming in the half-light. He caught sight of her just as she leapt from the truck's roof, over the head of a policeman. He held his breath until she landed safely with the help of friendly hands, and quickly disappeared.

Scanning the crowd, Henri's eyes locked on another figure, one with wide, frightened eyes, trying to keep her balance in the surging mass of yelling protesters. Claudia. He shoved through the by-standers and reporters standing on the steps below him and plunged into the crowd, elbowing and fighting his way to her side.

"What are you doing here?" he shouted. He didn't give her a chance to reply. "Come on." He grabbed her arm and pulled her, none too gently, fighting to get out of the crowd.

A policeman only a few years older than the students, a determined look on his round, flushed face, barred their way. He held a raised billy club in his fist.

"Press," shouted Henri, and pointed to the badge clipped to his shirt pocket.

A wild look in the young policeman's grey eyes, his arm slashed down.

Henri ducked, but the club grazed his forehead and struck his shoulder. "Press, God damn it," he shouted again, but the man had already pushed past, still slashing right and left, like he was wielding a machete in a field of sugarcane.

Shoving through the mass of bodies, Henri dragged Claudia in his wake. A bottle sailed past his eye, an elbow jabbed into his ribs, his ears rang with all the screams and shouts. Finally, they reached the cathedral steps. With curious looks, people drew aside to let them pass, and they climbed back to where Henri had left his camera bag.

He turned to her. "Are you okay?"

She nodded, but didn't speak.

"What are you doing here?" Henri stared at her, the muscles in his stomach tightened with an emotion he didn't want to acknowledge.

She gave a non-committal shrug. "Louise told me where to find you."

He needed to bend close to hear her soft voice. At her words, he straightened and scowled. "Work." Even to him, the word sound defensive.

He was suddenly conscious of the stale sweat under his arms and the jeans he should have changed a day or maybe two days before. He was also aware of the implied criticism in her eyes, though he didn't know why she should care how he spent his time. They hadn't seen each other in six months.

They'd once talked of getting married. When things began falling apart, he'd known the truth in her complaints. He was always working a story. When a deadline loomed or news broke without warning, there'd simply been no time. Still, he'd felt sure they'd work things out, hadn't dreamed she'd turn to someone else. Never dreamed she'd turn to Marc, his own brother.

"I heard you'd left Quebec." He frowned when someone bumped against him.

"You're hurt." She reached out to touch his forehead where the billy club had grazed him. He jerked his head to the side, avoiding her touch. She froze then dropped her hand. Her eyes traveled back to the square. "A few years ago, we would have been on top of that truck."

Henri eyed her, saw the unfamiliar lines of tension around her mouth, the way her fingers furled and unfurled. "Yeah, I guess you're right."

"Can you leave now? This will be over soon. Let's go find a place where we can talk."

"I can't." He had all he needed for the story, but seeing her again…lost and fragile-looking…. No. He couldn't go anywhere with her, not without time to prepare himself.

She stared at him, an indecipherable look in her eyes. Without another word, she turned and, with her usual grace, moved through the clusters of people remaining on the steps to the glass-littered sidewalk below.

His chest tightened, watching her mahogany hair swing against her narrow shoulders, longer now, but still clean and shiny. He knew how silky it would feel to run his hands through, how it would smell—like sunshine and strawberries.

★

The next morning, his eyes dry and red following a restless night, Henri pushed through *Le Journal Quotidien's* front door into a bubbling stew of activity. Several reporters were already at their desks, yelling into phones or banging on typewriters. The newsroom of one of the city's most outspoken French-language newspapers, an afternoon paper, was always loud and jangling and Henri loved it.

Louise handed him a piece of paper. "Claudia wants you to call her at this number." Her pale blue eyes danced with curiosity. "She called yesterday afternoon, too. Did she find you?"

"She found me." Without looking at it, he stuffed the slip of paper into his back pocket. "Feels like it's going to be another scorcher, doesn't it?"

The motherly receptionist, the wife of Henri's editor, wasn't about to be distracted by talk of the weather, no matter how unusual the late heat wave might be. Nor would she drop it once she had the scent of something. "She hasn't called in a while."

"She's been away."

"That's what she said."

Henri moved away from her desk.

"Aren't you going to call her back?"

"Later. First I need to write up last night."

At a table along the back wall, Henri filled a cup with coffee from the pot kept warm on a burner, adding enough cream to make it palatable. Minutes later, oblivious to the piles of magazines, books, old newspapers, and files stacked high on all four corners of his desk and on the floor beside it, he spun paper into the carriage of his typewriter. He'd already checked to see how many students had been arrested at the protest, and if any were still being held by the police. Tuning out the voices and noise surrounding him, he began setting down what he'd witnessed the night before. He didn't lift his eyes from the typewriter until he'd finished the story, forty minutes later. He read it through, sighed and leaned back in his chair.

"Want a warm-up?" Julien Amis stood next to him with the coffee pot.

Henri pushed his half-empty cup toward his co-worker. "Sure." Julien was fifteen years his senior, but Henri felt sorry for the tall, awkward man, with his thinning hair and shy smile, still living with his parents. Julien had been writing a book about an obscure jazz musician for years. He'd once confided to Henri that living in his parents' home made it easier to write.

"How's the book coming?"

Julien's eyes lit up. "I found a new record. Well, a new old record. I'm still in the process of analyzing it."

Henri knew from experience Julien could talk for hours about old jazz records. "Sounds interesting, but I need to get this to Maurault then go meet someone. Catch you later?"

"Sure," Julien said. "Later."

From a phone booth, Henri dialed the number Louise had given him. On the fourth ring, Claudia picked up. "Hello."

The husky quality of her voice had always captivated him. Now it gave an extra kick to his rapidly beating heart. "It's me." A sigh sounded in his ear.

"Henri. I'm glad you called."

He'd been tempted not to. He'd spent most of the night wondering what in hell she wanted—hadn't she gotten her pound of flesh? His mouth dry, he swallowed and said nothing.

"Could we meet somewhere? For lunch, maybe?"

"I have a lunch appointment." He shifted from foot-to-foot. "An interview," he added into the silence on the other end of the phone. "…but I can meet you after."

"Where?"

Good question. Wherever they met needed to be public, and yet private enough for a conversation. "How about Dominion Square?"

"What time?"

He saw her the moment he entered the park. "You're early," he said when he reached her side.

"I was anxious to see you."

He frowned and turned away, looking for a bench where they could talk without being disturbed. He pointed to one in a patch of shade, set back from the sidewalk. "How about we sit over there?"

"Anything out of the sun looks good. I always forget how hot Montreal can sometimes be, even in September."

"It can't be any worse than Chicago." Chicago was where he heard she'd gone.

Expressionless, she perched on the edge of the bench. "No, no worse."

For several moments, neither of them spoke, but Henri was so aware of her beside him he believed his skin might burst.

Claudia broke the silence. "I've missed you."

Henri breathed in her scent and memories flooded his brain.

She swallowed and her voice quivered when she spoke. "I want things to be like they were."

Her words created an emotional abyss, and he instinctively shied away before it sucked him in. "There's no going back."

Claudia blinked and shifted her gaze to a nearby statue of a soldier striding alongside a horse.

Henri stared at his hands, hanging loosely between his knees, giving the lie to his inner turmoil.

Finally, Claudia turned back to him. "Why didn't you call me? I was sure you'd call before I left—so we could talk things out."

"I was busy." Henri straightened and shifted his hands to his knees. He wouldn't tell her how close he'd come, how many times he'd gone to the phone and lifted the receiver. How many times he'd forced himself to set it down, resist the impulse to hear her voice just one more time. His eyes bored into hers. "Besides, we'd already said it all."

Claudia shook her head. "You always closed me out."

"Well, it didn't take you long to find someone else, did it?"

"I couldn't compete with your work, the people you surround yourself with."

On his tongue was the bitter taste of gall. "Why bring all that up now? It's over."

"What if I don't want it to be over?" Tears pooled in Claudia's eyes and she scoured them with her palms. "Damn it. I promised myself I wouldn't cry."

For the first time, Henri felt a stirring of sympathy. His throat ached. His hands itched to reach for her, stroke her hair, soothe her. He quickly smothered the feeling. "What you want doesn't make any difference. It's done." He pushed erect. "It was over and done when you went to bed with my brother."

Claudia surged to her feet and reached her hand to his chest. "But I didn't." Pleading filled her voice. "Henri, I told you. Nothing happened between Marc and me, nothing but a little flirting. It was harmless. It didn't mean a thing."

Henri stiffened and pulled her hand from its grip on his shirt. "You forget that I saw you. Sorry. I need to get back to work." He turned and walked away, every nerve and muscle in his body taut.

Chapter Three

Now that school had begun, only young children, their mothers or nannies were in the park. Marie-Catherine paced the graveled path while the three- and four-year-olds chased after one another. Periodically, the children stopped to feed bread crusts to a cadre of ducks that paddled among the reeds along the pond's edge, while their guardians watched benignly from shaded benches. Although leaves on the surrounding maple trees were starting to turn color, anticipating the approaching change of season, summer still reigned. The mid-September sun beat down on Marie-Catherine's unprotected head; it would be another hot day.

She glanced at her watch. Ten minutes after the hour. She knew it would be useless to protest, if or when Henri finally arrived—he always had an excuse for his tardiness: the demands of his job, a crisis of some kind. She felt torn between wanting him to get there, so she could tell him what she had to say, and wanting more time to rehearse. She'd give him another ten minutes.

Footsteps sounded on the gravel path. She turned once again, this time to see Henri coming toward her. The stone of dread in her stomach grew heavier. She tried for a breezy smile of welcome.

After he kissed her cheeks in greeting, she gestured to an empty picnic table, shaded from the sun by large, leafy branches. "Let's go sit over there."

Henri's eyes narrowed. "What's wrong?"

She shook her head; he knew her too well. "Let's sit down first." She led the way to the table.

When they were both seated, Henri wasted no time. "Okay, spill it."

She stared at her hands, twisted in her lap. "I'm not sure where to start."

Henri's voice held a hint of impatience. "Where every story starts—at the beginning."

Marie-Catherine took a deep breath and let it out slowly. The beginning. A mental image of their father sitting at the dinner table, thundering and thumping about the Anglos discriminating against French Canadians, formed in her mind. She'd been four, possibly five the first time she'd taken note of it. She hadn't a clue then what 'discrimination' meant, only that it was something bad. Over time, she'd learned.

She finally blurted out what she'd come to say. "I went to North Carolina with Marc."

Henri reared back as though she'd slapped him.

She hastened to reassure him. "It's okay. Nothing happened. We got back without a problem."

Henri struck the table with his fist. "Son-of-a-bitch." His lips formed a hard line. His voice was tight when he spoke again. "Tell me. All of it."

A squirrel skittered across a tree branch above their

heads. Henri hadn't interrupted her once, nor had he taken his eyes from her. Her feelings of discomfort intensified. She hurried to finish.

"We eventually crossed the border just north of Malone, New York. A freight-forwarding company in Syracuse had been going to send everything across with a shipment of goods, but they backed out at the last minute."

She didn't tell him why they'd refused, how one of their drivers was arrested near Toronto for carrying contraband cigarettes across the border and how all their trucks were now thoroughly searched when they crossed.

"At least they gave us some old furniture and things to cover the boxes." She straightened and attempted another smile. "That was it. After all the agonizing I went through, worrying about it, crossing the border was easy as pie. Marc told the inspector we were moving back home from Virginia. He just poked around the furniture and stuff then let us go."

Henri shoved up from the table and paced between the table and tree trunk. Several times he seemed about to say something, but each time he broke off.

"Henri, stop. It's done. I stayed in the cabin, away from everything—away from any danger—and we made it back just fine."

Coming to a halt in front of her, his breathing ragged, Henri opened and closed his fists several times. Finally, he spoke. "Jesus Christ, M.C. I can't believe this. Don't you understand how much danger you were in?"

"I think you're over—"

"Those men trade in everything—guns, explosives, drugs, people. They don't care who they sell to or what it is, so long as they make money. Don't you get that? They're ruthless. They could have killed both of you and kept every-thing to sell again. They have no loyalty to anyone."

"No honor among thieves?"

Henri gave her a scathing look. "Don't think it for a second. They'd kill you easy as looking at you—after sharing you with all their friends."

Marie-Catherine had an instant image of the big man with his hooded, searching eyes. She shivered.

"Yeah, you know I'm right."

Marie-Catherine didn't want to think about what could have happened. She quickly shoved it from her mind. "Oh, come on, Henri. It wasn't—"

"Or you could have been arrested. They're always stopping trucks and vans on the roads down there in the Carolinas, looking for bootleg liquor and cigarettes. That's why the car ran out in front of you—looking for road-blocks."

"I know."

"And I suppose you know it would have put an end to UQAM if you'd been caught. Can you imagine what it would do to Maman and Papa?" Henri didn't give her a chance to answer before he went on. "Then to make a border crossing with you. Jesus. How could you have been so stupid? How could you let Marc put you in danger like that?"

Marie-Catherine's cheeks burned. "That part wasn't his fault. He'd meant for me to fly home—I had a ticket. Things got messed up." Then she sighed and put her hand on his arm. "Come on, Henri. Don't be angry. You know

Marc wouldn't let anything happen to me. And I've never felt such a part of things. No matter how scared I got, it was worth it."

Henri jerked his arm away. "Worth it? Do you know what Marc's going to do with the explosives you brought back? Do you care? Bombs are built for one purpose, M.C. —to hurt people."

"Don't lecture me. You know the FLQ only targets property, not people."

"You don't even know how much you don't know." Henri's words were filled with disgust. "At least promise me you'll never do anything like that trip again."

Marie-Catherine crossed her arms over her chest. "I won't promise you that. I can't."

They stared at one another. Finally, Henri shook his head. "I have to get back to work. I'll talk to you later. Maybe you'll have come to your senses by then."

Marie-Catherine watched him go, determined not to call out after him. She didn't really want to go back to North Carolina with Marc. But why couldn't Henri understand how important it was to her to be part of the fight for Quebec's independence?

If only he weren't so pig-headed, so convinced Marc and the FLQ were wrong. Like Marc said, Henri could write newspaper articles until the cows came home, but action was what made things happen.

Chapter Four

For several days Henri tried without success to contact Marc. Each time he rang his brother's apartment, a woman answered the phone and told him Marc was out. At least the intervening days between meeting with Marie-Catherine and when Marc finally returned his call gave Henri plenty of time to plan what he would say to his brother.

"I won't be long."

Louise nodded and went on checking the lines of copy Julien had given her. Behind her, a reporter and a man who worked on the presses drank coffee and argued about the prospects for the newly formed Montreal Expos, who were playing Milwaukee that night at Jarry Park. It would be one of the last games of the season.

"Watch Mack Jones, his bat's red hot," one of the men said as Henri walked out the door, into the brisk afternoon air. The heat wave had broken.

He turned toward University Street and quickened his step, anxious to confront Marc. They'd agreed to meet at a restaurant near Eaton's department store. Henri arrived to find black-clad clerks from Eaton's and workers from the surrounding office buildings crowding the restaurant. He looked for a vacant table, then spotted Marc already seated.

Henri slid into the chair opposite his brother. "You're hard to get with these days."

Marc looked up from the menu in his hand. "I'm keeping busy."

"So I hear." A waitress handed him a menu. He gave it back without looking at it. "I'll just have iced tea."

Marc glanced up again. "You're not going to eat?"

Henri shook his head. "Go ahead, though. Don't let me stop you." His eyes tried to drill into Marc's. Marc gave him a benign smile in return.

When the waitress appeared with the tea, Marc gave her his order. Henri waited until she left. "I don't suppose you're wondering why I wanted to talk with you." The muscles in his neck jerked with tension.

Marc answered without a trace of apology in his voice. "I knew M.C. would tell you. I told her to."

The objective, dispassionate argument he'd planned to deliver flew out of Henri's mind. "God damn you, Marc. What in the hell were you thinking of?" He leaned forward, speaking low so his voice wouldn't carry to the surrounding tables. "She's just a kid, for Christ's sake. What if you'd been stopped? What if there'd been an accident? With all the shit in the back of the truck, both of you would have been blown from here to Timbuktu."

Marc smiled and shook his head. "Explosives don't work that way. They need to be primed."

Henri had always admired his brother's cool nerves, but he didn't like his fears dismissed as though they were foolish. His shoulders stiffened. "That's not the point. You shouldn't have taken her."

Marc shrugged. "I needed her for cover." He leaned

back and crossed his arms over his chest. "Besides, she wanted to come."

Marc's smug attitude and the casual indifference in his voice brought Henri upright in his chair. "I don't give a fuck what she wanted." He spat the words.

People seated at nearby tables glanced at him before quickly shifting their eyes back to their food.

Henri forced his voice lower once again. "She's our sister, Marc. It's our job to keep her safe."

"This is a war, Henri. Safe isn't the issue. Winning is."

"I don't buy that. I don't buy your win-at-any-cost crap." His hearted thudded.

Marc frowned, true lack of comprehension in his eyes. "What's happened to you? You didn't used to be like this. How come you're willing to sit on your ass and watch while the rest of us do the fighting for you?"

Marc's words stung. Although Henri believed his brother's methods were wrong, a part of him cheered whenever the FLQ struck against some symbol of the government's repression of French Canadians. He started to answer, to defend himself, but Marc wasn't finished.

"You write your articles and think you've done your part. But that's bullshit. *Le Journal Quotidien* and the other French-language newspapers should be behind us. All of you should be printing our *communiqués*, supporting our actions, recognizing that FLQ members who've been arrested are political prisoners not criminals." Marc leaned forward in his seat. "Do you? Do they? No, you all just piss and moan right along with the *Montreal Star* and the rest of the fucking English-language press."

The waitress set Marc's sandwich in front of him, and refilled his coffee. "More iced tea?" she asked Henri.

Henri shook his head and she left them. They were isolated now. Lunch hour traffic had ended and a pool of empty, littered tables surrounded them.

Henri stared at his brother. "That's always your answer, isn't it Marc? If someone doesn't see things the way you do, doesn't agree with your methods, he's the enemy."

"Damn right." Marc bit down on his sandwich.

Henri eyed his brother, disgust pulling down the corners of his mouth. "What about Marie-Catherine? Are you going to put her into the middle of this, just to prove you can? Are you going to make her more of an accomplice than she already is?"

Marc swallowed and took a sip of his coffee before answering. "You know I could."

The memory of Claudia passed between them.

Henri clamped down on the anger that spurted through his gut. "Maybe. Marie-Catherine's caught up in the excitement of things right now. But I don't think that's your game. I don't buy that 'cover' business, either." His eyes narrowed. "You're up to something. What is it and what do you want from me?"

Marc wiped his mouth with the back of his hand and took a folded piece of paper from his shirt pocket. He handed it to Henri. "I want you to use your influence and get this communiqué published in full in *Le Journal Quotidien*—in full, Henri, not just a few excerpts."

Without glancing at it, Henri set the folded paper on the table between them. "Maurault wouldn't print this even if I asked him. He wouldn't dare. Do you know how many times the police and the mayor have tried to shut us down, claiming we're a front for the FLQ? Printing one of your communiqués would be disastrous—it could spell the end of the newspaper."

Marc pushed his plate away, leaving part of his sandwich uneaten. "You exaggerate. You can make Maurault see the need to do it—you're his star reporter, his hot shot. You know you can talk him into it."

Marc's lips spread in a toothy grimace, but the smile, if that's what it was, failed to reach his eyes.

"And maybe when it appears in the paper, Marie-Catherine will see the need to apply herself to her studies."

"So, you're blackmailing me and using the safety of our sister to do it. That's the real reason you took her down there, isn't it, Marc? To get to me." Henri shoved back in his chair. "You fucking asshole."

Marc didn't even try to deny the accusation. "You're being melodramatic—we need to get the word out. You can help."

"And the explosives? Whatever it is you're planning, she can't be a part of it. I mean it, Marc."

"Don't worry. Get this done for us and our little sister can follow your footsteps into academia without interference from me."

Henri stared at his brother, not believing him for a second. With Marc, if a pledge got in the way of expediency, expediency always won. He never even tried to justify it. To cover his thoughts, he picked up the paper, unfolded and read part of it. "What does this mean, *The FLQ will proceed to eliminate all persons collaborating with the occupiers'?* You're declaring war on French-Canadians now, not just the Anglos?" He read further. "And what about here, '*We demand that our wounded and our prisoners be treated according to the statute of political prisoners and according to the Geneva Convention concerning the laws of warfare.*' You honestly think I can get Maurault to print this bullshit? You're crazy!"

Another smile, this one real, brought out the dimple in Marc's left cheek. "You can do it. I have faith in you, little brother."

"Fuck you, big brother." Henri refolded the paper and stuffed it in his pocket. "I'll get back to you." He stood and started toward the door, then turned back. "In the meantime, keep away from Marie-Catherine." He didn't wait for Marc's reply.

★

Sleep wouldn't come that night. Henri had too much on his mind, like how to convince Marie-Catherine their brother's methods were wrong. People could get hurt, had gotten hurt. Didn't she remember Jean Corbo? Sixteen-years-old and a courier for the FLQ...killed in a premature bomb explosion. Or Michele Duclos, arrested in New York City trying to deliver explosives to the Black Liberation Front. Those were the kinds of things Marc could get their sister involved in. He didn't know how she could not understand that. *"The FLQ targets property, not people,* Henri." What a load of bullshit. Tell that to the parents of Jean Corbo.

A breeze from the open window rattled the blind. Henri punched up the pillow and rolled onto his side.

It wasn't just that he wanted to keep Marie-Catherine safe from harm, although that remained his primary reason, of course. Nor was it politics. A separatist himself, he wanted many of the things the FLQ wanted. No, it wasn't just the politics or his sister's safety that concerned him. In honesty, he had to admit he resented Marc's power over Marie-Catherine. His brother had never done one thing to earn her loyalty.

He ignored the little voice in his head telling him his feelings might also have something to do with Claudia. For some reason, he'd been able to put his anger about Claudia in a separate chamber, hardening whenever he thought about her and his brother together. He and Marc had never talked about what Henri had walked in on, the scene that had changed his life. Was it so insignificant to Marc that his brother had forgotten it? Maybe—until he wanted to use Henri's jealousy to needle him, as he'd done that afternoon.

The next morning, feeling punch-drunk with exhaustion, Henri tapped on Maurault's open door. His editor put down the sheet of paper he'd been reading and waved Henri inside.

Though airless and reeking of stale cigarette smoke, Henri closed Maurault's office door against the steady hum and clatter from the newsroom. He didn't want anyone to barge in or overhear what he planned to say.

Minutes later, Maurault looked up from the creased paper Henri had given him. "You can't be serious. You don't expect me to print this jeremiad, do you? Where did you get it? No, never mind. I don't want to know." Maurault looked back down at the typewritten sheet. With his elbow on the desk he held his thumb to his forehead and rubbed his fingers across the expanse of creased pink skin, a gesture more of habit than fatigue, and continued reading.

"I thought maybe we could print it as a warning to French Canadians. Like a public service announcement." The idea sounded lame, even to Henri. His right eye twitched from nerves and lack of sleep.

Maurault gave him a look and dropped his heavy glasses on the desk in front of him. He leaned back in the chair, his fingers laced behind his head. "You think Drapeau would buy that?" Skepticism filled his voice.

Henri knew Maurault was right. Montreal's mayor not only would not buy it, he'd jump at another excuse to try and shut the paper down. "Actually, I've been thinking about something else."

Maurault dropped his hands from behind his head and shoved the communiqué away. He took a cigarette from the nearly empty pack on the side of his desk, next to an overflowing ashtray. Then he tilted back in his chair again, the unlit cigarette hanging from the corner of his mouth. Not for the first time, Henri was reminded how much Maurault, except for being taller, resembled René Lévesque, the leader of the new Parti Quebecois, even down to the perpetual cigarette and combed over bald spot.

"Go on."

"The FLQ has been protesting for months how their members are treated when they're arrested—beaten up by the police, held incommunicado and without legal representation."

"Shit, Henri, they're terrorists and crooks. What in hell do they expect, a red carpet? Oh, I forgot, they want to be treated like political prisoners." Maurault lit his cigarette and drew in a lungful of smoke then blew it out through his nose. "Christ, police beating up on prisoners is an old tradition in Quebec. You know that. The FLQ are treated no different in that respect."

"What would you think of me joining the FLQ— maybe get myself arrested?" He'd been thinking about it all night. If he could expose the corruptness of the present system, enough of it, it would surely bring wider-based support for independence. It would also show Marie-Catherine what responsible political action looked like. And if they'd just see it, it would show Marc and others in the FLQ they could achieve what they wanted without the bombs and violence.

Maurault's eyes narrowed and Henri knew he had to be remembering Louis Simard— he'd known he would have the memory of *Le Journal Quotidien's* former lead reporter to contend with. Maurault took another long drag from his cigarette. Henri waited for the reply, surprised when it finally came.

"Could you do it?" Maurault exhaled smoke as he spoke. "You think they'd let you in?" Henri's pulse quicken-ed. Maybe this would fly after-all. "Yeah, I think they would. They already know I'm a separatist. To them it would be a natural progression."

Maurault nodded. "Let me think about it. I'll let you know."

"Sure. What about the communiqué?"

"I'll let you know about that too."

Chapter Five

Everyone had left for the night, including Louise, leaving Henri and Maurault alone in Maurault's small office. Maurault's desk, piled with old copy, files and the perpetually overflowing ashtray, occupied the space between the two men.

"Even though you were here at the time, you were just an errand boy Simard took under his wing," Maurault said, lighting a cigarette from the stub of his previous one. "You don't know what we went through, how close we were to being shut down."

Henri nodded. "Times are different now. The separatist movement has much broader support—not only students and a handful of intellectuals. Doctors, shopkeepers, even housewives are becoming activists. And I think everyone needs to know what happens behind those prison walls."

Maurault breathed heavily, still appearing unconvinced.

Henri rubbed the back of his neck, trying to ease the tension that had been growing there since the day in the park when Marie-Catherine told him about her trip to North Carolina with Marc. "I think people are ready to hear it."

Maurault pursed his lips a moment or two before speaking. "Supposing I buy off on this, who's going to cover your desk? Who's going to finish that article you've been working on—the one about the Minister of Justice?"

A glimmer of light. Henri fought to keep the eagerness from his voice. "I can finish it. I have all my research and notes—it's practically written. And why not give Julien a shot at something a little tougher? He knows the ropes."

Maurault smirked. "He may know the ropes, but he's not as aggressive as you are, Henri. He doesn't push."

Henri caught his lip on a smile. Maurault didn't often pass out compliments, even back-handed ones. "He won't need to take my place for long. I'm not going to do anything crazy—I'll just make a few speeches, plan some demonstrations. Then get myself arrested. At least that part won't be hard." Detective Jeffers of the North Montreal precinct would relish having him behind bars. Henri quickly pushed that worry aside. "I'll be in jail a week. Two at the most."

They printed the communiqué. The mayor called. Henri sat across the desk from Maurault listening to his end of the conversation. "I'm sorry you feel that way, Mr. Mayor." Maurault glanced at Henri and winked. "We felt it important to print, important to let French Canadians know they might become FLQ targets." Maurault held the telephone receiver away from his ear and Henri grinned as Mayor Drapeau's loud but indistinct words flowed into the room.

Maurault picked up a cigarette and rolled it between his fingers. He suddenly jerked upright and the cigarette snapped in two. "The hell you say." Maurault's face turned grim as more verbal abuse poured out of the phone receiver. "No, sir, I will not." His voice was as harsh as Henri had ever heard it. "No. *Le Journal Quotidien* will continue printing what we think the public has a right to know, so long as there's freedom of the press in this country." Maurault slammed down the receiver, cutting off the flow of vitriol from the other end. "God damn him. I don't care if he is the mayor, the son-of-a-bitch doesn't make the laws."

Henri had worked long hours the night before, putting the final touches on an article sure to bring further wrath down on the newspaper. "Are you going to be able to hold him off until we can print the next installment?"

"Yeah," said Maurault, still frowning.

Henri wondered if his editor might be having second thoughts. "We don't have to go through with this. It's not too late to back off."

Maurault sighed. "No. It's a good plan. We'll do it."

Henri's article went on the front page, above the fold—the same spot the communiqué had been placed the day before. He'd been researching the story for several months. A Chicago businessman bought a prime piece of Montreal real estate from the Catholic Church at half its market-value. He put up a building. Less than two years later and well above market-price, the city bought the building for administrative offices. The Chicago businessman made a killing. The land purchase, building plans and sale to the city passed through the regulatory process without a whimper of protest. Henri used the transaction as a platform to call once more for change, starting with Quebec independence.

"I'm going to scream if that phone doesn't stop ringing." Louise took the fifth call in less than three minutes. "Just a moment please." She transferred the call to Maurault's office then turned to Henri. "Everyone's calling because of your article. I don't know what André was thinking to run it right after the FLQ *communiqué.*" She kept her voice low and her back turned to the always-inquisitive Julien and the rest of the newsroom. "They'll close us down."

Shortly before noon Henri looked up from his typewriter and felt carried back in time. "What do you want, Jeffers?"

"Just here for a short visit, Morais. Where's your boss?"

Without making eye contact, her hands trembling, Louise rose from her desk. "He's in his office, Lieutenant Jeffers. I'll tell him you want to see him."

One-by-one typewriters went silent as people grew aware of Jeffers' presence. Even the phone stopped its persistent ringing, leaving only the steady hum of the presses in the back room to fill the void.

Jeffers smirked. "No hurry. I'll chat with Morais while I'm waiting."

Jeffers' beefy red complexion ran up over his forehead to a shiny bald dome ringed with short, gingery hair. Since he'd been made a detective he no longer wore a uniform—his suit jacket stretched tight across his shoulders and under his arms. He lifted a ham-like buttock onto the edge of Louise's desk where he picked up a phone message, read it and put it down again then looked over at Henri. "You've been writing things they don't like downtown."

Henri stared into the man's watery, red-rimmed blue eyes. "It's my job. It's called investigative journalism."

Jeffers didn't comment on the jab but responded with one of his own. "What's going on with those FLQ bastards you hang out with?"

The first time Jeffers had asked Henri that question, Henri had just begun working for the paper. He remembered it like yesterday.

Louis Simard stood. "Leave him alone, Jeffers. He hasn't done anything. He's just a kid."

Jeffers ignored Simard's request. "What are you doing here, boy." He'd been sitting on the edge of Louise's desk that time, too.

Henri, just turned seventeen, tried to hide his nerves with bravado. "I work here. I work for Mr. Simard."

"Doing what? And don't lie to me. If you're involved with those FLQ bastards, I'll find out. If you're honest with me now, it'll go easier on you. Well?" The word hung in the air.

"I run errands and do research for Mr. Simard. Get him coffee, answer the phone when Louise isn't here. Things like that." Henri lifted his chin and looked directly into Jeffers' eyes. "Is there a law against it?"

Weary-voiced, Jeffers sneered. "Don't be a smart-ass, kid. You're out of your league."

Louise came out of Maurault's office bringing Henri back to the present. "You can go in, Lieutenant."

Jeffers slid off the corner of her desk, sauntered past Henri and across the room to Maurault's door, disappearing inside.

"He hasn't changed one iota," Henri said into the unaccustomed silence. "A bastard ten years ago, he's still a bastard." A sudden surge of activity had people busying themselves, but the air remained alive with speculation.

When Jeffers left, taking a bulky list of subscribers with him, Henri went in to see Maurault. "What did he say?"

Maurault looked up from studying the end of his cigarette. "Exactly what we knew he would, that I should fire your ass."

Henri sat still for a minute, thinking about the magnitude of what he was undertaking.

Maurault eyed him from across the desk. "You still have time to reconsider."

Henri shook his head then leaped to his feet. "I quit," he shouted.

"You don't quit," Maurault roared back. "You're fired."

Louise whipped her head around and stared when Henri slammed out of Maurault's office. "What happened?"

"You heard him. And why should it surprise anyone? It's just like happened to Simard." Henri glanced across the room to Julien. Julien quickly turned away, but not before Henri saw the look of anticipation on the man's face. *He'll hate my guts when I take my desk back.* Henri closed his eyes and took a deep breath. "I need a box for my stuff."

Henri told Marc that a casual family dinner might give them

an opportunity to talk without danger of being overheard. Marc agreed.

"You don't come home for dinner often enough," his father said when Henri arrived Saturday afternoon, in time to watch the Canadiens play an exhibition game on television.

His father looked older than he had just a few months before, more grizzle in his beard, a deepening of the lines carved in his cheeks. "How are you doing, Papa? You feeling okay?"

"Sure. Why wouldn't I be feeling good with the hockey season just getting underway and us a sure thing for the Stanley Cup again this year?"

Henri laughed. "I hope you're right on that one, Papa. I'm always ready for another win." He lifted the lid of the big pot at the back of the stove and sniffed. "It smells good, *Maman.*"

His mother, a short woman and stout, not given much to laughter or soft words, sat at the table with a cup of tea in front of her and a pair of scissors next to it, scanning the newspaper Henri had brought, searching for coupons to clip.

"Did Marc say when he'd get here?" Henri hadn't told his parents about his job, still not sure how to explain it and not wanting to lie to them more than he had to. But he wanted to get it done before his brother arrived.

His father sat in front of the television set, about to turn it on. "Not until later."

"What about Marie-Catherine?"

"She has a test..said she has to study." His father patted

the seat next to him. "The game is about to start, Henri. Come and sit down."

"I need to talk to you first, Papa. You and *Maman.*"

His mother looked up, alarm written on her face. "What's wrong?"

Henri's stomach churned, but he was determined to get the telling over with. "I'm frustrated with how slowly the separatist movement is going and I've been thinking about what I can do about that."

His father eased himself down in a chair next to Henri's mother. "You're right to be angry about it. It's long past time we have our freedom."

"Don't start about that, Emile. Let Henri tell us what he has to say." Agitation sounded in his mother's voice and her hand shook when she pulled her teacup closer.

Henri drew a deep breath, then spoke in a rush. "I've decided to do something more direct. I've left my job at *Le Journal Quotidien.*"

His mother's eyes widened. "Henri, how could you be so foolish? You've left to do what? What can you accomplish for separatism others before you haven't already tried to do and failed?"

"Hush, Anne-Marie. Henri is a grown man. Leave him be. What are you going to do, son?"

"I'm exploring things, Papa."

"You mean you don't have something else, another job to go to?" His mother turned to his father. "This is your doing, Emile. I wash my hands of it." She stood and in her agitation, knocked over the teacup, sending its contents across the newspaper. When she tried to blot the spilled tea with a dishtowel, she knocked the scissors to the floor.

"I'll get it, *Maman*." Henri picked up the scissors and returned them to the table then tried to wrest the dishtowel from his mother's hand. "I'll get it."

"I already have it." His mother jerked the towel away, dripping tea across the floor. She threw the towel into the empty dishpan. "I don't want to hear any more of this. I'm going to the market."

Henri watched her leave the house. He should go to the door and call her back, tell her the truth, but the words stuck in his throat. Reluctantly, he turned back to his father. "I'm not sure what I'll be doing, Papa. But I'm going to get closer to the action."

His father nodded. "It's time."

"I don't want you and *Maman* to worry. No matter what happens or what you hear, okay?"

"No, you're a good boy, Henri. I trust you to do what needs to be done."

The more understanding and encouragement his father heaped on him, the guiltier Henri felt. When his father finally suggested they have a glass of wine and watch the hockey game, he was glad to agree.

Marc arrived just as the hockey match finished. Later, after a mostly silent dinner during which his mother refused to look at Henri, their parents went to bed.

Just as Henri and Marc had done so many times growing up, the two brothers sat on the front steps. Both wore jackets. The days were getting shorter and little warmth remained after sunset. Henri dreaded the cold winter months ahead, imagining them ready at any moment to blast into Montreal and cover the city in an icy blanket. He shivered in anticipation.

"It isn't that cold."

"Not yet." Henri fell silent again, waiting for Marc to begin. A breeze rustled around the base of the lilac bush in the middle of the yard and swept across the porch, bringing with it the smell of decaying leaves and last spring's faded blossoms.

"Papa's looking old."

"I know." Henri was surprised his brother had noticed.

"It makes me think we've wasted enough time."

His cue, Henri thought. No more planning, no more practicing his lines, time to step out on the stage. "Not anymore. I'm ready to get down off the fence you're always telling me I'm sitting on and get my hands dirty."

Marc lit a cigarette. "You still haven't told me why. After all you've done for him, why did Maurault fire you and why do you suddenly want to be part of the FLQ?"

Henri swallowed, taking care to keep his voice even. "Remember Louis Simard?"

Marc shot him a glance. "Sure."

"Same reason; Jeffers and Drapeau applied enough pressure, so he let me go."

"What a chicken shit. He should have told them to get fucked." Marc stubbed out his cigarette on the porch step. "But why not go to work for *La Presse* or one of the other newspapers? They'd hire you. Why come to us now?"

"Because it's time." Henri's heart beat so hard, he thought he could feel the blood surging through his veins. "You know I've always wanted the same things as you—sovereignty, independence, justice. My way hasn't worked; I'm ready to try it your way." When Marc nodded and grinned, Henri felt giddy with relief. "So, what do you want me to do?"

"I've been thinking about that." Marc lit another cigarette and drew on it. "I don't think your usefulness is in operations. Though I hate to admit it, your articles about the establishment and about our need for independence have helped. And they've made you well known—in some parts of the city, at least."

Henri resented the skepticism in his brother's voice. *Le Journal Quotidien* was a first-class newspaper, one of the oldest in Montreal, and he'd worked hard to become its lead reporter. Instinctively, he started to protest, but then kept his mouth shut. Careful, he told himself.

"I think you need to be where even more people will hear you. The right people."

Henri lowered his head to keep the rain out of his eyes as he and Marc both reached for the door handle of the Black Cat, a 'men only' tavern on Pie IX Boulevard. They had come to the tavern in north Montreal to see Charles Pelletier, an electronics manufacturer Marc claimed supported the FLQ.

Inside the tavern, Henri shook the rain off his wool cap and stuffed it in his pocket. His gaze darted around the crowded room. The air was nearly blue with cigarette smoke and full of voices talking above the blare of the television on the back of the bar. Over the din came the crack of pool balls hitting against each other.

Marc jerked his chin toward the rear of the room. "There he is."

A steely-haired, heavy-set man sat alone at a table facing

them. Henri had heard about Pelletier, but not about his FLQ connections. "What do you think the chances are of getting more money out of him?"

"Good. Like I told you, he thinks we need more upbeat publicity."

"And that's why he wants to talk to me?" Excitement had Henri's stomach jumping, wondering what they wanted him to do. No violence, no bank robberies. He'd told Maurault all bets were off if they tried to get him into anything like that.

"Right. Let's go on back." Marc started moving toward the man at the table.

A woman carrying a tray of drinks sauntered past them. "Hey, Marc."

Marc turned his head to watch the woman, whose swaying hips were full of promise. Henri nudged his brother with his elbow. "Later." Marc grinned and shrugged. Two men at the end of the bar looked up and nodded as they passed. With his chin, Marc gave them a flicker of recognition.

Pelletier's eyes were on them as they approached. "I've been hearing about you," he said to Henri when they got to the table and Marc introduced them. He indicated two empty chairs. "Sit down and name your poison."

Marc pulled a chair back and slid into it. "I'll have a beer."

Henri pulled out the remaining chair. His mind raced, trying to remember everything he and Maurault had talked about and planned. "Beer works for me."

An ashtray next to Pelletier cradled the remains of a half -smoked cigar and a lit cigar was hooked under the index finger of his left hand. He picked up an aluminum holder from the table beside the ashtray and offered it. Henri declined, but Marc took a cigar and reached for the lighter Pelletier slid across the table to him.

"Thanks." Marc bit off the cigar's tip and spit it on the floor.

The same waitress appeared with two beers and another glass of whiskey on a tray. Smiling at Marc, she served the three men and then replaced the full ashtray with an empty one. Marc returned her smile with a wink.

"I've read your stuff." Pelletier's voice was rough with smoke. "Too bad Maurault let you go."

Henri didn't reply. After the waitress left them, Pelletier went on, not mincing words.

"As you know, we're at a juncture where we need to turn up the heat on Ottawa. Our friend here," he nodded to Marc, "your brother can provide the firepower to get Ottawa's attention."

He coughed to clear his throat then took a sip of whiskey, looking at Henri over the rim of the glass. He set the glass back on the table.

"But we need someone to tell the story, someone articulate, someone who knows and agrees with the FLQ's goals, but who hasn't been compromised by any of its past operations."

Henri glanced at Marc, who was tilted back in his chair, his arms folded across his chest. Smoke from the cigar Marc held in his hand drifted upward, gathering in the darkened rafters above their heads. Curious, Henri looked back at Pelletier.

"What do you have in mind? A Sinn Fein equivalent

for the FLQ? A separate public relations wing?" The possibility of it intrigued him.

"Something like that, but on a smaller scale. To start, we need the right man to make our case heard—a man who can get the attention of all the newspapers in the city, including *La Presse* and *The Montreal Star*, and make them print what he says. You." He jabbed his chin toward Henri. "We need you."

"I'm flattered you think I can generate that amount of interest just making speeches and writing articles." In spite himself, a flush of pride came to Henri's cheeks.

"You're good, Henri," said Pelletier. "Don't try to hide your light under a bushel now. Despite your youth, you've built a solid reputation because what you say makes sense to a lot of people. You use logic to make your case without getting bogged down in emotion."

Pelletier took another sip of whiskey, his eyes never leaving Henri's face.

"Though in my mind you've never gone far enough. But that's about to change, right?"

"I know what Marc does," Henri said, stalling for time. "What's your role in all this?"

A smug look spread across Pelletier's face. "I pay the bills."

There were plenty of rumors going around about where Pelletier had gotten his money. Henri had heard most of them. He knew the man had started out as a worker in an electronics plant. Bright and aggressive, he'd worked his way up the ladder into management. Then Pelletier left the company and started one of his own. His new company had been successful from the beginning. Along the way Pelletier must have had help people said; some said that help came from the Mafia.

"What do you say?" Henri asked Marc once they were again outside on the sidewalk. It was a little before midnight.

Marc shrugged. "Why the fuck should I care where his money came from as long as he wants to pass some of it along to us?"

It had stopped raining. Henri glanced upward. Big piles of clouds had pulled back, exposing a three-quarter moon, but the sidewalks and streets were still rain-slick. "Want me to drop you off?"

"Nah. I'm meeting someone."

"The waitress?"

Marc laughed. "She gets off in ten minutes."

"What about the woman who answers your phone?"

"Bunny? What about her?"

Twice Henri saw or imagined he saw Claudia. One morning on University Street a slim woman with dark, swinging hair just like hers walked down the sidewalk a block ahead of him. Heart thudding, he quickened his pace. He lost her when she disappeared into a crowd of office workers. Another time he thought he saw her in the window of a passing bus.

When he got home he dialed the number she'd given him, but hung up before anyone had time to answer. It had been easier when he thought she was in Chicago.

Chapter Six

Marie-Catherine climbed down from the city bus and pulled her thick wool jacket closer against the blistering-cold December night air. She tugged her knit hat over her ears and wound its long tail around her neck. When the bus pulled away from the curb, she crossed the boulevard and headed up the hill toward the University of Montreal campus. She didn't want to miss any of Henri's speech, the third one he'd made since Maurault fired him, and the first one on campus since he'd graduated from the university years before.

Looking toward the cluster of lighted yellow buildings, their oxidized copper roofs looking like small green caps, buildings that reeked of Quebec's past, Marie-Catherine wondered if she'd made a mistake in her choice of schools. Perhaps she'd be happier at this school, with its long history of student activism. She rejected the idea even as it came to her. Plodding along in Henri's footsteps would be a mistake. She didn't want to become a pale, female version of her brother. Better that she forged her own trail, make her own story.

Fine crystals of frozen snow stung her cheeks. She tucked her chin down, huddling deeper into her collar. The wind brought the rumbling voices of a crowd. She easily followed the growing noise to where two- or three-hundred were milling about. Together with its two classroom wings, the building formed three sides of a large square, the fourth side open. In the center of the building a sweep of steps ran up to a set of double-doors. Six-foot high marble walls flanked the bottom of the steps like giant white wings.

Marie-Catherine glanced around for Marc, who'd said he would meet her, but she didn't see him. Several classroom windows were thrown open. Young people leaned out and called to friends below. Anticipation crackled in the frigid air.

Most of those gathered looked to be in their late teens or early twenties, but here and there Marie-Catherine spotted some who were older, professors, maybe, and a few she recognized as reporters, including Julien Amis, the man who'd taken Henri's job at *Le Journal Quotidien*.

Julien looked miserable, shivering and hunched into his jacket, a bead of moisture hanging from the end of his thin, red nose. He started pushing toward her when he caught her eyes on him, but Marie-Catherine deliberately turned her back. He was no better than Maurault. Henri joining the FLQ pleased and delighted her, but it still made her furious her brother had been fired.

She wiggled her toes inside her heavy snow boots and slapped her gloved hands together against the cold as she searched the crowd. It didn't surprise her when she still couldn't find Marc. He often didn't show up where and when he'd said he would. But at least she saw no sign of the Provincial or the Montreal Police.

Shushes and *quiets* moved across the crowd. Henri had

suddenly appeared on top of one of the marble wings at the foot of the stairs.

Henri's good looks, his thick, brown hair curling over his ears, serious dark eyes under straight, black brows, were a frequent topic with Marie-Catherine's girlfriends in high school. They were often flushed and tongue-tied in his presence, then giggling as soon as he left the room. Marie-Catherine suspected Henri only pretended not to notice their reactions.

Tonight, his standard uniform, green army jacket, a plaid shirt and faded blue jeans, made him indistinguishable from many of the young people gathered. He didn't call out or whistle, but stood quiet and still. His hands were tucked into his armpits and his breath created a slight halo around his head. Although it had stopped snowing, droplets of moisture in the air were picked out in the light streaming from the security lamps mounted on the buildings. When the crowd finally grew quiet, Henri began to speak.

"Until a few years ago, a billboard welcomed visitors to our airport which read *'Invest in the province of Quebec, where labor is cheap and docile.* We got rid of that sign, but we haven't gotten rid of the attitudes that put it there. We still have businesses in the United States dictating economic policy in Quebec."

A man in the crowd began shouting: "Down with the U.S." Others soon joined him, but Henri raised his arms and they quieted.

"We still have U.S. businesses teaming with our government and championed by the Church. In private meetings, they strike real estate deals that are destroying our environment. They line their pockets with gold at our expense." The crowd grumbled and Henri's voice raised a notch. "We must wrest our future from the grasp of bloodsucking businessmen who dictate to us with impunity. They suck the life from us and treat us no better than slaves."

Marie-Catherine joined her voice with the crowd's angry roar.

"We have wasted too much time waiting for them to see French Canadians as men and women, not just as cheap labor to be used as they see fit." Henri's gaze swept the crowd. The crowd growled its agreement.

Marie-Catherine thought of their father, working for little more than half the pay English-speakers earned doing the same job. She thought of her mother, saving pennies to make ends meet. When she considered the house and neighborhood where they lived, nausea roiled her stomach. Only the pride she felt for her brother, standing above them on the wall, tempered her anger.

"What are we going to do about it?" When Henri took a step forward Marie-Catherine realized the wall was deeper than it appeared.

"Stop them," yelled the crowd.

"How are we going to stop them?" Henri almost chanted his response.

"Close the borders," said a woman.

"Kick the bastards out of office," said another.

Henri shook his head. "Solidarity is the answer. We must join our union brothers, and arm in arm we need to stand together and fight for workers' rights."

"Solidarity," the crowd echoed.

"We must help the Native people of Quebec, the Montagnais, the Cree, the Algonquins. We must help them save their homelands from exploitation by U.S. capitalists."

"Solidarity," yelled Marie-Catherine.

"Solidarity," roared the crowd.

"Together," Henri shouted. "We must destroy the present government, tear it down brick by brick, institution by institution, bureaucracy by bureaucracy, and rebuild a new government for Quebec—a separate government of responsible men and women who are bound together in solidarity."

The crowd surged forward, chanting Henri's name. "Morais! Morais! Morais!" Marie-Catherine no longer heard Henri's voice. She felt a push from behind and staggered, then quickly righted herself. She was caught up in the crowd's mounting fervor. Thinking she heard Marc yelling to her, she turned and caught sight of him, but the press of bodies kept her from turning back and reaching him.

Police whistles sounded. Over the shoulders of those behind her, Marie-Catherine saw a phalanx of uniformed men in riot gear pour around the corner of one of the building's wings before moving out to encircle the crowd. Marie-Catherine's breath caught in her throat.

Pandemonium erupted. Shouts and cries along with rocks and bottles started flying. Marie-Catherine didn't know where the rocks came from since concrete and tarmac paved the square, now partially covered with packed snow and ice from weeks of harsh, snowy weather. Some of the crowd must have come armed for a fight. Most of the missiles were deflected by the upraised shields of the police.

Pushed first one way then the other, Marie-Catherine struggled to keep her balance as everyone fought to escape the unyielding line of police. Tears blurred her eyes. The double doors at the top of the flight of stairs offered the only escape. The walls of the buildings on three sides served as a funnel. Using clubs and shields, the police had only to press forward.

More than once, Marie-Catherine needed to grab hold of an arm or shoulder to keep herself upright. Suddenly she slammed up against the icy marble wall, bare now of its speaker. At the same time, she spotted a young woman struck to the ground by a policeman's club, then kicked. She started to work her way toward the woman, but was grabbed by the arm and jerked to safety behind the wall. Henri.

"What are you doing here? Is Marc here, too?"

"Yes. I saw him, but I couldn't reach him."

"You shouldn't be here. Marc knew there'd be trouble tonight. He shouldn't have let you come."

"There's a woman on the ground. I need to go to her." Marie-Catherine was surprised they could hear each other in the din coming from beyond the wall.

"You'll only get yourself beaten. I'll go."

But when they looked out, the woman was gone.

"I didn't see Marc until the riot started because I got too caught up with what you were saying. I'm so proud of you, Henri. I'm so glad you're one of us now."

Henri studied her face a moment. "Marc should have been with you. You shouldn't have come alone. You shouldn't have come here at all."

"You worry too much Henri."

The noise beyond the wall slowly quieted. Only an occasional shout rang out. Marie-Catherine looked out once again. The most ardent students had been hauled off in vans and the police moved through the thinned crowd. They appeared to be searching for someone. Finally, the rest of the crowd dispersed. The few remaining police climbed into vans or cars and took off. Only two stayed behind, standing next to a dark sedan.

Without a word, Henri stepped out from behind their wall of safety.

"Henri, don't! Wait!" Marie-Catherine followed him, clutching his arm.

Henri shook himself free and while Marie-Catherine watched, anxiety knotting her stomach, he walked up to the two officers. They grabbed him and, jerking his arms behind his back, fastened on handcuffs then pushed him into the back of the car.

The slamming of the door released Marie-Catherine from whatever had been holding her at the wall. She rushed forward to protest, but Marc appeared from nowhere and grabbed her shoulder. "Not now. Let's go. He'll need a lawyer."

Snow began to fall again, this time in earnest.

Chapter Seven

Henri sat alone in the middle of the back seat. The two policemen in front, on the other side of the metal grill, said little to one another and nothing to him. The car smelled of stale cigarette smoke and disinfectant. The windshield wipers swung back and forth like a metronome, pushing the snow aside with a dull mechanical click, click. *Don't think. Don't think.*

Henri peered through the streaked windows as the car crawled down the hill, past the ghost city of monuments and tombstones that was Mount Royal Cemetery, before turning onto Rue St. Laurent, the street dividing Montreal's English-speaking haves from its French-, Spanish-, Greek-, Italian- and Polish-speaking have-nots.

He leaned back against the worn seat. Instead of the police station nearest the university, they were taking him to one on the north side of Montreal. Jeffers' precinct. His stomach wrenched.

The windshield wipers went on clicking: *Don't think, don't think, don't think.*

Chapter Eight

Marc watched his sister wearily climb out of his cab, her dark eyes filled with apprehension. "Let me know whatever you find out. As soon as you find out, okay?"

"Don't worry," he said. "I'll have a lawyer for him by morning."

Before she could reply, Marc reached across the seat and pulled the car door closed, put the car in gear and drove off. Framed in his rearview mirror, Marie-Catherine stood motionless on the curb in front of her apartment, gazing after him while snow fell around her.

Two hours later, Marc put the phone receiver back in its cradle. At least he'd taken care of the lawyer part.

"Come to bed. There's nothing more you can do for Henri, but you can do something for me." Bunny looked at him from black, deep-set eyes above sharp, high cheekbones that spoke of her Mohawk heritage.

"Not tonight."

She ran her hand up the inside of his thigh. "Come on, Marc." She moved her hand higher and began to stroke him.

Marc moved away from the side of the bed. "No. I told you, I'm not interested tonight."

"Well, fuck you." Bunny rolled over. Twenty minutes later, still dressed, she lay in a sleeping sprawl. Her straight black hair fell in a curtain over half her face.

Sex with Bunny was like waging war. Her goal was to conquer, and what she lacked in technique she made up for in enthusiasm and ingenuity. Any other night Marc would have enjoyed one of their protracted battles. They'd been together almost six months, longer by far than his usual relationships, because she gave as good as she got in bed. Out of bed, his indifference to her feelings never seemed to bother her. At least not for long.

Marc liked it that way. The last thing he needed was more drama in his life. He had enough of that from his family, namely Henri. He couldn't figure out what had made his brother give himself up like that. It gave Marc cold sweats just thinking about being locked up, but Henri had practically begged for it.

The two of them had always been poles apart in how they operated. Growing up, Henri insisted on doing every-thing the hard way, arguing with his teachers and every other authority figure, over issues he had no hope of winning.

"Screw the bastards," Marc had told his brother when-ever Henri started on one of his crusades. "You're not going to change their minds by talking. You being right and them wrong makes no difference. Believe what you believe, do what needs to be done and tell anyone who disagrees with you to get fucked. That's my motto."

Marc padded into the kitchen on stocking feet. Henri had never gotten it. Instead, his brother had made a career of tilting at windmills, real and imaginary.

As he reached into the refrigerator for another beer a light tapping sounded at the door. He went to it and paused a moment. The tapping sounded again. "Who is it," he asked, his voice low.

The reply was equally soft. "LeGuin."

Marc opened the door a crack. When he saw LeGuin standing alone on the threshold, he opened the door wide enough to let the man inside. He returned to the kitchen, LeGuin close behind him.

"Want a beer?" Marc waved his bottle in the direction of the refrigerator. "The opener is on the counter."

"I heard about your brother." LeGuin followed Marc to the living room, beer in hand. Even though he spoke in low tones, the hard edges of the sparsely furnished room and the uncarpeted tile floor made his voice sound louder.

"News travels fast." Marc sat in an over-stuffed vinyl-covered chair and took a cigarette from the pack on the tray-table next to it. "Who told you?" He flicked the lighter twice before a flame sprang up.

LeGuin lounged against the wall. "Theresa. I don't know where she got it." He paused, his dark eyes questioning. "What do you plan to do about it?"

"I just talked to Blanchard. He's going to see Henri tomorrow."

"You're not going to leave it there. What else?"

LeGuin's heavy jacket hung open. Beneath it, he wore the same uniform of baggy army pants and dirty white t-shirt he'd worn the day they'd met at the warehouse near the airport, when Marc and Marie-Catherine had returned from North Carolina in the explosives-laden rental truck.

Marc frowned. "I haven't decided yet."

"With that load you brought up from North Carolina, we've got all we need to get the flics' attention."

"I'd like to light some of it off under that shit, Jeffers." Marc stubbed out his cigarette and reached for another.

"Why don't we?" LeGuin's pale eyes lit with anticipation.

Marc shook his head. "Later. Fighting the *flics* directly will come later." More soldiers needed to be recruited into their army before they could declare all-out war on the police. The sooner that happened, the better.

"So? We've got the stuff. Where are we going to use it?" LeGuin spoke eagerly. He had even less patience than Marc. "What about doing something for the construction workers unions? We're beginning to get support from them. The needle trade is always ripe, too."

Marc pursed his lips. "I hear trouble's brewing at Arrow Shoe Factory."

"You think they'll strike?"

Marc shrugged. "Wouldn't you at a dollar-five an hour?"

LeGuin straightened from the wall, finished his beer then headed toward the door. "I'll check it out."

Marc sat on in the empty living room after LeGuin left, lighting one cigarette from another, and made his plans for Arrow Shoe Factory. He didn't need LeGuin to investigate. He knew they'd strike and he knew the strike would be long and bitter.

Eventually, daylight seeped in around the lowered blinds in the living room. Marc leaned back in the chair. Against his closed eyelids, he once again saw Henri walking out from behind the marble wall and up to the police. He didn't want to contemplate what Jeffers or someone like him might be doing to his brother. He stubbed out his cigarette, sending the ashtray scraping across the table's metal surface.

"God damn it to hell," he muttered. "The stupid fuck." He wasn't sure if he meant Henri or Jeffers.

Chapter Nine

Marie-Catherine paced the carpeted floor of the small living room in the apartment she shared with two other young women, also students at UQAM. For the zillionth time, she rehashed the events of the evening, once more seeing Henri walking out from behind the safety of the wall into the hands of the police. He'd acted so fast there'd been no way for her to stop his madness. Surely, he'd known what they'd do to him, what they were no doubt doing to him at this very moment. She scrubbed at the tears in her eyes and on her cheeks.

Her watch showed the time to be nearly two a.m. Earlier the snow had stopped, but only briefly. A snowplow passed by on the street below. Marie-Catherine paced on, checking the time every few minutes, willing the night away. She tried but failed to take comfort from Marc's promise to get Henri a good lawyer.

Chapter Ten

The two arresting officers led Henri into the precinct building. Jeffers' smirking face greeted him.

"You just couldn't stay away, eh?"

Henri refused to answer, but his hands were clammy and sweat sprang out on his forehead.

Jeffers shoved him toward a stairwell. "Come on, Morais. I've waited for you long enough." Another man silently followed them up the stairs. When Henri stumbled on a tread, Jeffers prodded him in the back.

"Pick up your feet."

The sound of their footsteps pounding on the linoleum-covered stairs, along with Jeffers' rough voice, filled the narrow passageway.

Could they smell his fear? *Don't think*.

In an interrogation room on the second floor, Jeffers pushed Henri into a straight-backed wooden chair. He unlocked Henri's handcuffs, took the cuff off his left wrist, and looped it through the back of the chair before reattaching and clicking it shut.

Henri looked over his shoulder. "What's the matter? You think I might be too much for the two of you to handle?"

As soon as he said the words, his stomach tightened, expecting retribution. He relaxed, but only marginally, when Jeffers ignored the jibe.

Jeffers tested the handcuffs before walking around the table. Williams, Jeffers new partner—Jeffers seemed to go through a lot of partners—took one of the two chairs facing Henri. Jeffers remained standing. They both stared at him for what felt like several minutes.

Then, without warning and seemingly without consulting one another, they both began firing out question after question.

"How long have you been in?"

"I'm not 'in' anything."

"What's the name of your cell?'

"I don't have a cell."

"Who's in the cell with you?"

"I told you, I don't belong to a cell." Henri was beginning to feel like a tennis ball.

Jeffers put his hands on the table and leaned in, his face mere inches from Henri's. "What's the FLQ's next target?"

"I don't know."

"Liar. Who's the FLQ's new leader?"

"I don't know.

"Where does their money come from?"

On and on they went, first one, then the other, often repeating themselves. Henri's answers remained the same.

"I've committed no crime."

He said the words for what the thousandth time. He hoped they were as sick of hearing them as he was of saying them.

"Inciting the overthrow of the government is called

sedition." Jeffers' voice rasped. "Starting a riot is a crime. So is planting bombs and robbing banks." He stared down at Henri.

"I've planted no bombs and robbed no banks. I've done nothing illegal. And the riot didn't start until you *flics* showed up."

He hated being kept in the chair, having to look up to see Jeffers' ugly face.

"You pink-o bastards are all alike," Williams said. "When are you going to give it up, Morais? The Canadian government is not going away. The Canadian people—the non-French Canadian people, who are the majority in this country—don't want a separate government in Quebec."

Taller, thinner, and younger than Jeffers, Williams remained slouched in his chair, a sneer on his face, while Jeffers now prowled the room like an underfed cat, picking at his teeth with a wooden toothpick.

With an effort, Henri pulled his eyes away from Jeffers and looked wearily at Williams.

"Of course they don't. Why would they want to change anything when they're in charge and benefiting? But how would they like to earn half their present salaries, eh? How would they like to see all the best jobs go to someone else— just because that someone else speaks a different language at home?"

Henri jerked his head toward Jeffers, who'd come to stand behind his chair. Jeffers' hard paunch rode against his shoulder.

"How would you like to earn half of what your fat partner there earns?"

"Shut up." Jeffers hit Henri with the heel of his hand, slamming his head down against the table hard enough to jar his teeth.

The interrogation didn't stop. Henri lost track of time. The adrenalin that had kept him defiant ebbed away as exhaustion set in.

"I want a lawyer," he mumbled through swollen lips.

He was so tired. He didn't care what he said anymore or if it made any sense, he just wanted the nightmare to end.

Jeffers hit him again.

Outside the barred window, the sky lightened enough Henri could make out the brick wall of the building next door. At some point in the night it had stopped snowing. Jeffers and Williams were gone. Ten minutes? An hour? He had no idea. His head drooped. His eyes felt like grit-encrusted slits and a coppery taste filled his mouth from where his front teeth had cut into his lower lip. He rolled his shoulders, trying to ease his cramped muscles. He needed to use the toilet.

A man, someone Henri hadn't seen before, stuck his head through the open door and peered around the room then withdrew, closing the door behind him. The sound of his footsteps retreated down the hall.

After a while more footsteps sounded and the man reappeared. This time he came into the room and walked around behind Henri. Henri braced himself, waiting for another blow.

Instead, the man fumbled with the handcuffs and in a moment his arms dropped to the sides of the chair. For what must have been ten hours, maybe more, Henri's arms had been tightly bound behind his back. Now the released muscles in his shoulders shrieked in sudden pain, and the room began to spin and go dark at the same time.

"Put your head between your knees."

The voice sounded distant and hollow. A hand came down on the back of Henri's head. Expecting to be slammed into the table again, he tried to resist the pressure forcing his head down, but his body refused to respond to the commands his brain gave it. After a moment, the darkness receded and the room stopped turning.

His throat felt like a metal band was tightening around it. He drew a deep breath and straightened in the chair. He tried and failed to lift his arms. On the third attempt, he got his hands into his lap. They were numb. He stared at them, feeling as if they belonged to someone else.

The man cleared his throat. "When you can stand up I'll take you down to a holding cell. Your lawyer called. He'll be here in an hour."

The guard unlocked the door and a man walked in. Henri stood.

"I'm Paul Blanchard, your attorney, assuming you want me." He extended his right hand. In his left, he carried a black leather briefcase.

After a moment's hesitation, Henri wiped his palm on his jeans then reached out and shook the man's hand. The muscles in his shoulder protested the movement. He struggled to keep from grimacing.

"Who contacted you? How did you know I was here?" His swollen lips slurred the words.

"Your brother called me. It took me a while to find out where they'd taken you—at first, they weren't going to let me see you. I had to pull some strings."

Although he'd stretched out on the bunk when they put him in his cell, Henri hadn't slept. His brain felt fuzzy and dull. "They brought me here, to Jeffers."

"Yes." Blanchard's voice was smooth and reassuring. "It looks like he worked you over a bit."

Henri nodded.

"I wish I could say you were the first." Blanchard looked at the bunk. "Shall we sit?"

Henri looked from the lawyer's meticulous khaki-colored slacks to the rough gray blanket on the bunk. "Okay."

When they were seated, Blanchard put his briefcase on his knees and pressed the buttons to release the locks. A half -inch of starched white cotton extended beyond the cuffs of his navy-blue blazer. He took out a file with Henri's name neatly printed in blue ink on the tab. Inside the file was a single piece of paper with Marc's name and phone number at the top and the letters "F L Q" printed opposite.

Blanchard took a pen from inside the briefcase then closed the lid and laid the file on top of it.

"I should explain that I've handled FLQ cases before."

Henri nodded. "The Huliene brothers, Marcel Pondi, Serge Damion." He knew all about Blanchard. The man liked to dress like a member of the establishment, except for the long, wavy blond curls hanging to his shoulders, but he'd made a name for himself representing high-profile FLQ prisoners.

Blanchard took the cap off his pen. "I'm also representing some of those arrested during the limousine riots."

Henri nodded again. The recent limousine drivers' strike and the subsequent riots in Murray-Hill. He began to feel more in control. It wouldn't all be Jeffers' way, now he had someone on his side. Especially someone as good as Blanchard.

"Okay." He clenched and unclenched his fingers, trying to drive the remaining numbness out. At the same time, he fought to bring his brain into sharper focus. He needed all his wits about him.

"So, what happens now?"

"May I call you Henri?" When Henri nodded, Blanchard went on. "To start, I'll ask you some questions and you answer them, as truthfully and fully as you can."

"And then what?"

"Then I begin the paper-chase to get you out of here. So…shall we begin?"

Henri answered all of Blanchard's questions. Most of his answers were true, the rest were well-rehearsed. Even through his exhaustion, he realized Blanchard questions were like a reporter's, establishing who, what, when, where, and why.

Noise from outside his cell interrupted one of Blanchard's questions. A guard carrying a tray of food approached.

"Looks like it's time for lunch. I guess this will do for now."

Blanchard put the cap back on his pen, closed Henri's file on the sheet of paper, now covered with cramped scribbling, and returned the file and pen to his briefcase before closing the lid with a snap. He stood.

Henri looked up, too tired to move from his seat on the bunk.

"Have they told you what I'm charged with?"

Blanchard moved to the door of the cell. "I don't think they've decided yet." He motioned for the guard to unlock the cell door. "I'll be in touch, Henri. We'll have you out of here in no time."

Chapter Eleven

Years before, Marc had stopped working on the docks with his father. Driving a cab gave him more flexibility, and no flics questioning why he was in one place or another. Three days after Henri's arrest, he parked his cab at the end of the taxi rank and got out to talk with several other drivers circled around a small, hotel-provided kerosene heater at the edge of the sidewalk. It had snowed hard in the night, but the plows had been out early. Now the sky was crystal blue. Also biting cold.

"Hey," Marc said to the group when he joined them. His steps buoyant, he felt full of purpose.

"Morning," said several others, shifting to give him space around the portable heater.

Marc put a cigarette between his lips and lit it. "What's new?"

"Not much," said the man next to him. "We were just saying maybe we should have waited until spring to settle the strike."

Marc chuckled and stamped his feet to keep the circulation going. "I know what you mean. The cold is without mercy this morning."

A sharp whistle sounded. Down the block a green-coated bellman signaled for a cab. The first cab in the rank of half-a-dozen drove forward and pulled up next to the bellman. Another liveried man carried suitcases from the hotel lobby to the back of the cab while the bellman helped a man and woman get in.

"Lucky shit," said one of the men in the circle. "The airport."

"Yes," said another. "I'm next in line, but with my luck it will be a two-block ride. *C'est la vie.*" Amid laughter he left the circle of men warming their hands and went over to get into his idling cab now leading the rank. At the same time, another cab turned the corner and tucked in at the end of the row.

After fifteen or twenty minutes of waiting, Marc was at the head of the line, and a minute later lifted the trunk lid to accommodate a single suitcase. He took his fare, a businessman, to the airport, dropped him off and returned to the rank at the hotel. He had two other short fares. At eleven-thirty, once more at the head of the rank, the bellman again whistled and lifted his arm.

A short, muscular man climbed into the back of Marc's cab, setting a briefcase on the seat next to him. He wore leather gloves and an expensive-looking wool coat over his suit, but his close-cropped hair, bent nose and scarred face didn't fit his businessman attire.

"Where to?"

"St. James Street," the man said, breathing heavily and speaking in an American accent. "Here's the address." He handed Marc a card. Marc glanced at it and handed it back then put the cab into gear and moved away from the curb. At the end of the block he turned left, toward the river. He turned left again onto a street that was once a bustling commercial center, but was now lined with second-rate shops and vacant buildings. When he found the address, a narrow, seedy-looking shop, its plate-glass windows painted black, he looked for a place to pull up to the curb.

"Just stop and let me out. I'll leave the briefcase on the seat." The man opened the door and stepped from the cab.

Though tempted to turn and check his back seat, Marc kept his eyes on the street ahead of him as he drove down the block. He turned right on Peel then several blocks later he turned right again, onto Sherbrooke. He took little notice of the beauty surrounding him, the clear sky arching over the city, the snow-covered monuments in the park, the architecture of the old buildings he passed. His mind was focused on the briefcase lying on the seat behind him. It took twenty minutes to get to his apartment building.

"How much?" said Bunny when Marc finished counting the bills.

"Seven thousand. The amount Pelletier promised."

Chapter Twelve

For three weeks Blanchard promised Henri a quick release. But *by the end of the week* had become *you'll be home for Christmas*, and just that morning he promised *before the end of the year*. Henri no longer listened to him.

Two weeks maximum, he and Maurault had figured. Talk about naïve. Pacing back and forth across the cell, Henri stopped each time at the barred door to peer down the empty hallway. He saw no one, even though there were three other cells along the hall, two across from his.

They mostly stayed empty during the day. Henri's jailers had taken his wristwatch, but he knew when night arrived because that's when they brought the drunks in. In the morning, they let them go. About the only other activity Henri could count on was someone coming down to mop up the puke after the cells had been emptied. They never got rid of the smell.

Nothing else relieved the tedium of eating, sleeping, and pacing his cell, except for Blanchard's occasional visits and the more frequent visits by Jeffers and Williams, alone or together. Sometimes they interrogated him in the cell. Sometimes they took him back upstairs. The questions were always the same, as were his answers.

Jeffers' violent responses stayed the same, too. Henri had taken his fair share of licks as a kid. From his mother most often, sometimes from his father. There'd been the frequent so-called disciplining at school, too. Ruler-whacked hands from the nuns and worse from the priest who'd been headmaster.

But nothing had prepared him for Jeffers' brutality, the relentless pounding to his kidneys and chest, the arm wrenching, the never-ending threats of worse to come. Henri didn't know how much longer he could hold out before he told everything he knew and more besides.

Crossing the narrow cell to his bunk once again, he threw himself down and stared at a spot on the green painted ceiling over his head, well able to understand the frustration leading a previous inmate to throw food at it. At least he hoped it was food. His head ached. Footsteps sounded above him. Then something, chair legs maybe, scraped across the floor. Footsteps followed again, a far-off door slammed, then silence.

Henri closed his eyes, forcing his mind away from his surroundings and back to a more innocent time. Answers, then, had been so much clearer.

Henri awakened with a start. For a minute, he imagined he lay on his narrow childhood bed at home. Then he smelled the toilet in the corner of his cell and heard footsteps and the scraping chair overhead. He hit the wall with his balled fist, winced and shook it.

"Hey, Morais. You've got a visitor."

Henri jumped off the bunk as the cell door opened. Marc stood behind the guard.

The guard stepped aside for Marc to enter the cell then slammed the door shut. "You got twenty minutes."

Henri waited until the guard's footsteps retreated down the hallway. "What are you doing here? Is it safe?"

Without answering, Marc glanced around the cell.

Henri saw his brother's involuntary shudder as he took in his surroundings. "It's not so bad," he lied. "How are they taking it? *Maman* and Papa? Marie-Catherine?"

"Our sister has been driving me nuts, wanting to know why Blanchard hasn't succeeded in getting you out. She's threatening to storm this place if they don't let you out soon, or let her in to see you."

Henri shook his head. "You need to keep her out of it. Tell her I don't want her to get involved, okay? I don't want Jeffers getting his hooks into her."

He stared at Marc, but only got a half-hearted shrug in response. He'd have to be satisfied.

"What about *Maman* and Papa?"

"Papa is angry. You know. Thundering about the provincial government first then the federal government, claiming they're all being run from the grave by Maurice Duplessis."

"I can just hear him." Henri was forced to smile at the image of their father Marc evoked.

"*Maman* is angry with Papa. She claims your arrest is his fault—for filling our heads with nonsense as we grew up." Marc sighed. "Same old shit."

"Funny. I was just thinking about that. When we were kids, I mean. Remember when we painted slogans on the government printing office and almost got caught? I think I was eleven, maybe twelve. That cop chased us for three blocks, blowing his whistle and yelling for us to stop—scared the hell out of me."

Marc nodded. "Yeah. I remember." He slumped down on the bunk.

Henri frowned. "What's wrong? What's going on?"

"It doesn't look good for you getting out right away."

"Why not?" Henri lowered himself onto the bunk next to Marc. "I said nothing at that rally I haven't said before, in speeches and even when I wrote for *Le Journal Quotidien.*"

"There are editorials about you—some people are saying you need to be made an example of."

Marc's head was tilted, his eyes questioning when he looked at Henri, as though he was trying to figure something out.

"That sounds like *The Gazette*," Henri said. "Or *Montreal Star.*"

He stood and began pacing between his bunk and the opposite wall, his mind racing. This isn't bad. It may even be good. He and Maurault had planned for only a couple of weeks, but he could handle a few more days. Even a week or two, if it came to that.

He needed to be careful, though. Marc was too good at reading his thoughts. He drew a deep breath to settle his nerves and let it out slowly.

"They're just reactionaries. Always have been—calling for the government to come down hard on the FLQ and other separatist groups. Why should this time be any different?"

Marc stared at him, a calculating look in his eyes.

"That's not all. I've heard they may move you to Parthenais next week instead of the Montreal jail."

Panic surged through Henri. His stomach tightened and he felt as though he couldn't breathe. The *Rue Parthenais* Detention Center, a fourteen-story prison set in a concrete jungle of cheap duplexes and shops in east Montreal, had a reputation for what they called aggressive discipline.

He took a deep breath. "I don't know how they justify keeping me locked up at all, much less sending me there." He tried to regain control of his emotions, make his hands stop shaking. "I've been here since the first of the month and they still haven't charged me with anything. That's not even legal. Besides, *Parthenais* is provincial police and it was the Montreal police who arrested me."

He sat on his bunk for a moment, next to his brother, but then stood and continued pacing. It didn't make sense.

"Why did you do it?"

"Why did I do what?" Henri swung around to face his brother. His heart thudded. What did Marc suspect?

"You know what." Marc didn't take his eyes from Henri's. "Why did you let them arrest you? Hell, you didn't just let them, you fucking asked for it."

Henri's heart beat faster than ever. "Don't we have to stand up to them?" It took all he had to keep his voice even. "It's not just about taking action, Marc. Principles are involved. I was standing up for what I believe in."

He sat once again, but on the edge of the bunk, ready to spring to his feet.

"Have you ever thought, Marc, that the more of us they

wrongly imprison, the more people will come to our side in the end?"

Marc snorted. "That's bullshit. What good is being a martyr? Who the hell cares about you when you're not out there spitting in their faces?"

"Lots of people."

Henri knew Marc would freak out if their positions were reversed, if Marc was the one locked up in a cell. Henri didn't much like being locked up either, but it was the only way. At least the only way he could think of.

"When people hear how I'm being treated, and know I'm just one of many, they'll flock to the side of separatism and justice."

Marc stood, his head thrown back and his arms crossed. "I don't buy that crap and if you do, you're crazy." His eyes blazed his disbelief. "The public will forget about you by next week. Then what? Will your high-flying principles console you then?"

"I won't let people forget about me." Henri wished he felt as confident as he tried to sound. He stood and faced his brother. "Blanchard is making them let me have something to write with. You can bet I'll use it."

Footsteps sounded, coming toward them.

"For whatever good that will do you," Marc said. He shrugged. "Well, when you get to Parthenais, look for a guy by the name of Albert Drill."

His voice was low and Henri had to lean forward to hear.

"Tell him you're my brother," Marc said.

"An inmate?"

Marc shook his head. "A guard actually. At least we won't forget you, Henri. If they don't let you out soon, we'll make them pay."

"What do you mean? Is something planned?" Henri had to work to keep his voice a whisper, to keep from showing his alarm.

Marc shook his head and gave him a look to discourage further questions.

Henri leaned in close to his brother. "Whatever it is, keep Marie-Catherine out of it. You agreed, remember."

Keys clanked when the guard inserted one in the lock and opened the cell door.

"Time's up."

The brothers stared at one another then Marc turned and went through the door without a backward glance. Henri stood at his cell door and watched his brother walk down the hall, next to the guard, until he turned the corner.

Chapter Thirteen

Henri looked at the unappetizing meal on the metal tray balanced on his knees. Cold oatmeal, cold toast, and cold coffee. When he'd finished as much as he could choke down, he set the tray on the floor and crossed to the sink to rinse his mouth and splash cold water on his face.

"Okay, Morais," the guard said, opening his cell door. "Get your shit together. They're here to take you to your new home."

Henri dried his face on his sleeve. Blanchard had told him the day before to expect the transfer. Before breakfast, they'd given him a cardboard box for his things. Besides his toothbrush and empty razor, he'd put into it two pencils, an orange plastic sharpener, the supply of paper Blanchard had given him, a pocket dictionary, a letter from his father and three from Marie-Catherine, some newspaper clippings, and a calendar.

Escorted by the guard, Henri, shackled, carried his box down the hall and up the stairs at the end of it, to where two provincial policemen leaned, hip-shot, against a desk. Moments later Henri was out on the pavement and being pushed, shivering, into the back seat of a police car. Sleet fell, mixed with snow. In his cell, he'd had no idea of the weather.

Twisting on the slick, plastic-covered seat, he gazed through the car's fogged rear window, barely able to discern the red brick precinct building. When he could no longer make it out, he turned and faced the heavy metal grill that separated him from the front seat. *Don't think, don't think, don't think,* the clicking windshield wipers repeated.

On Pi IX Boulevard they rolled past one familiar landmark after another. A tavern where only last month, though it seemed like a year ago, he'd met with some of Marc's contacts to plan a demonstration. A hockey arena where he and Marc had skated as kids—he was the better skater, but Marc, of course, the more aggressive. They passed the park where he and Claudia had spent long summer evenings making love on a secluded grassy bank. He wondered if she was still in Montreal or if she'd gone back to the States. Thoughts of her no longer filled him with anger. When he thought of her now, it was with a deep, empty loneliness, along with the knowledge he may have lost something he should have treasured.

Sleet gave way to snow as the car turned into the ragged neighborhoods of Montreal's East End, a part of town familiar to him. His family had once lived on Elmont Street, in an apartment over a tailor shop. They'd sublet from the tailor, a fussy widower who lived behind his workspace. The man had no children of his own and no patience for anyone else's.

Getting away from the irascible old man and the gangs of kids who roved the streets, with little to do except get into trouble, had been his mother's aim. Moving to what he thought of as the country had been his father's dream.

The car turned onto Parthenais Street. Through the

falling snow the detention center loomed. A tall chain-linked fence topped with several strands of barbed wire surrounded the building. Henri had passed it many times before. Now he saw it with a new appreciation for its foulness, an ugly scab on an equally ugly neighborhood.

Don't think, don't think, don't think.

Two uniformed men, looking cold and bored, stared through the window of the guard shack as the police car rolled to a stop. The driver cranked down his window. "We have prisoner Morais," he hollered to the men in the guard shack.

Taking his time, one of the guards emerged from the shack and walked over to the car, his boots squeaking in the fresh snow. He leaned down and glanced into the back seat at Henri, then at the clipboard in his gloved hand. His nose and cheeks were red with cold. "Okay." He straightened and turned to the other guard. "Open it."

The big gate slid back. When the way into the parking lot was clear, the driver moved the car forward. Henri closed his eyes and leaned his head back against the seat. Oh, Christ, what am I doing here? *Don't think, don't think.*

First, they sat him in a chair and cut his hair, zipping over his skull with electric clippers. He was told to strip. When he'd complied, one of the guards handed him a bar of brown soap and a small wooden scrub brush. "Don't forget your neck."

After Henri had showered, under the watchful eyes of security cameras and the guards, his skin still raw and tingling, he was told to bend over and spread his cheeks. He flinched and gritted his teeth when an ungentle latex covered finger probed his interior. Allowed to straighten, Henri's face flamed.

They weren't finished with him. He was meticulously photographed and measured, including the birthmark on his left shoulder. They gave him a number. He was now 176-649P. They took his fingerprints. Finally, they handed him a set of prison clothes and allowed him to dress.

No one asked him what he stood accused of, and neither did anyone ask him if he'd done it. No one cared. Henri's gut tightened. Never had he felt so alone.

Once in a cell, he found that drug addicts and the mentally ill were his closest neighbors. A less than subtle attempt to isolate and dehumanize him. He tried to tune out the sound of the man in the cell opposite his. It was a futile effort. The man stood for hours at a time banging his head against the bars of his cell door. A matted beard and disheveled hair obscured most of his face. Henri caught only glimpses of it when the man raised his head to strike again.

At night, the steady clunk, clunk, clunk of the man's head echoed along the gallery. Every ten or fifteen minutes a different voice would yell 'cut it out' or 'shut the fuck up'.

Finally, when the man began to punctuate his head-banging with high-pitched screams, two white-coated men arrived with a gurney. Following a brief struggle, they got the man onto the gurney and out of his cell. His arms were in a canvas jacket and wrapped around his middle. His wild, feral eyes stared straight into Henri's.

"Save me... They're trying to kill me..." The man

struggled to get the words out. "Save me," he said again, this time in a whispered whimper.

Without glancing at Henri, the white-coats wheeled the man down the hall.

That night, Henri lay on his bunk thinking about the man, wondering if he'd been crazy to begin with or if this place had driven him mad. Although he sympathized with him, wondered where they'd taken him, he was relieved the head-banging had stopped—it had filled every crevice of his own skull with pain.

The crazy man's absence didn't cause the noise of the place to diminish by much. Whether two o'clock in the afternoon or two o'clock in the morning, outside his cell rang a cacophony of noise. Inmates whistled or yelled to guards, each other, or demons known only to them. Doors slammed open or shut. Footsteps thudded.

Henri slept in snatches. He'd drift off for five or ten minutes then jerk awake. Finally, exhausted, he'd fall into a deep sleep, but even that only lasted for an hour or two. Then he'd jerk awake and the process began again. All night. Every night.

Henri had grown adept at identifying the guards by the sound and rhythm of their footsteps, but one morning shortly after the crazy man's removal, he heard steps he didn't recognize. The staccato tapping came down the gallery's concrete floor, halting outside his cell door.

"Warden wants to see you."

It was the man who'd been at the desk with all the

security cameras the day Henri had arrived at Parthenais, the man who'd ushered him into Hell.

"What does he want?"

"Warden don't consult with me about our guests. Get your ass moving, you can find out yourself."

Henri stood and carefully re-tucked his shirt, smoothing the wrinkles. He rinsed his face and took a drink of water before crossing to his cell door.

"Warden don't like waitin' either."

Henri walked out the open cell door. "He's kept me waiting long enough."

The man led Henri from the cellblock area through a labyrinth of doors and passageways and up two flights of stairs.

Parthenais wasn't only a jail. A forensic laboratory and a morgue were located within the building, which also housed the headquarters of Quebec's provincial police force.

"Stop here," the guard said.

They were in front of a door at the end of a short hallway. The guard knocked. A woman's voice called for them to come in. The man opened the door and nudged Henri forward into a small room that served as an outer sanctum to a larger room visible through a set of open double doors.

"Thank you, Drill," said the woman seated behind a desk to the right of the doors. "I'll call you when the warden has finished with him."

The woman told Henri to sit down in the chair facing her desk then returned to typing. Henri sat, his mind on the name she'd used. Drill. Albert Drill...it must be. He must be the man Marc had told him to contact.

He settled into the chair and, feet extended, crossed his ankles, attempting to appear nonchalant. He wasn't surprised when the silent hands of the clock on the wall moved from five minutes to ten minutes, and finally to fifty minutes past the hour.

Naturally, the warden would keep him waiting. Henri had quickly discovered that in jail, power and control were the basis of every interaction.

In a way, the same happened on the outside. The English-speakers guarded the status quo, making sure the balance of power remained on their side, while French Canadians stayed captive in their cells of inequality.

"He'll see you now," the woman said. Henri wondered what invisible means of communication had been used to deliver that message.

The warden sat behind a large desk, covered with stacks of papers and files. He didn't look up when Henri stopped in front of his desk, but went on studying a file. Henri's file. Finally, he tossed it aside, pushed back in his chair and looked up.

He was younger than Henri expected, not more than forty. And nothing about him could be called soft, from the steel grey color of his eyes to the coarse black hair standing like stiff bristles on the back of his hands. The silence drew out while the warden studied him.

Ensnared by the intensity of the man's eyes, Henri felt like an insect on a pin. Anger, fierce and unexpected, blazed up in him. He inwardly shook with its ferocity, but forced himself to stand still under the warden's inspection, refusing to lower his own gaze.

"Sit down," the warden said at last.

Henri looked down at the chair a moment before making up his mind to lower himself into it.

The warden nodded, as if acknowledging Henri's reluctance to obey. "You were a journalist." It wasn't a question. "Why did you make the move? Why wasn't being a reporter enough?"

Henri shrugged. "Times change."

"That's a bullshit answer." The warden picked up a pencil and tapped the eraser on Henri's open file. "Tell me something else."

Henri shrugged again. "It didn't seem to be going anywhere."

"What wasn't going anywhere? Your career or the FLQ?"

"What does the FLQ have to do with anything?"

"Are you telling me you aren't a member of the FLQ?"

"If I tell you I am, will you start treating me as a political prisoner? Start treating me, and the others, according to the Geneva Conventions?"

"Cut the crap. Just tell me the truth. Are you a member, or aren't you?"

"What if I am? It's not against the law." He wouldn't let the man intimidate him. "Nor have I done anything against the law. I told Jeffers when they arrested me and I'll say it again. I've done nothing illegal, unless it's now unlawful to speak the truth in Canada. Anything else he's said I've done is trumped-up bullshit."

"I don't believe you, Morais." The warden threw the pencil down. "I think you're in it and always have been—maybe not with the bombings and bank robberies, but with the union strikes, the Murray-Hill riots and everything else the FLQ has their fingers in. I want some names."

Henri scoffed. "Believe what you want. I can't give you anything. I don't know anything."

The warden shifted gears, his voice becoming conciliatory. "Life could be easier for you here. You could get some privileges—like working in the library and having real people to talk to. You don't have to be locked up with the druggies and the loonies."

Despite the placating tone, Henri had no trouble hearing the implied threat: if he didn't cooperate things could get worse. He felt an almost lunatic obstinacy. "I shouldn't be locked up at all. I didn't do anything."

"Give me some names, Morais. Cooperate and you might even get off with time served. You could go home— where you can make sure that sister of yours isn't getting tangled up in things she shouldn't be involved with."

At the unexpected mention of Marie-Catherine, Henri felt as though something with the power of a huge fist had slammed into him, nearly taking his breath away. Reflexes alone allowed him to answer the warden. "What are you talking about? Marie-Catherine's just a kid. She hasn't done a damn thing. Leave her out of this."

It was the warden's turn to shrug. "Whatever you say, Morais." He leaned back in his chair, his hands interlocked behind his head, his left ankle resting on his right knee. Henri stared. Without warning, the warden dropped his relaxed pose. His hands and leg came down and he slapped the desk. "I'm through with you. Bella." He made his voice loud enough to be heard over the clattering of the typewriter. "Call up Drill and get this man out of here."

As Henri reached the door the warden said, "Let me know when you do have something for me."

"Go to hell," Henri muttered under his breath.

Henri waited until he and Drill were well away from the warden's door before he spoke. "I was told to look for you."

Drill continued walking down the hall, his face pointed straight ahead. "Who?" he said, barely moving his lips.

"You know my last name." Henri kept his voice low as well. "Think about it."

Drill nodded imperceptibly and continued down the hall to the stairs. After they'd descended the first flight he indicated with his head for Henri to follow him. Drill singled out a key from the ring attached by a cord to his belt, next to where his baton hung threaded through another ring, and unlocked a door beneath the stairs. "In here."

A light came on when the door opened. The room gave barely enough clearance for them to stand. Television monitors and camera equipment were stacked on shelves and wedged into the spaces under the steps. A tripod leaned up against the door jam.

"He said you'd be contacting me. Why did you wait so long?"

"I didn't know who you were."

"You can't read a name badge?"

A. Drill was on the badge over the man's left shirt-pocket. Henri hadn't looked. "Even if I knew who you were, how was I supposed to contact you?"

Drill ignored the question. "What do you need? Smokes? Dope? What?"

Henri didn't know how much to trust the man. "I need

to know what's going on. They're keeping me isolated. I haven't talked to anyone and I haven't had any visitors since I got here, outside of my lawyer."

"They're trying to break you down." Garlic punctuated the man's warm breath.

"They're doing a damn good job of it." Henri shifted to put more space between them. "What's happening outside? What is my brother planning?"

Drill didn't know or wouldn't say what Marc was up to, and Henri decided his lawyer did a better job of bringing him up to date on whatever events went on outside the jail.

"I can get him a message if you want."

"Tell him the warden wants me to give him names. And remind him of his promise."

"What promise?"

"He'll know."

"That's it?"

Henri nodded.

"Okay." Drill started to push the door open so they could go back out. He held up his hand. "Wait a minute. Someone's coming."

Henri listened and heard the approaching footsteps.

"Get that one," said Drill, his voice filling the confined space. He pointed to one of the television monitors. "Hurry up, I ain't got all day."

Henri picked up the monitor Drill pointed to.

"Come on. I got to get this hooked up before the end of my shift." Drill gave him a shove when Henri started down the hall toward the second flight of stairs, his arms around the cumbersome piece of equipment. A guard, who'd often escorted Henri to and from meals or to the exercise yard, walked toward them down the passageway, heels clicking on the tile floor.

The guard nodded to Drill, but his gaze slid over Henri without acknowledgement, as though he wasn't there. A non -person. Henri tightened his grip on the monitor. The man's footsteps carried down the hall then faded away. Drill urged Henri forward.

Later, when things had quieted as much as they would for the night, Henri lay on his bunk and wondered what the warden had hinted at.Did he know about Marie-Catherine's trip to North Carolina with Marc, or was he simply fishing?

Chapter Fourteen

As her bus crossed the bridge over the St. Lawrence River, Marie-Catherine peered through the window at the rows of boxcars lined up on rail sidings along the river's bank. Ships were tied up to the quays or farther out, riding at anchor, waiting to be loaded or unloaded. From this height, the men on the docks and on the decks of the ships looked like ants. When she'd been eight, her father had given her a small piece of camphor wood from a ship he'd helped unload. She still had it tucked away in a drawer and would sometimes take it out and inhale its spicy, exotic scent. It reminded her of the river, the ships and especially of her father.

Across the river from Montreal, Longueil spread south and east along the shoreline. On the outskirts of Longueil was the place where she'd grown up, a place without a name, without a discernable town center or clearly defined boundaries. Its residents referred to the area by the name of the boulevard running the length of it.

When her family had moved here, they'd believed they lived in the country. "There was a field east of the boulevard where your brothers played baseball with their friends," her father told her. "And only a few miles away was a farm with cows." Marie-Catherine vaguely remembered the cows.

Now, rather than farms and empty fields, she looked out the bus window on traffic-clogged streets that were bordered by shops with cheap merchandise in the windows, pawnshops and taverns, barbershops and Chinese restaurants. Young boys with skates over their shoulders lined up outside the ice arena for hockey. Little girls in thin winter coats followed their mothers from shop to shop.

Marie-Catherine sighed. Another typical Saturday morning on the boulevard. She stood and retrieved her overnight case from the rack above her seat then pulled the cord. When the bus lumbered to a stop, she stepped to the curb in front of Mr. Tiburg's market.

A moment later, she left both sidewalk and paved street, onto the graveled lane leading to her parents' house. A deep ditch, originally meant to be an underground sewer, ran next to the lane, but the government had abandoned the project years before. "The politicians weren't getting enough 'payola', so they left it and went back to Longueil," her father claimed whenever the subject came up.

The ditch filled with weeds in the summer and snow in the winter. In the spring, muddy water gushed through it. When the water spilled over the banks of the ditch, which it often did, their yard became a swamp. As children, her brothers had delighted in building dams and floating boats in it. They hadn't cared how wet and dirty they became or how much *Maman* scolded.

After long weeks of gray skies, the sun now warmed the frozen earth. This brief flicker of spring wouldn't last—everything would be refrozen in the morning and the snow would return, weeks of it, perhaps—but for now, it was glorious, allowing Marie-Catherine to forget for the moment how much she hadn't wanted to make this visit.

The soles of her shoes were caked with mud and melted slush from the road by the time she reached the planks serving as a footbridge over the ditch in front of their house. She scraped them on the boards, and the falling clods broke through the snowy crust revealing a thin, clear stream of water rushing along the bottom of the ditch.

An eight-foot lilac tree stood in the exact middle of what, in some neighborhoods would have been a lawn, but here, when the snow melted and weeds replaced the water in the ditch, hard-packed earth filled the space.

As a child, Marie-Catherine often sat beneath the lilac tree and waited for her brothers and her father to get off their bus and wearily trudge down the hill—Marc had left school and joined his father fulltime on the docks as soon as he turned fourteen, Henri worked there summers.

Although she had girlfriends her own age to play with, Marie-Catherine's father and her brothers were like gods to her. Her father had indulged her, much to the displeasure of her mother. Marc had been twelve when she was born and had plenty of friends and interests other than a baby sister. His indifference to her as the years went by only seemed to make her crave his attention more. Henri, on the other hand, she could rely on. As a child, she'd followed him everywhere he allowed.

As Marie-Catherine passed by the leafless lilac tree now, she could almost see the shadow of the little girl she'd been, still watching, still waiting.

She scraped her shoes again before opening the door. "Hello. I'm home," she called and walked into the kitchen.

No one answered, but she knew at least one of her parents was nearby because the door had been left unlocked and a fire burned in the stove. She carried her overnight case to the ladder leading to the loft above her parents' bedroom.

Under a roof of plywood and tarpaper, the loft stayed hot in the summer and cold in the winter. But from the time she was old enough to leave the cradle until only a few months before, she'd slept there nearly every night of her life. She smiled, remembering the comforting rumble of her father's snores coming through the loft floor, accompanied by the mumble of her brothers' voices. Marc and Henri had slept on bunks Papa hinged to the walls of the front room. During the day, they were pushed up and latched out of sight. Henri said their father had gotten the idea from a ship.

Heavy foot-stamping sounded. The door opened and a gust of cold air filled the room before Marie-Catherine's mother could slam the door shut.

"You're home." Her mother crossed to the squat, black stove dividing the kitchen from the front room. She opened its door and stirred up the embers with a long, metal poker before adding a piece of wood. "We need more firewood."

Marie-Catherine climbed part way up the ladder and shoved her case onto the floor of the loft. "I'll get it, *Maman.*"

"Don't wear your good coat. Put on that old jacket of Marc's." Her mother motioned to the row of jackets hanging from hooks beside the door.

Marie-Catherine pulled off her coat and replaced it with her brother's worn jacket. Following the path around the side of the house, she made several trips from the woodpile to the porch and back again, slipping often on the melting snow.

The sun's heat burned through the heavy jacket and before long she needed to stop and wipe the sweat from her forehead. When she'd stacked enough wood beside the door, she carried an armload into the house and dumped it into the barrel beside the stove, took Marc's jacket off and hung it back on its hook. She kicked off her shoes and set them near the stove to dry.

Her mother sat at the kitchen table with a mug of coffee, her feet propped on a chair. Deep ridges were in the mottled flesh where her mother's felt carpet slippers cut in.

"Stuff some newspaper in the toes so they'll dry evenly," her mother said. "You should have worn boots."

Marie-Catherine frowned at her mother's feet. "Have you been taking your blood-pressure medicine?"

"I just need to put my feet up for a bit."

Marie-Catherine knew there was no point in saying more. She got a cup from the shelf above the counter, after she'd followed her mother's instructions with the newspaper. A pile of unpeeled carrots and potatoes stood next to the sink.

"Where's Papa?"

"It's Saturday."

Marie-Catherine filled her cup from the pot on the stove and sat across from her mother, who moved the pitcher of milk closer. "Most Saturdays he's home from work by noon."

Her mother always communicated in terse statements. Marie-Catherine thought she should be used to it. Still, her mother's taciturn manner bothered her. Why couldn't they have a normal conversation, like her friends did with their mothers?

"*Maman* conserves her words just as she does her affection," Henri said when Marie-Catherine once tearfully complained to him. "She doles both out like water in a drought."

"The union," her mother said. "They're having a meeting after."

"On Saturday?"

"I told him he shouldn't go, but he never listens."

"It must be important, Maman. You know how Papa feels about the union."

Her mother sipped her coffee and didn't answer.

Her father walked into the house two hours later, just as Marie-Catherine was setting the table for supper. He greeted her with an enthusiastic hug. She smelled the alcohol on his breath and cast a nervous glance toward her mother, stirring soup on the stove.

"Pour me some wine, Marie-Catherine," her father said as he kicked off his boots and hung his jacket next to the door. "We've something to celebrate." He hesitated, his eyes on his wife's back. "The union has voted to strike."

Her mother turned from the stove, her face as pale as Marie-Catherine had ever seen it. "I can't believe all of you would be so simple," her mother said. "Tell me it isn't true."

"It is true." Her father's tone was defiant. "The vote unanimous. We're striking."

Her mother's eyes narrowed and her mouth formed a rictus of disapproval. "If you think you can win, you are fools. They'll just fire all of you and hire replacements who are willing to work."

Her father shook his head. "We should have done it years ago. If we back down again, how can we hold our heads up as husbands and fathers? The union is in solidarity on this, Annemarie. We stand together." He took a large swallow of the wine Marie-Catherine had poured. "They won't fire us. We won't let them."

"Just like those postal delivery drivers tried, I suppose." Sarcasm filled her mother's voice. "And what will we use for money in the meantime?"

"We'll get by," her father said, though with less enthusiasm in his voice. He dropped down in his chair at the end of the table and gestured to Marie-Catherine to refill his glass.

"I can't believe you've been so foolish. What will we do?" Her mother's grip tightened on the wooden spoon she had been using to stir the soup. "Why can you never leave it alone, Emile? We have a house. You have a job. Isn't that enough? Why must you always be talking about politics and workers' rights and the injustices done to French Canadians? Look what we have from all that talk. Our son is in jail." She banged the spoon on the side of the pot.

Marie-Catherine jumped, startled by the loud noise.

"In jail, Emile. I hang my head in shame when I go to the market, see Mr. Tiburg behind the counter, our neighbors shopping and gossiping. But do you care? Do you, Emile? No," she answered for him. Her mouth worked and there was a glitter of moisture in her eyes. "You're proud of Henri. Proud he is in jail."

Marie-Catherine had never heard her mother talk so to her father, never heard her give such a long and impassioned speech.

"And what of Marc? Do you know what he's doing? The people he associates with? When will he be arrested, Emile?" Her mother's usual ruddy complexion had gone pasty white then splotchy red. She took a deep, shaking breath.

"Now, Annemarie," her father began.

"Don't say another word, Emile. I don't want to hear it."

Marie-Catherine froze in place, the bottle of wine still in her hand, while her mother poured more words onto her father's drooping shoulders.

"For years you've been filling the children's heads with things that will get them nothing but trouble. And it didn't matter I begged you not to." Her mother wiped a hand across her eyes and drew in another ragged breath before going on. "Now this! We will lose everything! I know it. And it will be on your shoulders, Emile." With that she threw down the spoon, marched into the bedroom and slammed the door behind her.

Marie-Catherine remained mute. Her father stared at the closed door for several moments before straightening his shoulders. "She'll get over it." He lifted his chin. "The union is right on this. She'll see. And I am proud of my boys for doing what needs to be done."

"I'll help with the money, Papa. I'll quit school. I don't need to go to university—none of my friends go. I'll get a job."

Her father didn't respond, instead he stared into his wine glass.

★

Marie-Catherine pulled the blankets up to her chin, trying to stay warm. When she'd first climbed into the loft, the heat rising from the stove had gathered beneath the low ceiling, making the space warm and cozy. Before long, the fire died and her space had gradually grown cold. It was well past midnight, and still her mind remained in turmoil. She tugged the covers tighter to her chin and shoulders and tried to imagine who would hire her.

After Henri graduated from secondary school, their mother had urged him to seek work in a bank, but Marie-Catherine doubted she could qualify. They'd no doubt claim her too young. Most tellers were men, anyway. During the summer, several of her friends worked in the canneries. What else was there for a girl who didn't know how to type? It wasn't summer though. She supposed some factories might be hiring, but she'd heard so many stories about the poor pay and working conditions in most of Montreal's factories, the thought of such work didn't thrill her. The longer she lay stewing about it, the more she despaired.

Despite misgivings, in the morning she told her parents what she'd decided during her long and sleepless night. "I'll apply at the factory where my friend Marguerite works." Her fingers twisted and tugged at an errant curl as she worked to make her voice sound calm and confident. "And if I can't get on there, I'll go around to some of the shops."

Her mother nodded her head in approval, but her father disagreed.

"No, you stay in school. We'll get by. The union will give us some money."

"How much?" said her mother.

"Enough to get by," her father answered.

Marie-Catherine looked from one to the other. "But, Papa, I want to help."

Chapter Fifteen

Relieved but feeling guilty that her father had turned down her offer to drop out of school and help with finances, on the bus ride back to Montreal, Marie-Catherine turned her morose thoughts to the unfairness of Henri being in jail while she remained free to go wherever she wished.

She wanted to support him, be there, as he'd always been there for her. Like running interference with *Maman,* when her friends began wearing lipstick and shaving their legs and Marie-Catherine wanted to as well. He'd taught her to read. Later, when she was older, he'd patiently drilled her on her multiplication tables.

Like Henri, learning came easy for her. Unlike Henri, however, she learned early to avoid confrontation. Even though it was ten years since he'd been in any of their classes, many of her teachers remembered her brother. Those who did were quick to express relief when they perceived Marie-Catherine to be more malleable. She'd graduated with honors from secondary school then nearly exploded with excitement when offered the opportunity to be in the first class of the University of Quebec at Montreal.

Her mother, however, had said any more education would be wasted on a girl. She forbade Marie-Catherine to accept.

Once again Henri came to her rescue.

"Why should she get any more schooling?" her mother said. "You spent four years at the university, and what good is it? You make less money than you would on the docks with your Papa. So tell me, what good it is, those four years you spent studying."

Marie-Catherine knew Henri was sensitive about the amount of money he made—too little in their mother's estimation—but he didn't get sidetracked with another explanation.

"She needs an education, *Maman*. Otherwise, she'll never be able to compete for a decent job."

"She could do like I did. Get a job for a while then get married and raise a family. What's wrong with that?" Marie -Catherine clenched and un-clenched her fingers. She wanted to scream at her mother's lack of comprehension. Her wonderful opportunity was about to be thrown away— even Henri lacked the persuasive skills to change their mother's mind once it was set.

"Nothing's wrong with what you did, *Maman*," said Henri. "But times are different now and Marie-Catherine is a smart girl. It wouldn't be fair to keep her from going on to school when she wants to go. She shouldn't have to go to work yet."

"Your papa and I have worked hard since we were children. He hasn't died from it, nor have I."

"Maybe not. But look at this place, *Maman*. A slave would live better than this."

"You think we are like slaves?" Her mother's face flushed redder than normal and she heaved her bulk up from the kitchen chair where she'd been shelling peas. The flesh of her heavy jowls quivered. "You think we are a couple of idiots, your father and me, working all our lives to give you and your brother and sister beds to sleep in and food to eat? You look down on us?"

"No, *Maman*. Nothing like that. You know I love you and Papa. I'm proud of what you've accomplished." He tried to put his arm around her shoulders, but she shook him off. "It's just that the future is going to require education, for women as well as men. I know you want Marie-Catherine to have a better life than you've had, with fewer hardships. I know the last thing you want for your daughter is that she'd have to scrub some other woman's floor like you had to do. I'm right, aren't I, *Maman*? That's not the life you want for your daughter, is it?"

Marie-Catherine had stood near the door, not speaking, not moving, almost not daring to breathe, but she took in every nuance of the argument, and mentally begged her mother to see that Henri was right.

Though reluctant, in the end her mother agreed. She'd even agreed to Marie-Catherine being allowed to live in an apartment near the campus with two other girls. Marie-Catherine later went to Henri with tears in her eyes.

"I'll never forget what you've done for me, Henri. You've given me a life."

She hadn't lied that morning when she'd told her father she wanted to help. But she didn't want to throw her life away, either; she wanted to do something important with it. Maybe she'd be a teacher or a lawyer. Or maybe she'd write books, books revealing the wrongs done by Quebec's ruling class, including the treatment of French Canadians like her brother, jailed for making a speech. Her mind raced with possibilities.

★

Marc called and asked her to meet him for a beer. Surprised and flattered, not to mention curious, Marie-Catherine wondered if he planned to ask her to go on another trip with him.

Students and workers from nearby offices and stores crowded the tavern where she and Marc met, laughing, arguing politics, and calling to one another in a polyglot of Montreal's many nationalities and languages. Above their voices, speakers blared the Rooftop Singers' *Walk Right In*.

Marie-Catherine wondered if Marc was going to ask her to go on another trip with him. He didn't. Instead, they talked about Henri. She needed to lean forward to hear him.

"He doesn't want you there, M.C. I told you that when he was still being held at Jeffers' precinct."

"I know he said I wasn't to visit him, Marc. But it's been ages since his arrest. Almost two months already." She tugged at a curl next to her ear. "I have to do something or I'll go crazy. What's Blanchard doing, anyway? Is he even trying to get our brother out?"

Marc took a swallow of beer then wiped his mouth with the back of his hand. "Sure, he's trying."

Marie-Catherine frowned her disapproval. "Then he should be trying harder. Anyway, I can't believe he's not part of the establishment. Look at the way the man dresses—every time I see his picture in the paper he looks like he just stepped out of Eaton's, always in his fancy blazers and school tie. I think he even has his fingernails manicured."

Marc laughed. "Don't worry. He's one of us, even though he looks like one of them. If anyone can get Henri out, it will be Blanchard—unless Henri has told him not to try too hard."

"What? Why would he tell Blanchard a thing like that?" Marie-Catherine ignored the glass of beer on the table in front of her.

Marc drained his glass and reached across the table for hers. He took a sip before he answered her. "It's only a hunch. We talked about it the last time I saw him, before they transferred him to Parthenais—about the more of us wrongly imprisoned, the more people will come to our side."

Marie-Catherine didn't think for a minute Marc had come up with that idea. It was too subtle and too time-consuming. Marc favored more direct action. "Do you really see that happening?"

Marc shrugged. "You've read the editorials and the letters-to-the-editor in the newspapers, especially the ones in *Le Devoir* after the letter Henri wrote about how he and other political prisoners were being denied their basic rights of citizenship. Blanchard got that letter out and mailed it for him, by the way. But what do you think?"

Marie-Catherine pushed her fingers through her hair as she pondered Marc's question. She'd been proud to hear her classmates praising Henri and his letters, but she didn't think a bunch of young people identifying with her brother answered the problem—it was their parents who needed to be convinced.

"I don't know. I don't see any measurable changes in position. I mean, the left-leaning French press backs Henri, the conservative English press backs the government, and the rest, the moderates, are in the middle—like they always are." She wished she felt more optimistic.

"I think things are changing. I meet people—other taxi drivers, I still see guys from the docks, truck drivers, people in the streets. More are for us now. We have lawyers on our side—lawyers besides Blanchard—and doctors. And some businessmen have given us money."

Marc took another swallow of beer.

"So maybe Henri is doing more for the cause by sitting in jail writing his letters to the newspapers than he would be giving speeches and marching in demonstrations. And he's sure as hell accomplishing more for us than he did cranking out shit for *Le Journal Quotidien*, preaching to the choir."

"Okay, I'll take your word there are more people on our side now—you get around a lot more than I do. And there should be more—our cause is right. But Henri shouldn't have to go to jail for people to see it. That's just wrong." Tears sprang to Marie-Catherine's eyes. "I feel so bad for him, Marc." She felt guilty, too. If anyone should be in jail, it should be her and Marc. Not Henri.

"Well, I know one thing, M.C. I could never do what Henri's doing—just the idea of being locked up like that makes me sweat." He shifted in his seat.

For a minute or two, neither of them said anything. Marie-Catherine tapped her fingers to Candy Man.

"So, how's school? Still the teacher's pet?"

"Hardly." She was relieved to set the subject of Henri's incarceration aside, at least for now. "Not with all the competition I've got. But I'm doing okay—despite all the disruptions."

Marc's eyebrows went up. "What do you mean 'disruptions'?"

"Well, after all the broken desks and run-down buildings in my first twelve years of schooling, I never thought I would complain about new buildings and new furniture." She laughed. "That's just it, though. Everything is brand new. No one knows how anything works—when and if it works. Yesterday we had no heat in any of the buildings. My roommate, Roseanne, said her chemistry professor dismissed lab one day and walked out in a huff because the burners weren't staying lit. It's one thing after another."

"What does the Student Union have to say about it?"

"I don't know. I haven't been to one of their meetings yet. I haven't had time."

Something always came up, things like meeting friends in coffee houses to talk about literature and poetry. Or attending a lecture she wanted to hear. Or going to a Bob Dylan concert with her roommates. Now that she had freedom, there didn't seem to be enough hours in the day to experience it all.

Marc's head tilted to one side and he looked at her through narrowed eyes. "I thought you wanted to be part of the movement. Aren't you the one saying you're tired of sitting on the sidelines?"

"I do, but what does the Student Union have to do with it?"

"Are you kidding?" Her brother's eyes bore into hers. "Don't you pay any attention, M.C.? My God, they're one of the most powerful groups around. And they've got money."

"From where?"

"Everyone has to pay into it. It's part of your tuition."

"Oh. So, what do they do with it?"

"You're the student. You should be telling me."

"Well, if I knew I would." She was stung by his tone and the look he gave her, like he pitied her ignorance.

He took another sip of beer, studying her above the glass.

"What?" she said, filled with impatience.

"Revolutionaries have been to our training camps in the mountains. They've come from all over—Algeria, Ireland, Palestine, Germany, Jordan. They've taught everything from how to make a Molotov cocktail to how to blow up a bridge. Want to know how they got here? The Student Union invited them to Canada to give speeches, even paid their way. The Student Union organized the demonstration in the computer center at Sir George Williams in February and the one at McGill in March. They've paid money for Valliere's and Gagnon's defense."

Marie-Catherine had seen pictures of the mess rampaging students had made at Sir George's computer center. It had looked like the aftermath of a tickertape parade. School officials said over a million dollars' worth of equipment had been destroyed. The students had defended their action with claims of racial discrimination.

Before she'd relented, her mother had cited the uprising as another reason Marie-Catherine should be content to stay home. "They are nothing but hooligans and trouble-makers." Marie-Catherine had countered with the argument it was a different school and had nothing to do with UQAM. Now she wondered how she had been so clueless.

"Hell, M.C. The Student Union organized the rally for Henri that got him arrested."

"You're kidding." She hadn't given much thought to the organization part before, but still it astonished her. "Are they paying Blanchard? He can't be working for free. Or is the FLQ paying? And what about all the other FLQ members in jail? Does the Student Union pay for their defense, too?"

Marc shook his head. "Don't ask me those questions. Go to one of their meetings and find out yourself." He drank the rest of her beer. "And then you can tell me. It would be interesting to know what else they have on their agenda."

Chapter Sixteen

Henri had been locked up nearly three months. Most of that time he felt he'd accomplished nothing by transforming himself into an FLQ member, that day-by-day his life was draining away. It was on one of those depressing days that Drill appeared outside his cell with the message the warden wanted to see him again.

The warden, his eyebrows moving up and down on his forehead like black caterpillars, once again demanded names and once again Henri told him he had no names to give. He also maintained he was being held illegally.

The warden scowled. "You're being stupid, Morais. Dumb-ass, fucking stupid. Do you think your brother and his friends would keep quiet to protect you?"

Henri shook his head. He knew Marc wouldn't betray him were their situations reversed. The warden's inference was wrong, though. Henri wasn't trying to protect Marc or any other FLQ member.

Instead, he was trying to keep his sister from rushing headlong into something that was sure to destroy her.

He was also trying to prove to his brother there was another way of achieving what they all wanted, Quebec's independence. He was doing it in the only way he knew how, by uncovering the injustices in the system and exposing them to public scrutiny. And even though each day he felt less certain of success, he'd come up with no other solution. No matter how hard he wracked his brain, no bright idea came to him.

He remained silent until the warden, disgusted, dismissed him.

Drill escorted him back to his cell. On the way, they ducked into the storage room under the stairs. "Did you deliver my message?" Henri asked.

"Yeah, I told him."

"What did he say?" Henri tried to keep the impatience out of his voice. He didn't want to alienate the man.

"Nothing much. Just said to tell you to hang tough."

"Great. That's a big help."

In his cell once again, Henri flopped down on his bunk. The warden was right. Marc did plan something. His brother had inferred as much before Henri got transferred to Parthenais. He had no idea what, nor why Marc didn't communicate anything of importance, only for him to 'hang tough,' whatever that was supposed to mean.

He considered using Drill to contact Maurault, to see if Maurault knew anything, but he and his editor had agreed Henri would be on his own here. He could trust no one.

Then his mind lit on Claudia. Would she help or would she laugh in his face? She'd always liked Marie-Catherine. On the other hand, she probably didn't think she owed his family anything. He didn't even know if she was still in Montreal. For several minutes, he went back and forth, debating.

The hell with it, he thought. He got up from his bunk, crossed to the metal sink built into the wall and splashed cold water on his face. He straightened, eyes closed. He had to do something. He wiped his hands on his pants before digging into the cardboard box next to his bunk. He pulled out a sheet of paper and pen, then picked up the box, sat and set the box on his knees.

Dear Claudia….

Chapter Seventeen

A single bulb dangled from a cord above Marc's head. He had removed the white glass globe surrounding it and the stark light glared down on the objects covering the Formica-topped table in front of him. With quick precision and without taking his eyes from the wires he held in one hand, he reached for a pair of needle-nosed pliers with the other. Behind him, Bunny lay on the couch reading a movie magazine.

Two quick knocks sounded at the door.

Marc looked up. "Get that, will you?" He stretched his neck and rolled his head from side to side. Bunny pushed herself off the couch and slouched toward the door of the East End motel where members of Marc's group, the Liberty Cell they called themselves, were meeting. It gave Marc ironic pleasure that the detention center where Henri remained imprisoned could be seen from the motel's parking lot.

LeGuin entered first, followed by Paul Gould. "Theresa's here, too. She's parking the car." Paul and Theresa were brother and sister. Several years before, Marc had worked with Theresa's husband, Alain Dumas. Marc had been out of the country when arrest warrants were issued for Dumas and several other FLQ members, charging them with bank robbery. Dumas said he wouldn't go back to prison. Instead, he'd fled to Cuba. Theresa had declined to go with him.

Marc put the lid on the shoebox containing what he'd been working on.

LeGuin, in his usual faded army fatigues, baggy t-shirt and jacket, gave it a quizzical look. "What's that for?"

Marc swung around on the chair. "A present for the warden."

Gould's long face split into a grin. "Can I deliver it?"

"This one will be my pleasure." Marc took the unlit cigarette from his mouth. "Did either of you bring beer?" When both men shook their heads, Marc gave Bunny a bill. "Go get us a couple of six-packs. The car keys are on top of the TV."

After Bunny left, Theresa shrugged out of her jacket. "It's hot in here."

"Feels good to me." LeGuin sank down on a chair.

Theresa smirked. "That's because you're always cold."

LeGuin sent her a disdainful look.

"Can't you two go for five minutes without arguing?" This night, Marc had no tolerance for their petty quibbling.

Theresa took the chair next to LeGuin. "He's always cold because he's such a skinny little shrimp." She glanced downward and brushed imaginary crumbs from the sweater covering her ample chest.

"Knock it off, Theresa." Marc left the shoebox on the table. He sat on the couch next to Gould and lit a cigarette.

Gould lit up as well. "How come we're meeting here?

Most of the time we meet at somebody's apartment or the warehouse."

Marc briefly closed his eyes. "We don't want anyone getting suspicious. Moving around keeps them guessing."

"Oh. Good idea."

Marc turned to LeGuin. "What's the word on Arrow?"

"They've voted to strike, just like you predicted."

"Good. We should get someone inside."

"One of us?"

Marc fought down his exasperation. Gould was dependable, but a little thick, not nearly as quick as his sister or LeGuin. "I'd rather get someone else." Theresa gave him a puzzled look. Marc exhaled a stream of smoke. "I have someone in mind."

LeGuin nodded. "When should we hit them?"

Marc flicked ash from his cigarette. "Let's give them a few weeks. Give their moods a chance to get good and foul."

"What if they settle?"

"If they settle and the terms are good, that's great." Theresa's impatience with her brother was in her voice. "We'll choose a different target." She glanced at Marc, her eyebrows raised. "But you don't think they will."

Marc shook his head. "No. The owners live in Toronto. Arrow is just one in a string of companies, and they have a history of not conceding to labor demands." He stubbed out his cigarette and leaned forward. "Okay. This should be pretty straight-forward. LeGuin, your job is to get us a contact—someone who can get our person inside." He turned to Gould. "We'll need your help later, when we're ready to move. Yours, too, Theresa."

Gould frowned. "Doing what?"

"Wiring a telephone. Logistics. The stuff you always do."

"Okay." Gould rubbed his hands together.

"And we need to find an observation post. LeGuin?"

LeGuin nodded. "I'll handle it."

"When we finish with this we'll need another target." Theresa rose and walked over to the sink outside the bathroom door. "Have you got something in mind?" She rinsed out a glass, filled it and drank.

Marc scratched his chin. "I've been thinking about it. We should go for something symbolic."

Theresa put the empty glass back on the counter. "How about the railroad? We could hit another CNR bridge. Those bastards deserve it if anyone does."

Gould bounced forward. "Or we could go for one of the banks. That way we'd get some money, too."

"We'll leave that to Hudon's group, or the Belgian." Marc again fought his exasperation with the man. If Gould didn't have his uses, he'd get rid of him.

"I don't know why we can't do one." Gould looked past Marc to the others.

Theresa narrowed her eyes at her brother then turned back to Marc. "What about the Palace of Justice?"

"The Palace of Justice." A smile spread across Marc's face. "Jesus, I like that." He stood and began to prowl the room. "Scout it out. Go see what you can learn—how accessible things are, the hours it's open to visitors, stuff like that."

"Sure." Theresa nodded, looking pleased with herself.

"LeGuin, you concentrate on Arrow. Paul, stay with your sister. I'll call you when I need you for something."

He threw himself back on the couch, extending his arms along the back, and put his feet up on the coffee table. He felt charged up. Planning a new attack always made him feel good. And now he had three targets.

The door opened and Bunny came in. "I had to drive for a mile. Everything nearby is closed or boarded up." She put the beer on the coffee table next to Marc's feet and helped herself to a can. "Don't let me keep you from talking." They all looked at her. "I can be as deaf as that doorknob over there."

"We're finished. They're just leaving." Marc took his feet off the table and rose.

LeGuin stood, too. Gould remained on the couch. "Aren't we going to have a beer? I'm thirsty."

Theresa rose and slipped her arms into her jacket. "Come on, Paul. We'll stop and get one on the way home."

"But—"

"Come on. See you later, Marc."

When the three had trooped out, Bunny took Gould's place on the couch. "I didn't mean to break up the party." She grinned up at him.

Marc didn't answer her in words; he reached down and took the beer can from her hand, taking his time in setting it on the table before looking at her. An acknowledging gleam flashed in her eyes.

When they left the motel, well after midnight, Marc told Bunny to drive. The shoebox was on the floor between his feet.

"How do you know you have the right house?"

"The fucking idiot is in the telephone directory." He had her drop him off three blocks away. "Wait twenty minutes. If I'm not back by then, get the hell out."

She nodded. Marc got out of the car and quietly closed the door, pushing until it clicked shut. When he looked back a minute later, he saw the top of Bunny's head and the glow of her cigarette. He almost ran back and told her to put the damn thing out, but decided not to bother. At two o'clock in the morning everyone would be asleep, not looking out a window.

The night was overcast, but periodically the moon emerged and cast its light on the houses lining the street. Marc stayed to the lawns edging the sidewalk to avoid the sound his shoes made on the sidewalk. A dog barked, momentarily startling him. He hoped it didn't belong to the warden.

A couple of minutes later he checked the number on the front of a house. This was it. And there was the mailbox, right next to the front door. He slipped along the side of the house toward the alley running through the middle of the block, thinking the warden's car might be a better place to leave his present. At the back of the house, a door led to the cellar with a coal shoot next to it. Bushes grew up around both. Leaning against the wall, Marc listened, but heard nothing beyond his own heavy breathing. He stared across the alley to the garage. Inside would be the warden's shiny, maroon Chrysler, a perfect target.

He wished he had the tools to jimmy the lock. "Shit," he muttered. It would take too long and make too much noise to force the garage door open. He looked at the coal shoot for a minute then turned and made his way along the side of the house to the front. The mailbox would have to do.

His foot was on the first step leading to the front porch when a light came on in the upstairs window of the house next door. Marc froze, his heart beating wildly. A toilet flushed. A moment later the light went out. Marc drew a deep breath then listened for any sounds coming from inside the warden's house. Nothing. He moved cautiously up the steps and across the porch to the metal box next to the front door. He stopped and listened once more. Still nothing.

It took only a minute to set the device and slip it into place. When he finished, he tiptoed down the steps and hurried back up the street, again keeping to the grass.

He climbed into the car and collapsed against the seat. Bunny started the engine. "I was getting ready to leave."

"Let's get out of here." As the car started forward, Marc leaned his head back. Visualizing the mess the bomb would make when it blew, a satisfied smile tugged at his lips. He'd set it to go off in two hours, knowing no one was apt to be around then. It wasn't very powerful, but it would scare the shit out of everyone, including the neighbors. "Henri better appreciate this."

Bunny turned onto Pie IX.~"I thought he didn't approve of bombs."

"He's coming around. Besides, that's why I set it to go off at four in the morning—to make sure no one gets hurt."

Bunny raised her eyebrows and speared a glance at him.

"Don't give me that look. The FLQ isn't responsible for any deaths. It's not our goal to kill anyone."

"How can the FLQ not be responsible when six people have died or been hurt?"

It was an old argument and he knew she said it to needle him, but he answered all the same.

"Because we're the victims. What we're doing is fighting back. It's the Anglos fault there's a war and people have gotten hurt."

"Well, I'm glad to say I'm a Native Person and don't take either side. We are routinely screwed by both."

"Whatever you say."

Marc had long before given up trying to figure out her logic. Everyone knew the Native People of Canada had been treated much worse by the Anglos than by the French, right from the start. They still were. Just look at all the Cree villages that would be wiped out by the hydro-electric dams the Anglos and a few rich French Canadians wanted, dams that would benefit the eastern United States as much if not more than Canada.

Ahead of them his apartment building stood out against the glow from the streetlights. "Go around the block once." While she drove, he examined the surrounding buildings and looked down alleys. When he was certain no one watched, he told her to pull into the parking lot.

Chapter Eighteen

Marie-Catherine walked into the crowded cafeteria. Cigarette smoke and voices filled the air. She looked around for a place to sit and saw a vacant spot at a table near the back of the room. When she got to it, she reached for the chair at the same time a bespectacled young man laid his hand on it.

"Go ahead."

"No, you take it. The meeting should start in a few minutes."

She nodded and sat.

This would be her second meeting of the UQAM Student Union. She guessed there were close to a hundred students gathered.

A young woman came to the microphone first. Marie-Catherine had seen her before, in the library and in one of her classes. A wide smile spread across the young woman's face. "I have wonderful news. Charles Gagnon has been freed on bail."

The room erupted in cheers and whistles. The woman held up her arms to quiet them. "Our next step…" The cheering continued unabated. The woman tried again. "Our next step is to get Pierre Vallieres out," she shouted, and the level of noise in the room rose even higher.

Henri had written several articles about Vallieres and Gagnon, when he still worked at *Le Journal Quotidien*. The two men had founded a magazine advocating the overthrow of capitalism and an end to imperial colonialism. Blamed for the bombing of LaGrenade shirt factory, they fled Canada. Later, they were arrested on the steps of the United Nations building, where they'd gone to seek asylum. Despite having valid passports with them at the time of arrest, they were convicted of illegal entry into the United States and deported to Canada. Once back, they were arrested and accused of murder along with a string of other crimes.

Marie-Catherine had read Vallieres' book, *White Niggers of America,* a call to arms of French Canadians, but she hadn't made up her mind about him. He was a hero to many, including Marc. At one time, Henri had admired him as well.

The meeting over, the young man who'd given up his claim to the chair held the door open for her. Walking down the stairs, Marie-Catherine wondered if she should call Marc.

"Are you going to the demonstration for Gagnon this afternoon?"

"What?" She hadn't realized the young man was still at her side. "Oh, sure."

"You don't seem too excited about it."

"Oh, I was just thinking. Sorry. Are you going?"

"Of course." He stopped at the bottom of the stairs and turned to her. Other students moved around them. "I'm Roger Oberle."

"Hi." She smiled for the first time. "I'm Marie-Catherine Morais."

"Want to get some coffee or a Coke? Do you have time?"

She glanced at her watch then nodded. "Yes." She'd call Marc later. He probably wasn't home now anyway. A blast of wind sent a shower of snow off the building's eaves. She pulled her collar tighter.

"There's a café a block away. Let's hurry before we freeze."

He was easy to talk to. In the crowded café over their coffees, they chatted about classes and professors, friends in common, the new campus.

Back in her apartment an hour later, Marie-Catherine called Marc.

Bunny answered. "He's not here."

Marie-Catherine bit her lip in frustration. She knew from experience not to expect Marc to return her call any time soon. "When will he be back, did he say?"

"Nope. Sorry."

Marie-Catherine hung up the phone. "Damn it," she said to the empty apartment. "I don't know what he expects to learn from me when he's never around so I can tell him anything."

Although she planned to join Roger and the others gathering at City Hall, Marie-Catherine didn't feel as excited as she'd been going to hear Henri speak. She felt torn, wondering if Gagnon, and Vallieres, too, were indeed responsible for the bomb that killed that woman at LaGrenade.

She didn't buy Marc's declaration that the factory's Anglo management bore all the responsibility. Whoever planted the bomb should have been more careful. If that had been Gagnon and Vallieres, like the police said, they were at least partially responsible for the woman's death.

In a way, she did look forward to the rally. Perhaps she could see the answer in Charles Gagnon's face, see if it held guilt or innocence.

Roger waited for her at the corner of Sherbrooke and St. Denis. A bus, already crowded with students from UQAM and nearby McGill, lumbered to a stop and they climbed aboard. The bus driver shouted to be heard over the noise of young voices. "Move back."

With all the seats taken, Marie-Catherine and Roger stood in the packed aisle. When the bus moved forward, Marie-Catherine grabbed hold of the seat next to her to keep from lunging into Roger, who put his hand on her waist to steady her. The humid air smelled of sweat, wet wool and rubber. Everyone talked at once, laughing and calling from one end of the bus to the other. Before they'd gone three blocks Marie-Catherine wanted to take her coat off.

The bus swayed and she felt Roger against her side. "It's hot in here," he breathed into her ear.

There were looks of bewilderment and anger on several faces when the bus went by its regular stops without pulling over. Some of the students laughed and waved to those on the sidewalk. Marie-Catherine fought the urge to reach up and yank the cord so she could get off. She didn't understand why she felt so tense. She'd never felt claustro-phobic before.

Roger leaned in even closer. "Have you been to any-thing like this?"

She nodded, thinking of Henri's rally, the rally where

he'd been arrested. She felt queasy and leaned against the seat to keep her balance while she searched in her bag for some gum.

"We're almost there."

She looked out the window. They were only a block from Notre-Dame. She put the straps of her bag back on her shoulder and took a steadying breath. The bus slowed and turned. People stood, some shoving their way into the already jammed aisles. Marie-Catherine and Roger pressed forward.

Roger stepped off the bus first, turned and reached his hand back for her. Pleased, she smiled at him. The cold air dried the perspiration on her face. She took a deep breath and her light-headedness disappeared as quickly as it had arrived.

In the oldest part of town, two-hundred-year-old buildings, mostly warehouses and made of brick, lined the cobbled streets down to the waterfront. Marie-Catherine glimpsed the river's slick, icy sheen. Wind gusted up the streets and tore at her hair, whipping it around until it stung her cheeks and eyes. She tucked her chin and nose into her coat collar. Her hand still in Roger's, she let him lead the way.

She soon found herself caught up in the growing excitement of the crowd in front of City Hall. Someone had a transistor radio turned on high. The Chambers Brothers singing *People Get Ready* poured out of it, heightening the anticipation. When Gagnon finally appeared, though, Marie-Catherine didn't join the others in their shouting, foot-stomping support.

Later, over dinner in a small neighborhood restaurant near her apartment, she tried to explain her feelings to Roger. "Do you ever wonder if they're guilty?" she asked over a forkful of spaghetti.

In the background, Joni Mitchell sang her newest release, *California*. Roger looked at her, his eyebrows raised in question.

"I mean what if Gagnon and Vallieres really did plant that bomb? Aren't they responsible for killing that woman? Shouldn't they be punished, even though her death wasn't on purpose?"

Attracted to his fresh, blond looks and the way his eyes crinkled at the corners when he laughed, Marie-Catherine was curious to hear his ideas.

He answered her question with careful consideration. "I don't think anyone condones what happened at LaGrenade, but I think we have to take action of some kind. If we don't stand up for what we believe, with marches and strikes—things like that—nothing will change."

Marie-Catherine nodded. "I know. And I agree with you. But I do wonder about Vallieres and Gagnon. I wonder if they deserve our support."

"No one has ever proved they were involved. Think about it. Vallieres was a journalist before he joined the FLQ. Then he spent his time organizing picket lines and demonstrations. Making speeches. I don't see him as a killer, not even an unintentional one. Do you?"

Marie-Catherine had an instant vision of Henri on the marble platform at the University of Montreal speaking to the crowd in front of the administration building. The similarity between Vallieres and her brother struck with such force she dropped her fork, splattering her sweater with spaghetti sauce. Shocked and then embarrassed by her clumsiness, a flush spread across her cheeks. She dabbed the front of her sweater with her napkin.

"There's another spot farther up." Roger held out his napkin. "Here, this one's clean."

"Thanks." Still chagrined, she finished mopping up. "Well, that was graceful, wasn't it?" They both laughed. She liked him more. "I haven't told you about my brother."

"Henri Morais?"

She nodded. Joni had moved on to *Both Sides Now.*

"When you told me your name this morning, I wondered if you were related. You look a lot like him."

It didn't seem possible they'd met only that morning. Marie-Catherine felt like they'd been friends forever.

"You must be very proud of him. I've followed his career, read his articles since I was fourteen. *Le Journal Quotidien* was foolish to let him go like that. That letter in *La Presse* yesterday was terrific. We should get the Student Union to organize a rally to support him, like the one this afternoon for Gagnon."

Marie-Catherine thought once again of the rally at the University of Montreal and its disastrous results, Henri's arrest.

That night she stared into the dark above her bed. Why hadn't she wanted to tell Roger about Marc, only Henri? Why hadn't she probed to find out if he supported everything the FLQ did, if he believed in going beyond protest marches? Maybe she didn't want to know.

Chapter Nineteen

When Henri heard he had a visitor, his pulse quickened. He felt in his pocket and touched the letter to Claudia. Her phone number, the one she'd given him, the one he'd memorized and dialed a hundred times in his head, was written on the front of the envelope.

Blanchard sat at one of the four visitors' tables. The other three were unoccupied. Always impeccably dressed, Blanchard sat with one gabardine-clad leg crossed over the other. Looking at the tasseled loafer on the lawyer's idly swinging foot, Henri doubted he made enough in a month at *Le Journal Quotidien* to pay for such shining perfection.

Blanchard stood and reached out his hand. "How are things?" Henri shook the offered hand then shrugged and sat. Blanchard retook his seat. "They settled the dock strike. Unfortunately, your father and his co-workers didn't win many concessions—no input on contracts, no across the board increase in pay, no additional sick days. But no one lost their job, even those with little seniority. And they'll get a pay raise in four months rather than a year."

Henri hadn't heard. "A slightly better resolution than in the postal delivery drivers strike last year." Scores were fired from their jobs in that strike, jobs many had held for years.

Blanchard crossed his leg over his knee again. "Or some of the construction workers' strikes."

Six months earlier a member of a striking construction workers' union was found dead in the trunk of his car, his lips sewn shut. Henri had covered the story for the paper. "Don't remind me," he said, shuddering slightly.

Blanchard changed the subject. "Did you hear about Robert Bourassa being elected head of the Liberal Party? He'll be running for Premier."

"No, but I'm not surprised. He's been gathering strength for some time. Do we know when the election will be?"

"April 29th."

Their conversation went on in desultory fashion for a few more minutes before Blanchard made moves to leave. "That's about it, Henri. I was here to see another client and just wanted to let you know I hadn't forgotten you." He handed Henri copies of several newspapers. "Your latest letter-to-the-editor is in the one on top."

Henri couldn't put it off any longer. "Can you get a letter to someone for me?" He wiped his suddenly sweaty palm on his pant leg before reaching into his pocket and drawing out the envelope with his note to Claudia.

It had taken him a long time to compose the letter. He knew it must sound curt and doubted Claudia would do what he asked—try to find out what Marie-Catherine was up to with Marc. If she refused to help, or didn't even bother to answer him, he wouldn't blame her. "I don't have her address, but I've written a phone number down and whoever answers should be able to tell you where to send it."

Blanchard looked down at the envelope Henri handed him. "Will there be a letter back?"

"I don't know. I hope so."

"If there is, it will have to go through the censors."

"Shit, I'd forgotten." Henri thought fast. Weeks before he'd hinted to Blanchard about his fears regarding Marc's hold over Marie-Catherine, although he'd never told Blanchard she was the main reason for his being in prison— his desperate gamble to save her from her own foolishness. "It's about my sister. I need to make sure Marc's keeping her out of trouble like he promised."

The lawyer frowned and pursed his lips as though he was considering something. Once more Henri wondered what or who Blanchard really worked for, how much to trust the man. If this got Claudia into trouble with the *flics* or the FLQ he would never forgive himself. It was too late, though. He'd already given Blanchard the letter.

Blanchard tapped the envelope on the edge of the table, appearing deep in thought. Then his face cleared and he looked at Henri, his eyebrows raised in question. "And this friend could find out for you?"

"I think so. If she's still in Montreal and if she'll do it."

"Well, no harm in trying."

Once back in his cell, Henri tried not to think of what Claudia would do if she got the letter and didn't tear it up without reading it. Instead he sat on his bunk with the copy of *The Montreal Star* Blanchard had brought him. He turned a page and adrenalin shot through his body. A picture of Jeffers, standing next to Montreal's mayor, glared up at him. With jaws clenched and the muscles in his cheeks twitching,

Henri scanned the caption underneath the picture then began to read the article alongside it.

According to Montreal's mayor, Jean Drapeau, Quebec's Combined Anti-Terrorist Squad will be making use of the ten-point program Justice Minister Choquette put forward last summer.

Henri had a sudden mental image of Choquette, the pompous, heavyset man he'd interviewed on the steps of City Hall months before, sweating in the August heat as he defended his proposed program.

Mayor Drapeau states more money is needed to combat the terrorism and violence of the FLQ and says the Minister has promised more funding for that purpose. 'We'll put an end to them before the year is out,' stated Detective Bruce Jeffers of the Montreal Police and a member of the Squad.

The Combined Anti-Terrorist Squad had been formed several years earlier, with members from the Montreal and provincial police and the RCMP, to deal specifically with the FLQ. Jeffers, of course, had been a member from the beginning.

Henri jerked the paper in his hands, disgusted. Why wouldn't or couldn't people understand. No matter how many large-scale manhunts they conducted, no matter how many times they cut off the snake's head by arresting the entire FLQ leadership, the movement regenerated and grew because of the issues. If the government would spend all that energy, money, and time in fixing the problem, Jeffers and his ilk being part of it, the FLQ would go away. There would be no need for it. Henri threw the paper down in contempt.

Not for the first time, he wondered how his brother had escaped the many nets thrown out by the squad over the years. In the past, he'd half-believed Marc had some guardian angel protecting him, maybe someone high up in government. How else could he have escaped the notice of the police for so many years? But ever since the warden's mention of Marie-Catherine, Henri didn't know what to think. Were they toying with him? Had they known all along about Marc and Marie-Catherine's explosives and gun -buying trip to North Carolina? If so, what more did they know about Marc? It had long puzzled him why he, not Marc, had been singled out by Jeffers, but maybe Marc hadn't been as far off their radar screen as he believed.

Four days after his last visit, Blanchard came to see Henri again. He began speaking as soon as Henri entered the visitors' room, before he even sat.

"I got hold of your friend." His voice was low to prevent being overhead by two men at another table. "I didn't have to mail her your letter. She came to my office. Pretty girl."

Henri ignored the last remark. "What did she say? Will she do it?" It felt like his heart stopped beating as he waited for Blanchard's reply.

"Not only did she say she would, she did. She came by

my office again this morning to tell me." He leaned forward. "You're not going to like this, Henri."

"I want to hear."

"Your sister joined the Student Union at UQAM."

Henri waited for more but Blanchard stayed quiet. "That's it?" Henri almost slumped in relief. "What's so bad about that? I was in the Student Union, too. Weren't you? Weren't we all?"

"That's not all, Henri. She's reporting all their plans back to Marc."

"Son of a bitch." Henri flung himself back against the chair. "He promised to keep her out of it, but he's sucking her in. I knew he couldn't be trusted."

Once again in his cell, Henri paced the short distance between the bunk and the wall, back and forth, as he asked himself over and over why Marie-Catherine couldn't see where Marc was leading her. His temples pounded. He wanted to bellow his frustration and hear it reverberate off the bars and walls. If only he had someone to talk to, someone who would understand. But there was no one.

Under the tepid flow of water Henri tried to work up lather with the brown square of soap he'd been given to shower with. He stared at the rusty stains around the showerhead and remembered his childhood baths. Every Saturday after dinner he'd waited his turn to stand in the washtub in front of the stove. Once in, his mother would slosh water over his head and with soap and a rough cloth would work her way down until she came to what she called his private parts.

Then she would hand him the cloth and instruct him to wash himself. Even when he grew older and could scrub his own neck and ears, still, there'd been little privacy.

The water from the showerhead turned to a trickle and then stopped. Henri's five-minutes had elapsed. He reached behind him for the skimpy towel he'd left on the bench and scrubbed dry. He started to dress when a guard he hadn't seen before opened the door and spoke to the guard who'd escorted him from his cell.

"Warden wants you, Morais. Hurry it up."

Ten minutes later Henri found himself in the anteroom to the warden's office. Voices came from behind the closed doors at one end of the room. Henri sat in the chair in front of Bella's desk while he waited to be called inside, wondering who was with the warden.

"You can go in now," said Bella, and Henri was once again aware of the invisible method of communication stretching between her and the warden.

He rapped on the closed door.

"Come."

At the window, with his back toward the room, stood a figure Henri instantly recognized. "What are you doing here, Jeffers? I already told you I've done nothing wrong and I've told the warden I haven't got any names for you."

"Shut up, Morais. Wait until you're spoken to." Jeffers turned to the man behind the desk. "You must not be running a very tight ship, warden. Not when scum like this shows so little respect for his betters."

The warden ignored Jeffers and turned to Henri. "What's your brother up to?"

Henri glared from one to the other. "How the hell

should I know? I haven't seen or heard from him in weeks. Why?"

The warden hesitated a minute, seeming to consider his words. "He left me a message," he finally said, his voice grim. "In my mailbox."

"What message?"

"A bomb."

"Typical of you spineless cowards." Jeffers came to stand in front of Henri, his chin jutting forward. "What if it hadn't gone off at four in the morning but at nine, Morais? What if his wife or kid had opened the box?"

Henri inwardly winced at the prospect of such a scenario, but he tried to hide Marc's shame with blustering innocence. "So why are you asking about my brother? What makes you think he had anything to do with it?"

"We're not stupid, Morais. We know more than you think—such as your whole family is in this up to their eyeballs." Jeffers butted Henri with his paunch, shoved his face closer to Henri's.

Henri stood his ground. "I'm not impressed, Jeffers. You've had me wrong from the beginning. Why should I believe you about anyone else?"

"Shut up, both of you." The warden turned to Henri. "Bombers leave signatures. Each one has a certain way of doing things—twisting wires, connecting the timer, what they use for a timer. This one had your brother's signature."

It was obvious they knew more than he or Marc thought they did.

"If you know so much about him, or think you do," he added for Jeffers's benefit, "why haven't you arrested him?

It's not like you haven't known where he was. Hell, he even came to see me when I was being held in Jeffers's precinct."

"Knowing and proving are different things." The warden didn't give Henri any more time to think, nor did he wait for Henri to defend Marc further. "He and his cell are planning something. We want to know what."

"I don't know anything about what he's doing. Like I told you, I haven't talked to him in weeks—not since I came here. And what do you mean about proof? No one needed any when Jeffers arrested me."

"Don't give us any shit." Jeffers shoved into Henri's face again. "You two have always been tight. You know what he's planning, all right."

It didn't surprise Henri that Jeffers didn't comment on there being no proof when he'd been arrested.

The whole thing was so confusing—Henri had almost given up trying to figure out how they were defending their actions. He knew what he was trying to prove, but he sure as hell didn't know their game. It infuriated him to think they were using him, trying to force his hand, just as Marc had done when he took Marie-Catherine to North Carolina.

"Back off, Jeffers. I'm beginning to think he's telling the truth about not knowing. Answer me this, Morais. Would you tell us if you did know?"

Henri turned to the warden. "I might. I guess it would depend what it is—if, in fact, he's planning anything. If everything you suspect is based on Jeffers' information, I'm a long way from being convinced."

Jeffers snorted and went to stand by the window again.

The warden leaned back in his chair. "Why don't you talk to your brother, get him to tell you what he's planning."

"That might prove difficult from here." Henri folded his arms. "Like I told you, I haven't talked or heard from him for weeks."

"Have Drill take him another message."

Still stunned by the warden's revelation about Albert Drill, Henri paced his cell. Did Drill work for the FLQ and the warden knew about it? Or did the man work for the warden and Jeffers?

Either way, Henri didn't know what he should do. If he did what the warden asked and sent a message to Marc, it would be an admission of guilt on all their parts, an admission that Jeffers was right about him and Marc and Marie-Catherine. On the other hand, if he did nothing, he feared they would simply go after Marie-Catherine, considering her the weak link.

At this point, Henri didn't care about his brother. Marc could take care of himself. But he had to do something to protect his sister. If only he knew what.

Chapter Twenty

Marc stretched out on the bed and considered Henri. He could never endure being locked up, as his brother was. Despite all Henri's blathering about exposing the system from the inside, Marc still didn't understand why he'd gotten himself arrested. But then he hadn't understood his brother for years.

His mind drifted back to one Sunday evening in the spring of 1968. Henri was still in university and working part-time as a glorified errand boy at that newspaper of his. Marc had moved out by then, but he occasionally dropped by the folks' house for a meal.

He and Henri sat on the front steps, each nursing a beer. Henri was the first to speak. "I'm not joining the FLQ, Marc. I know we both said we would, but I've changed my mind."

As young teenagers, for months after they'd read the FLQ's first communiqué, announcing the organization's birth, they'd talked of nothing but joining up. They'd sworn to each other that they, too, were 'ready to die for the political and economic independence of Quebec.'

"Why?" Marc asked, although Henri's revelation didn't come as a surprise. He'd known by then of his brother's change of heart. He even knew when it happened: the day Henri got connected with that reporter, Louis Simard.

"I'm going to be a journalist, eventually a politician."

Marc snorted in derision. He had no use for politicians.

"I know you're in, though. You joined long ago—even though you didn't tell me." Henri's voice sounded odd to Marc, as though his brother was angry at being left behind. "So how did you get in? It's why I went to see Simard in the first place. I thought he was in the FLQ and I wanted him to get us both in."

Marc shrugged. "You meet people."

Henri's gaze was unyielding. "But why didn't you tell me? You knew I wanted to join then. We always did things like that together."

"Papa would have had my balls if you hadn't stayed in school."

Henri took a sip of his beer. "Yeah, I guess." He sounded only partially convinced.

"So, what's stopping you from joining now?" Marc watched Henri from the corner of his eye. "Hell, if it's journalism you want, you can write for *La Congee*."

Henri shook his head. "I can't write for the FLQ. I need to be objective. I have to listen and understand both sides to write what is true and what isn't."

"Bullshit. You already know what's true. You live it just like the rest of us. You know what's right. You've just spent too much time with those fucking politicians at school." Marc had no patience with self-righteous rhetoric, especially coming from his brother.

Henri's cheeks flamed, but he didn't acknowledge the jab in any other way. "Tell me about how you started. What was it like back when you first joined? You must have gone in when the FLQ was still pretty new."

"In sixty-three." Marc took satisfaction in Henri's look of surprise. "Yep, right after it started. Nobody knew what they were doing. Me either, I guess." He gave a rueful laugh. "I wasn't even sixteen."

"What was it like back then?"

"Why do you want to know? What difference does it make now?" Marc wasn't interested in dissecting past events. Henri liked nothing better.

"No difference. I'm just curious."

To satisfy him, and maybe to brag a bit, Marc told his brother a little about the first training camp he'd gone to— the FLQ had camps for training recruits in the Laurentian Mountains north of Montreal and on the Gaspé Peninsula. "It was so unorganized you had to laugh. Except I was scared shitless I'd get killed by a bear or something. Only a couple of people knew what the fuck they were doing. Like me, most were from the city or towns. They weren't much older than me, either." He shook his head then drew again on his cigarette.

"Did they teach you how to make bombs there? Is that how you learned?"

"What do you know about that?"

"I saw some of your stuff once—at that place on Vandervere where you lived for a while."

"So why didn't you say something to me then?" Marc was more curious than angry.

Henri shrugged. "I guess I didn't want to think about it. But is that where you learned, at the training camp?"

"Why do you want to know? Are you researching for some paper you're going to write?" He wouldn't put it past Henri to show off his knowledge that way.

Henri looked wounded. "Of course not. I can keep secrets, too. Haven't I kept this one?"

"I don't know. Have you?"

"Yes, I have. But if you don't want to tell me, forget it."

Marc hesitated for only a second or two. "They taught us how to make Molotov cocktails—firebombs. When I got back to Montreal I tinkered for a while. A few of us did. But most of what we made didn't work—or it worked too well." It had been scary. They'd made some colossal mistakes. Marc had learned from his errors, though, and now he took pride in what he built. He'd become one of the best.

"I hope you didn't have anything to do with the bomb that killed the policeman in Westmount. Walter Leja."

The way Henri looked at him when he asked the question made Marc know his brother had no stomach for what needed to be done. "If it had gone off when it was supposed to, no one would have been hurt. But to answer your question, no, I had nothing to do with that."

He flicked the cherry-red butt of his cigarette into the darkness and watched the trail of sparks.

"I had nothing to do with it," he said again, disgusted to realize he still cared what Henri thought of him.

"So how *did* you learn to build them?"

"At first, like I said, it was trial and error. I learned a few things from others, but most of it was experimenting on my own. Then I went to Jordan. In the desert in Jordan is where I learned."

Shock registered on Henri's face. "You were in Jordan? I can't believe you were out of the country—so far away as the Middle East—and I didn't know."

"You've always been more wrapped up in yourself than in anyone else." Marc didn't try to hide his disdain. "Even now, your surprise is you didn't know, that I didn't tell you. Grow up, Henri. The world doesn't revolve around you."

"Maybe not, but I still don't know how you can put something together knowing it might kill someone." Revulsion sounded in Henri's voice.

"There you go with that bleeding heart of yours, little brother." Marc lit another cigarette. "We could cause a lot more damage. A lot of people would die if we meant them to. But we don't. We're just trying to get the world's attention."

Henri threw up his hands. "Get the world's attention? Are you nuts? The world thinks you're a bunch of crazy zealots. Is that the kind of attention you want?"

"We'll take what we can get. Instead of lecturing and letting us do all the dirty work, why don't you set the record straight by writing for us."

Henri shook his head. "Sorry. You push the line too far. Your hatred of the Anglos doesn't justify the things you do."

"No. You draw the line too close, little brother. This isn't a game we're playing. You can't have a revolution without casualties."

They hadn't resolved the argument. Instead their differences festered and afterwards Marc had taken every opportunity to needle and discomfit his brother. The girl-friend, Claudia, had been one way.

A year or so after Henri graduated and went to work full-time for *Le Journal Quotidien*, Marc saw Claudia waiting for a bus. He stopped at the curb, leaned over, and rolled down the window.

"Want a ride?"

They'd stopped for coffee, and after that it had been easy to occasionally just happen to be in the neighborhood. Marc hadn't known at the time why he kept up the pretense of friendship with her, and he didn't know what she told Henri about it. But Henri being Henri, he'd known the girl was being neglected.

The sound of the apartment door opening brought Marc back to the present. His eyes still closed, he heard footsteps and the rustle of paper. Then more footsteps sounded and suddenly Bunny dropped onto the bed, a knee on either side of his hips. Marc's eyes flew open. Bunny grinned down at him. "Ready or not, here I am." An hour later she stretched and looked across the rumpled sheets at him. "I brought home a couple of roast beef sandwiches. They're in the kitchen."

"I guess you want me to get them," said Marc, sitting up and pulling on his jeans.

She grinned. "Bring me a beer, too."

Marc came back to the bedroom a few minutes later. "I've been thinking about Henri. I can't understand how he's changed so much since we were kids."

"Changed how?" Bunny lay on the bed balancing a bottle of beer and the sandwich on her taut stomach.

Marc wasn't used to explaining himself. He had to take a minute to get his thoughts together. "When we were kids, Henri was adamant he would join the FLQ. Hell, the flics arrested him when he was thirteen for standing on the corner of University and Sherbrooke yelling 'down with the government'. God, *Maman* was angry. She wanted to kick Papa she was so furious."

Marc chuckled over the memory before turning serious again.

"Then he got connected with a reporter, Louis Simard, and everything changed. He didn't want any part of the FLQ. I had to blackmail him to get that *communiqué* printed last fall. Then a month after that he does another flip-flop and now he's with us. I don't get it. How can he change like that?"

"Maybe he hasn't." Bunny took a bite of the sandwich and chewed. "There's gristle all through this." She frowned, her words muffled by the meat and bread.

"What do you mean?" Marc paced to the window then back again to stand next to the bed.

Bunny went on chewing. "This is terrible." She put the half-eaten sandwich back on the plate then leaned over and put the plate on the table next to the bed.

"What do you mean?" Marc said again.

She took a swallow of beer. "I don't know, Marc. I guess what I mean is…maybe he hasn't changed all that much. Maybe he's always been one way or the other— always agreed with the FLQ, but thought he shouldn't. Or maybe it's the other way around. He didn't then and doesn't now, but for some reason is acting as though he does. You know him better than I do. What do you think?"

Long after Bunny had fallen asleep, Marc lay in the dark and pondered that question.

Chapter Twenty-One

Marie-Catherine had never had a boyfriend before. She'd never even gone on a date, much less been kissed by a boy. Now she had Roger.

"I can't believe you didn't have a string of boys after you," he'd said the second time he took her out. "You're so beautiful."

She'd blushed when he said it, quite liking the idea of herself as a femme fatale, but now she stared at her reflection in the mirror above the bathroom sink looking for the beauty he'd claimed to see. Cute, maybe, but hardly beautiful. Her face was too round and her nose too short for beauty. And her hair...well, that was its own sad story. If only she had sleek, straight hair like Claudia's instead of this thick, curly mess that frizzed up at the slightest excuse. She wouldn't mind having a long, graceful neck, as well.

She gave up searching for whatever Roger saw, and began brushing her teeth.

They'd gone to another Student Union meeting and to another protest rally, this time for the striking workers of a soft-drink bottling factory. She'd harbored no doubts about the second rally. Her heart was solidly with the striking workers.

She leaned down to rinse her mouth, splashed the cold water on her face, and groped for a towel to wipe her tired eyes. Sleep had evaded her the night before. She'd finally told Roger about Marc and the FLQ, but not about her own involvement. Roger hadn't condemned the FLQ outright, but he hadn't exactly praised them, either, which surprised her a little after his outspoken support of Charles Gagnon that first night at dinner. When she'd told him about Marc, he'd only nodded his head, as though he already knew about him. She'd spent the night trying to decide if she should tell Roger of her own involvement.

Claudia would know what to do, she thought, pulling a brush through her disheveled hair. It had been great running into her like that. She'd forgotten Claudia's parents lived near the UQAM campus, so hadn't expected to climb aboard a bus and find Claudia sitting in one of the seats.

It seemed like she'd always known Claudia. She and Henri had been a couple since their university days when they worked together on the school newspaper. By rights, she supposed, Claudia should have resented her hanging around, monopolizing Henri's time, chattering her girlish nonsense, but for some reason Claudia hadn't minded. Instead, she'd treated Marie-Catherine with indulgence, just as Henri did.

It had hurt when Claudia left Montreal without saying good-bye. And though she was back now, nothing felt the same. How could it, with Henri in jail? And Claudia wouldn't talk about it.

Marie-Catherine gave the brush a final yank as her roommate, Roseanne, rattled the bathroom door.

"Hurry up in there. I need to pee."

Marie-Catherine opened the door. "It's all yours," she told Roseanne, who brushed past her without answering.

It had threatened to snow earlier, but now the sun shone. It was one of those early spring days when whatever she put on in the morning, she'd either be too hot or too cold at least part of the day. For the moment, at least, she was just about right. "Let's go in here and get some coffee," she said to Claudia as they passed a café on a side street off Ste. Catherine Avenue.

They'd planned to visit a bookstore where an American writer was scheduled to speak about the Black Power movement, but Marie-Catherine knew she wouldn't be able to concentrate on what the man had to say. She didn't think Claudia was in the mood for it either.

"I need to talk to you about something," she said as soon as they'd placed their orders. Claudia had always been a sympathetic listener and before long Marie-Catherine had confessed everything about her trip with Marc and her worry about how Roger would react if he knew.

"What do you think," she finally said. "Should I tell him what I've done? What I'm still doing… reporting the Student Union's plans to Marc?"

Claudia looked pensive. She tapped her long fingernails on the table next to her coffee cup. "I don't know, M.C.," she said, using the same pet name as Marc and Henri. "You should know the answer to that question better than me. I've never even met him, though he sounds nice. But I guess I'm always on the side of honesty in relationships."

Marie-Catherine had known Claudia would say that,

had been waiting for it. "You're right. I have to tell him." It wouldn't be easy.

Claudia smiled at her. "Good girl." She glanced at her watch. "I have twenty minutes before I need to get back to work—time enough for another cup of coffee, I think."

"Good," said Marie-Catherine, pushing aside her worries about Roger. "Time enough for you to tell me why you and Henri broke up."

"I can't, M.C. Maybe Henri will one day."

"Well, you can tell me what your plans are, at least. I know your job's temporary. When it's over are you going to stay in Montreal?"

"Oh, I'm staying." Claudia spoke with what Marie-Catherine at first thought was a defiant look. Then she examined Claudia's face more closely and reconsidered. Not defiant, determined.

Roger stared at her as though he couldn't comprehend what she'd told him. They were once again at a table in the school library.

"You said we had to act. That first night, when we were having dinner, you said we had to fight for what we believe in. And you went to that rally for Charles Gagnon— he's FLQ. Why did you do that?"

"Because I don't think he or Valliéres did what they've been accused of doing. I don't think they were involved with that bombing. I told you—it would have been out of character for either of them. And when I said we had to stand up for what we believe in, I was talking about taking responsible political action." His voice was low and intense, just as Marie-Catherine's had been. "Marches. Demonstrations. Support for striking workers. Not bombs and stuff. Jeez, I can't believe you'd condone that sort of thing, much less participate in it."

Nettled, Marie-Catherine responded. "What do you think all the demonstrations and rallies we've been to have accomplished? I'm not sure they've done a thing."

"We've shown our support. We've shown support for justice." He shook his head. "Look how much Henri has accomplished with his articles and speeches."

"What, getting thrown in jail? That's accomplishing something in your mind?"

Roger ignored her sarcasm. "He's raised the consciousness of people through civil disobedience. He's raised awareness of the problems French Canadians face. People talk about Henri Morais—they quote him in class, in the newspapers, on the street. They compare him to people like Gandhi and Sadat."

At Roger's words of praise for Henri, Marie-Catherine's face flushed with pride for her brother.

Roger went on. "Henri hasn't planted bombs. He hasn't destroyed things. It's Henri whose example you should be following, not Marc's." He leaned forward in his chair, his brow furrowed and his eyes drilling into Marie-Catherine's. "Marc could get you killed."

"Don't be ridiculous. Marc would never let anything happen to me. I'm his sister."

"Then he should treat you like one. He shouldn't let you get involved with those people. They're crazy."

Marie-Catherine kept silent because she didn't know

what to say. Although part of her was angry, the other part of her, the part that thought he might be right, was afraid to say more.

"I have to go to French Lit," Roger finally said, picking up his books. "I'll see you tomorrow." He didn't kiss her goodbye. He didn't even look at her.

"Roger…." Her voice trailed off as he walked away, disappearing around the end of a long bookcase in the direction of the library's main doors. He was wrong about one thing, she told herself. Marc would never let anything bad happen to her.

Chapter Twenty-Two

Roger had gone back to Quebec City to spend time with his parents. He said he'd see her when he got back from spring break. But the way he avoided looking at her and the edge in his voice made Marie-Catherine know things wouldn't be the same. She sat alone, staring at the window. Rain struck the panes like marbles.

Roseanne had left for home the day before and her other roommate, Nicole, had gone off with her boyfriend. For the first time in her life Marie-Catherine had all the room she could want, an entire apartment at her disposal. So why did she feel the walls were about to close in and slowly squeeze the life out of her?

On impulse, she grabbed her coat from the end of the couch and left the apartment, ignoring that she'd just put off going to see her parents for another day.

Running down the stairs, she tossed a long blue scarf over her hair and wound it around her neck. Once outside she strode down the sidewalk to the corner and stood with her back to the buffeting wind and icy rain, waiting for a Saint Leonard or a North Montreal bus.

It would probably be a fruitless journey. She didn't even know if Marc was in town, much less at his apartment. And why should he be any more interested in her now than he'd ever been? Well, he seemed to be paying a little more attention to what she did and what she thought since their trip to North Carolina. Or maybe she kidded herself. Probably. The bus splashed to the curb and she climbed aboard.

At some point in the past, grass had been planted in front of the building where Marc lived, but only patches remained. A mountain of grungy, melting snow now filled the barren space, the remains of a winter's worth of sidewalk snow removal. It was surrounded by muddy puddles, their surfaces dashed with raindrops.

Marie-Catherine hurried up to the building's entrance, the glass in the door smeared with fingerprints. Struggling against the wind, she pulled the door open and stepped inside then pulled off her scarf and gloves while she paused to catch her breath and warm up. The week before it had rained off and on, but there'd been sun breaks to remind her of warm weather ahead. This week, the weather more nearly matched her mood. A cold wind blew out of the north, bringing with it a reprise of winter.

She passed the stairs leading to the second floor and stopped in front of the door to Marc's apartment, one of three on the ground floor. When she raised her hand to knock, she caught the murmur of voices coming from inside the apartment. She hesitated for only a moment then rapped on the thick layer of paint covering the metal door. When it swung open Marc stood framed in the entrance. They stared at one another for what seemed like a full minute, but must have been only seconds.

Marc stepped back. "Come on in."

Two men and a woman were seated in Marc's living room. She immediately recognized the man from the warehouse. He nodded to her.

Marc introduced a man whose long, plain face, small close-set eyes and big nose made her think of a cartoon caricature of Charles de Gaulle. "Paul Gould," Marc said. Gould nodded his head but didn't stand.

"I'm his sister," said the woman, whose face was a faintly softened version of her brother's. "Theresa Dumas."

Gould and his sister didn't take their eyes off Marie-Catherine. The man from the warehouse, LeGuin, lit a cigarette and leaned back in his chair; he was so thin he almost disappeared into his clothes. Marie-Catherine sensed excitement in the air. And purpose. Yet no one spoke until the woman stood. "Okay." As though she'd given them a signal, the woman's brother and LeGuin stood as well.

Marc walked out of the apartment with the others. A moment later, he came back inside, alone.

"I didn't mean to spoil your meeting."

"No problem. They were leaving anyway."

"Oh." She'd been standing by the window mindlessly fiddling with a strand of her hair and watching the cars drive by. Now she came back and curled into a fake-leather chair across from Marc.

Even though his head was leaned against the back of the couch and his legs stretched out in an attitude of careless ease, she saw he watched her from beneath half-lowered eyelids. "What's up?" he finally asked.

"Nothing special, I guess." She picked at the edges of a tear in the arm of the chair. "I just don't know what to do with myself, Marc. I feel so directionless. No, that isn't the right word. It's more like I have no control over my life—I'm like piece of flotsam in a stream, being swept along by the current." She picked at the chair arm again and sighed.

"What do you want me to do about it?"

Not looking at him, she shrugged. She didn't blame him for the irritation in his voice. She wasn't very happy with herself, either. Things were so confusing, though. She'd felt confident, filled with purpose when she'd gotten the chance to go to UQAM. She still loved school, the excitement, the freedom, meeting new people. But it didn't seem to be enough. "I guess I just want to be more like you and Henri. Things don't simply happen to the two of you. You make things happen. Henri even seems able to make things happen from jail. You both know exactly what you're doing and why. And what you do matters."

Marc straightened and frowned. It was a moment or two before he answered."The things you've done matter, M.C. I couldn't have made it back from North Carolina without you."

"Yes, you could. I was only along for the ride. You know that."

Marc shook his head. "You're wrong. I could have been stopped any number of times."

"I don't think so. When?"

"How about the state trooper who came into the all-night diner in Malone, just before we crossed the border? He gave me the once over, but passed me by because you were there, too. And don't forget that deputy sheriff when the truck broke down in Virginia." Marc shook his head. "He was so busy trying to impress you, he didn't have time to be more suspicious of me and what was in the van."

Marie-Catherine remembered how frightened she'd been when the truck sputtered and died and a few minutes later the sheriff's car pulled to a stop behind him. Just one more thing she hadn't told Henri when she'd confessed to him about making the trip. She stopped fingering the upholstery and leaned her chin on her hand.

"Maybe you're right, but I feel like I should be doing much more. I'm confused, Marc. I mean I want to go to school. And I want to graduate. But sometimes it just seems pointless. What does it matter what Charlemagne did? Who cares how Canadian hawkweed differs from spotted hawkweed or any other hawkweed?"

"What about what you're doing with the Student Union? Haven't you been taking part in protests?"

"I'm no more than a speck of dust to them. There are hundreds of students willing to march. I don't think one person would notice if I failed to show up at the next meeting."

"But you keep me informed. I like knowing what they're up to."

"I don't know what good it does you when I'm the last one to know anything." Marie-Catherine knew she sounded pitiful. She straightened her shoulders, ashamed of her poor spirit.

."Maybe you need a little break from school, get some real-life experience before cracking the books."

"Oh Marc. I couldn't quit after all *Maman* and Papa have sacrificed. You and Henri, too. Not to mention how hard I've worked."

But she was tempted, even though she knew Roger's anticipated defection had something to do with the way she currently felt. Everything just seemed flat to her now. Not like when she and Marc had gone to North Carolina. It frustrated her that Roger couldn't understand that.

"The thing is, I want to do something important. I want to do something that matters now."

"You can. And you don't need to quit school to do it, either. Unless you want to, of course."

"How? What can I do?"

"While you're on spring break you can get a job at the Arrow Shoe Factory."

She couldn't imagine what her brother was thinking. "Doing what? I don't know how to put shoes together. I can't even type. If I could type maybe I could get a job in their office."

"You can get a job there, all right. The workers are out on strike and they're hiring scabs."

"Then won't they want someone who can run the machines?"

"They'll have all sorts of jobs you can do—sorting, filling boxes, stuff like that. If you hate it, you can quit whenever you want."

She began to feel more positive. Still…. "Papa would have a cow if he heard about me working as a scab when the workers are out on strike. How would it matter anyway, especially for only two weeks?"

Marc gave her a long, calculating look before he spoke. "We want to find out what's going on inside, how bad off they are and what management is planning. And don't worry. Papa won't hear about it…you won't be there that long. But if he does hear, he'll understand. I'll explain you're doing it for us."

Marie-Catherine stared back, stunned by what he'd said. The idea of being a spy, because that's what Marc described, sounded glamorous and exciting. She nodded. "I think you're right—that's just what I need. I'll do it. Like you say, it's only for two weeks."

Marc smiled. "Good. I'll write down the name of the man you should ask to see."

Marie-Catherine watched her brother scribble the name on a scrap of paper. "Did I tell you I ran into Claudia a while ago?"

"Who?" Marc looked up, distracted.

"Claudia. You know. Henri's Claudia."

Marc frowned. "I thought she'd left Montreal."

"She's back. And you know what? I think she still loves Henri."

Marc handed her the scrap of paper. "I hope you haven't told her anything. I don't trust her."

When Marie-Catherine stepped off the bus in front of the factory the next morning, a mob scene greeted her. Men and women jammed the sidewalk. Many carried babies or led small children by the hand while also carrying signs declaring Arrow Shoes unfair to labor. All of them were shouting and chanting slogans. One man stood in front of the others, waving a sign that read "No Union...No Work." He seemed to be the ring-leader, encouraging the crowd to yell louder.

A truck pushed its way through the crowd toward an alley between the factory and the building next to it. Two strikers jumped up on the truck's running boards and pounded on the rolled-up windows. A scared but determined look was on the young driver's face. When he started driving forward into the narrow alley, the men on the running boards jumped down.

Marie-Catherine wasn't sure how to get through the crowd to the factory door. Before she could turn tail and run, she drew a deep breath and started forward. A woman with a baby in her arms scowled at her.

"What do you want here?" the woman asked. "You aren't planning to work for these bastards, are you?"

Another woman glared and said, "Shame."

A man gave her a shove.

Marie-Catherine stumbled into a young child before catching her balance.

A guard standing next to the factory door saw her struggling, but did nothing to help her. When she finally reached him, she shouted the man's name she had come to see.

The crowd booed.

The guard opened the door enough for her to squeeze through. She told herself to relax, they didn't understand she was doing this for them.

Her self-righteousness didn't last long. By the end of the day she worried each step might be her last. Never had she worked so hard and so long without stopping.

First, they'd put her to work helping unload the hides from the truck that had arrived from the tannery, carrying them to where they'd be sorted and cut. From there she'd been sent upstairs to load empty boxes onto a handcart, which she pulled onto an open elevator.

The elevator shook its way down to the main floor, near the end of a row of sewing machines. After she unloaded the empty boxes, she filled the handcart with stacks of filled boxes. These she took to a stack next to a conveyor belt at the other end of the room, where the shoes were inspected, wrapped in tissue, and put back in the boxes.

Then off she would go for another load of empty boxes. This routine kept her busy until the middle of the afternoon.

A plump, middle-aged woman with red hair and a creamy complexion looked briefly at Marie-Catherine then back to her task of wrapping a pair of men's shoes in tissue paper before inserting them back into the empty box on the conveyor belt.

"You look beat," the woman said. Her quick, deft movements told Marie-Catherine she'd been doing the work for a long time.

Marie-Catherine straightened. "I am. I feel about to drop."

The woman took the lid from another box with one hand and picked up a piece of tissue with the other. "When did you take your last break?"

"I haven't taken one. No one told me I could."

"You've at least eaten lunch, haven't you? You're not going to tell me these shits haven't even told you when you could stop for lunch?"

At this point, Marie-Catherine began to feel foolish, knowing she should have been more assertive. "I'm fine. I'm just not used to working like this. Tomorrow I'll be up to speed."

"Honey, you're doing fine right now. You go on into the break room—through that door over there." She jutted her chin over her shoulder to a door behind her. "You get some tea and put your feet up for twenty minutes, and if anyone gives you any trouble about it, you tell them to see Dora." She inspected and wrapped two more pairs of shoes while she spoke.

"Thanks, but I'm fine." Marie-Catherine picked up the handle of the handcart.

"Suit yourself. Nobody else is going to care if you keel over, you know. They'll just shove your body under a table and pull in some other sucker off the street."

Marie-Catherine stared at the woman a moment, then turned and left, dragging the handcart behind her.

Getting out of the factory seemed almost more difficult than it had been to get in, Marie-Catherine thought when she joined several other workers gathering to leave.

The guard stood inside now. "Soon as we get enough people together I'll open the door and you can all go out at once."

Through the grill-covered window in the door, Marie-Catherine saw most of the women and children had gone, leaving only the men to jeer and yell. She pulled the collar of her jacket up and hunched her shoulders.

"Put your arm through mine." Marie-Catherine turned toward the voice. "It helps," Dora said. Marie-Catherine nodded and slipped her arm through the crook of Dora's elbow. The guard opened the door.

The crowd on the sidewalk let out a roar and surged forward to meet them. Marie-Catherine and Dora tucked in behind three men. Forming a wedge, they forced their way through the strikers. Hands tugged at Marie-Catherine's jacket. One reached under it and pinched her right breast. She jerked her arm up to protect herself. She tried to close her ears to the words. "Scabs" and "sluts" were the mildest. She still had her arm through Dora's when they got to the other side of the street.

"Thank you." She turned her head as though searching for the bus. She didn't want Dora to see her tears.

"No problem. Which bus are you taking?"

"The one to St. Leonard. How about you?"

"My husband works near here. He'll pick me up in a few minutes. We'll give you a ride if you want. Not all the way, but we can drop you off near Pie IX."

When she looked back at the jeering crowd across the street waiting for the next group of people to come out the door, like cats outside a mouse hole, Marie-Catherine felt tempted to accept. Before she could say yes, she saw her bus half a block away.

"Thanks, but I see my bus coming now." When it lurched to a stop in front of her, Marie-Catherine climbed aboard and dropped coins in the glass box beside the driver. The seats in front of the bus were full. By the time she got settled, halfway to the rear, the bus had pulled away from the curb. She turned to look out the rear window in time to see Dora sliding into the front seat of a rusty brown station wagon.

That night at Marc's apartment, her brother quizzed her for an hour about what they had her doing and what the factory looked like inside. "Tell me again about the machinery. How many machines are they running and what do they do?"

"I don't know what all of them are called." Marie-Catherine was puzzled by his interest in the physical plant. She'd thought he only wanted to know what the people were doing inside. "Like I told you, they have machines that stamp out the leather, machines that sew the shoes together. It looked to me like lots of the work is done at work-benches—gluing or stitching the soles of the shoes on, stuff like that."

Marc nodded.

"And there's a long conveyor belt where they inspect the shoes and wrap them in tissue." She thought about the woman who'd helped her. Dora.

"Where's the conveyor located?"

"The factory is just a big room." She almost swallowed her words in a yawn. "It's at the south end. Marc, we've been over and over this. I have to get some sleep or I'll never make it to day two."

"Sleep here, tonight. You can sack out on the couch."

Too tired to argue and not wanting to face the long bus ride back to her apartment, Marie-Catherine agreed.

Chapter Twenty-Three

Blanchard didn't wait for Henri to sit down. "She's gone to work at Arrow Shoe Factory."

Henri was stunned. "What do you mean? How could she? She's still in school." Surely Marie-Catherine wouldn't do something so foolish, not after all her effort to get into UQAM.

"Claudia came by this morning. She said your sister claimed it was just over spring break, but that I should tell you right away. You know Arrow is out on strike."

"Yes, I read it in one of the papers you brought me." Henri's thoughts moved at a furious pace. At least she hadn't dropped out of school—but that must mean Marc planned something within the next two weeks. It also meant his aim to show Marie-Catherine responsible civil disobedience was a complete fiasco; nothing had gone according to plan.

Once again Henri sat in front of Bella's desk, waiting to see the warden. The summons came quicker than usual. Bella nodded to him then tilted her head toward the door.

Henri started talking as soon as he entered the room. "I'll find out what he's up to. Let me out of here and I'll find out for you."

The warden agreed. Without further discussion and after more than three months in prison with no trial and only vague charges, they were going to set him free, free to spy on his brother.

Blanchard came to bring Henri the official news.

Henri hadn't told his lawyer the truth about why he was in prison and he certainly wouldn't tell Blanchard of his deal with the warden, though surely the man must suspect something.

Part of him felt guilty for his lack of honesty, but the rest of him knew Blanchard couldn't be trusted. No matter how pleasant Blanchard might be, how responsive he'd been when Henri asked him to serve as a go-between with Claudia, at heart Blanchard was still the FLQ's man.

"It's about time they release me. I can't believe they've kept me here so long without charging me for something."

Blanchard brushed a speck of lint from his tailored lapel. "It's politics, my friend, just politics."

"When does it happen?"

"You have one more night here." Blanchard's shiny long blonde hair was pulled back in a club, tied at the nape of his neck with a black silk ribbon. "The Judge signs your release order in the morning. Congratulations, Henri. This time tomorrow, you'll be a free man."

Henri tried to clamp down on the wave of disappointment he felt at needing to wait, to not being released that very moment. He closed his eyes and focused his thoughts on the next day. Freedom: how precious when you don't have it. I'll always remember how this felt, he promised himself—these past few months, this moment—and no matter what else happens I won't give up the fight for Quebec's freedom.

"…get hold of him," Blanchard said.

"What?"

"I've asked my secretary to let your brother know you're getting out, but she's having trouble reaching him."

"There's no telling where he is." Henri was still distracted, thinking about his impending release. "He'll turn up. He always does."

Blanchard stood to leave. "I need to get a few more papers signed to assure your release, Henri. I'll see you in the morning."

Henri looked at the crowd of men and women on the sidewalk, holding up cameras and thrusting microphones in his face, yelling stupid questions like how it felt to be free. How did it feel? After three months of repeated beatings, rotten food and being locked up, how did they think he felt? He could hardly breathe with the excitement of it.

But his giddiness at being free fought with his desire to turn-tail and run back inside—away from their cameras and their prying questions, away from what awaited him at the hands of Jeffers if he didn't produce what he'd promised, away from the knowledge of his own duplicity.

Blanchard spoke for him. "Mr. Morais isn't ready to issue a statement right now. My client will be granting interviews in the days to come, but right now he wants to get home and be with his family." He held Henri's arm, and together they pushed through the crowd to a car waiting at the curb.

They drove away in Blanchard's sleek gray Buick. Henri tried to relax. "I don't get it. I know you must have arranged all that, but how? There must have been a dozen or more reporters there. How did you get so many to show up?"

"You don't realize how important you've become, Henri. You're a hero to French Canadians and a symbol of the separatist movement." Henri could only stare at his lawyer in disbelief.

His father wiped tears from his eyes, and Henri felt his own throat tighten.

"It's about time those bastards let you go, but you don't look so good, Henri. What did they do to you, son?"

"I'm fine, Papa. I'll feel even better with some of *Maman*'s cooking inside of me."

"The food was bad?"

"It was terrible, Papa. So bad I had to force myself to eat it."

"Bastards."

Henri watched his mother's back. She stood at the sink peeling carrots and potatoes. "*Maman*, you don't have to do that now. I'm not so hungry I can't wait. Come sit with us, have some tea."

His mother reached for another potato. "When I'm finished, then I'll sit."

Henri started to go to her, make her join them at the table, but his father shook his head and Henri sat back down.

Later, when he and his father were alone, Henri asked why his mother appeared so upset. "I'm out of jail now."

"It's Marie-Catherine. Your mother is worried why she hasn't been coming to see us."

Henri gripped the receiver, listening to the distant ringing. Just when he started to hang up a breathless voice answered. "Hello?"

"It's me."

There was a long pause before Claudia answered. "Henri." A whisper of a sigh followed. "I just heard the news. Have you seen your family?" Her voice sounded flat to Henri. Cautious.

"I've seen *Maman* and Papa. No one else."

"Oh."

He gripped the telephone receiver tighter. "Look, I need to talk to you. Can we meet?"

"Yes. There's something I need to tell you."

"What?" His heart pounded at the reluctance in her voice. "What's happened?"

"I'll tell you everything when I see you."

They arranged to meet at a coffee shop in a quiet neighborhood off Sherbrooke. Henri watched her come through the door, her eyes searching until she found him. She hurried forward. He stood and pulled a chair out for her. He'd already ordered two black coffees.

"She's going to drop out of school, Henri."

Henri closed his eyes, forcing his body to relax. "Jesus. How can she be so stupid? Did she tell you what she planned to do? Where is she staying? How can I reach her?"

"I don't know where she is and I haven't talked to her since spring break." Claudia put her cup down. "I stopped by her apartment. One of her roommates told me she'd moved out and is withdrawing from school."

She reached across the table and covered his hand.

A spasm jerked through Henri's arm. He turned his hand over and clasped Claudia's. "Thank you. I appreciate all you've done. If it hadn't been for you…" He didn't know what else to say.

"I wish it could have been more, Henri."

He let go of her hand. "She's fallen into Marc's trap." I should never have dreamed up such a stupid scheme, he thought. I should have been on the outside, watching out for my sister. "It was my job to protect her." His voice choked with emotion—if something happened to her he'd never forgive himself. And he'd never forgive Marc. Not ever.

★

It took some effort, but Henri finally broke through the pack of striking workers on the sidewalk in front of Arrow Shoe factory. The guard refused to let him inside. He wouldn't even confirm that Marie-Catherine worked there.

Henri shouted to be heard over the yells and taunts of the placard-bearing strikers. "I'm her brother. I know she works here. Just tell her Henri wants to see her. Tell her to call me." He gave the guard a scrap of paper with his new phone number. "Tell her I'll be there all evening."

The guard stuffed the paper into his shirt pocket along with the bill Henri passed him.

Marie-Catherine didn't call. Not that evening and not the next. Henri contacted everyone who might know her whereabouts, all her old friends, one of her ex-roommates, but no one knew anything, or if they did, they weren't saying.

"I've only talked to her on the telephone. Just the one

time. She didn't tell me where she's staying," Marie-Catherine's old roommate told him. "Don't you have a brother? Maybe he knows."

Henri replaced the phone, muttering to himself. "I'll just bet he does."

He put off broaching the subject with his parents. Already upset, it would kill his mother if she knew what Marie-Catherine had done. He thought back to his argument with her over Marie-Catherine being allowed to move into an apartment and attend UQAM. *Damn it. I should have minded my own business.*

For two days, he tried to reach his brother, two days before Marc finally answered the phone. "Where's who?"

"Don't give me that crap. Where's Marie-Catherine?" He would have hit Marc had they been face to face.

"Couldn't tell you. She's a big girl, though, Henri, plenty big enough to take care of herself."

"Have her call me, Marc. It's all I ask. Just tell her to call me." Henri hung up the receiver with so much force the phone gave a chirp of protest. *The son-of-a-bitch knows exactly where she is.*

Once again Henri wondered how Marc always got women to do what he wanted. He closed his eyes and saw Claudia, smelled the perfume of her hair. Trying to fill the empty hours in prison, he'd entertained himself, maybe tortured was a better word for it, by mentally dialing the phone number she'd given him and holding imaginary conversations with her, conversations in which she assured him of her innocence. He didn't believe her, of course. He'd seen the evidence with his own eyes, the two of them on the couch, her hair tousled, her blouse unbuttoned.

Then he thought about all the dates and plans he'd cancelled at the last minute because of work or meetings, and he wondered if things would have worked out differently if Marc hadn't come between them.

What he couldn't understand was how Claudia had been so willing to help him after he'd repeatedly told her his feelings for her couldn't be rekindled.

Disgusted with himself for thinking about her, for acting like a love-starved puppy, he slammed out of his room and sprinted down the stairs.

Chapter Twenty-Four

Marie-Catherine couldn't keep avoiding the inevitable. Telling her parents wouldn't be so bad. Her mother would say it's what she should have done from the beginning. Her father would be disappointed, but his drive had been for Henri's education, not hers. The person she dreaded facing was Henri.

When Marc had given her the news of Henri's release from prison, she'd been relieved, happy, and ecstatic. She'd felt all those things, but she'd been too ashamed to call him or go see him. She knew he was looking for her. The guard at work had given her Henri's phone number, but she hadn't used it. He would scold and disapprove of her decision to quit school, treat her like a disappointing child.

Why did it have to be so hard to please everyone and still do what she wanted to do, the things important to her? In the end, she felt like she pleased no one, including herself.

She went to see her parents, arriving at the house late on Saturday afternoon in time to help her mother with dinner. No one spoke during the meal—her father surprisingly refraining from his normal diatribes. Marie-Catherine picked at her food, barely tasting it. Several times she started to say something then fell silent. In the end, she pushed her plate away and blurted it out.

"I've dropped out of school."

"What? What did you say?" Her father put his spoon down and directed his full attention to her.

"I said I've left school."

"Why? What were you thinking? Were the courses too hard? Weren't you studying enough? Why didn't you tell someone you were having trouble?" One question tumbled over the next. He looked confused and hurt. "If you were having trouble, Henri would have helped you." He was apparently forgetting Henri had been in prison.

"No, that's not it, Papa. I think I'm just not ready. I want to experience life first."

"Doing what? Working in a factory or a cannery earning a dollar an hour? That is experiencing life?" He scowled at her. "If it is, let me tell you I've experienced enough life for both of us."

Marie-Catherine wasn't used to being on the receiving end of her father's anger. She defended her decision. "There's nothing wrong with hard work." She didn't tell him about already having a job in the shoe factory.

"The girl's right, Emile. Leave her alone. It's her life."

Her father ignored her mother. "You've thrown away an opportunity we never had, your *Maman* and me. You worked for it, but so did we. I can't believe you've thrown it all away."

He pushed himself from the table.

"Why do you think I've worked so hard all my life, eh, letting everyone piss on me and putting up with it. For you and your brothers, is why. So you could be what I'm not: an educated person—a free person."

"I'm sorry, Papa." She swallowed to keep the tears in check. She started to explain, but he cut her off.

"Don't say anything more. I don't want to hear excuses." He crossed the kitchen and went out, slamming the door behind him.

Marie-Catherine pressed her hands to her burning cheeks. "I wish things weren't so hard."

Her mother stood. "He'll get over it. Help me clear the table."

★

When Marie-Catherine heard Henri's voice on the other end of the line she panicked and almost hung up the phone.

"M.C., is that you? What's going on? What are you doing at Marc's?"

"I'm staying here for a while, a few days." She tried to sound defiant. "Marc told me you were released. I'm glad you're out."

"I saw your roommate. She told me you quit school. Why?"

"It was my decision, Henri." She lifted her chin.

"But why?" She heard the bewilderment in his voice. "And why are you staying with Marc? If you're not going to school, why not move back home?"

"You know I can't go home. *Maman* would smother me. We'd just end up fighting and I'd leave anyway. Better to stay away."

Henri was silent for a moment. "I suppose you're right." They both remembered his own arguments with their mother. "But why didn't you call me? Why didn't you at least let me know where you were staying? I've been worried as hell about you."

"I know." The defiance seeped away and she struggled to keep the threatening tears out of her voice. "I'm sorry, Henri. I should have called. But I know how important it was for you—me going to school. I'll never forget how you convinced *Maman* to let me go. I'm a coward, I guess. After all your efforts, after all you've done for me, I didn't want to disappoint you."

"But I thought you wanted to go to school."

"I did. And maybe I'll go back someday. Just…not now." Before he could respond, she went on. "I'm really glad you're out of jail."

"Thanks. It feels pretty good. So, what's going on? Why are you working at a factory that's out on strike?"

"Making money, for one thing."

With all her might, Marie-Catherine wished Henri would just leave it alone, but she knew he wouldn't. He always had to dig.

"You think that justifies crossing a picket line? Papa wouldn't think so."

Hearing the disapproval in his voice, she knew she'd been right not to call before this.

"And you're as bad as Papa. The two of you don't run my life."

They all needed to understand she'd grown up. She could make her own decisions about what to do with her life. Anger made the hand holding the telephone shake, but she forced herself to explain.

"It's not like you think, Henri. I'm just keeping an eye on things. Marc says they need to know what's going on inside. And you of all people should know how important our work is."

First Roger, then Papa and now Henri. Damn them all. She wanted to cry.

"Is he there?" Henri's voice sounded flat and controlled. "Is Marc there?"

"No." Marie-Catherine kept her voice equally flat. "He and Bunny are both gone. He had a meeting, he said."

"Did he give you any idea when he might be back?"

"No, he didn't. And you know Marc—his meetings might last an hour or a week." She heard Henri mutter a frustrated oath and again felt guilty.

"Well, have him give me a call when he gets back, M.C. No matter what time he gets in. Tell him it's important."

Chapter Twenty-Five

After he hung up the phone Henri stood for a minute with his eyes closed and his chin resting on his chest. No matter how much Marie-Catherine denied it, he knew Marc had drawn her even further into his world. He toyed with the idea of going over to Marc's and talking to her, but he knew it wouldn't do any good.

He needed to see Marc. Though he doubted that would do any good either. If he asked his brother how he could care so little for their sister's safety, Marc would say something like 'desperate times called for desperate measures, Henri.' Or he'd make light of it, telling Henri not to sweat the small stuff and that nothing bad would happen to her.

When Henri had gotten out of Parthenais, he'd rented a room in a rundown boardinghouse off Pi IX, in order to keep up the pretense of no longer being on *Le Journal Quotidien*'s payroll. The telephone hung on the wall outside his door. By one o'clock he gave up hearing from his brother and went to bed.

Two hours later he still hadn't fallen asleep. Frustrated, he stood and pulled on his jeans then went to fill the teakettle. When he came out of the bathroom, where he had a hotplate balanced between the sink and the tank of the toilet, he heard footsteps on the stairs then a faint tapping on his door.

"Who is it?"

"Me."

Henri opened the door and his brother sauntered in. Drops of rain glistened on the shoulders of Marc's black imitation leather jacket, and his black hair shone in the light from the hallway. "You called. What's up?"

"What are you planning at Arrow?" Henri tried not to show the depth of his anger.

"Who said I'm planning anything?"

The teakettle's urgent whistle interjected and Henri went into the bathroom to turn it off. It gave him time to tamp down on his ire before returning to where Marc stood.

"Why else have Marie-Catherine working there?"

Marc dropped his previous attempt at innocence. "They're bastards, Henri, and you know it."

"So, you are planning something."

Marc nodded and pulled back a chair from Henri's worktable. He slid into it. "Yeah."

"What's Marie-Catherine's role? What does she have to do?"

"Put your brotherly hackles down. She doesn't have to do a thing."

"Then why is she there? Why did you get her a job there?"

"Because she wanted to have a role in what's going on. I figured she'd make a little money and feel like she was doing something for the cause. You know how she is."

Henri refused to be drawn in by Marc's patronizing

attitude. "They know about the bomb in the warden's mailbox. They know it was you."

Marc grinned. "I'll bet it scared the shit out of him."

"What if it hadn't gone off in the middle of the night? What if his wife or one of his kids had been on the porch?"

Marc's face flushed. "It went off when I planned for it to go off. I know what I'm doing."

Henri felt his face flush as well, but not with pride. "They know you're planning something." He tried to keep calm. He didn't want to lose his temper and end up blowing everything.

"Yeah, but they can't prove it."

"I could help them." Henri kept his voice even despite the fury roiling inside. "You haven't kept your word to keep Marie-Catherine in school and out of trouble, so why should I keep mine?"

Marc gave Henri a measuring look. "You won't tell them anything. She's my insurance. You won't tell Jeffers anything and you know it."

"You bastard." Marc was right, though. He wouldn't tell Jeffers. He couldn't.

"Nothing's going to happen to her, Henri. For Christ's sake, man, lighten up."

Henri stared at his brother. "You'd better make sure nothing happens to her or anyone else, Marc. I'm not kidding."

Marc shook his head as he stood and walked out the door, ignoring Henri's threat. Henri listened to his brother's footsteps on the stairs, the sound of the front door as it opened and shut, then Marc's heels clicking on the sidewalk below his window, until they faded away.

He kicked his shoes off and threw himself back on the bed. Marc had him by the short hairs. No way could he keep his bargain with the warden and Jeffers, not with Marie-Catherine dead center in the middle of whatever their brother was up to. God damn it to hell. He's done it to me again.

★

Footsteps sounded on the stairs, the treads heavy. Then a fist pounded on the door.

"Who is it?"

"Open up Morais."

Sunlight seeped around the edges of the blinds. Henri looked at his watch: six-thirty. "Shit." He got up and tugged on a shirt over the jeans he still wore before unlocking the door and opening it. His eyes were dry from lack of sleep. "What do you want?"

Jeffers shouldered past him and gave a scornful look around the room before he answered. "Your brother came to see you last night. What did you find out?"

Henri tried not to show his surprise. He thought Marc would have been more careful about being followed then he realized they must have been watching the boardinghouse.

"Nothing important."

"In the middle of the night, he just shows up?" Jeffers thumbed through the pile of papers next to Henri's typewriter without looking up. "Don't give me that shit, Morais. What did he tell you?"

"Marc keeps his own hours." Henri's hand remained on the door. "And I told you, he didn't tell me anything about his plans."

"Then what did he say? He was here long enough."

Jeffers tossed the papers down and sauntered back over to where Henri stood.

"I've been locked up for three months, Jeffers. We talked about family, about what I missed. Like I said, nothing important."

"You're lying."

"Prove it."

Jeffers narrowed his eyes but didn't say anything. After he left, Henri put on a jacket. He needed fresh air to clear his head. Locking the door behind him, he went down the stairs and out of the building. The rain the night before had left puddles on the sidewalk.

At Pi IX Boulevard he had to wait several minutes for a break in traffic. Buses and trucks roared past, spewing out gas and diesel fumes. Cars and vans swerved in and out between the buses and trucks. Horns honked, brakes squealed, engines downshifted or sped up. A rich cacophony of sound and smell.

Montreal was a dynamic city with its own rhythms and sounds. Even though the English-speakers controlled most of the wealth and power, French Canadians were beginning to own the excitement and intellectual power and Henri reveled in being part of it.

Once across the boulevard he entered Maisonneuve Park and soon veered off the sidewalk onto a dirt and cinder path, away from the noise of traffic. A lacelike tangle of vines bordered the path, and beyond them Henri saw branches studded with pink and yellow buds. Signs of spring. He'd missed winter. In jail, seasons weren't in evidence.

He thought about the warden again and the bargain they'd made.

There had to be a way out of the morass the FLQ was creating with their bombs and hatred, just as there had to be a way out of whatever Marie-Catherine had allowed herself to be dragged into.

"Find out your brother's plans, Morais," the warden had said at their last meeting, "and you can stay home and keep your sister out of trouble."

Between them, Marie-Catherine as much as Marc, they'd put her square in the middle of it. He couldn't tell the warden and Jeffers anything about Arrow Shoe Factory. Not with Marie-Catherine working there, spying for Marc.

Henri didn't know how to get around it. For a minute, he pondered giving the warden and Jeffers someone else, like Pelletier, wondering if having the moneyman would satisfy them. Probably not. Besides, he had no proof. It would be his word against Pelletier's. Chances were, they knew about him anyway.

"Shit." He clamped his jaws together so tight they hurt. He had no choice—he had to get closer to Marc and find out his brother's plan. Only then could he figure a way to extricate Marie-Catherine. Jeffers and the warden would have to wait until he'd accomplished that.

But did he have enough time before Marc acted? He turned and retraced his steps out of the park.

The phone rang several times before Henri heard a sleepy female voice on the other end.

"Hello?"

"Marie-Catherine, is that you?"

"No, she isn't here. She's gone to work."

"Is Marc there?"

"He's asleep."

"This is his brother. I'll be right over. If he wakes up, don't let him leave before I get there."

Twenty minutes later Henri pushed his way through the glass front door of Marc's apartment building, past the staircase leading to the second floor, and rapped his knuckles on Marc's door. He waited a minute then knocked again.

Marc opened the door. "What's up?"

"We need to talk."

"Half the night wasn't enough for you?" Marc shrugged and opened the door wide enough for Henri to enter. "Want some coffee?"

"I just had a cup." Henri's gaze went over the room. There was no sign of the woman.

Marc yawned. "Well, I need some. You'll have to hold your horses for a few minutes." He waved Henri to a chair then went into the kitchen.

The window shades were closed, casting the room in golden shadows. Cupboard doors banged and the sound of running water came from the direction Marc had disappeared. Henri breathed deeply to steady his nerves.

A few minutes later, Marc strolled into the room with a steaming mug in his hand. "So? What's the deal?"

"I was wrong to yell at you about Marie-Catherine. You know I won't tell that shit, Jeffers, anything. I just don't want her to get hurt."

"You think I do?"

"No, I know you don't. It all just caught me off-guard."

Marc nodded his head and sipped at his coffee.

"We haven't talked about what I should be doing, now I'm out." Henri drew another deep breath. Marc's face was in shadow, but Henri saw his eyes over the rim of the mug, staring at him.

"Isn't Blanchard setting up some interviews for you?"

"A few."

"Say the right words and that should be enough." Marc set the mug on the TV tray beside his chair and reached for a package of cigarettes lying next to an ashtray.

"Jeffers came to see me this morning."

Marc frowned. "What did he want?"

"He knew you'd been there. He wanted to know what we'd talked about."

"What did you tell him?"

"Nothing, of course. But, I think I should know what your plans are." Henri hoped his voice sounded normal, maybe a little detached.

"Why?" said Marc from behind his cigarette. He held a lighter to the end of it and cupped his free hand around it as though protecting the flame from a draft, but his eyes never left Henri's face.

"So that I don't say the wrong thing." Henri leaned forward in his chair. "I don't want to step into something I should avoid."

Marc appeared to consider his words a few minutes. He drew on his cigarette and blew out the smoke. He finally shook his head. "I think it's better if you're in the dark. Then your innocence won't be faked. You've never been much good at lying."

Chapter Twenty-Six

Marie-Catherine laughed until her sides ached at Dora's imitation of one of their supervisors.

"What a pig," said Dora when they'd both caught their breath. Then her tone went from mocking to disgust. "Back when Mr. Strand owned this company, the likes of him would have been thrown out on his arse the day he walked through the door. Mr. Strand, he cared about us, treated us with dignity. The new owners—sitting on their fat behinds over in Toronto—do you think they care how we're treated?" She scowled then answered her own question. "It's plain as can be: the only thing they care about is squeezing however much money they can out of this place and be-damned to the workers."

The two women drank tea in the break room. They sat close to hear over the sound of the machinery on the other side of the wall. Marie-Catherine had to struggle to understand some of what Dora said in the best of circumstances. Dora and her husband had immigrated to Canada fifteen years before and Dora still spoke with the accent of someone who'd grown up in the wrong part of London.

Marie-Catherine knew that some of Arrow Shoe's employees, Dora among them, had worked at the plant for many years, but had refused to join the union when it formed. "You hate these new owners so much, why didn't you go with the others, Dora?" Marie-Catherine's voice was hesitant. She felt torn between her curiosity and not wanting to pry.

"'Cause the union won't do us any good." If Dora thought Marie-Catherine's question out of line, she didn't show it. "If them striking are lucky, they won't get fired. At least not right away. But they'll lose plenty of money and those bastards in Toronto won't respect them any more for it." She shook her head. "We have four kids to feed, my husband and me. Much as I'd like to black their eyes, the owners I mean, I can't afford the satisfaction." She spoke without apology or regret in her voice.

Marie-Catherine nodded, understanding the dilemma produced by conviction meeting reality.

"And what about you? You've not been used to work like this. What brings you to Arrow Shoe Factory?"

She should have been prepared for the question, but Marie-Catherine struggled for an answer. She finally shrugged. "Same as you, I guess. I need the money."

"Don't we all? Well, time's up. I'd best be getting back on the line." With a tired sigh, Dora heaved herself out of the chair.

Marie-Catherine had grown used to the routine of the factory and could move around the building with ease. She saw new faces every day as people came and went, although the women who worked with Dora stayed the same. She wondered if they'd been promised a bonus for remaining. Dora had hinted at it, though she hadn't come right out and said so. Marie-Catherine didn't begrudge them. They deserved a bonus—a big one for what they were going through.

Together, she and Dora left the break room.

As they entered the main part of the factory, a man glanced their way before he quickly pushed through the door on the other side of the building. Marie-Catherine stopped in her tracks.

"What's the matter? Forget something?"

"It's nothing. I just thought I recognized someone." The man from the warehouse where she and Marc had left the explosive-laden van when they came back from North Carolina. He'd been in Marc's apartment the day her brother convinced her to come to work for Arrow Shoes, too.

Although she kept looking as she moved about the factory throughout the day, she didn't see LeGuin again.

Marc frowned when she asked him about it later. "Are you sure it was LeGuin?"

"I got a pretty good look, Marc. What was he doing there?"

"Beats me, kid. If it was him, which I doubt."

Marie-Catherine didn't try to pursue it further, though she remained sure of what she'd seen. Showering and putting on clean clothes—she'd promised to meet Henri for dinner—she wondered why Marc tried to hide from her whatever LeGuin had been doing at the factory.

After looking over the menu she ordered a hamburger, then told Henri about stopping at a restaurant in North Carolina where the waitress had asked if she wanted her hamburger 'dressed or undressed.' She giggled. "I had to order it dressed. Like I told Marc, Maman would never approve of me eating something naked."

Henri didn't join in her laughter. "Speaking of Marc...."

Marie-Catherine's answer was hesitant. She didn't know how much she should confide. "I don't know what he's planning, Henri."

"You need to quit. Something's going to happen there and I don't want you anywhere near it."

"We've been over this before, Henri. I can't walk away now. It's important to me to be doing something—like you and Marc. And it's not just for French Canadians. It's for the other workers, too." She glanced at the nearby diners and lowered her voice. "Besides, I told you, he's promised me no one will be hurt."

"How can he possibly guarantee no one will be hurt?" Henri's voice was as low and intense as hers. "That's crazy and you know it. He builds bombs for God's sake."

"None of the things Marc's done ever resulted in someone being hurt. That's not the intention of the FLQ, Henri. You know that. We target property, not people."

"It's *we* now, is it? He's made you one of them?"

Disapproval was in his voice, but she refused to feel guilty. "You don't understand. We have to do something. The owners are such bastards, Henri. You should hear my friend, Dora, talk about them." She put her hamburger back down on the plate. It tasted like sawdust and she'd lost her appetite anyway.

"The owners may be bastards, M.C., but they live in Ottawa."

"Toronto."

"Toronto, then. You're right here at ground zero."

"And I like being here, Henri. I do." She lifted her chin and stared at him.

"He's using you, M.C. Using people is what Marc does. And when you need him, he won't be there." The sadness in her brother's voice matched the sorrow in his eyes. Suddenly the defiance drained out of her.

Although they left the topic of Arrow Shoe Factory and spoke of other, lighter things, Marie-Catherine was glad when the evening ended and she could return to Marc's apartment. Curled up on the couch and about to drop off to sleep, something Henri had said drifted through mind: '*so he's made you one of them*'. She came instantly awake. The way he'd said it—as though he wasn't part of the FLQ, too, and never had been. After only a few minutes reflection, she realized he'd spoken that way all evening.

Marie-Catherine pulled the loaded wagon onto the elevator and hit the lever to go down. As the elevator began its shaky descent, she stretched her arms above her head, happy to be making the last trip of the day and looking forward to a day off.

With a final shudder, the elevator came to a halt. She opened the cage door and backed out, pulling the wagon with her.

"Watch where you're going."

She turned and faced her supervisor, a wiry, compact man with short gray hair and deep frown lines between his thin black eyebrows.

"Sorry." She started to step around him.

"Wait." He scowled at the clipboard he held in his hand. "I'll need you to work tomorrow. You'll have to come in after all."

"But it's been nine days. I haven't had a day off in over a week." She planned to spend the entire day on the couch.

"Can't be helped." The man tuned and shouted to someone going into the break room. "Be here at the usual time," he said over his shoulder to Marie-Catherine as he scurried away.

She fumed while she watched him cross the floor. Bastard.

Marie-Catherine didn't see Marc when she got back to his apartment, but Bunny was home. They ate Chinese take-out and played gin rummy until Marie-Catherine's eyes burned and she couldn't focus on the cards.

She yawned. "Sorry, I've got to get some sleep."

"Okay." Bunny unfolded her legs and stood. They'd been sitting cross-legged in the middle of the living room floor. "I think I'll go see a friend."

Twenty minutes later, curled onto her side on the couch, Marie-Catherine thought about Bunny and discovered despite her ridiculous name she liked her.

When her bus came to a stop the next morning, Marie-Catherine leaned down and peered through the steamy, rain-spattered window. Dora stood on the corner, huddled inside a yellow rain slicker. Marie-Catherine smiled, knowing how her friend liked bright colors. She had grown used to the gauntlet she ran every morning and evening when she came to work and again when she left. They couldn't make her cry anymore, but whenever possible, she still made use of Dora's elbow. The bus door hissed open and the smell of wet pavement rose to meet her.

She stepped onto the sidewalk. "Hi."

Dora smiled in response. "Ready?" Arm in arm the two women crossed the street.

If anything, the men and women crowding the sidewalk in front of the factory had grown more strident. They were getting desperate, Marie-Catherine thought. The strike has been going on for two months, with no sign of either management or the workers giving in.

Several uniformed policemen were there, but standing to one side of the crowd, just like they'd been since she started working there. Standing by and watching, doing nothing to help the workers trying to get into the building.

"Coppers are the same everywhere," Dora said when Marie-Catherine commented on it. "Worthless when you need them, falling all over you when you don't."

The guard opened the door part-way and the two women squeezed through.

Chapter Twenty-Seven

Marc jimmied the flimsy lock on the door of an office for lease in a building across the street from Arrow Shoe Factory. It took Gould less than five minutes to have the telephone operating.

Theresa sat at the desk that filled most of the room, the phone receiver pressed to her ear. "The maid says she'll get him," she whispered to Marc, who leaned against the wall next to the window. Her fingers tapped the bare wooden surface of the desk. Suddenly, she sat up straighter. "Who's this?" She paused, throwing a glance at Marc, before looking down at the sheet of paper in front of her. She began to read. "At precisely 8:05 A.M. a bomb will detonate at Arrow Shoe Factory in Montreal. You have exactly fifteen minutes to have the building evacuated. If the strike is not settled in the workers' favor within the next three days, another bomb will be placed at one of your other properties and you will not be notified. Do you understand what I have told you?" Theresa paused again then hung up.

"What did he say?"

"He said he understood."

"Good." Marc turned to look out the window. A woman in a yellow slicker stood on the sidewalk below.

Gould began pacing.

"They'll hear you downstairs."

Gould stood still. A minute later he began to crack his knuckles. Theresa continued tapping the desk.

Marc looked through the rain again to the factory across the street. "I don't hear any sirens." A bus pulled up to the curb. "And people aren't coming out of the building. What's the matter with that guy? Do you suppose he didn't call and warn them?"

Theresa and Gould gave identical shrugs.

Marc looked back at the scene below. The bus pulled away from the curb after a single person had stepped off. He jerked to his feet.

"This was supposed to be her day off. Shit!"

He ran to the door, knocking into Theresa and Gould when they rushed toward the window to look. Marc tore open the door and raced down the hall to the stairs.

He ran down four flights, passing several startled people making their way to offices on the occupied first three floors of the building, their coats and jackets glistening with rain. At the bottom of the stairs Marc burst through the front door onto the sidewalk. Rain quickly soaked his hair and sweatshirt as he searched the faces of the crowd in front of the factory. Marie-Catherine had vanished.

"God damn it to hell." He kicked the side of the building then pulled open the door and took the steps two at a time to the fourth floor. When he reached the office, Theresa and Gould were still at the window. "Get your stuff. It's time to get out of here."

Chapter Twenty-Eight

Dora shrugged out of her raincoat. "Whew! I'm glad to be out of that mess."

Marie-Catherine shook the rain from her jacket as they walked across the large room, heading for the lockers in the break room. They passed the already chattering black machines stamping out the leather, and the heavy-duty machines that sewed the leather together. Beyond the sewing machines stood the bank of workbenches where the soles were glued then laboriously hand-stitched in place. Several of the machines and benches were empty of workers—they either hadn't arrived yet or the operators were on strike and hadn't been replaced.

Dora paused. "What's that doing there?"

A box, little bigger than a loaf of bread, appeared to be wedged into the machinery at one end of the conveyor belt.

An image of LeGuin flashed through Marie-Catherine's mind. She lunged toward Dora as her friend reached for the box.

"No!"

Chapter Twenty-Nine

The ringing telephone pulled Henri out of a deep sleep. He'd been in a meeting with Maurault until three in the morning, mapping out the series of articles he planned to write, and it was almost five before he'd finally gotten to sleep.

"Unh," he grunted. His eyes still tightly closed, he groped for the phone. Not on the bedside table. Oh, right, he wasn't in his old apartment. He got up and shuffled to the door and the phone hanging on the wall outside it.

"There's been an accident."

He didn't recognize the voice.

When he got to the hospital where they'd taken Marie-Catherine, he found Jeffers waiting.

"Why didn't you tell us, Morais?" Henri tried to push by, but the ruddy-faced detective barred his way. "You were supposed to tell us."

"I've got to get to the elevator. My sister is upstairs."

Jeffers ignored Henri's plea. "Your brother and his cell are responsible." He thrust his face forward. "They've killed a woman. Maybe your sister, too."

Henri shook his head, his thoughts swirling. No, that wasn't possible. He wouldn't let it be true.

Jeffers stood like a mountain in the center of the hospital rotunda, his arms crossed. "They even called the owners before it went off."

Henri shook his head again, this time with incredulity.

"What was your sister doing at the scene? Was she planting it and it went off?" Jeffers' eyes narrowed with contempt. "I should have known we couldn't trust you. You can't protect her. How long has she been with them?"

"She isn't. She never has been." Henri's hands shook. He balled them up, aching to smash Jeffers' face. "Why didn't they evacuate the building if they got a warning? What kind of idiots run that place?"

"Tell me, Morais. What was she doing there?"

"She worked there, Jeffers. Do you think I'd have let her do that if I'd known what was going to happen? God damn it, there's nothing more I can tell you. Let me pass. I need to see my sister."

Jeffers searched Henri's face before stepping aside. "Go ahead, Morais. But I'll want to talk to you later. Be available."

Henri didn't bother to answer. He ran to the elevator and punched the Up button. He got out on the third floor and quickly spotted the nurses' station. A nurse stood behind the chest-high counter.

"Where do you have my sister, Marie-Catherine Morais?"

"She's in intensive care. You'll have to wait. The doctor and your parents are in with her right now."

Henri grabbed the edge of the counter. "How is she?"

"She's just come back from surgery. She's still unconscious. You'll have to speak to the doctor to find out more." Although she spoke with courtesy, disapproval radiated from her pale blue eyes. Jeffers must have talked to her.

"Will she live? Will she be okay?"

"I can't tell you, Mr. Morais. Only that she's suffered a severe head trauma."

"When can I see the doctor?"

"He'll come out when he's finished. I can let him know you're here. There's a waiting room across the hall."

In the waiting room Henri sank into a deep armchair, leaned his head against the hard plastic back and closed his eyes. His stillness lasted less than a minute. He stood and paced around the room, picking up a magazine, putting it down, turning on the television then turning it off. A coffeepot and cups stood on a table in the corner of the room. He filled a cup, scooped in a spoonful of sugar, and poured in some cream. After stirring the mixture with a plastic spoon, he took a sip and nearly gagged. He set the cup down without taking another. After circling the room twice more, he left it and went back to the nurses' station.

"Did you let the doctor know I'm here?"

"I did, Mr. Morais."

"And?" Henri resisted the urge to grab the woman by the front of her white polyester uniform. "Is there any change?"

"He didn't tell me."

Without saying another word, Henri crossed to the big double doors and looked through the eye-level windows. He scanned the large room. On its perimeter were curtained walls separating individual beds. A nurse stood in the center of the room next to a desk writing something on a piece of paper attached to a clipboard. Another nurse scurried across the room carrying a metal pan. She ducked behind one of the curtains. Henri put his hand on the door.

The woman behind the nurses' station moved around the counter toward him. "You can't go in—two family members are already with her."

Henri pushed through the doors, leaving the woman sputtering a protest behind him. He spotted his parents through an opening in one of the curtains. They looked stunned. His mother's shoulders slumped, her black plastic purse dangled from her curled fingers. The purse would be empty except for her identification, a comb, and a small change purse. He'd never seen her leave the house without it. His father, too, appeared stunned. The sudden fragility of both frightened Henri.

With tear-filled eyes, his father reached out a hand to Henri. His mother didn't acknowledge her son's presence in any discernable way. She stood trance-like, her eyes seemingly unfocused.

A tall man in a knee-length white coat bent over the still figure on the bed. Marie-Catherine. Henri stared at her small, sheet-draped figure. She looked so vulnerable.

The doctor flicked the tube hanging down from the glass bottle above her head, adjusting the bubble of liquid dripping into a vein in her arm. Lights flickered on a piece of equipment set on a table next to the bed. A constant beeping sound came from it. The head of the bed was raised high enough to put Marie-Catherine nearly in a sitting position. A large dressing covered half of her face.

The doctor, his face grave, turned toward Henri and his parents.

Henri could scarcely breathe. "Will she live?"

"FLQ Bomb Explodes in Shoe Factory—Kills One, A Second Critically Injured," read the headlines. *"Dora Greene, wife and mother of four, killed instantly."*

Part of the bomb pierced Dora's forehead, lodging in her brain along with bone fragments from her skull. Her once-pretty face had been destroyed. The red hair, her vanity, was matted with blood and gray matter. The blouse she wore had vanished, revealing the fleshy white body beneath it covered with craters, large and small, and a huge wound in her right chest where a piece of metal had ripped through her breast.

The gory details hadn't been printed in the papers, but when Henri went in for questioning, Jeffers showed him pictures, appearing happy to fill in what the newspapers had left out.

"We've got witnesses putting your brother in the area, Morais. You could have stopped it."

Henri shook his head, attempting to deny culpability. Jeffers was right, though. He could have stopped it.

Jeffers fingered the photos. "The warden is disappointed. He thought the two of you had a deal. I told him not to trust you." He picked up the photos and put them into a file. "You'll be back in. It's just a question of time. You can settle it with him then. In the meantime, think about these pictures when you try to fall asleep tonight."

A week later, the doctors still couldn't answer Henri's question about Marie-Catherine. She was in a coma, they said. Her brain shows activity. That's good, they said. The longer it takes for her to wake up, the worse are her chances for a full recovery, they said. There's a problem with her right eye. She may not be able to see out of it, they said. If she lives, they said.

Henri stood at the foot of his sister's bed. The head of the bed was elevated, her head held stationary by an awkward-looking metal contraption that reminded Henri of a cage.

Marie-Catherine's nurse had explained. "Keeping her head elevated helps the swelling in her brain and eye go down."

She also assured Henri that his sister was holding her own. But every time he entered her room, Marie-Catherine looked smaller and smaller under the sheet. He feared one day he would come to the hospital and there would be nothing left of her.

His mother, always there, always in the same chair next to Marie-Catherine's bed, still said nothing, her eyes blank. Not once had she cried. Henri thought he would feel better if she would just say something. Accuse him. Berate him. Curse him. Instead, she looked through him.

Chapter Thirty

Marc sat on a bench in Maisonneuve Park. In the distance, he saw a horse cantering along a trail. The rider, a woman dressed in riding togs and helmet, moved with the gray horse as though part of it. Anglo bitch, Marc thought.

Though almost May, the wind blew sharp through the hollow, bringing with it the smell of diesel exhaust fumes from the buses on Sherbrooke Street. The horse and rider disappeared into the trees while Marc listened, intent now on what the red-haired man sitting beside him said in his thick northern Irish accent.

"You're sure it will work? I don't want the thing blowing up in my own hands."

"We've been using it for three months. It works."

Marc nodded. "Okay then. Thanks."

Without another word, the red-haired man stood and walked away, leaving Marc to remain on the bench, his mind following the twists and turns of wires and timing fuse the man had described. When the time came, he knew where he'd use it.

Chapter Thirty-One

The doctor who'd seen Marie-Catherine that first day pulled Henri to the side one afternoon. "Your mother needs to go home and get some rest. I think she's close to a breakdown."

Henri rubbed his hand across his dry, tired eyes. "I know. She doesn't eat. She hardly even sleeps—maybe a few hours sitting up in the chair. She ignores me when I tell her she should leave."

"How about your father? Has he tried?"

"Of course, but she won't talk to him, either."

"Well, keep working on her. I'll order some sleeping pills for her. Sleep is what she needs most right now."

"I'll try," said Henri.

Henri and his father both tried. They cajoled. They demanded. Nothing seemed to penetrate.

His father's shoulders sagged in defeat. "It's like she's in the coma with Marie-Catherine."

"I'm going to get Dr. Rynard. I don't know why we didn't think of him sooner."

Henri remembered the first time he'd met Dr. Rynard. He'd knocked on their door one afternoon when Henri was twelve or thirteen and introduced himself to Henri's mother.

"I've come from Quebec City to start a free clinic in your neighborhood," he'd said.

Henri had been stretched out on his cot, absorbed in a book about Louis Riel, a Metis Indian leader who had rebelled against the Canadian government and been executed in 1885.

Excited to have such an exalted guest, Henri's mother invited the doctor to come in for tea. Before he left, Dr. Rynard had given her some medicine for high blood pressure. He also talked to Henri about Louis Riel. His depth of knowledge on the subject surprised Henri. He'd even read the same book.

Over the years, Dr. Rynard had become a frequent and honored visitor to their home. His interest in Henri and his influence on Henri's mother had enabled Henri to continue in secondary school past the usual age of fourteen, when most boys and girls left school to work in factories or on the docks. More than once, Dr. Rynard was called upon to intercede with Father Francis, Henri's headmaster, on Henri's behalf.

Henri never knew what the doctor had thought of the priest, but he knew what Father Francis had thought of Dr. Rynard. Father claimed the doctor was a communist. His old headmaster may have been right, Henri thought now. Dr. Rynard may have been a communist. Might still be. He was also the holiest man Henri knew, living what Father Francis and the rest of them only preached.

The doctor's powers to influence Henri's mother didn't fail. "Annemarie," he said. "There's nothing you can do here. You must take care of yourself. You must go home and sleep."

Henri watched his mother's face lose its frozen, blank look. She gazed up at Dr. Rynard and her face crumbled.

Great sobs, long suppressed, rose from deep within her body.

"There, there." Dr. Rynard, patted her shoulder. "Yes. You can cry now. It's all right. I'll watch over your little girl while Emile takes you home to rest. I'll stay right here next to Marie-Catherine."

Henri watched, silent and amazed, while his mother stood and wiped her eyes. His father took her arm and gently led her from the room. She didn't even look back.

Dr. Rynard settled into the chair his longtime patient had occupied.

"Her faith in you is remarkable," Henri said.

The doctor sighed and leaned back, his arms folded across his broad chest. "Trust is a grave responsibility."

"Does it ever get too much for you?"

Dr. Rynard gave a tired smile. "Oh, yes."

"What do you do when that happens? What do you do when you're full of doubts and the burden seems too heavy for you to carry any longer?"

Dr. Rynard shook his grizzled head. "I go on, Henri. Like you, I just go on."

Though Marie-Catherine was still unconscious, they'd moved her out of intensive care, into a room with three other patients. Earlier, breakfast trays had been delivered from multi-tiered carts rolled down the hall, and later, the empty or partially finished trays had been removed. The odor of scrambled eggs, French toast and syrup still lingered, but made little impression on the overpowering and ever-present smell of alcohol and disinfectant that seemed to lay like a pall over the entire hospital.

Marie-Catherine's nurse came into the room. Henri had heard her coming. The squeaking of her crepe-soled shoes sounded the alert. A cheerful, no-nonsense woman, she gave Henri a friendly hello before checking Marie-Catherine's pulse and blood pressure, something they checked frequently. She adjusted his sister's pillows, changed her IV and emptied the bag of urine hanging from the bed frame. Henri was grateful it hadn't been time to change the dressing. He hated seeing the gory, oozing wound of her eyeball. Despite all their 'maybes', he knew his sister would never see with it again.

The nurse washed her hands once more, then dampened a cloth and bathed what she could reach of Marie-Catherine's face, the part not covered with bandages, careful not to dislodge the metal frame keeping her head stationary. Through it all, through all the poking and prodding, the shifting and turning, Marie-Catherine remained motionless.

After the nurse left them, Henri sat next to his sister's bed, bending first her thumb, then fingers, wrist and elbow the way the physical therapist had showed him, and half-watched the game show the young woman in the next bed had turned on the television. The young woman had been riding behind her boyfriend on his motorcycle when it slid out of control and landed on her, breaking her pelvis.

The television screen suddenly went blank. It flashed to a man sitting behind a desk, rolled, and went blank again, then flipped back to the man behind the desk. The man's face looked solemn, but his voice was filled with tension and excitement. He appeared to look straight into the camera, but his eyes flicked back and forth as he read from the teleprompter.

"An explosion has ripped through the Palace of Justice. Experts say the bomb went off in a cloakroom by the main entrance to the building, killing a demolitions expert from the RCMP as he was attempting to disarm it. The demolition expert's name is being withheld until his family can be notified. No other deaths or injuries have so far been reported, but the building has suffered major structural damage. It is believed the FLQ will claim responsibility. It is also believed the bomb was booby-trapped so it would explode when the attempt was made to disarm it."

"Independence or death," muttered the young woman in the next bed.

Henri carefully put Marie-Catherine's arm down and tucked it under the sheet. He looked from Marie-Catherine's unchanging face to his mother's.

He touched his mother's shoulder. *"Maman."* She didn't move. "I have to go now. I'll be back later." He had no idea if she heard him.

Henri left the hospital and drove back to his boardinghouse. He wondered how the sun could still be shining when he felt such utter anger and defeat. No one had to tell him what he already knew. The courthouse bomb was Marc's.

He pulled into the parking lot next to his building, turned off the engine and lowered his forehead to the steering wheel. A cloud passed over the sun, blocking out its warmth, and a slight breeze started up. An empty paper drink cup rattled across the patched tarmac and came to rest with a pile of other debris at the base of the building. None of it registered.

In jail and standing up to the guards, defying the warden and the rest of them, Henri had been halfway to believing Marc was right and violence might be justified, or at least there was enough wrongdoing on the Anglos part to outweigh some of the FLQ's violence. Now he felt sick to death of what his brother and others like him had unleashed. Maybe we don't have to answer to a higher authority, as some claim, but surely, he thought, we need to answer to each other.

Four days later, Henri heard the phone ringing from the sidewalk. He fumbled for his keys and unlocked the front door. The phone didn't stop ringing. The two other tenants on his floor must not be home yet. He took the stairs two at a time.

"Hello."

"She's awake," said his father.

Henri squeezed his eyes tight then opened them wide. His heart swelled and for the first time since Marie-Catherine's injuries, the restrictive vice clamped around his chest released and he could breathe freely. He wanted to shout out his joy at the news. But when he opened his mouth to speak, no sound would come out. Finally, he put the telephone receiver back into its cradle as though it was a newly hatched chick, leaned against the wall and slid into a sitting position on the floor. Several minutes passed before he could rouse himself.

By the time he arrived at the hospital Marie-Catherine had drifted back to sleep, but his father assured him she'd spoken. "To *Maman* and me. Right to us. She knew who we were." Henri's mother sat in the chair she'd occupied for weeks, holding Marie-Catherine's hand. She'd barely glanced at Henri when he walked into the room.

"She doesn't remember the explosion," said his father. "She doesn't even remember working at the factory."

"Good," said Henri. "It's just as well she doesn't remember. What about her eye? Can she see?"

"We don't know yet," said his father.

"God damn it. Sorry, *Maman*," he said with a brief glance at his mother before she could reprimand him for his language. He turned back to look again at his sister's thin form. "Does Marc know?"

His father shrugged. "I told that girl, Bunny. But I'll call him again, later."

"She shouldn't have been there, Papa. She was in harm's way and Marc put her there."

His father replied in a harsh whisper. "What are you saying? He didn't know anything would happen to Marie-Catherine. You know that Henri."

"I know what I know, Papa. Like I said, she shouldn't have been there."

"What do you think you 'know' little brother?" Marc stood in the doorway, still and watchful.

At the sound of his brother's voice, Henri spun around.

"I told you to keep her out of it, Marc. I warned you what would happen if she got hurt."

Marc walked into the room and stood in front of Henri, his hands stuffed into his pockets, casual in his defiance. "You know you don't have the balls to do anything. What have you ever done besides talk and get yourself arrested?"

"Marc," his father said, his eyes darting from Marc to the door. "You shouldn't be here. They've been asking for you."

Henri's eyes narrowed. Blood pulsed at his temples. "I've done plenty. Tell us what you've accomplished, Marc. Tell us what you've accomplished besides destruction. And this." He pointed to Marie-Catherine's bed.

His father put a placating hand on each of their shoulders. "Now, boys, this isn't the time or the place."

Marc ignored his father's hand. Henri shook it off. "Go on. Tell us, Marc. We all want to hear what it is you think you've accomplished."

"You've never been one of us, have you?" said Marc. "It was all a lie, wasn't it?"

Henri was glad to have it out in the open at last. "Yes. Damned right I've never been one of you. It was a set-up. I lied about losing my job. I meant to get myself arrested."

Marc stared at him for a moment, his face expressionless. "I knew it. You make me sick."

"Stop it," his mother hissed at them. "Stop it. It's bad enough Marie-Catherine is lying here, maybe blind, because of the three of you." She glared at his father first, then at Marc and Henri. "Don't make things worse."

Henri stepped back, his body still rigid with tension. "She's right," he said through tightened lips. "We'll settle this later."

Chapter Thirty-Two

Henri returned full-time to his job at *Le Journal Quotidien*, happy to give up any pretense he was part of the FLQ. When he stepped into the newsroom the first morning and heard the voices, the clatter of typewriters and the ringing phones, adrenalin surged through him. God, how he'd missed this place. Before he could pull the chair out from his desk and sit down, Louise told him he had a call.

"So that stupid prick Maurault hired you back."

"What do you want, Jeffers?"

"I want to talk to you. I'm sending a car."

Jaw clenched, Henri hung up the phone. An hour later, he walked into the North Montreal precinct.

"Don't think it changes anything," Jeffers said. "In my book, you're still guilty as shit. Maybe you don't build the bombs or rob the banks. What you do is just as bad. Maybe worse—you feed them ideas. You make their whining legitimate."

They were back in the same room where Jeffers had interrogated him in December and again after the bombing at Arrow Shoes. At least there were no handcuffs. Jeffers paced the room, just as before.

"And then again," he said, swinging around in front of Henri and planting his palms on the table. "Maybe the fact the shoe factory bombing didn't happen until after you got out of jail wasn't a coincidence. Maybe your brother was just waiting for you to get out and give him the go-ahead."

Henri stared at Jeffers. "We've been over this a hundred times. I wasn't involved. If I had been, do you think I'd have let my sister work there?" The fact Marc had done exactly that caused a muscle in Henri's jaw to twitch. It disgusted him that despite everything his brother had done, he still instinctively defended him.

"But you're not saying you didn't know about it, are you? You knew," said Jeffers. "And you didn't keep your part of the bargain. I should throw you back in your cell and let the warden deal with you." He paused then leaned across the table again. "What about the courthouse bombing? What did you know about that?"

On that one Henri could honestly answer. "Nothing."

Jeffers let him go, but not without twisting the knife. "You can tell your sister we'll be questioning her again, too. There's no way she wasn't mixed up in that mess and you know it."

Henri's evenings were divided between visiting Marie-Catherine and sitting in front of his typewriter, trying to write about his experiences with the FLQ and prison. He wasn't succeeding. He knew Maurault would be calling him into his office, pushing for the story. Still nothing came.

Henri jerked another piece of paper out of the machine, wadded it up and threw it into the growing pile around his feet. Damn it, he thought. Usually, once he'd done the necessary research, he could write a story start to finish without stopping. Not this time.

He knew why. It wasn't finished, it was still happening. Marie-Catherine was still part of it. Shit. He rolled another piece of paper into the typewriter then stared at his fingers on the keys, willing them to move. Finally, after another fifteen minutes of futile effort, he grabbed his jacket and stormed out the door, slamming it behind him.

On the walk to the small nursing home where Marie-Catherine had been transferred, he thought about Marc. He hadn't seen his brother since the night their sister had awakened from her coma. He knew Marc avoided him. Part of him was glad. The other part of him wished they could have it out in one of those free-for-all brawls they'd had when they were kids, feet and fists flying. But he knew that wouldn't settle anything. Their differences had grown beyond that simple solution.

"He came to see me last night." Marie-Catherine perched on the edge of the bed. "Late. He woke me up. He seems different—beyond my being hurt, I mean. Edgy, of course, that's Marc. But now in a grim kind of way. Are you two angry with each other about something?"

Henri stood by the window, looking out on a small patio set up with several picnic tables and bordered by shrubs. An elderly couple sat at one of the tables. "Don't worry about it. We'll work it out. You just concentrate on getting better."

Several days before, the doctor told Henri he thought Marie-Catherine would be ready to go home soon. He also said the loss of vision in her right eye was permanent.

"I'm surprised Maman isn't here," he said, turning away from the window and walking over to the upholstered chair beside the bed. He dropped into it, his arms hanging over the side.

"I sent her home," Marie-Catherine said. "I know she's exhausted. Her face gets so flushed sometimes I think she's going to explode or collapse."

Though his mother no longer sat in silent vigil at Marie-Catherine's bedside, Dr. Rynard had cautioned Henri that she still needed more rest. "I'm glad you convinced her."

"It makes me feel guilty. I used to think she didn't care about me. I've always had such a hard time talking to her, and she's always been so negative about everything. You know how she can be."

"She didn't leave your side."

"I know. I think she's scared, Henri. I think being scared is why she's so negative."

"I think so, too. It's why she gets so angry with Papa when she claims he's 'talking simple.' She's afraid of change."

"Change isn't so bad," said Marie-Catherine.

"You're right. I can't even imagine if this had happened ten or fifteen years ago. Without national health insurance, we couldn't have paid for all the specialized care you needed. Only the very rich could."

"Speaking of whom—well not that rich, but still comfortable—have you seen Claudia? You know she comes to see me almost every morning."

A nurse came into the room, her thick-soled rubber shoes making almost no sound. "I thought you'd left," she said to Henri.

"Not yet. Is it time?" He was relieved. He didn't want to talk about Claudia.

Marie-Catherine watched him, silent, but the question still on her face.

"Just about," the nurse said. "They're setting the tables for dinner in the dining room."

Henri leaned over and kissed Marie-Catherine on the forehead. "I'll see you in a couple of days."

She gave him a saucy, grin, lop-sided because of scarring and nerve damage. "If I'm still here—maybe they'll let me go home before then."

Henri bit his lower lip and punched her lightly on the arm. "Just see you behave yourself and don't give your nurses any trouble."

He stopped at a tavern for a sandwich and a beer on the way home. The evening news poured out of the television set mounted high on the wall behind the bar.

"Authorities say they have made an arrest in the bombing last month that damaged the Palace of Justice and left RCMP demolitions expert Walter Percy dead," said the announcer.

Henri, his eyes glued to the television, didn't notice the bartender set a glass of beer down in front of him.

"Inspector Bruce Jeffers of the Montreal Police Department has told this reporter of the arrest, but declined to give a name at present," the announcer continued. "When asked when he would be ready to reveal the name of the suspect in custody, Inspector Jeffers said tomorrow or the following day."

Henri looked down at the paper-wrapped roast beef sandwich the bartender had put down next to his beer.

He stood and pulled out his wallet.

"Aren't you going to eat the sandwich?" the bartender said as Henri laid some bills on the table.

"I just remembered something I need to do. I'll take it with me."

"Suit yourself," said the man.

Henri counted the number of times the phone rang in Marc's apartment—ten, eleven, twelve. When he got to fifteen he hung up. Of course Marc wasn't there. Probably hadn't been for days, maybe weeks. He wondered about the girl, Bunny.

Henri's mixed feelings dismayed him. If Marc had been arrested, he should be glad, if for no other reason than it would put an end to Henri's dithering. Besides, Marc should be punished. He should. Henri reached for the phone again. Again, there was no answer.

An hour later, Henri set a steaming cup of coffee on the table next to his typewriter. He started to sit down when he heard a faint scratching at the door. He stopped and listened. The sound came again. He crossed to the door.

"Who is it?" he said, his voice low.

"Me."

Henri opened the door and Marc slipped inside.

"I've been trying to call you all night. Where the hell have you been?"

"Not in my apartment. They're watching it. Can I have some?" He pointed to Henri's coffee.

"Take it. I'll make another cup. Are you sure no one followed you? I told you they were watching here before. Maybe they still are." He couldn't imagine Jeffers not having posted someone to watch him.

Marc shook his head. "I've been outside for over an hour. No one's there and I made sure nobody followed me." He took a swallow of coffee.

Henri sat on the end of the bed, mentally questioning Jeffers' obvious oversight. Marc sat in the chair. He looked terrible. Henri had never seen his brother's eyes so tired and bloodshot. "I thought you'd been arrested. When I heard them on the television say Jeffers had arrested someone, I thought for sure it was you."

Marc closed his eyes. "No. LeGuin. But he'll soon talk and then it will be just a matter of time."

"Maybe he won't."

"If they offer him immunity or a reduced sentence, he'll talk. He has the same revulsion I have for being locked up." Marc shuddered. "I'd rather be dead."

Even when they were children, Marc couldn't stand being confined. Henri remembered a day when Marc had been six or seven. Their mother had put him in her bedroom the only room in the house with a door. She'd told Marc to consider his misdeed—Henri had no recollection of what that had been—then she locked the door.

Marc almost destroyed the room. He pulled the blankets from the bed, pulled papers and clothes from drawers, kicked the door, yelled. Henri had watched his mother's face as she sat impassive through the crashing and banging until finally, when glass broke, she went to the door and opened it. Marc stood in front of her, his face streaked with tears and his shoulders heaving. Behind him, the bedroom floor was littered with blankets, clothes, papers, and a broken mirror.

"Don't ever lock me in here again." Marc had said the words with such ferocity that Henri, who'd been no more than five at the time, remembered like it was yesterday. She never did.

"What are you going to do?" he asked his brother now.

"I'm not sure." Marc said. "Maybe I'll head south. New York City. Maybe Buffalo or Chicago. Do you know anyone who can put me up?"

"Maybe. I'll check around in the morning. Maybe by then we'll know if LeGuin talked. You could be worried for nothing."

"If he hasn't talked yet, he will." Marc leaned back in his chair, his face grim.

"Marc, do you ever regret any of this?"

Marc turned his head and looked at Henri, his eyebrows raised. "What, joining the FLQ?"

"All of it. From the time we were little kids, one way or another, it seems like we've been caught up in this fight. Do you ever wonder what other kids thought about when they were growing up, how they spent their time?"

"Those little pussy-whipped bastards living in the big houses in Westmount, with their plutocrat, pompous bastard parents? Who gives a shit what they thought about?"

Henri shook his head. He would never understand his brother. "It's always the same with you, isn't it? There's no doubting you're right and they're wrong. No compromise in you."

"You're damn right," Marc said. "Why should we compromise with them? They've lorded it over us for decades. Centuries. I'd like to grind them into dirt." The tiredness in his voice belied the aggression in his words. He leaned back in his chair and closed his eyes once more.

"But don't you feel any remorse or regret?"

"Everything the FLQ has done was necessary." His eyes still closed, Marc's face revealed nothing but his fatigue.

"Sack out here," Henri said with a sigh. "I'll make some phone calls in the morning."

Twenty minutes later Marc's voice came to Henri through the dark. "That night you walked in on us—on Claudia and me—nothing happened. I'd given her a ride and she invited me in for a glass of wine. I knew she expected you, but you were late, as usual. She got a little drunk and started crying on my shoulder. One thing led to another, but nothing serious happened. I let you think the worst. I wanted you to."

Henri's heart started to thud in his chest. His stomach clenched. Without a doubt, he knew Marc spoke the truth. "Why?"

"Because you're such a self-righteous ass, Henri. Besides, what do you need with someone like her? Her kind is worse than those rich Westmount bastards. At least they're true to their own. Not like rich French Canadians— they're traitors to the rest of us."

Chapter Thirty-Three

It had been a long day. After lunch, Marie-Catherine's doctor dropped by to see her.

"Was the soup good?" he asked with a smiling glance at the red spots on the front of her gown.

She refused to return his smile. "I didn't taste much of it."

"You'll do better," he said, looking at her chart.

"I can't believe all this rehabilitation stuff is so hard," she told him a minute later while he peered into her right eye. "I'm weak as a baby."

"You're getting stronger each day, though, aren't you?"

"I guess." She felt bored and frustrated, with no inclination to be agreeable. "I can't remember things." She knew she sounded like a brat, but didn't care. "When I try, it's like my mind turns to mush."

"You're likely not to remember what happened just before the accident." His face was close to hers as he peered into her eye, his warm breath on her cheek.

His gentle patience irritated her more. She felt the muscles in her shoulders knotting.

Finally, he stepped back and put the little flashlight into the breast pocket of his white coat. "It's your mind's way of protecting itself. As for the rest of it, relax. You're more likely to remember when you're not trying so hard."

Easy for him to say, she thought after he'd left.

Marie-Catherine lay quiet, listening to the nighttime sounds of the hospital. Her mother and father had gone home, she'd eaten dinner after someone had cut the tough meat for her, and now the television and the lights were off, leaving only the light from the hall to seep into the room around the door, slightly ajar. An old woman slept in the bed next to her. The woman's snoring comforted Marie-Catherine, reminding her of the rumble of her father's snores coming through the floor of her loft at home.

She wondered again what Marc had done to make Henri so angry. Although Henri wouldn't say, she knew him too well—whatever it was, he couldn't hide it from her for long.

"You might as well be upset with the sun," she'd told him a few days before. "Or with the moon and stars. Marc is Marc and we're never going to change him."

Henri refused to be drawn into a discussion about their brother. "Let's just concentrate on getting you out of here and back to school in the fall. I've talked to the Dean. He said they'd let you start over."

The thought of going back to school filled Marie-Catherine with dread. People would stare at her. Even Roger's eyes had filled with pity the day he'd come to the hospital to see her. She didn't blame him. Whenever she looked in the mirror, the strange young woman she saw startled her. The scar around her right eye was puckered red and angry-looking. Even though the doctor had taken the stitches out ages ago, she still saw the telltale track-marks they'd left behind. She looked like a little bird had walked across her face.

Her eyelid drooped. Fortunately. It covered the ugly mess on her eyeball. Though she'd gained back a few pounds, her face remained thin, with bruise-like smudges beneath both eyes. Her ribs and hipbones pushed against her skin.

She supposed she should feel lucky to be alive. Everyone told her so. But she didn't feel lucky at all. She felt confused and angry. When she'd demanded to know exactly what had happened to her, the doctor explained a part of the gear where a bomb had been wedged broke off and hit her in the temple, and a piece of the conveyor belt had torn loose, slapping into her face, across her eye.

A bomb? A bomb had done this to her? And what was she doing working in a shoe factory and not in school. Either no one knew, or they were keeping the reason from her.

I hate this, she thought, plucking at her blanket. I'm never going to feel like myself again.

Marie-Catherine sat next to her mother in the back seat of the taxi—the last time they'd ridden in one together, they'd been going to a restaurant the night Henri graduated from secondary school. It was old enough, it might even be the same cab. The seat where she and her mother sat had a lump in the middle from a broken spring. The cab driver, a friendly-faced Middle Easterner, had started out talking, English first then French, but soon gave up when neither woman responded beyond "*oui*" or "*non.*"

"You can let us out here," her mother finally said. "We'll walk the rest of the way." The driver brought the taxi to a halt at the curb. Her mother carefully counted out the exact change and handed it to the driver. He looked at it and sighed before putting the money into a cardboard cigar box. He then closed the box with a rubber band and returned it to the floor beneath his feet.

Out on the sidewalk, Marie-Catherine looked around and drew comfort from the familiar sights.

"We could have come on the bus," her mother said and brushed an invisible speck from her coat, worn despite the growing warmth of the day. "Your father insisted on a taxi." She sniffed. "A waste of money if you ask me.'

"I'm glad you came to get me, *Maman*. Even though I need to go back Sunday night, it will be so good to be home."

Her mother sniffed again. "I'm going to stop at the market since we're right here. Do you want to come in?"

"I think I'd rather stand here and soak up the sunshine, *Maman.*"

Her mother nodded, then pushed open Mr. Tiburg's door and Marie-Catherine heard the bell above the door ring.

A few people nodded to her, but most either stared or averted their eyes when they walked by. And with good reason, Marie-Catherine thought, glancing at the pasty-white and scarred face reflected in the store window.

Walking up the street a few yards, she kept her chin tucked down and her shoulders hunched forward.

On the sidewalk in front of a tobacco shop was a stack of newspapers with a half a red brick holding the papers in place. She read the headlines, visible above the brick: "*Police Arrest Suspect*" and "*Ernest LeGuin Arrested for Palace of Justice Bombing*". Below the words Marie-Catherine saw a picture of a man she knew. She shivered. He'd been at the warehouse when she and Marc came back from North Carolina. And she'd seen him once at Marc's apartment. Somewhere else, too, she thought. She tried, but couldn't remember where.

"I'm done," said her mother, suddenly appearing at her shoulder.

"Can we get this, *Maman*?" Marie-Catherine pointed to the newspaper.

Her mother looked at the newspaper and frowned. "Why? These days the papers are always full of bad news— people doing bad things to each other. Why should we waste our money and our eyes on such trash?"

"I've lost track of things while in the hospital. I'd like to read the newspaper and catch up." She felt ashamed to be using her injury as an excuse, playing on her mother's sympathy. But it worked.

"Hold this." Her mother handed Marie-Catherine a bulging string shopping bag. "I'll go inside and pay for it."

When her father came home from work, Marie-Catherine stood at the kitchen sink beside her mother, trying to help peel vegetables for the evening meal. Marie-Catherine turned when she heard the door open. "Papa," she said, and went to him.

"*Ma petite fillé,*" said her father, enfolding her. The long, ropey muscles in his arms quivered in his effort to be gentle. When he finally loosened his grip and Marie-Catherine pulled back a few inches, she saw tears trembling on his lower eyelids. "It is good you're home."

"It's good to be home, Papa."

Later, when Marie-Catherine and her parents sat down to the table to begin their meal, Marie-Catherine again heard footsteps cross the porch. The door opened. When she turned this time, Henri stood framed in the doorway.

"Henri," she said with a smile. "I'm home."

Henri's face remained solemn. "I see."

"Come in, son," said her father. "You're just in time to eat. *Maman*, get another bowl for Henri." Her mother rose and moved to the stove to ladle out more soup. "Get a glass, Henri." He picked up the wine bottle to pour.

Henri didn't move, but from the look on his face, Marie-Catherine knew something was wrong. "Henri? What is it?"

PART TWO

Chapter One

A few kilometers south of Quebec City, Marc crossed the St. Lawrence River. Muddy from recent rains, the river flowed swiftly beneath the bridge. The lyrics to an old jazz song flashed through his mind—something about drinking muddy water and sleeping in a hollow log…"

Once on the other side of the river, he turned northeast, toward the Gaspé Peninsula. Every fifteen miles or so, along the riverbank, were cathedral-like churches with towering spires. A dozen or more houses and shops huddled around them. Like a flock of chickens scratching for corn around the skirts of Mother Church.

"Shit," he muttered. He was getting as fanciful as Henri. He wondered if his brother had discovered his car was missing. At least Henri wouldn't report it to the police. He'd know who'd taken it.

At Saint Flavie, he stopped at a gas station for fuel and to use the restroom before turning inland. The highway, glistening now in a flat drift of rain, stretched out in front of him. Before long he'd be in the peninsula's wooded, mountainous interior. In the meantime, he kept his eyes glued to the highway, gripping the steering wheel when a truck loomed toward him and passed in a rush of wind and noise and spray.

Late in the afternoon the drizzle ended and an unexpected sun break nearly blinded him. Squinting against the glare, Marc spotted the bridge that crossed a narrow stream of water. The water tumbled over moss-covered rocks and rotting logs. A low peak rose behind the few scattered houses on the other side, casting them in its shadow. Marc slowed and turned onto the bridge. He sucked in his gut, as he did each time he crossed it, hearing the wooden planks of the bridge deck slap back into position as the car's wheels passed over them.

The houses appeared empty, although a child's swing swayed beneath a tree branch in a side yard. Its rope looked new. He slowed further and rolled down the car window. From somewhere floated the unmistakable, throbbing voice of Elvis Presley singing *Return to Sender*. A door slammed shut. Marc stopped the car in front of the last house.

Raymond Latour stepped out on the porch. A huge handlebar mustache graced his upper lip, and two long gray braids hung over his shoulders. "I wondered when you'd show up."

"Where can I put the car? I don't want it to be seen."

Latour jerked his head to the left. "Drive around behind the house. I'll get something you can throw over it."

Marc put the car in gear and drove through the dirt yard to the back, where Latour waited with a dirty canvas tarp.

"I'll take you up in the morning," Latour said when they were both inside the little house.

Marc lit a cigarette. "I'd like to go in tonight." He looked around for somewhere to put his match. He settled on a dirty coffee cup.

"Suit yourself. I'm just fixing something to eat. Want some?" Bacon lay in the bottom of a black skillet on the stove, congealing in its own fat. An empty baked bean can stood on the dented metal counter next to the stove.

Marc hadn't eaten since breakfast the day before. His stomach recoiled when he looked at the fat-larded bacon, but he shrugged anyway. "Sure." He forced himself to relax.

"There's beer in the fridge." Latour picked up a knife and cut several slices from a four-inch slab of bacon, added them to the skillet then turned up the flame. The bacon began to sizzle. With a loud pop, grease splattered out of the pan and Latour jerked back. "God dammit," he said and sucked on the back of his hand.

From the small refrigerator, Marc pulled out a bottle of beer. "You?"

"Already got one." Still nursing his burned hand, Latour again reached out the fork and cautiously stirred the strips of bacon.

"Have you seen anyone?" Marc's eyes hadn't been still since he'd entered the house. His entire body felt like an antenna, stretched taut, listening, waiting for the sound of sirens.

"Naw, just another group of recruits. They've been up there for the last week. The Belgian guy is with them."

"Barins?"

Latour nodded. "Yeah. He's trouble, I think."

Marc studied Latour's profile. "Why do you say that?"

Latour shook his head. "Just a gut feeling. Nothing I can put a finger on."

Marc thought of what he knew about Barins. The man was at least fifteen years older than most of the FLQ members, who tended to be in their late teens or early twenties—other than a few exceptions like Latour. Himself, too. Barins claimed to have been in the French resistance when he'd been a teenager. As a Gaullist or a communist, Marc didn't know, but decided it didn't make any difference. Nothing Barins had done so far had aroused his suspicion. But he respected Latour's instincts enough that he determined to keep his eyes and ears open.

When he'd eaten as much as his nervous stomach would allow, he leaned back in his chair and watched Latour mop up the beans and the grease from the bacon with a piece of dense rye bread. When nothing was left on his plate, Latour wiped his hand across his mouth, smoothed his moustaches and belched. "You ready to go?"

"Yeah." Marc stood. The chair legs scrapped the floor.

"Anything you want out of your car?"

"I didn't bring anything."

Latour drove his beat-up Ford pickup along the dirt and gravel track bordering the stream. Rocks spit from beneath the tires and clattered against the underside of the truck. Across the stream, on the highway he'd driven in on, a truck, piled high with peeled logs, made its slow-going way up the grade.

Ten bone-jarring minutes later, the track veered left, toward a fold in the base of the mountain, where it disappeared. When they'd followed the track around the fold and into the pass, darkness seemed to swallow them. Latour flipped on the headlights.

Marc raised his voice to be heard over the noise filling the truck's cab. "Aren't you afraid someone will see the lights?"

"Bears, maybe," Latour shouted back. "No people out here except for our own."

In another twenty minutes, the walls of the pass receded, opening into a broad canyon. Visible at its end were the lights of several small campfires.

Marc lay on his back with his fingers laced behind his head and stared into the void above him, barely registering the musty smell of the canvas and the symphony of sleep noises coming from the three other men in the tent. He wouldn't be safe up here for long. Someone would talk and this refuge, too, would be revealed to the police. It seemed every training camp the FLQ ran eventually got raided, no matter how remote.

In the past, Marc had never allowed himself to worry about getting caught. Now he couldn't get Henri's pale face from his mind, the one time he'd forced himself to visit his brother in jail. He mentally cringed as he remembered the clank of the guard's keys hitting the iron fitting when he unlocked then relocked Henri's cell door, the click of the tumblers as they came to rest.

Though his body begged for sleep, Marc stared into the empty space. The sky outside the tent flap lightened from black to gray and the sides and roof of the tent emerged from their shadows. His eyes grit-rimmed and dry, he strained his ears, listening for sounds that didn't come.

A school bus, late in its career, had been painted olive green and converted to perform as a mobile kitchen. An awning extended from its side. The awning covered a long metal camp table where, at mealtime, platters and pans of food were set out and people helped themselves. After each meal, volunteers used the table to wash the dishes and scrub pots and pans.

This morning, Marc's second in the camp, about twenty people huddled three or four to a group, talking and waiting for someone to open the bus door and bring out whatever had been prepared for breakfast.

He'd stayed in the background the day before, watching as recruits were stirred up with anti-government slogans and shown how to passively resist during demonstrations. They were taught how to put together a Molotov cocktail without spilling gasoline on themselves, and when to throw it. A fuzzy-faced twenty-year old, who claimed to be a former Laval University law student, lectured them about the legal ramifications of resistance.

Someone had asked Marc to tell about his experiences, but he'd refused.

He hung back from the others again, not wanting to join any group, still not sure why he'd come to the training camp, except he hadn't known where else to go. He'd thought about going to Pelletier, but dismissed that idea. Pelletier wouldn't help for fear Marc would bring the *flics* down on him.

Maybe he should have waited for Henri to call his contacts in the U.S., but Henri could easily have come up empty. Or worse yet, turned him over to Jeffers.

Marc was somewhat surprised Henri hadn't done that. As usual, the workings of his brother's mind were beyond him. Still, Marc hadn't dared wait. He'd slipped out the door as soon as he knew his brother was asleep, picking up Henri's car keys on the way out.

"What do you suppose they're serving us this morning?"

Startled from his inward brooding, Marc glanced at the man who'd materialized at his elbow. Richard Barins was hunched into his unzipped jacket, his hands shoved into its pockets. He was taller than Marc, but his stomach ran to fat, bulging over the top of his jeans and belt. A tic in his right eye gave his remarks an oddly flirtatious air.

Marc shrugged and lit a cigarette.

"It's not their fault the food tastes like shit." A watery drop quivered on the end of Barins' red nose. He wiped it on the sleeve of his jacket. "We haven't gotten any food supplies or any other kind of supplies since we got here."

Still Marc remained silent.

Barins kicked at a stone. "How can I train recruits when we have nothing to train with—no guns, no ammo, no nothing?" He wiped his nose again. "You just came up. What's going on back there? Have they forgotten us?"

Marc shrugged. "Who knows? Things are confused right now."

He thought of the truckload of guns, ammunition, and explosives he'd brought up from North Carolina and wondered if the *flics* had confiscated it. LeGuin would no doubt have told them where to find the cache. Then he wondered if the police might be staking it out, waiting for him to come and get it.

"Confused? What the shit is that supposed to mean," said Barins, sniffing and winking.

"Look, I don't know anything, okay?"

"Don't give me that shit, man. I know who you are, what you do."

"I told you I don't know anything." Marc threw down his cigarette and ground it out with the heel of his shoe.

Just then the school bus-cum-mobile-kitchen door pushed open and a woman backed into the opening holding one handle of a steaming aluminum pot. A man stood a step above her holding the other handle and together they maneuvered down the steps then turned and carried the heavy pot to the table.

"Oh, shit. Oatmeal again." Despite his complaints, Barins joined the young men and women converging on the table. Marc shoved his hands into his back pockets and followed.

Chapter Two

Henri missed his car. It had been two weeks since he'd discovered it gone, along with his brother. The other members of Marc's cell, Gould and Gould's sister, Teresa, had been arrested and joined LeGuin in jail. Henri wondered if Albert Drill had played a role in the arrests, or if LeGuin had broken down and named them, as Marc had predicted.

He thought about his own treatment at Jeffers' hands. If LeGuin had broken down, he couldn't blame the man. But he did worry what LeGuin might have said about Marie -Catherine, about her involvement. He had no idea if LeGuin or the other two even knew about his sister. He hoped Marc had had enough sense to keep her away from all of them. He should have asked when he had the chance.

He was still deep in thought, when a thin, dark-haired woman fell in beside him.

"I'm Bunny."

Henri looked at her. "Am I supposed to know who you are?"

"I'm Marc's girlfriend. I know your sister, too. How is she, by the way?"

Henri ignored her question. "What do you want?"

"I want to talk to you. Can we go somewhere?"

Henri gave a brief nod. "There's a coffee shop on Ste. Catherine."

As they walked along Peel Street, Henri glanced back at the statue dominating Dominion Square and remembered meeting Claudia there. He thought again about what she'd done for him while he was in prison. He thought about what an asshole he'd been to her.

Bunny tried to keep up. "What's the rush?" she said, her breath coming in huffs.

Henri didn't answer, but slowed his pace so she could stay abreast. The sun had come out. A brisk wind blew off the river and threaded its way through the buildings to tug at Henri's jacket collar. Through a notch in the skyline he saw the flanks of Mount Royal where the indigo sky was reflected in the windows of an ornate stone house on Redpath Crescent.

Buses and cars clogged Ste. Catherine Street. He led the way, dodging between a yellow and green taxi and a tour bus. The cab driver honked at them. From the corner of his eye, Henri saw Bunny extend her middle finger. Halfway down the block he stopped in front of a door set into a red brick building. The sign above it said *Gabrielle's*.

It was late in the morning and the place was nearly empty. "So," Henri said when they were seated and the waitress had taken their order for two coffees. "What do you want from me?"

Bunny rested her forearms on the edge of the table and leaned toward Henri. "Have you heard from Marc?"

"No."

"I need to talk to him."

"Why?"

"It's personal."

Henri shrugged. "Personal or not, it doesn't make any difference. I don't know where Marc is and I don't know how to get a message to him. You should know better than me, anyway."

"What about your sister? Do you think he's contacted Marie-Catherine?"

"No." Henri voice was harsh and louder than he'd intended. The waitress stood behind the counter, wiping its surface with a damp rag, but she didn't look up. "My sister is still recuperating," he added, his voice lower. "I don't want you going near her."

"Don't worry. I don't plan to."

Henri noticed the way her bird-like fingers twitched when she hooked a strand of her long black hair behind her ear. He remembered how Claudia's hair swung forward when she read a book and how she'd used both hands to push it back from her face, tucking it behind her ears.

"She doesn't need to be reminded of the accident or be worried about Marc right now," said Henri, his voice gentling. When he looked in Bunny's eyes, he thought he detected something like uncertainty or fear, but she looked down at her coffee and he wasn't sure.

"I won't bother her," Bunny said again. "But I do need to talk to Marc."

Henri shrugged and shook his head. "I can't help you." The words sounded harsh in his ears and he tried to soften them. "All I can promise is that I'll give him your message when and if he contacts me."

"I guess that will have to do. Here. I've written down a number where I can be reached. If I'm not there, whoever answers will take a message for me." Henri took the slip of paper she pushed across the table and tucked it into his shirt pocket. "Don't lose it," she said and stood to go.

"I won't." Henri stood, too, and set a bill and some change on the table.

Back out on the sidewalk Bunny turned to him. "Thanks for the coffee, Henri." She gave him a twisted smile. "See you around."

Henri watched her small figure walk down Ste. Catherine Street before she crossed it and turned down Metcalfe.

As he headed back to the newspaper, his thoughts turned once more to Claudia. He couldn't go on like this. It seemed like everywhere he went and every woman he saw made him think of her and what he'd lost. He had to apologize, make her forgive him. He had no idea what to say to her. How could he tell her he'd been a complete asshole when he wouldn't believe her, but believed his brother instead, the one who lied as easily as he drew breath, the one who just stole his car. Sure. Good idea, Henri. She'll love hearing that.

That evening Henri once again heard the phone on the wall outside his room ring as he turned the key in the downstairs door. He pushed the door aside and ran up the steps, thinking something might have happened to Marie-Catherine, a set-back or something. "Hello?"

"Henri Morais?"

He didn't recognize the voice. "Yes. Who is this?"

"I'd like to meet with you."

Henri frowned. "Who is this? How did you get this number?"

"My name's Lanctot. I have a proposition for you."

"What kind of proposition?"

"I can't say right now, but other reporters will wish they were in your place. Do you want to talk?"

The next day, seated in a corner booth at a dingy little coffee shop, Henri listened to Jacques Lanctot, intent on his every word. When the man had finished, Henri asked the question he'd been pondering since Lanctot's phone call. "Why me?"

"I've read your articles for a number of years. We've seen all the interviews you've done since you got out of prison, too. We know you're not one of us, but you support the same causes we do."

Henri stared at the man, trying to read him. "I won't be part of any violence."

"We're not planning to do anything violent." Jacques Lanctot was a slender, handsome man, with a smooth, almost mesmerizing, voice. "I promise you, there'll be no bombs or explosives."

Henri decided not to press the issue, even though he was a long way from being convinced. "What exactly do you want me to do? I told you this would be strictly off the record," he added, sensing Lanctot's reluctance to fully confide in him.

"When the timing is right, I'll be getting a document to you. We want it published."

"Not another FLQ *communiqué*." Henri reached for his jacket, disgusted and disappointed he had wasted his time.

"I can't get one of those things published for you or anyone else."

"Wait a minute." Lanctot reached his hand across the table, placing it on Henri's arm. "I promise you, everyone will want to get hold of the document I'm preparing."

"Then why do you need me?" Henri cautiously settled into his seat again.

"Because at the time I want it published, my freedom may be restricted."

Chapter Three

Bit by bit, Marie-Catherine began putting the pieces of her memory back together, starting with the picture of Ernest LeGuin in the newspaper. One morning, about a week after she'd been discharged from the nursing home, on her way to a doctor's appointment, she saw a "For Rent" sign tacked to a wooden stake in the yard of a duplex. She had a sudden vision of a crowd of people on a sidewalk, carrying signs attached to wooden poles. She clutched her mother's arm.

"What is it?" her mother said.

Marie-Catherine shook her head. "I don't know. I...I must be imagining things." The vision had seemed so real, though.

At other times, when she least expected it, she'd get a mental picture of someone, a red-haired woman with freckles and a lively smile, or a thing, like a doorway, a strange piece of machinery, an open elevator.

She felt like Alice in Wonderland trying to put together a giant puzzle, but without being able to see the box lid to know how the finished picture was supposed to look.

Everyone told her not to agonize so much about it.

"Concentrate on getting well," her doctor said.

"Have more soup," said her mother.

"Don't worry," Henri said.

But she had no control over the visions, and when they came to her she seemed to have no control over the way they tugged at her memory, letting her see a tiny bit more of the picture. So, she nodded to her family's well-intentioned admonitions. When at last she felt strong enough to leave the house alone, she climbed the hill and boarded a bus to Montreal.

At the UQAM reference library, Marie-Catherine approached the desk. Behind it, a thin, balding man with rimless glasses stood looking over the shoulder of a young woman at a typewriter. More aware than ever of her scarred face, and not altogether sure she wanted to be there, Marie-Catherine waited to be acknowledged.

"Excuse me," she finally said.

The man frowned as he glanced at her and away from his task of instruction. "Just a moment."

Marie-Catherine waited another minute, her own irritation beginning to mount. She cleared her throat. "Excuse me. I need some help."

The man sighed and straightened. He came to stand in front of her. "Sorry to keep you waiting. How can I help you?" His smile was as insincere as his apology.

"I want back copies of *The Montreal Star, La Presse* and *Le Journal Quotidien.* I want to see all the articles on the bombing of Arrow Shoe Factory."

"I'll show you how to locate them." As he explained to Marie-Catherine the way the articles were filed and how to retrieve them, his irritation gave way to thoroughness. Within twenty minutes she was installed in front of a gray box with a large square magnifying lens on its top. Several sheets of microfiche were on the table next to her.

She thanked him and, after a brief pause, his footsteps receded. Then there was nothing to hear beyond the sound of the tray as, one after another, she inserted a sheet of microfiche onto it, pushed it into place and read.

Even though many of the articles contained her name, it felt as though they referred to a stranger. There was someone else, too. A woman named Dora Greene. She slipped in another sheet of film. As she moved the tray, a picture came into view.

The picture was in black and white, but Marie-Catherine saw it in full color. Dora's red hair, her milky white complexion, freckles scattered across her cheeks. She heard Dora's ever-ready laughter. Then she saw Dora walking ahead of her with her yellow rain slicker over one arm, reaching for a box wedged into the gears of the conveyor belt. And she saw Ernest LeGuin once more, moving through a door on the other side of the factory when she and Dora came out of the break room.

It felt as if all the air had been sucked out of the room. Her ears rang, the light faded. She grabbed the edge of the table and gasped for breath as she faced what they'd been hiding from her. Henri had been right about their brother all along. Marc had done this. He'd killed Dora—with the explosives Marie-Catherine helped him bring from North Carolina.

"Where have you been?" her mother said when Marie-Catherine nearly staggered into the house. "I was afraid you were lost or hit by a car. Why didn't you let me know you would be gone so long? You shouldn't have gone out on your own like that." Her mother's words tumbled over each other in their rush to get out. Without waiting for any answers, she bundled Marie-Catherine across the room to a chair at the kitchen table, then quickly prepared her daughter a cup of hot, sweetened tea.

"At first I didn't remember." Marie-Catherine struggled to get the words out, knowing if she didn't, they might choke her. "I read the words, but they didn't seem real, as though I was reading about another Marie-Catherine Morais, someone I didn't know, had never met. Then in a flash, it all came back to me. I remembered working at the shoe factory. I remembered the striking workers on the sidewalk, I remembered the smell of the leather and the machine oil, the noise of the machinery. And I remembered Dora. Oh, *Maman*," Marie-Catherine cried. "I remember Dora." She dropped her head into her arms, knocking the empty teacup onto its side, and sobbed.

How her mother pulled herself up the ladder to the loft to sit next to the bed until Marie-Catherine fell into an exhausted and dreamless sleep, Marie-Catherine never knew.

Her shoulders squared and her fears held in check, Marie-Catherine listened to footsteps echo on the other side of the bright, parrot green door, so typically Dora. If possible, she was even more conscious than ever of the scars crisscrossing her sightless right eye and cheek. The door swung back and a haggard-looking man with tired, red-rimmed eyes faced her.

"Yes?"

Marie-Catherine froze.

"What do you want?"

With a tremble in her voice, she introduced herself. "I was in the accident that killed your wife, killed Dora." Her throat choked with tears. "I'm so sorry."

The man stared at her. His face and eyes, blank at first, filled with rage. "Sorry," he ground out. "I don't believe you. They were your people who did it."

His hatred crashed into her like a physical blow. She struggled to keep from reeling.

A boy, who looked to be about three, clutching a fuzzy blue blanket under his arm, leaned against his father's leg. She reached a shaking hand toward him. "You must be Billy," she said, her voice barely above a whisper.

The man jerked the boy's arm from beneath Marie-Catherine's fingers and backed away. "Get out. Get the bloody hell out and leave us alone."

The door slammed in Marie-Catherine's face. For a moment, she stood and looked at it, her mind blank, her shoulders slumped. She turned and retraced her steps down the avenue where Dora had lived, past all the drab duplexes with their drab front doors and their scraps of drab front yards.

★

She refused to talk to any of the others at the precinct in North Montreal while she waited for Lieutenant Jeffers to show up, just as she refused to let herself back down and go home. Then he was there. He opened the glass door and strode into the building. She didn't take her eyes from him as he crossed to the desk sergeant. After a few mumbled words, he turned and walked over to her.

"You wanted to see me?"

Marie-Catherine stared into Jeffers' watery blue eyes, knowing he was only pretending not to notice her scars, her distorted right eye. It was too late to change her mind. She stood. "Where can we talk?"

Two hours later Jeffers leaned back in his chair. He lit another cigarette with his big, square hands. "Tell Henri this lets him off the hook."

"What do you mean? What hook?"

Jeffers exhaled a lungful of smoke into the room. "He made a deal with me and the warden." He picked a piece of tobacco from the tip of his tongue then looked with distaste at the unfiltered cigarette before looking back at her. "That's how he got out of Parthenais—he promised to find out what Marc and his cell were planning." He stubbed out the cigarette in the overflowing ashtray resting on the table between them. "Henri didn't keep his part of the bargain. You did."

"You know why he couldn't tell."

Jeffers gazed at her. His eyes in their watery sockets didn't waver. "You. He was protecting you."

Marie-Catherine was conscious of Henri at her side, at the same picnic table where little more than a year before she'd told him about her trip to North Carolina with Marc. He must wonder why she'd called and asked him to meet her there.

"I went to see them," she said, her voice flat.

"Who, M.C.?"

A glowing kaleidoscope of fall colors surrounded them. Maples in red, orange and purple, withered red fruit dangled on thin stems from the bare branches of crabapple trees. Bright yellow leaves fluttered above the white trunks of tall alders. "Dora's family. I saw her husband. He slammed the door in my face, Henri. He said it was my people who did it, who killed Dora."

She'd cried all her tears; the weeping had left her feeling empty. She sensed his eyes on her, but he stayed silent.

"He's right, Henri. More right than he knows." She swung around and gazed at her brother, hoping he'd have the answers she hadn't been able to find for herself. "How could Marc do it? How could he?"

"I don't know, M.C."

"When I think about going to North Carolina with him...I thought it was...I was just so excited to finally be doing something important." She nearly spat out the last word. She'd spent hours remembering every detail of that trip, every detail of her role in it. "I get sick thinking about what I did."

"It wasn't your fault. Marc used you."

"I know he did. But it is my fault. Even with all your warnings, I let him. Even when I knew he was using me, I still let him." She paused, feeling the truth of her words. "Dora was a good person, Henri. She was my friend." She said the word friend like a challenge, and waited for Henri to contradict her. When he didn't she went on. "If we let him, Marc will keep on using people and building bombs. More people will die."

Henri leaned forward, his elbows on his knees, and she felt the tension in him. "Do you know where it is now? The stuff you brought up from North Carolina?"

"I know where we took it." Her voice was low. Henri had to lean in to hear it. "I don't know if it's still there."

He stood. She watched him walk a few paces away. He turned, came back, and stood in front of her. "So long as Marc has access to the explosives, he'll use them."

"I know."

"I could tell someone. I could let the police know where to look. Your name wouldn't have to come into it."

Marie-Catherine released her breath in a heavy sigh. "I've already told them."

Chapter Four

The granite cliff was short, but jutted straight up. Marc worked at finding toeholds to set his feet in as he ascended the ten feet to the top. The leather-soled shoes he wore were meant for city streets, not this precarious position on the side of a mountain. Above the sheered outcropping, the slope gentled, but even there the going proved to be dangerous. Loose shale crumbled and shifted with every step he took.

He inched his way upward, his shoes soon filling with bits of stone. Beads of sweat pricked his back and made it itch, but he didn't dare risk scratching. With each move, he feared he would lose his balance, slide back down the treacherous slope, and end up in a heap at the base of the cliff. Finally, nearing the top, he spotted a protruding tree root and grabbed for it. It held.

Exhausted, he slowly pulled his body out of the loose rock and onto a grassy verge. Panting, he rolled over and stared up at the tall trees towering above him. A cool breeze rifled through the long, dark branches, drying the sweat on his face.

He'd left the camp before breakfast, unwilling to spend another hour with the new recruits, whose enthusiasm was exceeded only by their ignorance. He hated the feeling of powerlessness that had descended on him when he'd arrived four days earlier. He'd go crazy if he remained much longer.

In the stillness a rock fell, sounding like a thunderbolt as it struck a rock and then another. He heard a thump when it reached the hard-packed dirt below. He pushed himself onto his feet, braced to fight, and peered down the way he'd come. Barins' head emerged first, then his shoulders. Wordlessly, Marc watched as the man swung his foot over the top edge of the granite outcropping before the rest of his body followed.

Just as Marc had done minutes before, Barins inched cautiously through the shifting shale. When he neared the top, Marc stuck out his hand. Barins grabbed it with his sweaty one. Marc pulled him up the rest of the way. For several minutes Barins lay face down, his breath coming in loud, rasping pants.

Marc studied him, his eyes narrowed. "Why did you follow me?"

Barins rolled onto his back and peered up at Marc. "Why the hell did you climb this fucking mountain?"

Marc scowled. "Answer the question. Why did you follow me?"

"Because you aren't finished with the Anglos. Whatever it is you're planning, I want in on it."

Marc squatted, considering his words before he spoke. "I need explosives." Barins nodded. Marc watched Barins' face. "I know where there's plenty. Weapons, too—that is if the *flics* haven't gotten it all."

"I knew it," crowed Barins. "I knew you'd have a supply hidden away…but what do you mean about the *flics?*"

"They arrested LeGuin. Gould, too." Marc threw a rock over the ledge and heard the faint plop when it hit the ground below. "Before long, they'll answer any question the *flics* ask and even some they don't."

"Then what the fuck are we waiting for? Let's go get it before they squeal like pigs."

Marc didn't want to use Henri's car, so five of them, Marc, Barins and three recruits—Alain Guenette, Giles Bizer and Yves Pruneau—drove down from the Gaspé in a car Latour found for them. For a day and a half Marc and Barins watched the warehouse, looking for any sign of surveillance. The place looked deserted and they saw nothing to make them suspect the police were watching.

Bizer, younger-looking than his nineteen years and a dropout from the University of Montreal, was elected to rent a van.

"What do I tell them at the rental place?"

"Tell them you're moving," said Barins. "Montrealers are always moving."

"Tell them you're moving a dead body," said Marc, irritated at such naïveté. "For Christ sake, man, they don't give a fuck what you're going to do with it."

They'd need a truck, too, and Guenette, whose past included knowledge of such things, promised to acquire one. But at the sight of the bright red pick-up he drove up in, Barins shook his head in disgust. "We want to avoid being seen," he said to the crestfallen Guenette. "Not advertise."

Marc brushed off Barins' concerns. "Don't worry about

it. If anyone sees anything, they'll remember the red pick-up, not the van we transfer the stuff to."

Now, except for the youthful-looking Bizer, who waited in the van three miles away, in a dark alley, they were gathered in a tavern a block from the warehouse, finishing their second round of beer.

It was going well, Marc told himself. In less than two hours they'd be on their way back to the camp. He hadn't told Barins or the others what he planned to do with the explosives, but it would be big and it would be symbolic, something the fuckers would never forget. He glanced at his watch. Ten-twenty. He drank the last of his beer.

"Let's do it."

Barins, Guenette and Pruneau tipped their heads to finish their drinks then set the empty glasses on the table.

Marc and Pruneau walked down the block toward the warehouse, their footsteps echoing behind them. In the distance Marc saw the lights of the tower at Dorval airport. Behind them the lights from the tavern spilled onto the empty street. The rest of the buildings surrounding them were dark.

He gave a momentary shiver and blamed it on the jacket he wore. The imitation leather may have been thick, but it didn't offer much warmth and the fall air had grown cold. A wind had blown up, too, carrying the ripe, slightly salty smell of the St. Lawrence along with the chill.

Pruneau stumbled over a railroad tie when they crossed the tracks running in front of the warehouse yard. "God dammit." He hopped on one foot and rubbed his ankle. "Hold up a minute."

"Here's the gate," said Marc, fishing keys from his pocket.

Pruneau limped over and grabbed the gate

Marc turned on the flashlight he carried, shielding the beam with his body. The chain and lock dropped to the ground. Pruneau slid the gate all the way back. They crossed the paved yard, Pruneau still favoring his left ankle.

"Wait here," Marc whispered. Singling out another key from his key ring he opened the office door. The beam from his flashlight cut across a desk then over a picture of a semi-nude woman tacked to the wall above it. Beyond the desk, the door to the warehouse stood ajar.

Marc went through the door and shone his light around the open space. Against the far side of the building he saw the shape of boxes covered with a canvas tarp. *Son of a bitch, LeGuin didn't talk. It's still here.*

After a quick examination to confirm they were the wooden boxes from North Carolina, Marc crossed to the barn-like sliding door, unlatched it, and pushed it open. He flashed his light. Guenette gunned the red pick-up across the railroad tracks, through the gate and into the warehouse. Barins followed in the car. Pruneau ducked into the building and Marc slid the door closed just as what sounded like a Boeing 720 roared overhead. The building and its contents vibrated from the noise, the ground trembled.

"The stuff is over there under the tarp." Marc pointed to the pile of boxes with the beam of the flashlight then switched the flashlight off. The space was lit by the moon and starlight shining through high, mesh-covered windows at the end of the building.

Barins pulled the tarp off the pile. "Give me something to pry the lid off this."

Marc shook his head. "We don't have time. I want to get this stuff loaded so we can get out of here."

"What's the rush? We've got plenty of time." The tic near Barins eye flicked faster than ever. "Let's see what you've brought us down here for." He pulled one of the long flat boxes off the pile. "Come on, Pruneau. See if you can find me a screwdriver or pry bar."

"God damn it, no. Get the fuck over there and start moving those boxes, Pruneau. You, too, Guenette. We can open them when we get back to camp. Then you can look all you want."

Guenette hesitated, but Pruneau picked up one of the boxes and, still limping, carried it to the back of the truck. A moment later Guenette picked up a box and followed Pruneau's lead. Barins grunted then he, too, picked up a box and carried it across the hollow-sounding cement floor to the back of the pick-up.

Fifteen minutes later Marc called a halt. "Okay, we've got all we need. The rest will have to wait for another time. Pull the tarp back over it," he told Guenette.

Pruneau held up his hand. "Listen, do you hear it?"

"What?" Marc scowled, then he heard it, too. "A train. What's it doing here at this time? He ran to the door and slid it open a foot. "Shit. Get the truck started. Barins, get the car turned around. Pruneau can ride with you. I'll go in the truck." Marc pushed the door all the way open and Barins backed the car out. Behind him, Guenette backed the pick-up out. "Pruneau, get in the car. Hurry."

Pruneau limped in the direction of the car while Marc began sliding the heavy door closed.

"Hurry up, man," said Barins to Pruneau, who hobbled toward him.

The clanging racket of cars bumping and grinding together grew louder as the train drew closer, its huge light washing over the open gate. Suddenly, just as Pruneau reached for the door handle, the old car shot forward, through the gate and across the tracks.

Marc stared after him. "That son-of-a-bitch."

"Come on, Morais." Guenette revved the pick-up's engine.

"Get in the truck, Pruneau," Marc shouted above the train's growing clamor. He ran toward the pick-up as Guenette started it moving slowly toward the gate. The train let out a blast of noise and diesel fumes. Marc reached the back of the pick-up, stepped on the bumper, and swung himself in, on top of the boxes. The truck tires spun and caught and the truck spurted forward then lurched to a standstill as the train moved in front of the gate and with a screech of metal on metal came to a stop.

Marc jumped off the back of the truck and sprinted across the yard to the fence. He shoved his feet into the links, pulling and clawing his way to the top, then rolled over and dropped to the ground. He heard running footsteps and shouting, but he didn't wait to see what happened with Pruneau and Guenette. He raced down the street away from the train and the warehouse, toward the airport. If he made it to the airport he'd be able to get a cab. International flights came in at odd hours, so there was bound to be a cab or two in the rank. With any luck, the driver would be someone he knew.

The passenger terminal was nearly empty. A young couple slept, the girl's head on the boy's shoulder, their baggage piled around them. An old man read a newspaper. An Indian woman in a sari sat next to a dusky-skinned young boy playing with a toy airplane. Passing the ticket counter on the way to the men's room, Marc saw a clock on the wall showing ten minutes to midnight. Just a little over an hour ago, everything had looked rosy.

In the men's room, he washed his hands and splashed cold water on his face. Staring at his reflection in the mirror, he fingered a two-inch triangular tear on the front of his jacket. "Shit," he muttered, before turning to leave, his leather-soled shoes sounding on the gray tile floor.

Moments later, in answer to his signal, a cab moved forward out of the rank. He climbed into the back and leaned his head against the seat. "Downtown," he said. The driver was a stranger.

Sirens wailed in the distance.

They reached the highway to downtown Montreal just as two police cars screamed past. "Someone's in trouble," the cabdriver said. He didn't sound concerned.

"Turn off here," Marc said a few blocks later.

The driver looked at Marc in his rearview mirror. "I thought you wanted to go downtown."

"I've changed my mind."

The driver shrugged and turned. "You're the boss."

Marc directed him to a street near the alley where Bizer waited—unless the *flics* had been onto them from the start and Bizer had already been arrested. "Let me out here."

The driver looked in his rearview mirror again. "There's nothing but closed shops. Are you sure you want to get out here?"

Marc pulled out his wallet and extracted some bills. "A girl I know lives over one. I wasn't planning to see her on this trip but she just got lucky." He laughed. "Keep the change."

The driver chuckled as he put the bills into a zippered pouch. "Thanks. I hope she's alone. Want me to wait?"

"Nah." A minute later, Marc watched the rear lights of the taxi disappear around a corner. Probably heading back to the airport, he thought. He turned and trotted down the street until he came to the alley where Bizer waited. He stopped and listened. All he heard was the far off and fading sound of sirens. Still cautious he peered around the corner and saw the silhouette of the van. His heart pounded, fearing another set-up. He took a deep breath and stepped into the alley. Nothing. Without daring to think further, he darted toward the van. He rapped on the partially fogged window in the passenger door. Giles Bizer turned a startled face in his direction.

Marc pointed to the lock.

Bizer reached across the seat and unlocked the door. "Where's everyone else? I didn't hear a car or a truck. What took you so long? I almost left."

"I don't know where they are." Marc pulled the door closed. "The whole thing got fucked up. Let's go."

"But where are the others? Where are the M-16's? The ammo? The explosives?"

"We couldn't get it out. It was a fucking trap."

"Shit." Bizer reached for the key and started the van then put it in gear and they shot forward.

Marc put a steadying hand on the dashboard. "Easy, dammit."

"Shit," Bizer said again. They reached the end of the alley and he pulled onto the street. "What should we do? Are they looking for us too?"

The panicky whine in Bizer's voice grated on Marc's nerves. "What the fuck do you think?"

"But what should we do?"

"Shut up a minute. I need to think."

Bizer slammed his fist against the steering wheel, but at least kept quiet.

"We're going downtown," Marc said.

"What? Are you crazy? They're looking for us. We have to get out of here, back up to the camp." Bizer's eyes darted from side to side, as though any minute something might jump out at them from a side street.

"Take the downtown turn," Marc said as they approached the Auto-route. "They'll be searching around the warehouse area for a couple of hours."

"But why do you want to go downtown?" Bizer asked, but he did as Marc directed and in twenty minutes they were approaching the heart of the city.

"Drive to one of the construction sites for the Métro. What I need is there."

Bizer did what Marc told him, but he wasn't happy. He

kept looking in the rearview mirror and readjusting it, his hand trembling. They turned up University Street.

"Let me off here." Sawhorses and construction signs barricaded one lane and part of the sidewalk and extended into the intersection of a side street, where crews had been working to extend Montreal's underground shopping mall. Down the side street Marc spotted a chain-linked security fence surrounding a small shack. There was no guard. "Drive around the block and see if you can pull in near the fence," he told Bizer as he got out of the van. "Move a barricade if you have to."

Dynamite would be inside the shack. Not a lot, but at least enough for the job Marc had in mind. He wasn't going to let the screw-up at the warehouse put a period to his plans. He tried to appear casual, like a sleepless apartment-dweller out for a late night stroll, curious about the progress of construction. He saw no one else on foot, but an occasional car cruised by on University Street.

Several wicked-looking strands of barbed wire crowned the fence, but when he got close enough he saw whoever put it up hadn't finished the job. Only one thin strand ran along the top of the gate. He looked around then tossed his jacket across the top and clawed his way up and over the gate. Jumping down, he ducked behind the shed just as lights bounced off the sides of buildings then slid over the walls and door of the shed. When he knew it was Bizer, pulling the van up close to the fence, Marc found a screwdriver in a toolbox and jammed it between the metal hasp and the wooden door of the shed.

The screws holding the hasp in place gave way with a mild screech of protest before the door canted and swung partially open. Marc stepped inside and flashed his light over the walls and dirt floor. In a corner were three clearly marked wooden boxes with rope handles.

Back outside, Marc whistled softly to Bizer. Moments later he heard Bizer's footsteps hurry toward him. "You'll have to climb up the gate. I'll pass the boxes over to you." Bizer scrambled up the gate and Marc met him halfway. Marc slid the first box over the top of the gate. "Careful, it's heavy. Don't drop it." When all three boxes stood on the cement sidewalk outside the gate, Marc flashed his light around until he found what he looked for, a closed metal box, painted orange, next to the fence.

"What's in that?" whispered Bizer when Marc reached the gate again.

"Blasting caps, time fuse and det cord." Marc scrambled to the top of the gate with the footlocker. "Here, take it." He jumped down, glad to be outside the enclosure once again. Bizer had already loaded two of the boxes into the back of the van. After grabbing his jacket off the barbed wire, he picked up the metal box. Bizer picked up the remaining wooden box. They loaded both then climbed into the front of the van.

"Now where to?" said Bizer, backing the vehicle out of the side street. Marc noticed he seemed less nervous, as though the physical activity had given him confidence.

"We need to get out of town first, then find a place where we can park this thing and not be bothered. Any ideas?"

Chapter Five

In the passenger seat, Marc tried to relax. Bizer drove, leaning forward over the wheel. They took the highway to St. Jerome before turning southwest, onto a rarely-used road. Marc played with the zipper of his jacket, running it up and down, his eyes darting into the darkened underbrush and the woods on each side of the road. After about ten miles, they came to a park, closed for the season. "Stop here." Bands of clouds filled the eastern sky—blood red, pink and yellow. Marc climbed out of the van and unfastened the chain that hung across the road. Bizer drove through. After traveling a short distance, they came to a deserted campsite and parked the van. They both got out. "Walk around for a while," Marc said.

"Can I light a fire? It's freezing."

Marc walked around to the door at the back of the van. "Better not. Somebody might see the smoke. Go use a tree branch to wipe out our tracks. That will warm you up." He climbed in the van and pulled the door shut behind him.

Forty-five minutes later, Marc squatted on a box, an unlit cigarette hanging from the corner of his mouth. He used the tip of a sharp knife to punch a diagonal hole in the side of a stick of dynamite. When the hole was large enough, he cut off a length of time fuse. Using a tool he'd taken from the shack, he crimped the fuse to one end of a blasting cap then plugged the hole in the dynamite with the cap's other end. He wiggled it around to make sure it wouldn't fall out. Satisfied, he dug around in the brown paper bag at his feet and pulled out another roll of black, rubbery electricians' tape. He gathered ten more sticks of dynamite around the stick with the length of time fuse, then taped them all together. Several other taped bundles lay on the floor. He'd need to stop at a store and buy a couple of satchels to hold them.

Bizer had been noisily stomping his feet and slapping his arms for some time. He opened the door and stuck his head inside. "How much longer? I'm freezing my balls off out here."

"Fifteen minutes."

Bizer glanced at the bundles surrounding Marc. He frowned. "Okay." He took a step backward and gently closed the door.

Before Marc had joined the FLQ, a cell led by Robert Hudon had fabricated a powerful bomb. They'd meant to blow up the bridge connecting the Province of Quebec to the city of Ottawa, but the two men who were meant to deliver the bomb panicked and returned with it to Montreal. The well-publicized episode had disgusted Marc. He put the final touches on the last bundle. "There's gonna be no turning back with these babies," he muttered, his tone almost a caress. He'd spent hours at the training camp planning just how he'd do it.

"Okay," he told Bizer as he climbed out of the back of the van. He stretched his arms upward and rolled his head left then right. He lit the cigarette that had been hanging from his lips, took two drags off it and flicked it into a snow-filled campfire pit. "We're ready to roll. I'll drive now."

Bizer climbed into the passenger seat. He looked over his shoulder into the back of the van. "What if we're stopped?" Once again, his voice was raw with panic.

"We'll cross that bridge if we come to it." Marc smiled at the unintended play on words. Like Barins, Bizer had no clue.

Marc eased the van along the rut-filled road back to the highway, then stopped for Bizer to get out and move the chain. When the chain dropped, Marc drove forward onto the pavement. He didn't stop. In the rearview mirror, he saw Bizer staring after him with a look of utter disbelief on his face. Marc chuckled. *What a stupid shit.*

A bell tinkled when Marc opened the door of the sporting goods store. The place smelled of Neet's Foot Oil and leather. The tables and counters were piled with hockey and ski equipment.

A tall man whose thick blond hair was speckled with gray, looked up from studying a sheaf of papers. "Can I help you?"

"I need a couple of gym bags. Sturdy ones."

"Over here." The clerk led the way to the back of the store.

Marc didn't take long to make his selection. "Is there a hardware store in town?" he asked, handing the clerk payment for the bags.

Marc slung his purchases onto the passenger seat of the van and climbed behind the wheel. Once again driving west, keeping well within the speed limit, he reviewed the plan in his head. He hoped the rope he'd bought was long enough to reach the spot where the bridge's concrete pillars met the steel girders. He intended to secure an explosives-laden gym bag to both sides of the pillar, one a few inches above the other and set them to go off simultaneously. The blast wouldn't take the bridge down, but it would do plenty of damage. There'd be no traffic crossing it for a long time. He tightened his grip on the steering wheel. His plan would work. He knew it.

In Gatineau, traffic slowed as buses, trucks, and cars crowded the roadway. Ahead, among the smoking factory chimneys of Hull, sunlight glinted off the bridge stretching across the river to Ottawa.

The closer Marc got to the bridge the more euphoric he became. He'd stopped earlier and transferred the bundles of dynamite into the gym bags. They lay on the floor behind the passenger seat, the rope coiled next to them. His left foot tapped the floor.

The truck in front of him downshifted.

Marc ran his fingertips along the steering wheel as he waited for traffic to pick up speed. The driver of the car next to him, a woman with two young children in the back seat, turned her radio on. The sound of a symphony came through the partially opened window.

Marc tapped the brake. The woman's car pulled ahead a few feet, then slowed when the car in front of it slowed.

They were side-by-side again. The woman glanced at Marc, raised her eyebrows, and smiled in assumed mutual resignation.

The truck ahead of him pulled forward.

Marc edged over in his lane, trying to peer around the truck, but he saw nothing. Pinching his lips together, he stepped on the gas then slammed on the brake as the traffic ground to a complete halt. The bridge lay less than twenty feet ahead. There were no turnouts. He was committed. "What the hell is the fucking hold up?" In his rearview mirror loomed the grillwork of a green and white bus. He put the van in park, set the brake and got out.

"See anything?" he asked the driver of the truck in front of him.

"Nah. Must be an accident or something—probably a fender-bender. Should be cleared out soon."

Marc walked back to the van and climbed in. By the time he'd gotten settled and shifted into gear, the truck in front of him had pulled forward a few feet.

For the next fifteen minutes, he stopped and waited then crept forward until finally he was well onto the bridge and could see the river over the side. Traffic stopped again. Vibrations came through the floor of the van. The sensation made him almost giddy.

The driver in the truck ahead leaned his head out his window. Marc leaned out as well.

Jesus Christ. The *flics*. He took a breath and let it out slowly. *There's nothing to see except two gym bags and some rope. Don't panic. It's just a routine traffic stop.*

The truck ahead moved forward again and Marc followed. A *flic* stepped onto the running board of the truck and spoke to the driver. Marc squirmed in his seat. The policeman stepped down and waved the truck forward then turned and motioned to Marc. That's when he saw the other three *flics*. They were two to a lane.

He put the van into gear and started rolling forward until he came abreast of the uniformed man who'd waved to him. "What's going on?" he said. Another policeman approached and stood on the other side of the van, next to the passenger door. Marc held his breath.

"Routine stop," the first flic said. "I need to see your driver's license."

Marc reached into his back pocket.

"What's in those bags?"

"What?" Marc fumbled with his billfold to stall for time. A rock seemed to have lodged in his chest. He extracted a license with his picture and someone else's name.

"The bags," said the man. "What's in them?" He took the license Marc held out to him.

From the corner of his eye, Marc saw the *flic* on the other side of the van reach for the door handle. He didn't think. He gunned the motor and shot forward. In the rearview mirror, he saw the startled faces of the two policemen. The truck ahead of him had begun building up speed. Marc spurted around it, cutting off the woman and her children.

When he got around the truck and crested the middle span of the bridge he saw all the federal government buildings lined up along the riverbank, their backs to him, braced, it seemed, against invasion. And he saw the futility of his efforts. A police car was being maneuvered into position crossways at the other end of the bridge.

Without lowering his speed, Marc aimed the van for the narrow space between the police car and the bridge railing. He took a firm grip on the steering wheel and leaned into it, bracing for the impact. He saw nothing but the narrow space. Everything else blurred.

Too late Marc realized he'd misjudged the size of the gap. Instead of pushing the police car aside, the van slammed into the bridge rail. It climbed a couple of feet then slipped back down. He was stunned for only seconds. He shoved open the van door and climbed out, his only thought escape. A hand clamped down on his shoulder. At the touch, he lost control. He spun around and in a frenzy, began hitting and pummeling.

"Hey," shouted the man who'd grabbed him.

Marc dimly heard the man's repeated shouts. He kept up the barrage until he felt an explosion of pain behind his ear.

When he came to, he found his arms handcuffed behind his back. From somewhere came the crackling noise of a two-way radio. He winced when he opened his eyes into the glare of sunshine beaming through the side window of a police vehicle. He moved slightly. Pain filled his head and a wave of nausea rolled over him. His stomach heaved. He thought he'd vomit.

Chapter Six

Marie-Catherine met Henri at the door. "I'm so glad you're here." She looked over her shoulder at their father, slumped in a chair at the kitchen table. "It's been like this every night since Marc's arrest. He comes home from work, picks at his dinner and starts drinking." She spoke in a whisper. "He doesn't rant and thunder about 'the system,' or about Bourassa and the government, like he usually does. He doesn't talk at all."

"Not even about Marc?" Henri asked.

"No. And he ignores me and *Maman*. It's like we aren't even here. He just sits in that chair and drinks until he can't remain upright any longer. Then *Maman* and I need to get him from his chair, one of us on each side, and maneuver him into the bedroom, hoping the three of us don't end up on the floor."

An hour later, Henri sat alone with his father, whose gnarled fingers clutched a glass of dark red wine. At Henri's urging, his mother and Marie-Catherine had gone to bed.

"Papa, no more."

"Leave it," said his father, but he didn't argue when Henri took the nearly-empty bottle of wine and put it in the cupboard.

"It's not your fault, Papa." He wondered when his

father's hair had gotten so gray. It seemed like yesterday they'd teased him about the first silver threads appearing at his temples. Now it covered his head. "Papa. Did you hear me? It's not your fault."

"Whose fault is it, Henri?" He spoke as though Henri had posed an interesting question to which he would wait, as long as was necessary, for the answer.

"Marc is a grown man. He made his own decisions."

His father turned his bloodshot eyes on Henri. "You know what it's like in prison. You, of all people, know what it's like."

Henri nodded. "Yes, I do."

"And you don't think those bastard Anglos are responsible?" His father started to push out of the chair, but then had to sit down again.

Henri saw he'd waited too long for meaningful talk. The wine had already done its work. There was no point in telling his father that Marc had put himself in jail with his hatred and his determination to impose his beliefs on others.

"Let me help you to bed, Papa." He hooked his arm under his father's and eased him out of the chair. "You've got to stop drinking so much, Papa. It doesn't help, and *Maman* needs you. Marie-Catherine, too."

Henri half-led and half-carried his father to the bedroom. When he at last got his father undressed and into bed, the old man opened his eyes and looked up at his son. "What are you going to do about it, Henri? What are you going to do about your brother?"

Henri tossed in his bed, stewing on memories and regrets.

Marc wouldn't be getting out of prison for a long time, if ever. Henri could do nothing about it, even if he wanted to, which, regardless of his father's plea, he didn't. Besides, it wasn't like he'd never tried to get Marc to change.

He pushed Marc from his mind and turned his thoughts in a more pleasant direction. Claudia. He didn't deserve her forgiveness, but she'd readily given it. He'd gone to her apartment prepared to beg for another chance, but he'd barely begun when she'd put her fingers to his lips and told him to stop, told him that when people loved each other apologies weren't necessary.

But what kind of future did they have, when he had so little to offer her? Her background was a world away from his. Her parents belonged to the minority of French Canadians who, if not rich, were at least well off. She hadn't grown up in Westmount or Mount Royal, the bastions of the English-speaking elite, but in a neighborhood of large and comfortable homes on Cherrier Street. Henri had been there once, and he'd felt awkward and uncomfortable. Claudia said all that made no difference to their feelings about one another. He prayed she was right.

His brother crept into his thoughts once again. Had he missed something he could have said or done, something to make Marc give up whatever drove him? There hadn't been, of course. Why keep thinking about it? He determinedly rolled onto his side.

Everyone at the newspaper had welcomed him back, congratulating him, slapping him on the back. Even Julien told him how much he'd been missed. Then everyone went back to work, including Henri. From time-to-time, someone asked to interview him about his prison experience, about what happened, why he'd been there and what he'd hoped to achieve. There'd been a renewed flurry after Marc's arrest.

Mostly life went on as usual—researching, interviewing, and writing articles. And the newsroom hadn't changed, the phones still rang incessantly, typewriters still clattered, the presses still hummed.

Henri's last thought before finally falling asleep was that despite all that, some of the old zest seemed to be missing.

Something brought him out of a heavy slumber. He rubbed his hands over his eyes and face, trying to think where he was. It felt like he'd just gotten to sleep. The banging that must have awakened him started again.

"Henri. Open the door."

Henri shoved the covers back, sat up and reached for his jeans, lying in a heap on the floor. "Okay, okay, I'm coming," he muttered. The banging continued. "I'm coming," he said again, louder this time. The banging stopped. Hitching his jeans over his hips with a short hop, he crossed the room barefoot and opened the door. Maurault stood in front of him.

"Turn on your television set," Maurault said, brushing past him into the room.

"I don't have one."

"The radio then. Where is it?"

"By the bed. What's going on?"

"They've kidnapped James Cross."

Henri spun the dial. "Who?"

"The FLQ. Here, let me do that."

"I've got it." A burst of static blared into the room. "Who's James Cross?" Henri tried to place the name, but his brain felt dull and confused with the lack of sleep, not to mention the bizarreness of the scene. Then he got a mental image of the man. "What does the FLQ want with a British commercial attaché?" He twisted the dial until he heard the voice of a newscaster.

"They haven't said yet. Let's listen." Maurault sat on the edge of Henri's bed and Henri squatted on his haunches.

The newscaster repeated in hushed tones what he'd no doubt announced several times. "Early this morning, a group of armed men broke into the Mount Royal home of James Cross, a trade commissioner in the British consular office, and kidnapped him. According to Mrs. Cross, now under a doctor's care, when she answered the door, masked men pushed her aside and raced through the house to the bathroom at the top of the stairs, where her husband was shaving, preparing for work. The men grabbed her husband, put a sack over his head and forced him outside to a vehicle waiting in their driveway on Redpath Crescent. The authorities have not released the kidnappers' note, but we believe it may contain a list of demands from the FLQ."

"My God. This must be what Lanctot meant."

"Where's an ashtray?" said Maurault, looking around Henri's small room.

"In the bathroom," Henri said, distracted. "There's a coffee cup next to the sink. Use it." He moved to Maurault's position on the edge of the bed and listened to the radio announcer repeat the story. "No violence," he called out. "Lanctot told me not to worry—no bombs or explosives—no violence. I'd like to know his definition of the word." The toilet flushed and Maurault returned. Henri looked at him. "I wonder what their demands are going to be."

"You should be the first to know, not counting the police after they read the note left with Cross's wife," Maurault said around the cigarette between his lips.

"You're right." Henri shoved his feet into his shoes and pulled a shirt over his head at the same time. "He'll contact me at the office. We'd better get down there."

Speaking over the intensified newsroom clatter, Louise told him he had a phone call. Twenty-four hours had gone by. Henri had been about to give up when the phone rang.

"Come to Gabrielle's on Ste. Catherine Street," said a man whose voice Henri didn't recognize.

"How will I know you?" Henri asked, but the man had already hung up. Henri grabbed his jacket and stuck his head in Maurault's smoke-filled office. "It came—the call." He didn't wait for Maurault to respond, but bounded across the room, slapping a hand on Louise's desk as he passed, and shoved out the door.

Twenty minutes later, Henri entered Gabrielle's. He paused inside the door and looked around. The place wasn't empty, as it had been that day with Bunny. Office workers filled the tables, drinking a mid-morning coffee or having an early lunch. The buzz of talk, the blue haze of cigarette smoke and the aroma of coffee filled the air.

A bearded young man nodded to him from a table near the window. Henri crossed to him. "You called me?"

"Sit down," said the young man who looked to be no more than seventeen or eighteen. He had shoulder length brown hair that hung straight and flat from a center part. With his knee and foot, he nudged a chair a few inches away from the table. "You can call me Igor."

Henri sat, his back to the other customers. He tried to avert his eyes from Igor's acne-scarred cheeks, somewhat hidden by sparse, blond whiskers, and instead eyed the black cloth satchel slung over the young man's shoulder, across his chest. "You have something for me, Igor?"

"There," said Igor with a slight nod at the vacant chair still pushed up to their table. "Give it a few minutes after I leave."

Henri nodded agreement. The young man finished his coffee and stood. Henri turned in his seat to watch him move between the tables as he crossed the room, opened the door, and went outside. A moment later he saw the moving drifts of Igor's long hair, seemingly disembodied, float above the top of the red and white checked curtain covering the lower half of the coffee-shop's window. He reached under the table for the package Igor had left on the chair seat.

Inside the cab he hailed to take him back to the newspaper, Henri gripped the paper in both hands and read through the list of demands the FLQ made for the release of James Cross: publication in all Quebec newspapers of the enclosed political manifesto; release from jail of almost two dozen political prisoners; a chartered airplane to fly the kidnappers and their families to Cuba—$500,000 in gold bullion was to be placed on the airplane; the 450 drivers for Lapalme Service who'd lost their jobs in a labor dispute with the Post Office were to be given Federal jobs; "squealers" were to be identified by name and photo; and, finally, Bourassa should call off the manhunt for the kidnappers.

"They'll never agree," he told Maurault when he'd handed over the documents. "It's ludicrous to think it. Four of the men in jail, including my brother, have been accused or convicted of murder. They'll never let them go. What will the kidnappers do then? Kill Cross?"

Maurault flipped through the papers Henri had given him. "The government could negotiate…the FLQ has some public opinion on their side. Robert Bourassa has only been in office a few months. He's young. He doesn't have a firm hold yet."

"I don't think they will. And what if they don't? What then?"

Maurault shook his head. "I guess I wouldn't want to be in Cross's shoes."

"They say the government has until noon tomorrow." Outside Maurault's office Henri heard Louise give directions to a new part-timer hired to run errands, do odd jobs, and help with phone calls. Maurault was already gearing up. Briefly, Henri thought of his own introduction to *Le Journal Quotidien*. He gave himself a mental shake and returned to the present. "And what are we going to do with their list of demands? Publish it?"

"Damn right, I am."

Henri frowned. "I wonder why the police haven't released it yet. Or why someone else hasn't—Lanctot must have given the documents to others besides us."

"Doesn't matter. We'll publish this afternoon."

The kidnapping hit the front page of the New York Times along with newspapers around the world. In Montreal, the police arrested sixty people and that evening a French language radio station read the manifesto over the air.

"They're famous now," Henri told Claudia when the broadcast finished. "But do you think that will satisfy them?"

Claudia looked grim. "I don't know what they think having it read over the air will accomplish." They'd just finished a quick dinner of soup and sandwiches at the apartment she shared with a roommate.

Henri helped carry dirty dishes from the table to the tiny kitchen. In ways, it felt as though they'd never been apart. "They want it read on all the stations. They want as many people as possible to read it and hear it. Actually, once you get past all the rhetoric about sold-out politicians and bankers, you have to give Lanctot credit. The manifesto does a pretty good job of identifying the problems of French Canadians."

Henri was right. Over the next several days, Quebecers, used to muttering under their collective breaths, now commented on how right it felt to have their grievances aired aloud.

"Who can deny there are hovels in the East End and château in Westmount?" he overheard a woman in the supermarket say to the man ringing up her purchases. "Who can deny forty percent of the country's unemployed are from Quebec, with the majority being French Canadian, including my nephew and brother-in-law?"

Henri set his jar of instant coffee on the counter while the cashier, nodding his head in agreement, put a can of peas and a box of cereal into the woman's knotted string market bag. "You're right, Nadine." He handed her the bag. "It's about time something's done about it, too."

"They're good boys," the woman said, putting the straps of her handbag over her arm and lifting her shopping bag off the counter. "They mean well."

Good boys. How often Henri heard those same words. Eating a sandwich at a downtown lunch counter he listened to a gray-haired couple sitting at a nearby table. "Most of them are good boys," said the woman. "And from good families, they say."

"I've heard that, too," said the man. "They're just young—a bunch of idealistic kids."

Henri shook his head as he walked back to the newspaper. Do these people ever read a newspaper, watch television, or listen to the radio? Idealistic kids don't bomb, kidnap, and threaten to murder. Surely, they can't hold the public's sympathy for long.

Chapter Seven

Blanchard's manicured hands rested on the table between them. "Do you want me to represent you?" His face and voice were without expression.

Marc slouched in his chair. He shrugged.

"You have to say it. Do you want me to represent you?"

"Yeah," said Marc, although he knew Blanchard could do nothing for him. "Might as well."

"You haven't heard the news. An FLQ cell kidnapped a man named James Cross, a British commercial attaché, and is holding him captive."

"Which cell?"

"They call themselves the Liberation Cell."

"Jacques Lanctot and Marc Carbonneau." For the first time in weeks Marc felt an interest in something other than himself. "Cab drivers. I've worked with them—we were on strike together last year."

Blanchard nodded his head. "You'll be interested in hearing about one of their demands." His eyes never leaving Marc's face, Blanchard paused a moment, like he was savoring the news.

Marc began to lose what little patience he had. "What?"

"The release of twenty-three political prisoners. Including you."

Marc sat up straight. "You're shitting me."

"I'm not."

"When?" The word came out in a whisper.

"They're negotiating. The first deadline was forty-eight hours, but now they've extended it to midnight tonight."

Marc took a deep breath. The pressure on his lungs eased, his heart slowed. "You mean I could get out of here tonight?"

Blanchard raised a warning hand. "Hold on. I don't think anything will happen that fast. These things take time. But if it works out, are you willing to go to Cuba?"

"Are you kidding? Shit yes. I'd go anywhere to get out of here."

Chapter Eight

Henri had wondered how long the FLQ could hold the public's sympathy. The answer: five days. Just hours after the Justice Minister gave a radio address claiming James Cross's kidnappers were blackmailers and the government wouldn't deal with blackmailers, the FLQ kidnapped Quebec's Labor Minister, Pierre Laporte.

"What in the hell is happening?" Henri shouted over the telephone. "Who's next? Pierre Trudeau?"

Maurault voice was just as strained. "Christ, Henri, don't yell at me. Why didn't you know about it? You're the man with the contacts."

Henri closed his eyes and rubbed a hand over his face. "You're right. I don't know why I should be yelling at you. Sorry."

"So, what do you know about Laporte?" said Maurault, sounding mollified.

"A bit. I interviewed him a year or so ago. But I'm on it. If Julien is there, have him do some more research for me—especially on the personal side. I'll call in later so he can brief me."

He phoned Claudia and told her they'd have to cancel their plans.

"But it's Saturday and you promised we could drive up to the mountains while the weather holds. I've made arrangements to use my parents' car."

"Claudia, I'm sorry, but I don't have time to explain. Turn on your radio and you'll know why all that's not possible." He glanced at his watch. "Look, I have to go. I'll try to call you later, okay? Maybe we can do something tonight."

Henri headed to City Hall, where he hoped to find out more. The building may have been a beehive of activity, but government officials, including Montreal's loquacious mayor, weren't talking to reporters.

After giving up on getting anyone inside to talk with him, Henri waited in the parking lot near City Hall on the off-chance the mayor, who made a fetish of driving himself, would show up. Even so, his eyebrows shot up when the man approached alone and unprotected.

"Mayor Drapeau, can you tell me what you know about Pierre Laporte?" Henri asked as soon as the man was close enough to hear. "Who has him? What are their demands?"

Drapeau unlocked his car door before responding to Henri's question. "This is a heinous crime. The perpetrators will be punished."

"Has there been contact? Do you know what they're demanding?"

Drapeau shook his head. "The provincial government is handling all negotiations."

Henri tried to keep his exasperation from showing. "But, mayor, aren't they keeping you apprised of what's going on?"

Drapeau's tone turned defensive. "Of course they're keeping me informed, but the contents of our discussions are for them to divulge to the press, not me."

Henri tried a different approach. "I understand there's a problem between the RCMP and the Montreal Police over who has jurisdiction. Can you fill me and our readers in?"

Drapeau shook his head again. He removed his charcoal gray fedora, threw it on the passenger's seat and got into his car. "I have nothing more to tell you." He slammed his door closed and started the engine, then backed the big black car out of its parking space and drove away.

Henri watched as the car disappeared into Saturday afternoon traffic. *Nothing more to tell you, he says. Damn it, he didn't tell me anything.* Well, at least he still had some FLQ contacts. Maybe one of them would be more forthcoming. He whistled to a passing taxi. It pulled over. He climbed into the back seat and gave the driver the name of a tavern off Pi IX Boulevard.

Henri and Maurault went out to grab something to eat before returning to the newspaper to plan for the following week. Henri took a swallow of beer. He picked up his sandwich then put it down, too keyed up to eat.

"No one even planned it. Last night on their car radio, four guys heard the Liberation Cell had granted another extension on Cross's life. They didn't think the negotiations were getting anywhere." Henri leaned forward. "According to what I've been told, the men planned this mostly on the spur of the moment. They got Laporte's name out of the phone book then called and talked to his wife, like they were party workers or something." He took another swallow of beer and wiped the foam from his upper lip with the back of his hand. "When they got there, Laporte was playing football on the lawn with some kid. His nephew, I think. They got out of the car and took him—forced him into the back seat and drove off with him." He shook his head in disbelief. "They had an appointment. Can you believe it? Jesus."

"Do you know who did it?"

Henri looked around to make sure no one was listening. "Like I said, there were four of them—or maybe only three. My contact was kind of muddled about that. A student from the University of Montreal, a couple of brothers, Paul and Jacques Rose—I've met them—and maybe another guy."

"What demands are they making?"

"So far as I know, the same as were made for Cross."

"And assuming the results are the same—the government won't capitulate—then what?"

"The Rose brothers are way out there, especially Paul. I don't trust him." Henri shoved the plate with his uneaten sandwich away, shaking his head. "If the government doesn't negotiate…I don't know, but whatever happens, it won't be good."

There'd been only a few minutes to call Claudia the day before, and he'd have little time for her in the next twenty-four hours. Maurault wanted a special edition ready for Monday afternoon, one that featured every bit of news they could pull together on the FLQ, from the first *communiqué*

announcing its founding on March 9, 1963 to the present. Everyone had a piece of it.

Church bells tolled throughout the city, as they did every Sunday in Montreal. Henri interviewed people on the phone or met them at coffee shops or on street corners, in parking lots or empty hallways—wherever anyone would agree to meet him—trying to find a way through, over or under the wall of silence the government had erected around the negotiations. By the end of the day he was frustrated and exhausted.

Reluctantly, he called Claudia once more and begged off for another day. "I'm afraid I wouldn't be much of a conversationalist. I'm so tired right now I don't think I could tell you my name without taking a minute to think about it. And then I'd likely fall asleep before I answered."

Claudia chuckled. "Okay, okay. Go home and get a good night's rest."

"I'll make it up to you. I promise."

"You better. I love you."

His voice rough with emotion, he answered. "I love you, too." His eyes burned with unshed tears as he placed the receiver back in its cradle.

Robert Bourassa and a special task force from the provincial government quickly converged on Montreal from Quebec City, the provincial capital. They set up temporary headquarters in the Queen Elizabeth Hotel. One of Henri's contacts told him that Bourassa wanted a meeting with all the opposition leaders. He headed to the hotel to see if he could find out anything.

Expecting a crowd of reporters and policemen in the lobby, he was surprised to see only a woman in a green and brown uniform standing behind the reception desk talking to the similarly clad bell captain, and an old man sitting in a chair, reading *The Montreal Star*, a cup of coffee on the table at his elbow. Other than that, the lobby was empty.

Henri crossed over to the elevators and pushed the up button. He glanced over his shoulder, still half-expecting to be told to stop, but no one hailed him. He pushed the button several times, tapping his foot at the elevators' slowness. Two of them appeared to be stuck on the fourth floor. Then the sweep hand above the third elevator began to swing: fifth floor, fourth floor, third floor, second. Finally, the door slid opened. He waited for a middle-aged couple to get off, then stepped inside.

When the elevator door slid open on the second floor, Henri stuck his head out. Nothing except for a woman pushing a laundry cart down the hall. Same thing on the third floor. On the fourth floor, he hit pay dirt. When the door slid back, three armed policemen stood facing the elevator. Along the hall, uniformed men were stationed in front of every door.

"State your business," one of the three men said.

Henri decided to brazen it out. "Henri Morais, *Le Journal Quotidien,* here to see Premier Bourassa."

The man smirked. "Get the fuck out of here." The other two took a half-step toward Henri.

He stood his ground. "I just have a few questions. The people have a right to know what's going on."

"Get out. Don't make me say it a third time." The man's companions moved in closer. Henri had no choice.

He stepped back into the elevator. The man leaned inside and pushed the button for the lobby. "Don't try it again."

When Henri stepped off the elevator on the ground floor, he recognized a reporter from *La Presse*. "Fourth floor," he said as the man stepped past him.

Henri crossed the lobby to several upholstered chairs facing a big fireplace. He chose one where he could keep watch on the elevator. The old man was gone.

When the *La Presse* reporter came back a few minutes later Henri waved for him to come over.

"Looks like a fortress up there," the reporter said, easing down onto the chair next to Henri's.

Henri nodded. "Yeah. I'd sure like to be a fly on the wall." The two men spoke for several minutes, until they were interrupted by the sound of the elevator dinging as its doors slid open. Henri straightened, surprised by what they revealed. René Lévesque, leader of the newly formed *Parti Quebecois*, was surrounded by several other men and a woman, all of them speaking at once.

Henri sprang up from his chair and crossed the lobby. "Mr. Lévesque," he called. "Can I talk to you a minute?"

"Me, too," said the *La Presse* reporter, sprinting after Henri.

Lévesque and his companions didn't appear to have heard. They continued talking rapid-fire as they walked across the lobby. Henri and the *La Presse* reporter chased after them.

"Mr. Lévesque," called Henri again, just before the group reached the door to the street. "Mr. Lévesque, I'm Henri Morais, a reporter with *Le Journal Quotidien*. This is

James Cartier from *La Presse*. Can we ask you a couple of questions?"

Lévesque looked at his watch. "I don't have much time. Two minutes, no more." He pulled a box from his coat pocket, took out a cigarette and put it in the corner of his mouth.

"Have you been to see Premier Bourassa?"

"I have."

"Can you tell us what you discussed?"

Lévesque talked around the unlit cigarette. "I have taken it on myself to gather a number of like-minded individuals," he said, indicating his companions, most of whom Henri recognized. "We wanted to tell the Premier with one voice that if he is looking for a non-violent solution to this dilemma, he can count on our complete support."

"Did he welcome your support, Mr. Lévesque?" said Henri, scribbling on his notepad.

"I believe he did," said Lévesque, taking the cigarette from between his lips then putting it back. One of his companions pointed to his watch and Lévesque nodded.

"Is there any movement in the negotiations?" said *La Presse* reporter.

"I'm not at liberty to talk about the negotiations, but I will say Ottawa appears to have the fearful impression the FLQ is a huge organization with thousands of rifles and machine guns in their possession as well as enough plastique to blow up the heart of Montreal. We know that is not so, in both the scale of the organization and its intentions."

Lévesque ignored another attempt by one of the men in his entourage to hurry him along.

"And I do state clearly here and now, the negotiations and the resolution must be from Quebec, for the people of Quebec, not from Ottawa." He wagged his finger at both Henri and the *La Presse* reporter. "You put that in your papers." He wrapped a scarf around his neck and buttoned his coat. "Now, gentlemen, I'm afraid I've given you all the time I have."

"One more question," said Henri. "Please. Have they heard anything more from Pierre Laporte since receiving the letter his kidnappers allowed him to send?"

"No, sadly they have not." Lévesque's face was grim. "Or at least, not as far as I'm aware." Lévesque took another step toward the door then turned back to Henri. "Glad to see you're putting your education to work, Mr. Morais. Reporting is a good way to get started in politics."

Henri had briefly interviewed Lévesque while still a student at the University of Montreal, but he didn't have time to be flattered that the man appeared to remember him. After Lévesque and his companions left, Henri raced back to the paper. When he got there Louise told him his contact from James Cross's kidnappers had just called.

"He said you should meet him at the same place. He said he'll wait twenty minutes for you."

Henri glanced at his watch. An hour to deadline. He felt tempted to skip going to Gabrielle's and concentrate on writing about his meeting with Lévesque, but decided he didn't dare, even though he guessed meeting with Igor would result in nothing more than another long-winded communiqué containing the same rhetoric and threats he'd read before.

Igor had tied his hair back, but otherwise he looked just as he had the last time they'd met, down to the black cloth satchel.

The police had identified Lanctot as a suspect in James Cross's kidnapping, but they hadn't released any other information. Henri didn't know if he'd been arrested or was simply lying low. He was more interested in the health and well-being of Cross. "Have you seen James Cross?" Henri whispered. "Is he okay?"

Igor shook his head. "I don't know. I just carry the mail."

"Right," said Henri. "You don't know anything about Pierre Laporte either, I suppose."

Back in the office Henri wrote and re-wrote the article about his brief and informative interview with René Lévesque, tossing half-finished pages on the floor and jamming fresh sheets into the typewriter in rapid order. Maurault extended the deadline fifteen minutes. Henri pulled the final sheet of paper from the typewriter and scanned over what he'd written. Seconds later, he threw the finished copy on Maurault's desk. "Done."

"What about your contact with Lanctot? Anything there?"

"It's in the article—another communiqué, another extension. And they seem to resent people thinking they kidnapped Cross for the money."

After work, Henri boarded a bus for home. Claudia planned to have dinner with her parents that evening, and had an early meeting the following morning. They'd made tentative arrangements for dinner and a movie the following night, though with all that was going on Henri doubted anything would go as planned.

Two trucks filled with soldiers rumbled past. Henri frowned when he saw soldiers had been posted in front of the government printing office. On a Sunday afternoon when they were kids, he and Marc had decorated the building with slogans. They'd even managed to paint a couple of slogans on the statue in front of the building—General James Wolfe astride a horse. To Marc and Henri and many other French Canadians, Wolfe symbolized their hatred of the English-speaking establishment. Henri shook his head at the memory, wondering why he and his brother hadn't been playing baseball or soccer with their friends. And he wondered why soldiers now seemed to be guarding the building.

Another truck filled with soldiers passed. Henri followed it with a puzzled eye until the bus turned a corner, onto the street where his boardinghouse stood. He reached for the cord to signal he wanted off. As soon as he unlocked the door to his room, he crossed to his bed and switched on the radio. He was just in time to hear a repeat of Prime Minister Trudeau ordering out the Army, to protect public buildings and senior government officials in Ottawa and Quebec.

"When will it stop?" Claudia had asked the other night. Henri wondered the same.

That night he tossed and turned thinking about James Cross and Pierre Laporte, the agonies their families must be going through, and he wondered what anyone could have done to prevent the kidnappings. Probably nothing; their selection had been random. And unlike him, Cross and Laporte hadn't knowingly made a hash of everything.

Henri had no doubt that if he'd cooperated with the warden and Jeffers, the bombing at the shoe factory would never have happened. Marie-Catherine would still have perfect eyesight. Her friend would be alive.

His sister knew that he could have prevented it, but hadn't because of his misguided ideas about family loyalty and his ambivalence about the FLQ. 'Tell Henri he's off the hook,' Jeffers had told her—which showed how little the man knew about anything.

The next morning, Henri felt dopey with exhaustion from his sleepless night. With no place to sit on the crowded bus, he stood in the aisle and gripped the back of a seat. An Army Land Rover swung around them. The driver looked no more than nineteen or twenty, and the two men in the back, maybe twenty-two. The three mirrored the ages of most in the FLQ. Only eight or nine years their senior, Henri felt much older; he guessed the battle for independence had made them all feel older than their years.

A woman walking along the sidewalk stopped to stare after the Land Rover, her face curious and slightly hostile. Something about her reminded him of Bunny. The slip of paper she'd given him was in his room. He should call her. She might not know of Marc's arrest.

Apprehension and fear hung in the air like wood smoke, made even more toxic by the inflammatory rhetoric of some of Canada's elected leaders. On a small black and white television in Maurault's office, Henri and his editor watched Pierre Trudeau respond to critics regarding his use of the military.

"What do you say to people who call this a military occupation?" asked a reporter.

"There are a lot of bleeding hearts around who just don't like to see people with helmets and guns," Trudeau said. "All I can say is go on and bleed. But it is more important to keep law and order in the society than to be worried about weak-kneed people who don't like the looks of..."

The reporter interrupted. "We're talking about taking away civil liberties here. How far are you prepared to go with that?"

"Well, just watch me."

Henri jumped to his feet. "What the hell is he trying to do? Start a civil war?"

Maurault snorted derisively. "You missed seeing the Premier of Ontario. He claims that terrorism in Quebec has already turned into a general war. He says the time has come to rise up and fight—compared to him, Trudeau's remarks are mild."

Henri shook his head in disgust. "And they call themselves leaders."

Chapter Nine

Marc lay on his stomach, his face turned to the wall. He'd lost track of the number of days since Blanchard told him there might be a chance he and the other FLQ prisoners would get out, days in which Marc had gone from eagerness to anxiety to rage, banging against the bars, shouting, yelling. Finally, apathy set in.

Blanchard hadn't been back to see him, had sent no message, and Marc hadn't heard from anyone else, not even that pig, Lieutenant Jeffers. He'd been forgotten. His mind seemed fixed on a single refrain: *I'll never get out of here.*

The shuffling sound of many feet approached down the gallery. A moment later the key turned in the door of his cell. He didn't raise his head from his bunk.

"Rise and shine, Morais," the guard said from the cell door.

Marc ignored him.

"You don't get off the fuckin' bunk and get out here, I'm comin' in," the man said.

Marc pushed himself up on one elbow. "What do you want?"

"I want you to get your ass out here and fall in. It's time to go out in the yard."

Marc got up and walked out of his cell. It seemed easier than resisting. Somewhere along the way, he couldn't remember exactly when, he'd gotten over his fear of being locked up. He didn't care now if he went outside or stayed in his cell. What was the difference? Either way, he was trapped.

In the yard, the men stood near the building, trying to keep out of the wind. It was cold, even for mid-October. Marc glanced up at the flat, gray clouds filling the sky. It would rain soon. Or snow. One of the other men, Jason something, offered him a cigarette, but Marc shook his head. The man, a boy really, lit one himself, shielding the flame with his cupped hand. "You hear about that guy, Laporte?" he asked once his cigarette was lit.

"Yeah," said Marc, wishing he'd accepted the cigarette offer. "I heard."

"What do you think it does for our chances to get out of here?"

Marc shrugged. He didn't want to think about it.

"Has Blanchard talked to you?"

"A while back. Why? Has something changed?" But Marc knew nothing had changed. They were all talk. Laporte's kidnappers would do the same thing as the ones who'd kidnapped Cross. They'd fumble around, caving in and granting extensions, just long enough for the police to find them. That would be the end of it. None of them had the guts to follow through on their threats.

"Nah, nothing's changed I guess. I was hoping you knew something."

Marc shook his head and leaned against the wall again. After a while the guard let them back inside.

Within an hour of returning to his cell, a guard once more appeared outside Marc's door.

"You got a visitor, Morais."

"Who?"

"Don't know," said the guard, turning the key in the lock. "I'm just here to collect you."

When Marc entered the visitor's room, Henri sat at a table, waiting for him. He felt an unexpected surge of gladness at the sight of his brother, but the feeling was fleeting. Before he reached Henri's side, the hopeless gloom he'd been living in returned.

"Hey, little brother," he said, trying to put some of the old devil-take-it bravado into his tone. "What's up?"

"Hey, Marc." Henri's voice was non-committal. "How's it going?"

"How do you think? Not so long ago, you were the one inside." Marc pulled out a chair and sat across from his brother. "The difference is, you knew you'd get out."

Henri nodded, but his eyes failed to meet Marc's.

"What's wrong? What are you not telling me?"

"What's wrong? Well, there's just a shit-pot of stuff going on."

"What about the negotiations?" Marc was unwilling to be distracted from the single thing that held his interest. He didn't take his eyes from Henri's. "Isn't that why you're here? What's going on?"

"Bourassa made a statement."

Marc leaned forward, his forearms on the table. "What did he say?"

Henri shifted in his chair. "It was pretty ambiguous, but it sounds like he might be interested in negotiating."

"Jesus," breathed Marc. Closing his eyes, he let his head sink back.

Henri shifted in his seat again. "I don't think you should build any hopes on Bourassa, Marc. The temper of the country is grim. There are tanks in the streets of Montreal, for Christ sake. I don't think Bourassa will get the chance to negotiate—I think Trudeau will take over. I think he already has."

"But still…" Marc closed his ears to what his brother was saying about Trudeau. He only wanted to think about getting out. "How much longer do you think it will take them to do something? How much longer will I be left to rot in this fucking hole?"

Henri shook his head. He said nothing.

Chapter Ten

Marie-Catherine sat beside her father on what once had been Marc's cot, and what now, with pillows against the wall, served as a sofa. The television flickered in the corner where the Beav found himself in one of his weekly predicaments, looking for help from his big brother, Wally. The French words he spoke didn't match the movement of his lips. *It's like my whole life, disjointed and surreal,* she thought. *Words don't match actions. Actions don't match words.*

At least her father had stopped drinking himself into oblivion every night, but he hadn't returned to his old self. She almost missed the thundering diatribes she'd grown up on. Politicians, Federal and Provincial alike, were all the same to her father, receiving his contempt in equal measure. According to her father, none of them did enough for French Canadians. Nothing escaped his notice, either…at least nothing had escaped his notice.

"How are things going at work, Papa? With the union, I mean."

Her father shrugged, not taking his eyes away from the television screen. "About the same. Nothing's changed."

"No trouble since you settled the strike? They haven't done anything to those who were on the picket lines?"

Her father shook his head.

"Have you been to see Marc, Papa?"

Again, her father merely shook his head.

Her mother came out of the bedroom, where she'd gone to rest after dinner. "Don't talk about Marc. He is no longer our son."

"*Maman*, you don't mean that."

"I do mean it. Don't mention his name in this house again."

"But, *Maman*..."

Marie-Catherine struggled once more with telling her parents the truth of the previous summer and her part in Marc's arrest, telling Lieutenant Jeffers where she and Marc had taken the cache of explosives and guns they'd brought to Montreal from North Carolina.

She wanted desperately to confess what she'd done to her parents, but Henri cautioned her not to. "It might ease your conscience, but it would only end up making *Maman* and Papa feel worse."

Henri was right. Still... No, she couldn't. She stood. "Guess I'll go to bed."

Like the night before and every night since Marc's arrest, Marie-Catherine had trouble falling asleep.

She brooded about school and wondered when it would get easier. With the start of the new term she'd enrolled at UQAM. However, she'd limited her classes to one titled French Women in History and a math class. Instead of sharing an apartment as she'd done before, she lived at home and took the city bus to school. She felt like everyone stared at her though. Who could blame them when half of her face looked like a road map?

Her former roommate, Roseanne, was the only friend she felt comfortable talking with, and even Roseanne didn't understand, couldn't understand, how it felt when she raised her hand in class and everyone turned to look at her, all polite, pretending they didn't notice her face.

One day she and Roseanne had seen two friends from the year before walking toward them, their heads huddled together. Certain they were talking about her, Marie-Catherine had turned on her heel and fled in the opposite direction, leaving Roseanne in mid-sentence. Roseanne later told her she needed to stop being overly sensitive.

"Why would they be talking about you? Don't you think people have other things that interest them?"

"You're right. I'm being foolish," Marie-Catherine said. She tried to do better, but she was still self-conscious.

She thought about Roger. She missed him. She hadn't seen him since the day in the hospital, when she'd been surprised to look up and see him standing in the doorway to her room. Joy had leaped into her heart and she knew it had to be written on her face. The joy hadn't lasted.

"I'm sorry about the accident." He wouldn't look at her. She sensed his discomfort, but hadn't known what to say. "Are you going back to school in the fall?" he finally asked.

"I hope so. Henri talked to the dean. He said I could go back." Marie-Catherine tried to smile, hoping to put him at ease.

"I'm transferring to Laval," he'd said.

She'd tried to keep her voice neutral. "Oh. Well, your family will be glad to have you nearer home."

Then he was gone. He'd sent her a card, but she hadn't answered back.

She wouldn't cry, she vowed once more, punching up her pillow and rolling onto her side. And she wouldn't quit. She owed it to Maman and Papa. She owed it to Henri. She owed it to herself. Most of all, she owed it to Dora.

Chapter Eleven

From somewhere not far away, a dog howled, the sound lonely and forlorn in the early hours of the morning. Then Henri heard the sirens. They seemed to come from all corners of the city. His first thought was that a large fire must have broken out somewhere. He threw back the covers, got up and crossed to the window. He raised the blind and scanned the horizon, looking for a telltale glow. He saw nothing. He returned to his bed, but between the dog's howls and the sirens, sleep was impossible.

"What the hell," he muttered, sitting up and swinging his feet to the floor once again. "Might as well get up." He felt around for his shoes and at the same time flipped on the radio. Static-filled music, something by Neil Diamond, played into the room. He turned it off.

Still in his underwear, with his feet shoved in and squashing down the backs of his shoes, he stood and shuffled into the bathroom. He switched the light on and looked at himself in the mirror before splashing cold water on his face. He turned the electric burner on under the teapot and a few minutes later, a steaming cup of coffee in his hand, he sat on the edge of his bed. A siren sounded on the street in front of his building then faded away into the distance. He looked at the clock beside the radio; not even five.

Something's up, he thought. He put the cup down and started pulling on his clothes.

The lighted interior of the bus illuminated the driver and half-a-dozen early-morning commuters when it swung around the corner and pulled to a stop in front of Henri. It was still dark when he arrived at the newspaper office, but Maurault was there ahead of him.

"What's going on?" Henri asked. "There are police cars all over the place."

Maurault looked up when Henri entered his office. "They're arresting people. Hundreds of people. Rounding them up and taking them in. No arrest warrants, no search warrants, no nothing. They're picking up anyone they even think might have a connection to the FLQ."

"You're talking martial law." Henri, scowled—never had a Canadian government taken such an action in peacetime. "I can't believe Bourassa did it—he hasn't been in office long enough. It's Trudeau. No one else has the balls."

Maurault leaned back in his chair and lit a cigarette, probably about his tenth of the day, Henri thought. By now, they weren't the only ones in the newsroom. A couple of pressmen were getting coffee and several other reporters and staff had begun trickling in.

"Do you know where they're taking everybody? I should be there."

Maurault blew out a stream of smoke. "Wherever there's an available cell."

Henri nodded. "I'll head for Jeffers' precinct. You can bet he'll be in the thick of things."

"Take my car." Maurault fished the keys from his pocket. "And stay out of Jeffers' way. I don't want you getting yourself arrested again. And keep in touch."

Henri headed toward the door. "Right. I'll give you a call in an hour. Maybe less."

"Take a camera!"

Henri grabbed one off a desk.

On the way to the precinct, Henri passed at least four police cars heading in the opposite direction, all traveling at high speed, sirens blasting. He had to swerve to avoid being hit as one swung into his lane to pass a taxi.

"Jesus! Watch it."

His breath fogged the rolled-up window.

The sky had lightened and streetlights were blinking off by the time Henri neared his destination. He parked on a side street two blocks away from the precinct, locked the car and pocketed the key. As he approached the red brick building where he had been held captive just nine months earlier, a police car slid past him and pulled to a stop in front of the entrance.

Jeffers opened the passenger door and pushed his bulk out of the front seat, then opened the rear door. At the same time Williams, apparently still Jeffers' partner, opened the door on the driver's side and climbed out. Henri brought the camera to his eye and started shooting while Jeffers and Williams dragged three people in handcuffs out of the back seat and hustled them inside the building. He ran to catch up.

Henri walked into the precinct and found what looked and sounded like bedlam. The place was jammed with people, many in handcuffs, and everyone seemed to be talking at once. Among them he recognized a couple of professors from the University of Montreal and one from McGill, several students, and activists. In the past few years, there had been an explosion of French Canadian artists, singers, and poets. That group, too, was well represented in the crowded room.

Henri approached a well-known jazz singer, surprisingly standing alone. "I'm Henri Morais, a reporter for the *Le Journal Quotidien*. May I ask you a few questions?" He needed to raise his voice to be heard above the din.

The woman nodded.

"Why have they arrested you, do you know?"

"Do they need a reason?"

Her eyes glared at Henri as though he was to blame for her being there. Henri said nothing. She turned her head and bit her lower lip. When she turned back, her eyes were less hostile.

"They came into the nightclub. They didn't even let me finish my song, but stormed onto the stage and arrested me."

"Why?"

"They said I had known connections to the FLQ, which is a lie. If by some chance they are correct, the connections are unknown to me. I have no time for politics."

The woman had nothing more to say. Henri interviewed others, but they were equally puzzled as to why they'd been arrested. Many had been awakened by pounding on the door. No one was given an explanation. Two admitted to sympathizing with the FLQ's goals, signing a few petitions, or marching in a demonstration. Nothing more. All were French-Canadian.

"My wife was holding our three-year-old daughter, who was crying and holding out her arms to me," the professor from McGill said. "She'll probably never get over being awakened in the night and having her papa hauled off in handcuffs." The man's cheeks reddened as he grew more agitated. "I teach history, for God's sake, not sedition."

Henri searched for Pelletier, the man he and Marc had met the night he'd gone over to the FLQ, but didn't see him. He'd described the meeting in one of the articles he'd written, though without identifying Pelletier by name as the man who 'paid the bills.' Jeffers had grilled him on it, but Henri had said he had no proof and it would only be his word. He'd ignored Jeffers' snort of derision. Still, Pelletier should have been on someone's list. Maybe he was being held at another precinct.

Interspersed among the handcuffed prisoners and uniformed police were a few reporters Henri knew. He nodded to the one he'd met at the Queen Elizabeth Hotel several days before, the reporter from *La Presse*, and made his way through the crowd to the man's side.

"What do you make of this?"

James Cartier shook his head and shrugged. "I wonder how long they're going to let us stay."

It was Henri's turn to shrug. Frankly, he was surprised they'd let reporters into the building in the first place.

His eyes narrowed as he gazed around the room. "I can't believe they're doing this. Most of these people have done nothing but march in a demonstration or sign a petition, if that."

"Yeah, I know. Do you recognize those people Jeffers brought in?" Jeffers and Williams had the three from the car lined in front of the tall desk in the center of the room.

Henri knew the one in the middle by his long dirty blond hair and the ever-present black cloth satchel he carried over his shoulder: his contact with Lanctot. "No. Do you?"

"No," Cartier said. Henri wondered if he lied, too.

The level of noise went up when Igor started to shout. "I don't have to tell you fascist pigs anything. *Vive le Québec libre. Vive le Québec libre.*" Others in the room took up the chant, which soon turned into a roar. "*Vive le Québec libre.*"

Jeffers yelled "Shut up," clipping Igor on the ear with the edge of his hand. Igor looked stunned and Jeffers jerked his handcuffed hands higher up on his back, then goose-stepped the boy through the door in the back of the room. The crowd didn't stop chanting.

Remembering his own treatment at Jeffers' hands, Henri's stomach clenched. He decided he'd seen enough. "I'm going back to the shop," he told Cartier. "You?"

"Not yet."

A policeman walked in from outside just as Henri reached the door.

"Who said you could bring a camera in here?" The man grabbed the camera from Henri's hand.

Stifling words of protest, Henri watched in frustration as the man exposed all the film before handing the empty camera back.

"Now get out of here."

"Bastard," muttered Henri, as the door swung closed behind him.

Driving back downtown, with the unbroken wail of sirens in his ears, Henri passed truckload after truckload of armed soldiers. According to the government's announcement, more than seventy-five hundred troops had been ordered to Montreal, not to mention the ten thousand policemen already in place. *So why don't we feel safer?*

Later, once again sitting with Maurault in his office, Henri listened to Prime Minister Trudeau explain to the public that Canada would not deal with the kidnappers of James Cross or Pierre LaPorte.

He then defended the *War Measures Act*, "to permit the full weight of Government to be brought quickly to bear on all those persons advocating or practicing violence as a means of achieving political ends."

Henri put his head in his hands, shaking it at the same time. "That's crazy. There are so few real FLQ members— and even fewer taking part in these kidnappings." He looked up. "Trudeau is using the FLQ to terrorize Quebecers into rejecting the idea of separatism. That's what's behind this— he isn't afraid of the FLQ, he's afraid of losing Quebec. But like Lévesque said, Quebec is already a nation, a nation of language and culture. If they'd let us go, there'd be no need for all this."

The Prime Minister wasn't through. He concluded his address by telling the nation that the *War Measures Act* suspended the *Canadian Bill of Rights*.

That night, Henri covered his ears with a pillow to block out the blare of sirens. He dreamed a police car slid to a stop in front of his building. Jeffers and Williams piled out and rushed across the sidewalk, inside the building and up the stairs to his room.

He heard pounding on his door and thought it part of the dream, but when he came fully awake, whoever was outside still knocked.

He pulled on his jeans and crossed to the door. "Who is it?"

"Henri, it's me."

Henri turned the lock and pulled open the door. "Hey. What are you doing here so early?" He opened the door wider.

"It's ten-thirty," said Marie-Catherine, walking past him into the small room.

"Oh. Well, it's Saturday." He looked around for a semi -clean shirt. "You didn't answer my question. What brings you here?"

"I thought maybe we could talk." She picked some papers off his chair, put them on the desk and sat.

"Sure. Hold on while I finish getting dressed. We can go get some breakfast."

"I don't have to ask if you saw Trudeau's speech last night," she said. "What did you think of it?"

"What could anyone think? We're living in a police state now," he said, pulling a shirt over his head. "You know they're never going to let Marc go?" He looked at her closely, trying to gauge how she would react to this.

She drew a deep breath. "Yes, I know."

He nodded. "What did Papa have to say about Trudeau's speech?"

"Papa was curiously quiet. He didn't say very much at all. Mostly he just stared at the television set."

"That doesn't sound like Papa." Henri sat on the side of the bed and tied his shoes.

"No."

He looked up. "What about *Maman*? Does she realize Marc will have to stay in jail?"

"I don't know, Henri. Neither one of them is talking."

He stood and put his hand on his sister's shoulder. "It must be hard on you, M.C. I'm sorry."

"I'm okay." She smiled, even as tears glistened. "You'd better hurry up, though. I need some coffee."

Half-an-hour later they sat across from each other in a café near *Le Journal Quotidien*. Henri didn't feel like eating, but he knew he'd better order something. It was bound to be another long day. "I'll have the scrambled eggs and sausage," he said when the waitress came to take their orders. "And coffee."

"I'll just have coffee and toast," Marie-Catherine told the woman, who winked familiarly at Henri and said she'd be right back with their drinks.

Henri wondered how things could appear so normal, as if what happened outside on the streets, the arrests, the still-wailing sirens, was the sort of thing they always woke up to. Marie-Catherine stared at the checked tablecloth. She obviously had something on her mind.

"Well?" He looked at her, his eyebrows raised in question.

"Yeah," she said, and took a deep breath, but went no further.

"Spill it."

"I want you to take me to see Marc."

Surprised, Henri sat back in his chair; he hadn't been expecting this. "Why? Why do you want to see him now?"

"I want to see him because he's my brother. And because I need to."

Henri shook his head. "I don't think that's such a good idea. It's a horrible place in a cruddy neighborhood. I don't think Marc would want you to see him there. Especially now."

"But I need to talk to him, Henri. Please take me."

Always reluctant to deny his sister anything, Henri finally agreed. "I guess I'd rather take you than have you go out there alone."

"When?"

"Tuesday or Wednesday afternoon, if either one works for you, and if I can get away. That will give me time to see if we need a pass or something. In fact," Henri brightened with the thought, "with all that's going on, they may not let us in."

Marie-Catherine smiled her confidence in him. "They will. And either day works. I'll come by your office."

"Tuesday, then, unless something comes up." Henri wished he could instill a little enthusiasm in his voice. The waitress set his breakfast in front of him. "Thanks," he told her.

"I knew I could count on you." Marie-Catherine reached for the cream and sugar. "So how are things between you and Claudia?"

"Pretty good, I think—at least most of the time." Henri put down his fork to talk. Marie-Catherine was young, but she was a woman. Maybe she could give him some advice. "But then other times, not so good at all."

"I thought you'd made up." Marie-Catherine's eyes were puzzled. "I thought all was forgiven."

"It isn't that. It's just that I never have time for her. Especially now, with these kidnappings and everything else that's going on. I love her. She says she understands, but I'm afraid it will end like it did before…this time it will be because she really has turned to someone else."

"What do you mean?" Marie-Catherine said, her brows drawing together in a frown. "Is that why you two broke up? I asked her once, but she wouldn't tell me."

"Something like that…she wasn't really seeing someone else, I just thought she was." Henri moved his coffee mug, spilling a little on the table. "Look, it's too complicated to go into."

"Well, I don't know what to tell you, except I think you shouldn't let her get away."

"You're right," he said and sighed. "I don't want to." He wished she had something more concrete to offer.

They talked again about their parents.

"At least Papa isn't drinking so much," Marie-Catherine said, spreading apple jelly on her last piece of toast. "But he isn't the same, Henri. Like last night, being so quiet. I miss hearing all the thump and thunder."

"I don't suppose it will get better any time soon. Not with the way things are with Marc."

She set down the toast, uneaten. "He didn't have that problem when you were in jail. Then, he was ranting and raving about everyone in the government."

"It's different with Marc. I was in there for making speeches—for the most part saying the things Papa has said since we were kids. Marc is different. He's hurt people— you for one. Just like knowing Dora put a face on the enemy for you, Papa can no longer hide from the violence his words may have caused. Just as I have to take responsibility for some of the things I've said."

"Maybe you're right." She took another sip of her coffee. "Do you worry about it, Henri? The things you said at those rallies? The things you've written?"

"Yes. I didn't before, but now I often worry that what I've written or said has influenced someone to violence."

"You shouldn't. When you gave those speeches, it was to get yourself arrested so you could show people how political prisoners are treated. You weren't advocating violence."

"My choice of words was meant to provoke a reaction. And does it make a difference what my reasons were? If the results were that someone committed a violent act in response to something I said or wrote, am I not still guilty?"

"Maybe in the eyes of the law."

"In my own eyes."

She didn't look convinced, but appeared ready to change the subject. "Did you see the letter Pierre Laporte wrote to Bourassa?"

"Yes." Henri shook his head once more, thinking of the fear he'd seen behind the words in the letter.

"What a lot of sadness he's had in his life—losing his two brothers and his father, being guardian to his brother's children—and now this." She pushed her cup away. "What do you think is going to happen to him, Henri? And to James Cross?"

"I don't know, but I don't think invoking the *War Measures Act* was the answer. I'm afraid it may push the kidnappers over the edge."

It had grown dark several hours earlier, but the long florescent lights along the ceiling made the room bright as daylight. Henri pushed back from the desk and stretched both arms above his head then rolled his neck from side to side. They'd worked all weekend again, researching Pierre Laporte, James Cross and everyone in their extended families, everyone they'd ever talked to it seemed, preparing for the week ahead.

Ready to call it a night, Henri stretched again. He sighed. Maybe he should take Claudia to a movie after dinner. They could make out in the balcony, pretending they were still in school. He smiled at the thought. At least now they could go back to his room. Soon, though, he had to find a new apartment. With the need to keep up the pretense of working for the FLQ gone, he was more than ready to move out of the cramped and dingy room he'd rented when he'd come out of Parthenais. As soon as he had the time, he'd start looking.

He looked over at Louise, pulling her handbag from the bottom drawer, ready to go home. "Can you believe they've already arrested over four-hundred people?"

The phone rang before she could answer him. Looking resigned, she picked up the phone. *"Le Journal Quotidien.*

One moment, *s'il vous plait,* I'll see if he's available." She held her hand over the phone and hissed at Henri. "It's for you. One of them, I think."

Henri picked up the telephone. "Hello."

"Pierre Laporte has been executed," said a harsh voice.

In the Won-Del Aviation parking lot near the St. Hubert air base, Henri stood a few feet from the upraised trunk lid of a navy-blue Chevrolet. Lights had the scene lit up. Focused on the trunk's grisly contents, cameras whirred or clicked.

Henri turned away. He'd seen enough—the bloated face, the bruised and torn neck, a gold chain hanging from it.

Besides Henri, a radio station had been contacted by the kidnappers. "They called around seven," Peter de Brose, the newscaster, said. Earlier, de Brose had been doing a remote broadcast, telling those Quebecers still awake, what happened, describing how two bomb squad officers from the air base had hacked at the trunk lock with a long steel-tipped rod before finally prying the trunk open. He nodded to his companion. "Martin took the call."

"I recognized the voice from when he'd called to announce Laporte's kidnapping," said the man named Martin. His voice and hands shook. He had a beard and wore wire-rimmed glasses. He looked to be twenty-one or twenty-two. Neither the beard nor the glasses could conceal his pallor.

"I hadn't talked to him before tonight," said Henri, his own hands shoved into his pockets. "And with the *War*

Measures Act in place, my editor and I weren't sure what to do—notify the *flics* first, or what."

"I know, the same for us," said de Brose. "But we had to find out." Avoiding one another's eyes, all three nodded.

A St. Hubert policeman approached. "We'll want to talk to you again tomorrow," he told them. "For now, you guys can go."

Henri didn't wait for a second opinion. "See you later." He left the other three and picked his way through, over and around bomb disposal trucks, mounted lights, short and tall, heavy cables, and police vehicles to get to Maurault's car. When he got there, he looked at his watch; two A.M. He closed his eyes and rested his forehead on top of the steering wheel. *Christ, when will the bloodshed and violence end? When will the FLQ admit they've done enough?* After a minute or so, he straightened and started the car.

Louise had taken a cab home, but Maurault was still in his office when Henri got there. "When this is over I'm going to sleep for a week," Maurault said, after Henri finished telling him about the discovery of Laporte's body.

Henri leaned back in the chair across the desk from Maurault and closed his eyes once again. He'd never felt so tired. "I just keep thinking of Mrs. Laporte and all those fatherless kids. And what James Cross must be thinking right now."

"If he knows about it," said Maurault.

"He may not know about it, but his wife does."

"You understand what this means, don't you Henri? If anyone had held out any hope after Trudeau's speech, which they shouldn't have, they'll know for sure now—none of the prisoners will ever be freed."

"I know." Henri's thoughts went to Marc. He'd been concerned at how withdrawn and remote his brother had looked when he'd last visited him. Then he thought about what he'd just seen in the trunk of the abandoned car, and about Mrs. Laporte and the young children in her care.

Henri saw shock and stunned disbelief on the faces of people he passed on the street, on busses, in coffee shops.

"It's as though everything they thought they knew had evaporated overnight," he told Claudia. "As though they awoke and found themselves in a foreign country, not in our beloved Montreal."

The radio stations played funeral music. The front pages of the newspapers, including *Le Journal Quotidien*, were banded in black ink.

The morning of the second day following Laporte's assassination, Maurault waved Henri into his office. "You haven't heard anything from Lanctot?"

Henri shook his head. He'd heard a rumor that Lanctot's cell had written a desperate communiqué assuring authorities Cross's death sentence was suspended indefinitely. If they'd received such a notice, the authorities weren't telling anyone.

"Now they've arrested Igor, I'm hoping Lanctot will find some other means of contacting me. Since we can't publish anything they give us anyway, maybe it makes no difference."

Grim-faced, Maurault rolled his unlit cigarette between his fingers. "At least we'd know."

"You're right," said Henri. "But we couldn't publish it. It will be six months before the *War Measures Act* expires. That's just staggering. For six months we have to let the government vet everything we write." He stood and paced in the confined space of Maurault's office. "We shouldn't have to put up with that. Why isn't the entire population of Montreal out in the streets protesting? Jesus, it's like we're living in a city of zombies."

Maurault held up his hand. "What's that noise?"

Henri listened and heard a roaring whump, whump, whump. As it drew closer, everyone in the newsroom, including Henri and Maurault, quickly moved to a window or out of the building and craned their faces skyward.

Escorted by a covey of troop helicopters painted dull brown and green, a shiny white helicopter with Royal Canadian Air Force markings skimmed over the tops of buildings. Trudeau. Come to town for the lying-in-state of Pierre Laporte.

"I've heard he's meeting with Bourassa and Drapeau before the ceremony," Henri told Maurault. "I'd better get over there and see what I can find out."

In front of City Hall, uniformed soldiers jumped from the back of a truck onto the sidewalk. Three soldiers, gripping rifles across their chests, ran up the stairs, turned and stood with their feet spread and planted, glaring at passers-by. Policemen and soldiers were scattered along the sidewalk in front of the buildings, spilling over into Place Jacques-Cartier.

Henri climbed from his taxi as a handful of tourists, no doubt exploring Old Montreal, cautiously walked past him.

They were scrupulously avoiding eye contact with any of the armed and uniformed men. Henri studied their blank faces. Even outsiders, non-Quebecers, were being affected by the events, he thought.

He started up the steps of City Hall, but a soldier moved forward and barred the way. "Stay back."

"I'm a reporter." Henri showed his press pass. "I need to get inside."

"Stay back," the soldier repeated. Without further warning he shoved Henri with the stock of his rifle. Unprepared, Henri staggered backward, down several steps. "God damn it!"

Before he could charge back up the steps, the doors of City Hall swung wide and Trudeau emerged at the head of a long line of men and women. The men wore black armbands on their suit sleeves and the women were dressed in black.

Police officers and soldiers flanked the phalanx of mourners trooping down the stairs, past Henri, who quickly fell in line behind them, to the nearby courthouse where Pierre Laporte's body lay in state. Several policemen and soldiers hovered near Trudeau, shielding him from possible attack.

After leading the mourners past Laporte's body and while television cameras whirred, Trudeau blasted the FLQ and promised swift justice. Without taking any questions, he was then spirited out the backdoor of the courthouse to his waiting helicopter and whisked back to Ottawa.

Henri approached Bourassa and Drapeau, standing with their heads close to one another, speaking in hushed, tense voices.

"Prime Minister, Mayor. May I ask you a few questions? What did you and the Premier discuss earlier? What are you doing to find the Rose brothers and bring them to justice?"

Both men turned hostile glares on Henri. "No comment," they said, in near unison. They turned and left the building.

Henri stared after them, his lips thinned and pressed together. He'd earlier been sickened by what he considered Trudeau's phony display of concern for Quebec and justice. Now he was equally disgusted with Bourassa and Drapeau. Neither man had given so much as glance at Pierre Laporte's body when they passed, nor did they stop to say a final goodbye to Mrs. Laporte, heavily veiled and surrounded by her stunned and grieving children and nephews.

Chapter Twelve

The bus pulled away and left Marie-Catherine standing on the curb next to Henri. The four remaining passengers, a man and three women, stared down at them, their faces pinched and closed. She wondered what they were thinking, wondered if they knew she and Henri were going to see their brother. The walls of the jail loomed over them. She felt puny and insignificant.

Henri must have sensed her growing panic. "Are sure you want to go in, M.C.?"

The concern in his voice made her feel guilty for dragging him into this, but she had to do it. She had to. "Yes, I'm sure."

Armed soldiers stopped them at the gate and again inside the building. Both times they showed their identification and the pass Henri had managed to acquire for their visit.

The guard inside the building examined both sides of the pass. He looked at each of them then handed the pass back to Henri. He pointed to her purse. "I need to look inside." He took his time looking through it, opening each compartment, taking out her billfold and examining it, even looking at the pictures it contained.

Marie-Catherine forced herself to stay calm while the guard continued his methodical search. Henri stood at her shoulder. She could almost feel the heat of his gathering anger. She reached for his clenched hand and patted it.

The guard returned her bag. "Through the door and up the stairs."

The walls in the stairwell were painted the same sickly green as the walls in the guardroom. The smell of disinfectant stung her nose and made her eyes water, but it failed to mask the pervasive odor of despair. At the top of the stairs another guard stood behind a tall desk.

They approached the desk and Henri showed the man their pass. "We're here to see Marc Morais."

The guard glanced at the pass. "He's only allowed one visitor at a time."

"We know that." Henri put the pass in his pocket. "I'll wait here. His sister has come to see him."

The guard looked through several pages of a list attached to a clipboard before he found Marc's name. "B-block, C-gallery," he said into the phone receiver and paused a moment. "Prisoner Morais has a visitor. Right."

Marie-Catherine could hear the voice on the other end, but couldn't make out the words.

"Yeah," said the guard, chuckling. He hung up. He glanced at Marie-Catherine then back at Henri. "It'll be twenty minutes or so. You can have a seat while you wait." He nodded his head to several rows of worn, wooden chairs. Most of them were unoccupied.

They sat in the middle of a row of empty seats. Marie-Catherine leaned over and whispered in Henri's ear. "There are children here. The woman in the back row has two little kids with her."

Henri glanced over his shoulder. "Probably come to see her husband or boyfriend."

"But how can she bring children? They said only one of us could go in at a time. What will she do with them?"

Henri shrugged. "I think it's different for families with kids. They must have a special room for them to meet."

"Oh." She turned and looked at the children again then faced forward. "Poor kids." She muttered the words more to herself than Henri.

A thin woman with graying hair, sitting in the row in front of them, methodically shredded a tissue in her lap. In the rows behind them were a heavy-set young man and two other women. No one spoke. At one side of the room, above a drinking fountain, a poster warned against contraband material.

As the minutes dragged by, Marie-Catherine went over in her mind what she would say to Marc.

The metal door next to the drinking fountain swung open. A guard stepped through it and crossed to the desk, spoke to the guard at the desk in a low voice then turned and said, "Morais visitor."

Marie-Catherine tensed and caught her breath. Henri squeezed her hand as they both stood. She tried to give him a reassuring smile. "I'll be fine. I'll see you in a bit."

She followed the man through the metal door and down a short hall. He unlocked a second door with a key he took from a ring on his belt.

Marie-Catherine immediately located Marc. Her brother sat at one of several tables, his head lowered, his forearms resting on his knees. She stood still for a moment, blocking out the echoing voices of prisoners and visitors in the high-ceilinged room with its high, mesh-covered windows. They'd cut his hair and he wore the same gray uniform and lace-less shoes as the other prisoners.

She crossed the room and came to a stop in front of him. "Marc." She barely whispered his name. He didn't lift his eyes from the floor in front of him. She said his name again, louder this time. When he looked up she tried to smile, but the muscles and skin around her mouth felt stiff. She pulled out a chair and sat. "Are you okay?"

He stared at her, his eyes devoid of expression. "Why did you come?"

"You're my brother."

"Do you have news? Are they going to let me go to Cuba?"

It was her turn to stare. "No. They've only offered that to Cross's kidnappers."

"Then why did you come?"

She forced herself to take a deep breath to calm her racing heart. "For one thing, I want to know how you are. I want to be able to tell *Maman* and Papa you're okay."

"I'm okay," he said, his voice flat.

"Good." She looked down at her hands, clenched into fists in her lap. "And I need to know how you feel."

"Like shit. I want out of here."

She tensed. "Not that."

"What then?"

"I need to know how you feel about the people you've hurt."

"What?" For the first time, an expression appeared on her brother's face. He looked puzzled, as though she'd spoken in a language he didn't understand.

"Dora was my friend, Marc. She was a good person and I liked her. I met her husband and one of her children. Billy is only three-years old. He won't even remember his mother. You've ruined their lives Marc—Billy and his brothers and sister. Dora's husband. I need to know how you feel about that."

For a time, she didn't think he would answer her. Then he did.

"You think I should feel something because some English-speaking bitch died? I don't." Neither his voice nor his face revealed any emotion. "It's not my fault the building wasn't evacuated. They were given plenty of warning. If someone should feel remorse for your so-called friend, it's the owners of Arrow Shoe Factory, the managers. Not me."

Marie-Catherine stared at her brother in disbelief. "And me? What about me?"

"What about you?"

"Look at me. Look at my face." The scars were healing, but whenever she looked in the mirror, she saw how the thin red lines crisscrossing her temple, eyelid and cheek stood out against the whiteness of her skin. A muscle at the side of her mouth jumped.

Marc's eyes moved over her face, impassive. "You weren't supposed to be there."

A roaring sounded in her ears. Her head began to pound. "That's it? That's your answer?"

Marc shrugged.

Marie-Catherine stood, knocking the chair over in her haste. She gripped the edge of the table. Her head felt ready to explode. In a panic, she turned and nearly tripped over the chair. She felt her throat close, felt sure she would choke. Escape. She had to escape.

"Are you all right, ma'am?"

Marie-Catherine pushed past the guard in her rush to the door. She grabbed the handle and tried to turn it. When the handle failed to turn, she pounded on the metal door with her fist.

"Ma'am. Step away from the door."

Marie-Catherine kept pounding.

"Step away from the door. Step away so I can unlock it."

Breathing hard, she took a step back and the guard reached in front of her with the key. A minute later she stumbled through the second door, into the waiting room.

Henri leaped to his feet. "What's the matter?"

Shaking her head, Marie-Catherine squeezed her eyes shut and cover her face with her hands. She couldn't stop shaking.

"What happened?" Henri asked the guard.

Marie-Catherine's mind whirled.

"Nothing," the guard said. "Must have been something he said."

"M.C. what's wrong?" She stiffened and dropped her hands, her eyes flew open when Henri put his arm around her shoulder. "Can you tell me what's wrong? Why are you shaking?" He tried to lead her to a chair.

She pulled back. "No. Just get me out of here."

"You need to sit down a minute and catch your breath."

"Henri, no!" Panic nearly choked her. She gulped, forcing it down. "Please, let's just go. I need to get outside."

"Okay, M.C. Relax." His voice went soft with reassurance. "We're leaving." He took her hand and led her across the room to the stairwell. Like a child, she followed, thinking only of the need to breathe fresh air. In a few minutes, they were out of the building, heading toward the gate.

"Now can you tell me what happened?"

She shook her head, her thoughts still crashing into one another.

They rode back to town in silence. Marie-Catherine sat next to the window, Henri beside her, on the aisle. He asked her again what Marc had said, but again she refused to answer him. It had grown dark. She stared out the bus's window at the streetlights reflected in the glistening surface of the *Rivière des Prairies*, which served as Montreal's northern boundary, before the bus turned and headed toward downtown. Before long, the slopes of Mount Royal loomed on the right. Lights gleamed from scattered windows in the old-fashioned European-style houses and apartment buildings. Marie-Catherine vaguely wondered about the people living in them.

Evening rush-hour traffic grew thicker as they neared Sherbrooke Street. Occasionally a truck or a Land Rover went by, filled with soldiers, their young faces pale, unsure and even a little frightened under the streetlights. Almost identical were the looks reflected on the faces of people hurrying along the sidewalks.

Henri stood and pulled the cord. "Our stop is next," he said.

Marie-Catherine gathered her coat tighter before stepping into the aisle in front of him. The bus pulled up to the curb and she got out, neither knowing nor caring where they were.

"Do you want to go home now?"

"No." She didn't want to face their parents. "Not yet. Could we go somewhere and have something to drink? A beer or something?" Maybe it would help. Right now, she felt dead inside.

They went into a tavern on University Street. Men and women from nearby offices and shops nearly filled the chairs and tables, while a small group of workers from a nearby construction site, dressed in canvas work clothes and heavy leather boots, stood or sat around one end of the bar.

Henri stopped a few feet inside the door. "It's pretty crowded. Want to go somewhere else?"

Marie-Catherine shook her head, feeling reassured by the buzz of activity. "No, this is good."

Henri led the way to a table in a corner with two empty beer mugs and a half-full ashtray. "Sit down. What do you want?"

"Just a beer."

"How about something to eat?"

She closed her eyes and shook her head again, unable to bear the thought of food. Around her, voices swirled. She heard Laporte's name and Trudeau's, but mostly the voices blurred together, indistinct.

Henri dumped the contents of the ashtray into an empty mug then carried both mugs to the bar. "Here you go," he said a few minutes later, setting a frothing glass in front of her. Marie-Catherine picked it up and downed a quarter of the beer.

When she set the glass down, the corners of her mouth relaxed and her shoulders loosened. She took a deep breath and let it out on a heavy sigh. "He's a monster."

A group of students at the table next to them were chattering in loud, high-pitched voices. Henri leaned closer, his eyebrows drawn together. "What?"

"Marc is a monster. He has no remorse, Henri. None." She stared at him, daring him to argue. When Henri opened his mouth to reply, she cut him off. "Don't even try to defend him. There's nothing you can say to excuse what he's done. I've blinded myself to it for years, but you know it's true."

Henri fingered a drop of foam running down the side of his glass. "I guess we're both guilty of not wanting to see."

He looked up and she read the sympathy in his eyes. Suddenly she wanted to cry. "I just don't know what to tell Papa. He knows I planned to see Marc today."

"What about *Maman*?"

"I didn't tell her. She won't hear his name spoken."

"We need to prepare them. Marc isn't getting out— not for a long time. Maybe never."

"I think they already know, Henri."

Chapter Thirteen

After Marie-Catherine fled across the visitors' room and the guard let her out, Marc stood and walked to the door he'd earlier come through. His steps were even and deliberate. Mechanical. At the door, he stopped. The anger, the revulsion, the terror he'd felt when he'd first been locked up had faded weeks before and been replaced by a boundless, interminable void. He felt like a human husk, empty and without purpose.

Silently, he waited while the guard inserted the key, turned the lock, and opened the door. He walked through and, still silent, submitted to being searched—an act that followed every visit.

When they'd finished with him, he straightened his clothes and followed the guard back to his cell. He knew now they'd keep him locked up until he died. He waited to feel some emotion, but none came. He sat on his bunk. Maybe I'm already gone, he thought. Already dead and buried inside these walls. He stared at his hands, examining the lines in the palms and the black hairs springing up on the backs, at his knuckles and fingernails. It was like they were foreign objects, not part of his body.

The guard shouted down the gallery for everyone to get ready for dinner. Marc stood and waited at his cell door for the line to reach him. When his door was unlocked, he fell in and marched with the others to the mess hall. Passing through the line, he held his tray out to be filled and then sat at his assigned table. He pushed the lima beans and ham around, taking only one or two bites.

"You going to eat that?" The man on his right pointed to the slice of bread on Marc's tray.

Marc shook his head. He put his hands in his lap and stared into nothing. The men on both sides of him helped themselves to his carton of milk and chocolate pudding, but he gave no complaint.

A whistle sounded and everyone stood. Dinner was over.

Back in his cell, Marc stretched out on his bunk and waited for the guards to make their final rounds before dimming the lights. A few people called to one another. He ignored them. Toilets flushed. Doors clanked open and shut. Someone called out again and a guard yelled, "Shut up, lights out." The lights flashed twice then the banks in the middle were turned off, leaving a steady glow from each end of the gallery.

He may have dozed. Later he heard footsteps, but they were far off.

He stood and began to unbutton his shirt. When he drew the shirt off, he tugged on one sleeve, to test its strength, and walked to his cell door, his eyes focused on the stretcher bar a few inches below the door's top edge.

Chapter Fourteen

The Catholic priest who'd baptized Marc, Henri, and Marie-Catherine, who'd confirmed them and still heard the weekly confessions of their parents, had refused to perform the ceremony.

"Suicide is a mortal sin."

In the unfamiliar Protestant church, Henri sat on the hard pew beside Marie-Catherine. Next to her were their parents, behind them Dr. Rydel and Claudia.

Although the smell of incense and candle wax was missing, Henri was reminded of the many hours he'd spent on a similarly hard bench, when he and Marc were boys. Dressed in white shirts and navy slacks, always an inch too short, their fingernails and necks scrubbed clean, their hair slicked down with water and a comb, they would sit side-by-side between their parents. When one of them squirmed too much or they got to poking at each other, they could count on a pinch or a twisted ear administered on the spot by their mother, followed-up by a cuff to the shoulder or back of the head on the walk home.

Marie-Catherine's shoulder pressed against Henri's. He felt her trembling as she tried to suppress quiet sobs. He stared at the closed casket in front of the altar, as though if he looked hard enough he'd see through its walls to Marc's body inside. He shut his ears to the minister's words. How could someone who hadn't known his brother have anything meaningful to say about his life? He squeezed Marie-Catherine's hand. Eventually the man finished.

Henri and his father sat on the limousine's jump-seat, facing his mother and Marie-Catherine. His eyes were fixed on his mother's callused hand resting on the seat cushion. The worn cuff of her black coat and the roughened skin of her hand were in stark contrast to the plush gray material of the limousine's upholstery. Her eyes were closed, preventing Henri from seeing the numb, deadened look in them. Marie-Catherine huddled in the corner of the seat and stared out the window. Beside him, his father cleared his throat, as though about to say something, but then he fell silent again.

The boulevard was congested with the usual Saturday morning traffic. Behind the limousine followed a train of cars, many of them taxis driven by Marc's co-workers, lights on to indicate a funeral procession. His parent's neighbors and some of his father's co-workers were no doubt among them. Claudia rode in one of the cars with Dr. Rydel.

Marie-Catherine broke the silence. "Nothing excuses what he did."

His father shook his head and glanced at their mother. "Hush."

Marie-Catherine flashed a teary look at Henri and then her father. "I don't care what you say, Papa. I don't care what anyone says. It was typical and selfish of him. I won't forgive him for it." She turned back to the window.

Henri didn't blame his sister, the last of the family to see Marc alive. She still hadn't told him what their brother had said or done to send her reeling that night.

The car slowed, turned, and drove through the wrought -iron gates of the cemetery, to the Protestant portion where Marc would be laid to rest, mostly among Anglos. How his brother would hate that. Again, the Church had been adamant.

Henri rested his hand on his mother's knee. "Maman, we're here." She opened her eyes and looked out. Her shoulders stiffened and her hand clenched and unclenched before she gathered the handles of her black purse. The driver came around and opened her door. She scrambled out. She seemed almost eager to have it over.

The minister stood beside the open grave, the wind tugging at his vestments. The coffin was lowered into the hole. If Marc had delayed a few months they would have been forced to wait until spring to bury him. Soon the ground would be frozen and too hard to dig.

Claudia refused to join them, to sit with them in church or ride in the limousine. She stood with the other mourners now. The Morais family's grief was private, she said. He'd tried to convince her she was now part of the family, but she'd remained firm, saying his parents didn't need anything more to worry about. Without her beside him, it felt part of him was missing.

Staring at a tree in the distance, Henri's mind drifted back to two boys floating boats in their springtime-flooded yard, boats they'd fashioned out of the butt-ends of two-by-fours, or playing war on long summer days. Or baseball.

"*Here. Here,*" *Marc yelled, jumping up and down. "He's going to try and score.*"

A long string trailed behind the ball Henri threw toward his brother, who stood over the piece of wood they used as home plate. The ball was lop-sided due to the yards of string and tape they'd wound around it. It waffled through the air, finally landing with a plop and a spongy bounce about three feet in front of the plate. Marc dove to pick up the ball and swung back around, holding the ball out, trying to make the tag. The runner was already up and brushing dust from the front of his shirt.

"*Shit.*" *Marc threw the catcher's mitt to the ground and kicked it.*

"*Hey,*" *called the redheaded boy playing first base. "Be careful with that mitt. It's the only one we've got.*"

"*So what. It's a piece of shit. So is the ball and everything else. How can anyone play a decent game with this bunch of crap?*"

As usual, Henri tried to calm his brother's anger.

"*Come on, Marc. Let's finish the game. And watch your mouth. She can hear you.*"

He nodded toward four-year-old Marie-Catherine, who sat in the shade of a lilac tree feeding her doll dirt with a rusty spoon.

"*Yeah, and if she repeats it, which she will, your mom will knock the shit out of you,*" *laughed the boy who'd just scored.*

"*Come on,*" *said Henri again. "Are we going to play or not?*"

The sound of dirt rattling against the coffin's lid brought Henri back to the present. Marie-Catherine rose and returned to stand next to him. His turn. He reached down for a handful of dirt and tossed it into his brother's grave.

Somehow, in the back of his mind, Henri always believed he could save Marc from himself.

"Why did I hang back, waiting for him to change?" he said, staring at the ceiling.

Claudia lay on the bed beside him, the sheet and blanket pulled up and tucked under her bare arms, folded across her chest. "I don't know why you have to keep beating yourself up like this. What could you have done differently? Your brother used everyone around him, including you and me, and he wasn't about to change."

"I know. So why did I hang back, hoping he would."

"Because you're an optimist, darling. It's one of the reasons I love you."

"Marie-Catherine should hate me."

"Henri, you're making me crazy. You can't change anything. You have to let it go."

"I know." She was right. He still brooded about it, though. If he'd quit straddling the fence and confessed to Jeffers years before, when Marc was still a kid, they wouldn't have been so hard on him. The part Henri had the hardest time reconciling, was knowing that deep down, he'd wanted Marc to win. Used him, used his brother's anger and hatred to do what he, Henri, hadn't the nerve to do.

The police arrested Bernard Lortie and the girlfriend of Jacques Rose, but they hadn't caught the Rose brothers. Nor had they caught the others in the cell that had executed

Pierre Laporte. Henri had received no word from Lanctot since Igor's arrest. There'd been nothing made public about James Cross, either. Henri wondered if Cross had suffered the same fate as Laporte.

He balked at writing articles the government had to vet before it allowed Maurault to print them. "Trudeau claims he's fighting communism," he complained to his editor. "But when the government stifles the press or dictates to it, it seems like a police state to me—one every bit as bad as in Russia or China."

"We still need to get a paper out."

"I know." Henri returned to writing a tepid piece about a mayor in Eastern Townships.

One afternoon he met Marie-Catherine at school. The weather was too cold to walk in the park. She took him to a room in the library, furnished with comfortable chairs and tables, good for quiet conversations and study groups. When they were seated, Henri asked how their parents were holding up.

Marie-Catherine sighed and shook her head. "Not good. Maman refuses to be in the room if Marc's name is mentioned. You remember what she said the morning after his funeral."

"Committing suicide is a sin against God and the Church. We'll not talk of it again," Henri quoted.

"And she hasn't," said Marie-Catherine.

"How do you feel?"

"I'm just so angry, Henri. Sometimes I can't stop shaking, I want so bad to scream and shout. I feel guilty, too. Marc must have read in my eyes what I thought of him and what he'd done."

Snow had been falling off and on since early morning. Visible through a window were thickly bundled figures, moving with care along the snow-covered sidewalks.

"I don't think what you thought of him, whether he saw it in your eyes or not, had anything to do with it, M.C." Henri shifted his gaze back to his sister. "I think Marc just couldn't face years of being locked up. Plus, he'd lost the game. There was nothing more he could do. No more hits against the Anglos. They'd won. At least that's the way he'd have seen it. He couldn't take that."

Tension showed in the skin around Marie-Catherine's eyes. The red network of scars stood out more than ever on her pale skin. With trembling fingers, she picked at a fuzzball on the sleeve of her sweater.

"You've no need to feel guilty," Henri said, his voice gentle.

"I can't stop."

Henri didn't know how to give her comfort when he had none to give himself. They both sat unmoving, unspeaking, as though in identical brown studies. Henri roused himself first. "What about Papa?"

"Like I said before, he's not the same. He hardly ever talks now, and he looks so old." Tears welled in her eyes. "Damn Marc. Damn him to hell for what he's done to all of us."

Henri bought another car, a Renault, similar in age and color to his old one. Driving back to his rooming house Friday night, he thought about his conversation with Marie-Catherine. He didn't blame her for feeling angry, although he knew much of her anger, like his, stemmed from guilt—she couldn't forgive herself for going to North Carolina with Marc and for playing along with his schemes at the shoe factory resulting in her friend Dora's death and he couldn't forgive himself for not being able to save either his brother or his sister from themselves.

His window fogged. He turned the defroster up. Rush hour should have been over several hours before, but traffic crawled. Henri, anxious to be inside but hemmed by a bus and a large white delivery van, drummed his gloved fingers on the steering wheel.

Briefly, he thought about an article he was trying to write. Nothing seemed to be catching his interest these days, making him eager to find the story behind the story. Especially with the government vetting everything he wrote. Maybe he needed a change.

One thing he did know. He needed to find an apartment. The single room he'd occupied the last several months was too cramped, especially now, with Claudia spending several nights a week. Claudia. Whenever she entered his thoughts he felt overwhelmed by his good fortune. Just don't screw it up, he told himself once again.

He turned off Pi IX onto a side street, leaving the slow-moving traffic behind. Snow was piled at the sides of the streets. Sidewalks had been cleared as well. Light poured out of the front windows of duplexes and triplexes, onto the small mountains of snow centered in each front yard. Leaves were long gone from the trees lining the streets, revealing bare, twisted branches reminding him of claws. He passed a scattering of shops, their fronts covered by wrought iron grills.

When he reached his boarding house, he turned into the lot. The car tires crunched over ridges of scraped and frozen snow. He pulled into the space he'd claimed as his, got out and reached inside for some notes he needed to go over.

"Henri."

He jerked upright, hitting his head on the doorframe. He backed the rest of the way out of the car and grabbed for the top of his skull. "Damn it," he said, rubbing his head. He turned around, his eyes searching. She stood in the building's shadow. He peered through the darkness.

"Bunny?"

"I need to talk to you."

"Sure." Puzzled, he closed the car door and locked it. The pain in his head began to subside. "Let's go inside. It's colder than hell out here. You must be freezing. How long have you been standing there?"

He didn't wait for her answer, but silently led the way around the building. He didn't know what to say to her. He hadn't thought to call her after Marc died. He should have. Surely, she knew.

He unlocked the door with his house key, stood back and indicated for her to go first. The light in the hall had burned out and no one had replaced it, but he could see she wore a thick heavy jacket and carried a knapsack. Her pace appeared slow, almost plodding as she walked up the stairs.

At the top, she stood back and waited for Henri to unlock his door. He flipped on the light. "Sorry about the mess." The blankets on the bed were thrown back, just as he'd left them, and dirty clothes lay like large gopher hills on the floor. "Do you want some coffee?" He kicked a pair of jeans under the bed.

"I don't have time. I just came by to give you something." She'd been unbuttoning her jacket with one hand at the same time she supported something underneath it. "I can't keep him."

"What?" Henri looked down and saw a tiny face with its eyes screwed closed, wrapped up in a plaid flannel blanket. "What's this? What are you talking about?"

"Marc's son. I'm giving you Marc's son."

She held the blanketed cocoon out to Henri like an offering. His hands at his sides, Henri took a step backwards.

"You can't be serious. What would I do with a baby?"

"I'm leaving Montreal. I can't take him with me." Bunny continued to hold the infant in her outstretched hands.

"You're crazy if you think I'm going to take him." Despite himself, he looked down again. "How do I know he's Marc's?"

"You don't. Except I'm telling you he is."

"You can't just walk in and spring something like this. I need to think about it, talk with the family. Maybe we can arrange something. Help you or something." His words, like his thoughts, dwindled off. Marc had a son.

"I don't have time to argue, Henri. My ride is downstairs." She put the baby on the bed, the knapsack beside him.

Henri stood motionless, staring at the baby, until he realized Bunny had walked out the door. He gathered up the baby and turned to follow her, feeling awkward with the nearly weightless bundle in his arms.

"Wait."

But she'd already clattered down the stairs.

"Wait," he shouted.

He was halfway down the steps when he heard an engine start up and a car door slam. By the time he got to the sidewalk, all he saw were taillights flashing red as a car braked at the corner, turned right, and disappeared.

Less than five minutes after Bunny disappeared, the baby awakened with a loud wail. Henri wondered how such a small body could emit such a piercing demand for attention. Thumping noises and curses came through the wall. Henri dug through the knapsack and found several bottles of formula along with half-a-dozen cloth diapers and a change of clothes. By morning, he was down to one diaper and one bottle.

Henri stared at the baby, finally asleep, and considered his limited choices. He could turn Marc's son over to the authorities or take him to *Maman.* No choice, really. Thirty minutes later, he looked down at the St. Lawrence River as he crossed the bridge to Longueil. The baby, wrapped once again in its flannel blanket plus two of Henri's warm shirts and a sweater, lay on the seat next to him. "Why weren't you sleeping like this last night?" he said, irritable with exhaustion. "That's when people are supposed to sleep."

In the winter, snowplows never maneuvered down the

steep road that led to their house, although a path had been cleared for foot-traffic. Henri parked on the boulevard and walked the rest of the way, holding tight to his burden, using more care than usual not to slip.

Smoke curled out of the chimney into a drift of lowering clouds. Someone was home. He crossed the plank bridge and kicked the snow off his shoes on the front porch steps. The door opened before he reached it.

"Hey, Henri. What has you out this early on Saturday morning?" Marie-Catherine gave a puzzled look at the bundle he carried. Over her shoulder he saw breakfast dishes still on the table. His mother stirred the fire with a poker before adding more wood. "Come in," said his sister. "You're letting in the cold."

He drew a deep breath then walked into the room. "Morning, *Maman*."

Without answering, his mother busied herself at the sink.

"Where's Papa?"

Marie-Catherine gestured to the rear of the house. "He'll be back in a minute—it's too cold to linger out there." She smiled. "What are you so carefully clutching?"

Henri looked down at the bundle in his arm. He'd been rehearsing what he would say, but now felt unable to utter a word. The bundle moved.

"What in the...."

Henri frowned and whispered. "Wait for Papa." The confused expression on his sister's face should have been laughable.

Footsteps sounded on the porch and Marie-Catherine reached for the door handle.

"*Bonjour,* Papa."

"Henri." His father said his name with a sigh and held out his arms.

Henri leaned forward and hunched his shoulders, instinctively protecting the baby from being squeezed between them.

When Henri drew back he saw the lines of grief etched deeper into the already creased and ashen skin on this father's face. Only the grayed stubble on his unshaved cheeks gave them color. Henri's heart broke for this pitiful residue in front of him. He longed for the vigorous, animated man he remembered. Anger stirred in him once more, anger toward himself as well as Marc.

"Sit down, Papa. *Maman*, you too." He nodded his head to the bewildered Marie-Catherine, whose eyes went back to the bundle in Henri's arms. "I have something to show you." He drew the blanket off the baby's face. "Marc's son."

"Bunny?" When he nodded Marie-Catherine plowed on. "Are you sure?"

He shrugged. "She says so."

His sister nodded her head. "I believe her. Where is she? Why isn't she here?"

"She's gone."

"What?"

Henri sat. "She brought him to me last night. Waited for me to get home from work, said she was leaving Montreal and couldn't take him with her."

"Just like that? How could she leave her own baby?"

"I don't know, M.C. She didn't take the time to explain."

"Marc left a son," she murmured. "I can't believe it."

Neither of his parents had uttered a word. His father's confused look distressed Henri even more, but when he saw the look on his mother's face, his heart sank.

"Conceived in sin of a sinner."

Marie-Catherine's face fell. "*Maman!* He's just a baby. You can't blame him for his parents, no matter what they did."

"He's the spawn of Satan."

Henri flinched. "He's your grandson, *Maman.*"

"No. Not mine. Take him away, Henri."

"You'd send him away? Your own grandchild?" Marie-Catherine stared at their mother.

"He is not my grandchild." His mother's voice rose. She shook her head and the flesh along her jaw shook as well.

Henri hadn't been prepared for this. "But where, *Maman?* I can't take care of a baby. Where should I take him?"

She wouldn't relent. "What you do is your concern. I want no part of it."

"What about you, Papa? Do you, too, reject Marc's son?" Henri thought he detected longing in his father's eyes, which were locked on the bundle in his arms. He felt the baby squirm against his chest then arch his back and a faint but explosive little rush of noise and wind erupted against his hand.

Marie-Catherine reached out her arms. "Let me hold him." He passed the baby to her. "Look," she said. "Look at those little hands and fingers. Look at those perfect fingernails."

Their mother refused to even glance at the baby. "I don't want him here." She stood as if to end the discussion. "Take him somewhere else. I don't care where."

Henri tried again. "*Maman*, please, you know I can't take care of him. What do you want me to do?"

"Not foist him on me, if that's what you were meaning to do."

"Who else will take care of him?"

"I told you. It's not my problem."

Henri looked at his mother, his eyes pleading.

"No."

"Papa?"

His father dragged his eyes from the baby in Marie-Catherine's lap.

"Papa, can't you talk to her?"

The old man turned his eyes to his wife then looked back to Henri. Without speaking he slowly shook his head.

Resigned, Henri stood and reached for his jacket. "I guess I'll have to take him to the Sisters."

Marie-Catherine grabbed his hand. "No. Henri, you can't. He's Marc's son, our nephew. I'll come with you. We'll think of something." She took the bottle from the baby's mouth and wiped the milky spit from his lips with the corner of his blanket then wrapped it tight around him. "Here, hold him while I get my things." She grabbed her coat from its hook by the door and put it on, then reached once more for the baby.

Outside, big flakes floated down, sticking to their coats and to the baby's coverings.

Henri held his sister's elbow as they stepped off the porch. "We'll have to stop and get some more stuff to feed him. You just gave him the last bottle Bunny left. He needs more diapers, too."

"What are we going to do, Henri?"

Chapter Fifteen

Marie-Catherine carried the baby up the stairs. Henri followed with the bags containing the diapers, plastic pants, formula and two changes of clothing she couldn't resist buying. At the top of the stairs she saw a note taped to Henri's door.

Henri read it then crumbled it in his hand. "Screw them."

"What did it say?"

"*No babies allowed.*"

"Oh."

Henri opened the door and they went inside. "Wait a minute." He put the bags he'd been carrying down, crossed over to the bed and pulled the sheets and blankets up. He smoothed the wrinkles out. "You can put him here."

The baby's warmth felt good against Marie-Catherine's chest and arms and she was reluctant to put him down. "It's cold in here."

Henri crossed to the radiator under the window, turned the black wooden knob and a faint hiss of steam sounded.

She pushed one of Henri's shirts off the chair and lowered herself into it, the baby still cradled in her arms. "How could Bunny just leave him? I don't understand how a mother could do that." She pulled the blanket back and gazed at the tiny face. Deep blue eyes, seemingly wise and all-knowing, gazed back at her.

Henri sat on the edge of the bed. "I don't know. Maybe something to do with the FLQ. Maybe she thought the *flics* were getting too close and felt like she needed to get out of Montreal."

Marie-Catherine recalled playing gin rummy with Bunny on the floor of Marc's apartment. "Bunny? You think she's in the FLQ?" It didn't fit with the woman she knew. "I doubt it. She wasn't very political. She used to needle Marc, claiming as a Native person, French Canadian problems didn't concern her."

The small room heated quickly. Marie-Catherine unwrapped some of the covering from around the baby and set him down on the bed next to Henri. "How old do you think he is?"

"Not very. His belly-button thing hasn't fallen off yet."

Marie-Catherine shrugged out of her coat. "Did Bunny tell you his name? We can't just keep saying him and he."

"If he has one, she didn't tell me."

Marie-Catherine dug in one of the sacks for a can of formula. "We need to give him a name."

"I thought about it last night," said Henri. "When I wasn't going crazy, trying to get him to stop crying. Why don't we call him Emile?"

She'd been reading the directions to make the formula. She lowered the can. "For Papa. I like that. And how about Marc as his middle name?"

"That would be good." Henri's voice cracked. She gave him a weak smile as tears flooded her own eyes.

She took the used bottles stacked on the bedside table into the bathroom and washed them, then filled the teakettle with water and set it to boil. When she came out of the bathroom Henri stood next to the bed staring down at their nephew. She didn't doubt for a minute the baby was Marc's son. "What are we going to do, Henri?"

Henri shook his head. "I don't know."

"We can't give him over to charity. We can't let him be raised in an orphanage or by people we don't know."

"Then what would you have us do, M.C.? I sure as hell can't take care of him. I have a job. I won't ask Claudia. Although she'd probably do it, she has a job, too, and she's already given more than enough to me and mine. And you have school. I hoped Maman would take him."

"She can't, Henri. I think she's shut her heart because it hurts too much."

Just then the baby started crying and Marie-Catherine bent to pick him up. As soon as she had him in her arms he fell quiet. Maybe he can read what's in my heart, she thought. "Hold him a minute, Henri. I'll get another bottle." But when she tried to put the nipple in his mouth, the baby turned his head away. "I guess he's not hungry." She started to lay him back on the bed. As soon as she withdrew her hands, he cried again.

Henri let out an exasperated sigh. "He did that all night."

"He probably misses Bunny. Do you think he knows she abandoned him?"

Henri shrugged.

"So, what are we going to do?"

Henri threw himself full-length on the bed. "Well, he can't stay here, *Maman* won't take him, and we don't want the Sisters of Charity to raise him. I guess that means we need to find someplace where the three of us can live. Do you see any other way?"

Marie-Catherine shook her head. She'd hoped Henri would suggest it. "What about Claudia?" she said. "Hadn't you better talk to her first?"

"She'll be okay with it," he said and Marie-Catherine didn't press further.

They decided to find an apartment or a duplex.

"I'll take a week off work. We should be able to find a place in that amount of time."

"With everything still going on with the police and James Cross and everything?" Marie-Catherine paced the short space between the bed and the window. "Why don't I look around?" She nodded at the baby drowsing in her arms. "I can take care of him and look for an apartment. When I find something I think will work, then we can look at it together."

Henri protested saying she shouldn't miss any of her classes, but Marie-Catherine reminded him she was only taking two and said her professors were sure to understand if she missed a week of class. In the end, he agreed.

"Can you keep him here at night while we're looking?"

Henri flashed her a look she assumed meant he didn't care what the landlord said about babies.

"I think it will work, though. This term is almost over. Next term I'll sign up for night classes. That way I can watch him during the day and you can watch him in the evening."

Henri frowned. "You're forgetting something. My schedule. I never know from day to day what it's going to be. I'll have to work some nights. Lots of them, probably."

"Those nights we'll get a sitter, then. Maybe Claudia can help. It will work. I know it will."

"Maybe," he said, though she didn't think he sounded as sure she felt. She would make it work.

Chapter Sixteen

Henri watched the mood and attention of the city shift. Time passed and most of the hundreds who'd been arrested during those few days in October were released. A slightly less restrictive *Temporary Measures Act* replaced the *War Measures Act.* Jacques Lanctot and his group were in Cuba after negotiating with police, who'd found and surrounded the apartment in north Montreal where they'd held James Cross for weeks. James Cross was reunited with his family.

"Even though the Rose brothers are still on the run, the death knell is tolling for the FLQ," he told Claudia. "There's no way anyone is going to forget Pierre Laporte and what they did to him." Henri would never forget the sight of Laporte's body.

Christmas came and went—for a while people put politics aside in favor of Christmas. Lampposts were trimmed, their tinseled garlands whipping in the gusting wind, and store windows were laid out to delight and entice shoppers. When January arrived, the spirit of the season quickly disappeared.

Henri stopped his car so a woman and a little girl could cross the street. The little girl looked lost in boots, snow pants, a coat buttoned up to her chin, a muffler wound around her neck and a cap pulled down around her ears. She stumbled and the woman gave her arm a sharp tug, jerking the little girl back to her feet, but barely paused as she hurried across the street.

God, he hated the cold.

Ten minutes later Henri walked into the newspaper office, pulling off his coat as he went. He picked up his telephone messages from the corner of Louise's desk and glanced through them on the way to his own desk. Several people said good morning. The day was just starting. By mid-afternoon the place would be jumping and no one would have time for such pleasantries. Henri slipped a message from Claudia into his pocket. He'd call her later. Marie-Catherine wasn't working at her new part-time job that night, so he and Claudia had plans.

Things with Claudia were better now that the FLQ crisis had settled down and he had more time to spend with her. He felt torn, though—maybe trapped was a better word for it—between his love for Claudia and his desire to begin a settled life with her, maybe have children of their own, and his commitment to helping Marie-Catherine raise Marc's son.

Marie-Catherine had encouraged him more than once to invite Claudia to move into their new apartment with them, but he resisted. Claudia spent plenty of time with them, even stayed over lots of nights; helped take care of Emile. She and Marie-Catherine had always gotten along well, too. But he couldn't be sure that would continue if their living arrangements were on a permanent basis. And though she showed no signs of it, he still hoped *Maman* would relent.

Maybe he was crazy, but he just didn't want to complicate things more than they already were. He flipped through two more messages then came to one that made him frown. Paul Carpentier. He'd heard that name before, but couldn't place it.

Claudia smiled a greeting when he walked toward her, but the smile faded as he drew closer. "What's wrong?" she said when he reached her side.

Distracted by his thoughts, Henri gave her a quick kiss. "Do you really want to see this movie? Can we go somewhere and talk?"

"Back to your place?" she suggested.

"No." He shook his head. "Not with M.C. and the baby there. I don't want us to be disturbed."

"Same problem with my place. The roommate and her boyfriend were watching television when I left. They didn't look ready to budge anytime soon."

"Damn," he muttered, running his hands through his hair. "Well, let's go find a quiet corner in a bar." Walking along the sidewalk, her hand in his, he suddenly laughed. "Makes me think of our university days when we were always looking for a warm place in winter—preferably one with a bed."

Claudia chuckled and squeezed his hand. "At least we had the park in the summertime."

Forty-five minutes later their young waitress brought a second mug of beer for him and another glass of wine for Claudia.

Henri still felt dumbstruck over what Paul Carpentier had told him that afternoon. They wanted him to come to

Quebec City to be the official spokesperson for the entire *Parti Quebecois.* He picked up his beer.

"Carpentier said René Lévesque himself had made the proposal. He said Lévesque has been following my career for years."

"Henri, it's so wonderful. I can hardly believe it."

"I know. Crazy, isn't it? I asked him if my connections to the FLQ might not cause problems—you know how well that FLQ=PQ, PQ=FLQ thing has been playing out, especially in the English language newspapers. Carpentier assured me it wouldn't be a problem. He said everyone knew my involvement with the FLQ had been a ruse."

But even as Carpentier had said those words, Henri's memories of the events that surrounded his imprisonment—what led him there and how he got out—prevented him from taking any pride in the accomplishment. Now he shook his head. "I'm afraid that's just wishful thinking on his part. Sure, some people will agree with him. Apparently, René Lévesque does. Still, I—"

Claudia couldn't contain her excitement any longer. "When do you start? When do we leave?"

"We don't." Henri rubbed his hand across his cheek and jaw. "Oh, I haven't turned them down yet, but I will. I have to."

"The hell you do." Claudia's voice was suddenly raw with emotion. "This is a fantastic opportunity for you. You've always admired René Lévesque. You've always wanted to be in politics. How can you even think about turning his offer down?"

"The timing's not right. I have responsibilities here

now. There's no way I'm going to leave Marie-Catherine with Emile to raise on her own."

"What about me? Don't I count? Doesn't what I want mean anything to you?"

"You know it does. I love you."

Claudia's huge eyes filled with tears. "It's just like before. You never have time for me. What I want or need isn't important enough to you. It's always about what you want. What you need. I can't go on like this, Henri."

Henri felt like he was in a four-way tug-of-war: he loved Claudia; he was responsible for Marie-Catherine and Emile; he felt loyalty to Maurault and the newspaper; and now something he wanted most dearly was offered—the *Parti Quebecois* and René Lévesque. It was impossible to satisfy them all. "Do you want to end it?" he finally said.

"No, but..." She shook her head. The tears overflowed and began to run down her cheeks.

Henri reached out and wiped them away with his thumbs. "Don't cry. We'll think of something."

Chapter Seventeen

Marie-Catherine finished drying a dish and put it on the shelf before reaching for another from the rack. "I think Emile tried to hold his bottle by himself today."

"He's growing," said Henri. He didn't look up from the book propped on the table in front of him, although she'd noticed he hadn't turned the page in fifteen minutes.

"What's the matter, Henri? Is something going wrong at work?"

He put his arm across the book. "No. Things are pretty much back to normal since the troops have been pulled out of Montreal and Lanctot and the others went to Cuba. I'll feel even better when catch the Rose brothers."

As usual, she gave a quick prayer of thanks James Cross had been set free, then turned her attention once more to her brother. "If not that, what is it? Is it Claudia?" She'd always been able to tell when Henri brooded about something.

He shook his head. "Nothing's wrong." He looked back at his book.

Marie-Catherine dried her hands on the dishtowel. "You might as well tell me. I'm just going to nag until you do."

With a sigh, Henri told her to sit down. The pulse in her temples thudded as she lowered herself into the chair across from her brother, no longer sure she wanted to hear.

"Someone from Lévesque's office came to see me," he said.

"René Lévesque?"

"He offered me a job." He didn't elaborate.

"Henri, that's wonderful." She knew her brother's interest in journalism had always been as a route into politics. "Congratulations. What will you do for him?"

"I turned him down."

"Turned him down!" The words exploded out of her mouth. "Why?"

"It's in Quebec City."

"Oh." She fell silent, thinking what it would mean to her if Henri left. How could she possibly manage Emile and school without Henri's support, both emotional and financial? "We need to think about this."

"There's no way, M.C. I'm not going to leave here. I'm not moving to Quebec City. Besides, I like my job."

"Don't lie. You've been dragging around here for weeks complaining about not being able to make an impact on enough people, or about the government interfering with the press."

"That part is over—the government interference part. Well, mostly it is."

"But this is your chance, Henri. It's what you've always wanted."

"I can do it later. The paper is still good experience for me."

"What about Claudia? What does she want?"

"Let me worry about Claudia."

"In other words, she's for it. You won't have another chance like this, Henri. To get in with someone you've always admired—on the ground floor. And the *Parti Quebecois* stands for everything you do, even if they are having an image problem right now. Think of the experience you'll get."

They argued some more, but then Marie-Catherine glanced at her watch and saw it was time to leave. "I have to go, or I'll be late for class. Just don't think I'm giving up."

"Forget it, M.C."

But Marie-Catherine didn't forget it. For several days, she thought about nothing else. Henri needs to take this job, she told herself as she tended the baby, washed clothes, and diapers. He needs to be in Quebec City. We need him there. Even as she studied, she worried at it like a sore tooth. Finally, she bundled Emile into a hooded bunting she'd bought at a thrift store—he'd grown and wiggled too much to keep him contained in blankets any longer—and left the apartment.

Saturday morning Marie-Catherine told Henri they were going out. "I have something to show you."

Half an hour later, she sat next to him in the car, Emile on her lap.

"Where are we going? What do you want to show me?"

"A surprise." She directed him across the river to Longueil.

"We're going to see *Maman* and Papa? *Maman* has changed her mind?"

"No, nothing like that." She hoped her voice didn't sound as anxious as she felt. "Turn left here." A People's Credit Jewelers stood on the corner across the street from a large church. Henri turned at a break in traffic then had to brake for a group of pedestrians.

"Where the hell are you taking me?" They passed several brick duplexes and one or two older houses. They came to a large, concrete building that took up most of a block.

"This is it. Stop here."

Henri found a parking place and by working the car back and forth a few times managed to get into the tight spot. "This better be good."

Marie-Catherine's palms were sweaty and her heart pounded in her chest as she got out of the car. "It is." A few minutes later, holding Emile in her left arm, she inserted a key into the lock of a door on the second floor, turned it until she heard it click then stood back.

Henri looked from her to the open door and back again. "What's going on, M.C.?"

She let out a breath. "Just go in. I'll explain."

Inside smelled of paint. Their footsteps echoed on the bare tile floor. There wasn't much to show—a narrow room with a kitchen in one end, a bathroom, and a small bedroom. It only took a couple of minutes for Henri to walk through, his eyebrows drawn into a frown and his mouth grim. He turned to her. "Okay, I've seen it. Now tell me what it means."

"This is government housing, Henri. It's cheap. Emile and I can live here and you can go to Quebec City."

Henri shook his head. "No. Even if it's cheap, you can't do it all and still go to school."

"I can, Henri. I've worked it all out. They even have a day-care center here." She didn't tell him it meant dropping one of her classes and taking on more hours in the restaurant where she worked part-time waiting tables, but in the end, she won. "Now you just need to go get that job back."

After Henri and Claudia left Montreal, Marie-Catherine busied herself settling into the new apartment. Henri had given her money to buy some used furniture, but the apartment was so small it didn't take long to fill it up with a bed, a table and two chairs, a sofa.

Before long she fell into a routine of caring for Emile, working at the restaurant and school. And even though she'd dropped a class, she kept the text and studied it. She wrote once a week to Henri, though most often she only got a brief note with the bi-weekly check he sent in return. He was too busy to write more, he said each time, and promised a long letter soon. He did tell her Claudia had found a job and liked Quebec City.

Marie-Catherine missed her parents. She called once a week from a payphone, but the conversations were always short.

"Hello, *Maman.*"

"Hello." Her mother had never liked to speak on the telephone her father had installed while Marie-Catherine was still in secondary school. Marie-Catherine hadn't been allowed to spend time on it, talking for hours as some of her friends did. The telephone was for emergencies, her mother had said. Not gossiping.

"How are you?"

"I'm good."

"And Papa?"

"He's good, too."

"Is he back to work?" The last time she'd called, her mother said her father was in bed with a cold.

"Yes."

"I had a card from Henri yesterday." Emile reached for the telephone cord. Marie-Catherine held it out beyond his reach and his fingers fastened instead on one of the big black buttons on the front of her coat.

"He's okay?"

"He's fine, *Maman*. Just busy. Claudia's fine, too." She didn't know if Henri wrote to their parents or if her mother knew he and Claudia planned to be married that summer. "He says he likes his new job." Emile tried to reach the button with his mouth. When he couldn't, he squealed his displeasure.

Her mother grunted a reply and Marie-Catherine decided she'd tried long enough. "Good-bye, *Maman*. I'll call you again next week." There was no answering farewell from her mother, just a click and silence. She set the receiver back in its cradle.

"I love you, too, *Maman*."

She pushed her way out of the phone booth, kissed Emile and held him close.

Spring came late. Rain lashed against the window as Marie-Catherine finished giving Emile his lunch—a jar of sweet potatoes and lamb. She washed his face and hands, changed his diaper, and carried him to his crib. She held out his bottle and he grabbed it. She smiled as he stuffed the nipple in his mouth and started sucking, his eyelids already drooping.

"It's just you and me, my friend," she murmured.

His brown hair had grown longer. It curled around the top of his ears now. And he had one bottom tooth that clinked against the spoon when she fed him.

"Sleep tight, little one."

He paid her no mind, concentrating instead on the bottle he held between his fists.

While the baby napped, Marie-Catherine planned to study. She hoped to get a couple of hours in before she had to take him to day-care. It had rained for three days straight and she'd turned the lights on to keep away the gloom. Baby food smeared the table and she wiped it with a wet cloth before setting her books out. Crossing from the sink back to the table, a knock on the door sounded. She stopped for a moment thinking it might be across the hall. The knock came again.

"Just a minute." She crossed to the door and pulled it open, curious to see who was there.

Her mother stood in the hall. Water dripped off her

raincoat and the folded umbrella she carried, collecting in a puddle on the floor at her feet.

Marie-Catherine stared.

"Aren't you going to invite me in?"

"*Maman*. What are you doing here? Yes, of course. Come in."

"Where can I put this?" Her mother held out her dripping umbrella.

"We can leave it in the hall. Open it back up and it will dry."

"Is it safe?"

"It will be fine, *Maman*. I leave mine out there all the time. Everyone does."

Her mother grunted and began to unbutton her coat, at the same time looking around the room. Marie-Catherine had tried to make it feel homey. She'd taped a Georgia O'Keefe poster of red poppies to the wall above the second-hand sofa, and one of a fountain in a courtyard next to the table where her school text and notebook were now spread. A glass vase with a clutch of spring flowers stood on a lamp table next to the sofa. Her mother nodded, but didn't say anything.

"Drape your coat over that chair by the heater, *Maman*, so it will be warm and dry when you're ready to leave. I'll make us some tea." Marie-Catherine crossed to the sink, talking as she went, knowing she was babbling. She filled the teakettle with water. "I can't believe you're out in this weather." She put the teakettle on the narrow stove and lit the flame. "This won't take long to heat."

"Sit down, Marie-Catherine. You're making me nervous."

"Shall we sit on the sofa, *Maman?*" Her voice was artificially bright. She scolded herself for behaving like a ninny.

"We'll sit here," said her mother, indicating the table. She pulled out a chair and sat then moved Marie-Catherine's things aside. Marie-Catherine sat as well.

"How's Papa?"

"He misses you. Why don't you come to see us?"

"You know why, Maman. I can't leave Emile."

"You've named him Emile?"

"Yes. Emile Marc Morais." Behind her, the teakettle whistled. Marie-Catherine jumped up and began to set out the tea things, wishing her hands would stop shaking. She scooped leaves into the pot and poured the boiling water over them, then took some cookies from a tin on the counter and put them on a plate.

Behind her, chair legs scraped the floor. Her mother moved around the room.

"I got another card from Henri. It's there next to the flowers." Marie-Catherine set the teapot, two mugs, the sugar and milk and plate of cookies on a tray to carry to the table. She looked up just in time to see her mother disappear through the door to the bedroom. She set the tray down and hurried to catch up.

Her mother stood next to the crib looking down at Emile. The baby stared back, unblinking, then he started gurgling and waving his fists in the air.

"Can I pick him up?"

"Of course, *Maman*. He's your grandson."

Her mother reached for the baby.

About the Author
TONI MORGAN

Born in Alaska, raised in Oregon, where she studied history at Portland State University, and married in Hawaii, Toni Morgan has lived all over the United States, from California to Washington, D.C., and the world, from Denmark to Japan. She now makes her home in southwestern Idaho. She is the author of six novels: TWO-HEARTED CROSSING (2017) and PATRIMONY (2018) published by Adelaide Books; ECHOES FROM A FALLING BRIDGE, HARVEST THE WIND, LOTUS BLOSSOM UNFURLING, and QUEENIE'S PLACE in the pre-press process. Toni's articles and short stories have been published in various newspapers, literary magazines, and other publications (authortonimorgan.com)